A Bargain Made in Hell . . .
or Heaven

"I will marry you, but . . ." Libby appeared agitated. Uncomfortable.

"But?"

"But . . . you will not share my bed."

Jackson touched her breast, eliciting a gasp from her, but she didn't move away. His thumb moved over the turgid nipple, and he felt her quiver beneath his touch. "Whatever has provoked you to insist on a chaste marriage will be the death of you, Liberty O'Malley."

Fear and distrust swam behind the desire in her eyes.

"Oh, don't worry. I'll honor your request, but you didn't ask that I not touch you."

"Don't . . . don't touch me." Her voice was a shaky whisper.

His hands roamed her hips, then her sweet, savory fanny. He bent to kiss her, using his tongue to gain entrance into her mouth. When she began to weaken and answer his kiss, he lifted his head and smiled down at her.

"Too late."

Books by Jane Bonander

Dancing on Snowflakes
Wild Heart
Winter Heart
Warrior Heart

Published by POCKET BOOKS

For orders other than by individual consumers, Pocket Books grants a discount on the purchase of **10 or more** copies of single titles for special markets or premium use. For further details, please write to the Vice-President of Special Markets, Pocket Books, 1633 Broadway, New York, NY 10019-6785, 8th Floor.

For information on how individual consumers can place orders, please write to Mail Order Department, Simon & Schuster Inc., 200 Old Tappan Road, Old Tappan, NJ 07675.

JANE BONANDER

Warrior Heart

POCKET STAR BOOKS

New York   London   Toronto   Sydney   Tokyo   Singapore

An *Original* Publication of POCKET BOOKS

POCKET BOOKS, a division of Simon & Schuster Inc.
1230 Avenue of the Americas, New York, NY 10020

Copyright © 1997 by Jane Bonander

ISBN: 0-671-52981-1

First Pocket Books printing March 1997

10 9 8 7 6 5 4 3 2 1

POCKET and colophon are registered trademarks of Simon & Schuster Inc.

Cover art by Lina Levy

Printed in the U.S.A.

For two of my favorite small-dog lovers, Evelyn Bonander and Donna King, and for Dorothy Lohman, whose Shih Tzu, Tashi, taught me everything I needed to know about the breed.

A special thank-you to my Michigan friends, Nancy Giggey and Peggy Wang, for their unwavering support and for the title of this book.

Let those love now who never loved before;
Let those who always loved, now love the more.

—Thomas Parnell

Prologue

Northern California Coast, 1879

VIGILANTES. THEY HAD COME OUT OF NOWHERE, HOODED,
cowardly, and without a salvageable soul among them. One
minute Flicker Feather had been industriously weeding her
garden, and the next, she lay dead, her blood soaking into
the earth.

Jackson stood over her grave, his head buzzing, his chest
and his throat burning with unshed tears. The smell of fresh
dirt drifted through the air, as did the scent of the wildflowers that showered the ground around the grave. A mourning
dove wept somewhere in the distance, the sound as melancholy as it was comforting.

Jackson heard the baby crying, but he couldn't move.

Time passed. Aeons, maybe. He didn't know and he
didn't give a good goddamn. Time meant nothing now that
his beloved was gone. The vision of her lying beneath the
dirt made him choke, and he gasped for breath, feeling as
though he were suffocating. He fell to his knees and rocked,
dragging in gulps of air.

Again he wondered why he hadn't sensed trouble with the
vigilantes. There had been plenty of it around, but Flicker
Feather's village had been far enough west that it had

1

escaped the vicious acts of the Whites who were so filled with hate. Even so, he should have felt the danger. He should have *known* they would ultimately find them.

He wondered if it would have done any good, if he could have prepared the villagers better. . . . Could he have insisted his wife not go out into the garden unless he was there to watch her? He attempted a smile. She'd been a sweet, generous girl, but she'd also had a mind of her own. She'd hated it when he hovered.

His gaze found a lingering robin perched atop one of the split redwood pickets that made up the fence that enclosed his wife's grave. The bird pecked at the decorative feathers Grandmother had fastened there. Finding nothing edible, it hopped to the storage basket that sat beside the fence and plucked at the woven reeds.

Jackson had never professed to have a "gift," but he'd predicted his wife's pregnancy, and it hadn't been a hopeful guess. He'd *known* the baby was growing inside her. Why couldn't he have "seen" the horror coming?

He groaned. God, he didn't know what he would do without her.

"Her spirit is gone, Warrior Heart."

He'd been so lost in thought, he hadn't heard the footsteps that scuffed across the grass, stopping behind him.

Pain tore through Jackson's chest and tears leaked, spilling onto his cheeks. "Why couldn't I save her, Grandmother?"

"Your energy must no longer be for my granddaughter. You have a child to think about."

A ragged sigh escaped. "What good am I to her? I couldn't keep my wife from harm, how can I be of any use to the daughter she bore?"

"That is not Warrior Heart talking; that is pity."

"It's the way I feel."

Her strong, bony fingers grabbed his shoulder. "You are being selfish. Think of what Flicker Feather would want you to do."

Staring into the distance, Jackson shook his head, unwilling and unable to put aside his pain. "If she's dead, she has no thoughts, Grandmother." He continued to stare, yet saw nothing.

"This was my fault. My being here has put the village in jeopardy."

Grandmother was quiet, but Jackson knew that deep in her heart, she too felt he was to blame, for he'd stood alone in his attempt to fight the prejudice against Flicker Feather's people, against all the Indian people. For decades the Whites, and before them the Spanish, had slaughtered the gentle California tribes, to gain their land and to rule over them. Resistance meant death. Passivity meant death or enslavement. To many, Jackson realized, bile forcing its way into his throat, death was the more honorable route.

His presence among these gentle-hearted people put them in danger. He had first thought that living among them would be a deterrent against those who wanted all remnants of the Indians and their old ways obliterated. Arrogance, perhaps, had led him to this hopeful belief.

"It's better if I'm gone, Grandmother. And better if you and the baby are gone, too. You'll be safe as long as you're away from here. And away from me."

Grandmother made a spitting sound. "You would abandon your own child?"

A shudder tore threw him. His destination was uncertain. But whatever it was, his daughter was better off elsewhere. "Where I'm headed, she can't go."

Grandmother squatted beside him and hesitated a moment before speaking. "Will you return to your other family, then?"

He shook his head. He'd tried that route, but in the end, he hadn't been able to tell his father what he wanted. He hadn't been able to tell him anything. The estrangement between them had grown wider, ever since he'd refused to settle down and work the ranch. Angry words had been spoken on both sides. Although his father was not a bigot, he didn't understand Jackson's need to be with the Indian people. He never would. When they couldn't reach an understanding, Jackson had gone back to the tribe, fallen in love with Flicker Feather, married her, and fathered a child. And no one knew. No one.

"I want *you* to raise Flicker Feather's daughter," he replied. "I want her to know the ways of your people, not mine."

Grandmother's expression was skeptical. "Your vision is hampered by your grief. Your people are good. They should know of your child."

In his heart, Jackson knew there was a corner that would agree. But not now. Not here. Not with this child. He hadn't the strength to face his father again.

Grandmother made an impatient sound with her tongue. "Where am I to take her?"

Jackson clasped the old woman's bony fingers and stood, drawing her to her feet. He towered over her in every physical way, but she possessed the strength that he somehow had lost when Flicker Feather died.

"I will make arrangements for you to take the baby and travel up the coast. To safety."

"I do not want to go. I will not." Grandmother folded her thin arms across her chest and set her toothless jaw firmly.

Jackson felt a knot of frustration twist through his grief. "Please, Grandmother. I can't guarantee your safety if you stay here."

"This is my home. I will not intrude upon the lives of others. If you want me to care for your daughter, then she will stay here with me." She waited a beat, then added, "And if you are the man I know you can be, you will not leave us."

Her disgust was evident. Jackson's own disgust with himself swelled. "You aren't safe here, Grandmother. No one is safe from the vigilantes."

"You are a coward to leave," she spat.

He couldn't argue with the truth. "Whether I stay or not, you are still in danger."

She was resolute. "They will not harm us. I have been in contact with the spirits, and they have promised us safety."

Squelching a sigh, Jackson pinched the bridge of his nose.

He had respect for her religion, but the reality was that no one was safe from the vigilantes.

"I'm going to the bank to talk with John Frost. Once I've set up a trust fund for you and the child, I'll make sure you have access to it. John is a good man. He'll make it easy for you, I promise."

There was a voice in his head that warned him not to leave, but he refused to listen. He knew he should stay and find the bastards who had murdered his wife. He knew he should exact some revenge. His head told him it was the right thing to do. But his heart was so filled with grief he had no room for any other emotion.

"Your religion speaks to you, Grandmother, I know that. But I need to know that my daughter will survive in spite of my absence."

Grandmother's black eyes pierced his. "Since the death of Flicker Feather you have not spoken your daughter's name."

He couldn't speak it aloud, for it had been Flicker Feather's choice, and each time he heard the name now, it intensified his personal pain. Their daughter's eyes, his wife had told him, held the faded tints of morning and the deep, rich colors of evening. She was named Dawn Twilight.

Northern California Coast, 1882

He had been born twenty years too late. Now, as the leader of the vigilantes sat astride his mount on Pinkers Bluff, gazing out over the burned and smoking village, he knew this had to be the last raid. Twenty years ago, other whites would have applauded him for the butchery of the small tribe of digger Indians. They would have looked at the grass where pools of blood sweltered in the heat, and at the huts, spattered with gore, and said, "Well done. Another filthy savage village returned to dust."

But not now. Now, although there was still prejudice, widespread massacres were frowned upon. He drew in a breath, the air pungent with smoke and burning flesh, and pulled out his tobacco pouch. As he rolled a cigarette, he glanced at his companion.

"This will be the last village," he instructed. "If we burn any more, we're liable to get caught." And in truth, he didn't know if he could stomach another slaughter. It was one thing to rid the countryside of the filthy diggers; it was quite another to watch their children die. Strange. He felt no shame after killing the adults. But the children, even though they were the nits of the lice-ridden diggers, softened his heart.

His companion shifted uncomfortably in his saddle. "I'm glad we're done. I never did like doing this. Hell, I almost confessed my sins to the priest last week."

The leader leaned over and shoved his cigarette near the man's brushy mustache. "If word *ever* leaks out about what we've done, I'll know who did it."

The older man pushed the cigarette away. "I don't have a death wish. I can keep my mouth shut."

The leader's gaze returned to the smoldering village. He'd done what had to be done, but he wasn't like the others. Not like those who went in and butchered the innocent, slicing and gouging and skewering the babes on their bloody blades . . . or roasting them over fires made from the flesh of their parents.

He swallowed hard. No, he wasn't like that. After all, he was a father himself. He could never harm a child. At least . . . not on purpose.

1

Riverside Boardinghouse,
Thief River, California, 1891

Hold still, dear. I can't get a straight hem when you wiggle."

Dawn's movements quieted and she expelled an exasperated sigh. "I'm sorry, Mama. It's just that I promised Mahalia I'd go into the woods near the river and pick her some berries for dessert tonight."

Libby took the last pin from her mouth and fastened it to the yellow flower-sprigged calico. She caught her daughter's glance and smiled, admiring how well the bright yellow color suited her dusky complexion.

"Walk to the door so I can see if the hem is even."

Dawn pirouetted away, her thick, dark braid swinging.

Libby scrutinized her work, satisfied. "It's nice of you to want to help, but you don't have to take orders from Mahalia."

Dawn giggled and studied her reflection in the mirror. "Why not, Mama? You do."

Libby caught her daughter's eye and winked. "I do, don't I?"

"It's almost like she's the boss and you're working for *her*

7

instead of the other way around." Laughter lingered in Dawn's voice as she twirled.

"Mahalia does have that effect on people, doesn't she?" Libby put the pincushion into the sewing basket and set the basket beside the rocking chair. She had mending to do tonight.

"I like her, though," Dawn mused as she swayed to some internal music. "She'll cook anything I want, and she bakes the most delicious apple pie in the whole world."

"That she does." Libby's hands automatically went to her hips, which had rounded slightly more than she would have liked since she'd hired Mahalia as her cook and assistant three years before. She couldn't call Mahalia a whirlwind, for her larger-than-life appearance and presence likened her more to a tornado.

"Have you finished your lessons?"

Dawn stopped dancing and wrinkled her nose. "I have sums to do."

Libby swallowed a sigh. Sums were Dawn's nemesis; this wasn't the first time she'd finished all of her other lessons, leaving the sums till last, hoping they'd somehow miraculously do themselves.

"You can take the dress off, dear."

Dawn stepped out of her new dress, and Libby noticed that the knee of one of her cotton stockings was torn. Dawn attempted to move away, but Libby caught her arm.

"What happened to your knee?"

"It's nothing, Mama. Really."

Again she attempted to leave, but Libby drew her close and examined the rip, noting that blood had soaked through the fabric. Gently pushing the cloth aside, she saw the ugly scrape on her daughter's knee.

"How did this happen?"

Dawn wouldn't look at her. "It was nothing, Mama. I . . . I tripped, that's all."

An angry ache settled in Libby's chest. "You were pushed, weren't you?"

Dawn finally pulled away and picked up her school dress. "I told you, I tripped."

Libby clenched her fist and pressed it against her mouth. This was the third time in a week that Dawn had "tripped" on her way home from school, ripping her stockings. But the stockings be damned. Libby refused to believe her daughter was that awkward and clumsy.

"It's those boys, isn't it? Willie Frost and his bullying friends. They're teasing you again, aren't they?"

Dawn stood before her in her muslin chemisette. The lace edging the hem of one leg was torn. "It happens all the time, Mama."

How could she be so calm? Libby rose, maternal possessiveness causing her blood to boil in her veins. "I'll get to the bottom of this if I have to—"

"Mama, please," Dawn pleaded. "If you interfere, you'll only make things worse." She hugged Libby's waist. "It's not so bad, really. I can usually outrun them. I don't mind so much. They'll get tired of picking on me one day and go after someone else."

Libby returned the embrace, pressing her nose against Dawn's shiny black hair. "But *I* mind."

Dawn patted her shoulders, as if Libby were the one who needed the encouragement. "I can take care of myself, Mama."

Leaning away from her daughter, Libby swallowed the lump in her throat and gave Dawn's braid a playful tug. "What will I do when you no longer need me?"

"That won't be for a long, long time," Dawn assured her.

Libby forced a smile. "I guess you need me to tell you to get out of those stockings and have Mahalia bathe your knee." She lifted an old brown cotton dress off the table. "Put this on before you go cavorting in the woods, please, and hang your school dress in the wardrobe."

Dawn shrugged into the dress while Libby folded the new one and draped it over the sewing chair.

"Perhaps you should do your sums before you go off picking berries. I know you. Once you're in the woods, you'll have no concept of time, and I'll have to come looking for you."

"But if I do my sums first, it'll be dark before I can get to the berry patch."

"Sums come before berry picking, Dawn."

Dawn's beseeching look was a well-practiced one. Although it confirmed her youth, there were times when Libby swore her daughter was twelve, going on eighteen. The realization filled her with bittersweet emotions.

"But, Mama, I—"

Laughter erupted on the porch below, and they both turned toward the open window.

Dawn skipped across the room, ignoring the cat that slept on the cushioned window seat, and peered outside. "Oh, look! How cute!" She sped past her mother, scrambling to button the last few buttons of her dress before she disappeared out the door. Her footsteps clattered on the stairs.

Libby frowned and stepped to the window just as a horse's rump disappeared beneath the porch roof.

Raising her battered head, the cat on the window seat made a raspy sound and glared at Libby with her one good eye.

Libby stroked her scarred ears, lingering on her neck. "I'm sorry, Cyclops. I didn't mean to disturb your nap."

The roof hid the Bellamy brothers from view, but Libby heard them chortling. She wondered how many decades Burl and Bert had been living at the boardinghouse; they'd been here when she arrived twelve years before.

Now, as every day, they rocked on the porch, snorting with laughter at something or someone Libby couldn't see. They passed most days that way, making running commentary on everyone, stranger and acquaintance alike.

"What the hell do ya call *that?*" Burl Bellamy's cackle turned into a fit of coughing.

"It's a dog."

The voice, rich and deep, tinged with a hint of indignation, reminded Libby of bronze and polished mahogany.

"A *dog?* That ain't no dog," Burl argued. "Hell, a real dog'd eat that'n fer lunch and cough up a hair ball bigger'n a stallion's testicles."

Bert Bellamy howled at his brother's witticism.

10

Libby's interest was piqued. She hurried down the stairs and went to the front door, pulling aside the short curtain that covered the window. She peeked outside, squinting at the stranger.

"Oh, my." The words came out on a rush of breath, and she put her hand to her chest, feeling an odd fluttering there.

He stood by his mount, big and luxuriantly muscled with a chest as wide as a door and arms as big around as porch pillars. His face was deeply tanned and as leathery as the saddle that was cinched around his horse's belly. Deep brackets were etched on either side of his mouth, and his jaw was square and hard. Unrelenting, Libby decided.

"Oh, what kind is it?" Dawn stood on tiptoe by the stranger's horse and peered at his saddlebag.

Libby's gaze was riveted on the man's face, which had softened slightly when he smiled at her daughter. He removed his hat, revealing sun-bleached streaks in hair that was as brown as strong coffee.

"It's called coyote bait, little gal," Burl suggested, obviously still having a good time at the stranger's expense.

"He's a Shih Tzu." The stranger's smile vanished, and his voice was gruff and defensive.

Burl guffawed again. "Hear that, Bert? It's a shit-soo!"

"A shit-Sioux? What's that?" Bert asked, clearly amused with himself. "Some kinda Injun dog?"

"Can't be, Bert. Ain't enough of him there to feed a whole tribe."

The brothers chortled again.

Dawn glared at the old men. "Shame on both of you. You know how I feel when you make fun of the Indians."

"I'm sorry, little gal," Burl apologized, still laughing, "but ya gotta admit it ain't much of a dog."

Dawn turned toward the saddlebag again. "I think he's adorable, especially with that leather thong holding his hair up on the top of his head. Is that to keep it out of his eyes?"

The stranger continued to study Dawn, a look on his face that Libby couldn't identify. She sensed he hadn't had much experience with girls Dawn's age. "That's right, young lady."

11

Dawn gazed up at him. "Can I hold your dog? Maybe play with him?"

He lifted the dog from the saddlebag and handed it to her. "I think Mumser could use some exercise."

"Oooh, Mumser. What a cute name," Dawn said with a giggle as the pup licked her face. "You're much more fun than our cranky old cat."

Dawn carried the wiggly pup to the grass, where she ran her fingers over its long, silky coat before it scampered away from her, obviously eager to play.

Libby's gaze lingered on her daughter as the child romped with the pup. She was grateful for Dawn's resilience. Somehow she had to keep her innocent and sweet, but with the world the way it was, she knew that wasn't possible. Prejudice against half-bloods was rampant, even in bucolic Thief River, California.

Dawn's laughter tinkled through the air. With such a playmate, her sums certainly would be forgotten, and perhaps even her promise to pick berries.

"Is this the boardinghouse?"

Again Libby was drawn to the rich timbre of his voice.

"Shore is. Riverside. Built in eighteen-seventy on the banks of Thief River by the late Sean O'Malley," Burl recited. "May God Almighty bless his Irish soul." He spat a stream of tobacco over the side of the porch, hitting one of Libby's prize chrysanthemums.

With an angry gasp, she flung open the door. "Burl Bellamy! How many times have I told you not to spit your disgusting tobacco onto my flowers?"

He turned and grinned, exposing his toothless mouth. "Well, afternoon, Miz Liberty, how long you been standin' there?"

"Long enough to see you do it." She put her fists on her hips and glared at him. "If you can't use the spittoon, then quit chawing tobacco."

Lifting her skirt with one hand, she grabbed the sprinkling can she kept on the porch with the other and hurried down the steps to the grass. With her fingertips, she gingerly held the stem of her beautiful pink mum, then doused it with water.

"There, there," she soothed, almost feeling the mum's anxiety.

"Who knows, Miz Liberty? Mebbe tobaccy juice is just what them posies need," Bert offered.

Libby rolled her eyes and swung around. "That stuff is poison. To my flowers *and* to you." The last three words lost their punch as she met the stranger's gaze. She swallowed hard, having momentarily forgotten he was there in the flurry over her mums.

His hat was still in his hand. His eyes were such a brilliant blue that they appeared to have been painted.

"He's wantin' a room, Miz Liberty."

"She don't rent to folks with dogs," Burl announced.

"Heck, Burl, that ain't no *real* dog."

Libby continued to stare at the stranger, her mouth working but nothing coming out. For anyone to render her speechless was quite an accomplishment, she thought, bemused.

"Mumser!"

Hearing her daughter's cry of alarm, Libby pulled her gaze to the other side of the path that led to the house, where more of her chrysanthemums grew.

"Oh, no!" The damned dog was digging in her precious flower bed!

Flinging away the sprinkling can, she flew at the dog, making threatening motions with her hands. "Get away! Shoo! Shoo!"

With his rump in the air and his tail wagging, the pup clearly thought Libby wanted to play. She disregarded him and fell to her knees next to the flowers. Ignoring the playful growling and the tugging at her skirt, she replaced the dirt the little beast had dug up around the stems, pressing it over the roots.

"I'm sorry, Mama. He just sort of got away from me." Dawn was contrite as she bent to help her mother put the flowers to rights.

13

"I don't think he did any real damage." Libby held a tight rein on her temper, which could be volatile. Although she never displayed anger in front of her daughter, she often felt as if she were going to explode. Like now. It was unreasonable to get emotional over flowers, but she'd worked so hard on them and they were truly the most beautiful mums in northern California. Everyone told her so. Why, perfect strangers would stop and compliment her on their beauty.

She took a deep breath and continued to pack the dirt when she heard the keening rip of fabric, followed by Dawn's gasp and cry.

"Cyclops! Mumser! No!"

Libby turned in time to see her battered one-eyed cat giving chase to what appeared to be, for all intents and purposes, a small shaggy mop racing over the grass. A length of her own lacy petticoat fluttered along behind the dog.

Jackson cringed as he surveyed the chaos and covertly studied the girl. When he'd ridden up, his emotions had been exposed like raw nerves, but he'd quickly shoved them into the corners of his mind, where they belonged. His first glimpse of the girl had nearly done him in.

What he'd expected hadn't been what he'd found. He'd been searching for her for a month, since his return from the Orient. His first discovery was the burned-out village where he'd left her and Grandmother. With mounting fear, he'd tracked her to a ranch, but learned she hadn't been there for six years. His gut had clenched when he discovered the rancher had been using her as hired help. A mere child, for Christ's sake! He'd expected to find the same thing here, but found instead a happy, beautiful child, well dressed and cared for by a woman she called Mama. What in the hell was going on?

It was hard for him to keep from staring at her. She was a beauty. More than that, she appeared to be sweet-tempered and compassionate. He felt a rush of pride, followed by a surge of guilt that washed every other feeling away.

Mumser raced past, breaking into his reverie, the cat not far behind. Mumser was trained to know the "come" and "heel" commands, but at this point, under these circumstances, Jackson wasn't sure it made any difference. Still, he had to try. He whistled a command, then called his dog. Mumser ignored him, as Jackson knew he would.

With his hat in his hand, he crossed to where the woman continued to fuss with the dirt around her posies.

When she first stepped onto the porch, he'd noticed her fire. White women were always full of fire. Always had their backs up about one thing or another. They never left a man in peace. But if Jackson thought she showed her temper when the old coot spat tobacco on her flowers, wait until she discovered why he was there. *Then* he'd see a damned inferno, he had no doubt about that.

He hadn't been drawn to a white woman in over ten years, for all the reasons that had just run through his head. Give him a geisha any day. Or, he thought, remembering painful years passed yet not forgotten, an Indian maiden. There was something soothing about women who knew how to please a man, and to his mind, white women hadn't quite gotten the hang of it.

And he was tired. Damned tired of getting paid to fight someone else's battles in dirty corners of the world. His years as a globe-trotting freelance mercenary had finally caught up with him. He was ready to retire and settle down. More than ready.

"You should really have a fence of some kind around those flowers, ma'am."

The woman stood, her hands on her hips, and gave him an icy stare, although her eyes were dark and hot. "Until today I didn't have need for one."

He cleared his throat. "The name's Wolfe, ma'am. Jackson Wolfe." He bit back another groan as the animals raced past.

"Cyclops!" The young girl continued to chase them, her braid, as thick as his fist, swinging from side to side.

"After all this," Jackson began somewhat hesitantly, "I . . . er . . . don't suppose you have a spare room, do you?"

Her mouth opened, then snapped shut. "After all this,"

she countered, throwing her arms wide with a flourish, "you actually think I'll rent you . . . and your *dog* a room?"

"Well, I . . . er . . . just came from the jail, and Vern said you might have a room available."

Her gaze was wary. "Vern Roberts?"

"Yes, ma'am. I'm acting sheriff until Vern gets back on his feet, and I'll need a room." This was where he wanted to stay. No other place would do. He'd camp outside if he had to.

She turned away, but not before he saw her jaw clench. "As Burl said, I don't rent to people with pets."

"I noticed you have a shed out back. That'll do."

She swung around to face him, her expression incredulous. "You want to sleep in my shed?"

Nodding, he added, "I'll pay you five dollars a week."

Her jaw dropped. "You'll pay me five dollars a week to sleep in my *shed?* My regular rooms don't even cost that much."

The young girl nearly skidded to a stop beside them. "Mama, we have two vacant rooms, and you said we needed—"

"Never mind what I said, Dawn. Has Mahalia looked after your skinned knee yet? And what about your sums?" Her voice was stern but not scolding.

"But, Mama, you said we needed the money for—"

"Ma'am," Jackson interrupted. "I'll be gone most days, all day. I'll take Mumser with me. Why, you won't even know we're here."

"Yes, Mama, we won't even know they're here."

The girl's eyes held a familiar twinkle in their depths, and the excitement he saw there weakened him. His gut clenched like a fist.

With her arms crossed over her chest, the woman continued to study him. During the fracas, wispy threads of dark hair had come loose from her neat bun and now blew gently over her forehead and cheeks. The rest of her hair shimmered with deep burgundy highlights.

Her mouth was rich and full, her skin creamy. There was the suggestion of a cleft in her chin, and a lushness about

16

her that reminded him of sultry Spanish nights. Warm wine. Willing women. His thoughts surprised him, for this one, with her snapping dark eyes, was anything but willing. Though her face was expressionless, those eyes told him she thought that anyone who would spend five dollars a week to sleep in a shed had ulterior motives.

If that was what she thought, she'd be right. He'd come for his daughter, Dawn Twilight, and he wouldn't leave without her.

2

LIBBY NIBBLED AT THE INSIDE OF HER CHEEK. "I'VE NEVER BENT the rules for anyone."

"Mama, please?"

She glanced at her daughter, whose beseeching look never failed to soften her, then at the stranger. What *was* the matter with her? He was merely another boarder; she'd had hundreds before him. The fact that he was polite and could pay should have made her eager to rent him a room. And the fact that he was easy on the eyes should have helped, as well. Her feelings confused her, and she didn't dare investigate them. But if Vern Roberts sent him . . .

"You're going to fill in for Sheriff Roberts?"

He continued to hold his hat, and the sun danced brightly on the golden strands that threaded through his dark hair. "Yes, ma'am."

Dawn tucked her arm through her mother's and squeezed. "He's gonna be the sheriff, Mama."

Dawn's gaze darted toward the wretched dog, and Libby knew that her daughter's enthusiasm had nothing to do with the man and everything to do with his pet. She'd always had a softer spot in her heart for critters than for people.

"We can't let him sleep in the shed. We just *can't*."

Libby looked past her daughter, toward the lawn. The animals had tired. Cyclops was nowhere to be seen, but the dog was merrily ripping the torn length of her petticoat to shreds.

She stifled a sigh. They did need the money. The nest egg Sean had left her before he died six years before was dwindling fast. And with Bert and Burl seldom able to pay their rent, there was little income and far too much outgo, especially when there were empty rooms. And that outgo included the repairs the Bellamy brothers did in exchange for their rent. Repairs she had to pay someone to do over properly, she reminded herself with a weary sigh.

Yet she was hesitant. "Well . . ."

"Oh, thank you, Mama!" Dawn sprinted across the grass and fell to the ground beside the dog.

"Much obliged, ma'am."

Libby stuck out her hand and he took it. His rough calluses slid over her own. "Liberty O'Malley," she stated.

"My pleasure." His hand held hers for a fraction of a second longer; then he released it.

She made a fist and shoved her hand into her apron pocket, sensing an odd tingling that burrowed through her palm. Giving him a jaundiced look, she mused, "Had that mutt of yours been big and ugly, you can bet I wouldn't have given in."

His smile was wide. It momentarily disarmed her, for it made him even more appealing.

"For the first time since he was given to me, I'm glad he isn't. It's hard to appreciate a dog that isn't even as big as my boot."

She hid her feelings, still unsure if she wanted to rent him a room. There was no sensible explanation for her reticence. Before she'd agreed, she'd decided the dog was merely a nuisance, and as long as it stayed away from her precious mums, she didn't give a diddly damn about it.

There was something about the man himself that caused the skin on her arms to pebble with gooseflesh. The sensation was new and it was pleasant, and it bothered Libby a great deal.

With an abrupt nod, she turned and took the steps to the porch, sensing that he was behind her. The Bellamy boys had been surprisingly quiet since the fracas between Cyclops and the dog had ended. Libby shot Burl a quick glance, noting that his rheumy old eyes held an unprecedented gleam. Bert chuckled quietly beside him. Narrowing her lids, she gave each of them a threatening look. Bert's restrained chuckle developed into a wheezing laugh.

Flinging open the door, she marched through and strode up the stairs, making her way to the third floor, where she kept a large bedroom. It was usually unoccupied; she rented it out rarely. The furnishings had been Sean's. Not that it was a shrine to his memory or anything like that. Theirs had not been that kind of union. The room tended to get hot and stuffy in the summertime and cold in the winter, so she kept it vacant during the hottest and coldest months. Now, with September behind them, the cool autumn breeze would keep the room comfortable—until December, when there could be frost on the inside of the windows.

Perhaps Mr. Wolfe would be gone by then. An unpleasant twinge darted through her stomach at the thought, and she scolded herself for her foolishness.

"The room is four dollars a week. I usually charge three, but since you have the dog, I'm tacking on an extra dollar." She didn't expect him to argue. After all, he'd offered to pay five to sleep in the woodshed.

Stepping inside, she gave the room an automatic survey to make sure everything was in order. She cringed at the sight of the dust that winked and danced in the air, clearly visible as the sun shone through the window.

He stepped in beside her, his size both intimidating and alarmingly arousing. She'd been showing male boarders bedrooms for over ten years, and never before had she been so acutely aware that they were rooms in which people did their most intimate acts.

The bed, which had been Sean's, was wider and longer than normal. It seemed the perfect bunk for this big man.

Sean's heavy rolltop desk and his big leather easy chair with the matching ottoman were bittersweet reminders of a life long gone. For obvious reasons, it was her most masculine room. She'd fought her feelings for months after Sean's death, wondering if she could bear to have someone else use his things, but in the end, she was too practical to do anything else with them.

Mahalia had once asked her why she didn't simply use the furniture herself. That would have been the sensible thing to do, of course. But with Sean gone, it was her first opportunity to have things of her own.

As the only daughter of migrant Irish farmworkers with four sons, Libby had been the least important person in the household. No one cared that she wanted a permanent home. Her brothers, rowdy boys all, had been delighted that they didn't have to attend school. Her father moved the family with every change in the seasons, going where there was work, careless of his daughter's thirst for a little knowledge and a place to put her roots. She barely existed, as far as he was concerned. The only thing she'd been good for was to work and bring in money. Money that he took from her. She'd even tried hiding a few dollars for herself, but in the end, he found that, too. She wore her brothers' hand-me-downs, not owning a dress until she married Sean. Even at that, he'd bought it for her, not her father.

Sean's arrival in her life had been like a prayer answered. A distant relative from Ireland, he'd sought them out after learning the family was picking peaches in the valley. To Libby, Sean had been a savior from the beginning. He was quiet and polite, a welcome change from her bawdy brothers and brutish father. He'd given her polish and taught her independence. Although she'd known how to read a little, he'd taught her more. He'd been a tutor and a mentor. He'd opened up a whole new world to her, a world in which she was important. And although he'd been kind, Libby had been forced to share what was his. Now she had things in her bedroom that she had chosen, and she chose nothing that had been Sean's.

The new boarder shifted beside her. "Looks fine. Real nice."

Pleased, she merely nodded. "Breakfast is served between five and seven." She crossed to the washstand and tidied up the towels that hung on the wooden bar, catching a glimpse of herself in the mirror. Her hair was a mess, and her cheeks were flushed. Her stomach dropped. She looked positively unkempt.

"The evening meal begins promptly at six. Mahalia, my cook, doesn't do lunches, so you're on your own."

Actually, that wasn't entirely true. There was usually a pot of stew or soup simmering on the back of the stove, fresh bread, and cookies in abundance, but Libby wasn't feeling generous. If Mr. Wolfe was the least bit clever, he wouldn't go hungry.

"You'll share the bath with the other tenants on the floor below. There's a gas-heated tub. The . . . necessary is outside, beyond the woodshed." She opened the wardrobe, revealing a clean chamber pot, and felt heat rise on her neck. She berated herself again, for never before had such things embarrassed her.

"I'll . . . ah, let you settle in, then. Dawn, my daughter, will leave a teakettle of hot water for washing outside your door each morning. It's one of her responsibilities before she goes to school." She marched to the door.

"Ma'am?"

Libby stopped but didn't turn around.

"She's a pretty girl, your daughter."

Hearing no derision, Libby was momentarily shoved off-balance. "For a breed, you mean?"

"That's not what I said." His voice was hard, as if he was angry with her.

Libby turned, noting the coldness in his eyes. Again her balance was threatened, but she owed him no explanation, nor would he get one. Dawn's skirmishes with her white classmates need not be blabbered to strangers.

"I apologize. Thank you," she said as graciously as she could. "Yes, she's a pretty girl, although around here, Mr. Wolfe, a breed is a breed is a breed. Her looks, pretty or not, mean nothing at all. She may have the face of an angel, but she must fight off the demons, just the same."

With a slight nod, she left the room, closing the door quietly behind her.

Jackson stared at the door long after she'd gone, her words ricocheting in his brain. He'd been so single-minded in his purpose, he hadn't given much thought to anything else.

Who was this child he had sired twelve years before? When he last saw her, she'd been an infant, void of personality. She'd been the dependent child of a widower on whom she could not depend. She'd been a helpless little angel.

And he'd been a coward. A spineless whiner whose tears had been as much for himself as for the woman he'd loved and lost. And he'd been running from his grief and guilt ever since.

He flung his travel bag onto the bed and crossed to the window, raising it to let in some air. The curtains caught the breeze, billowing slightly.

Scanning the lawn, he felt his heart clutch when he saw his daughter. And he had no doubt that she was his. None. His gut told him. She had Flicker Feather's smile. The same dimple in her left cheek. The same tinkling laughter, which had always reminded him of chimes in the wind.

He laughed softly, knowing that to look at him no one would believe he had the soul of a poet. Truth to tell, he hadn't felt poetic for a very long time.

He had questions aplenty. Among them, how did Dawn Twilight come to be at this place, with this woman whom she called Mama? Maybe his questions would be answered in the morning, when he paid a visit to the bank. And John Frost. It had been five years since he'd received the last verification of funds he'd mailed. Sometimes it had taken two or three years for his mail to catch up with him, but five . . .

Time had softened the pain of his wife's death. It no longer dug at him with serrated edges, bloodying his conscience.

He still hurt, probably always would, but finding Dawn Twilight was like pressing a cool, healing compress over a wound that refused to heal.

Now he had to find a way to announce who he was. He would need time. Couldn't simply blurt it out, for that would drive the girl away. And, he thought with a scornful smile, he would no doubt find a stake driven through his heart by Liberty O'Malley if he moved too quickly. But he would make his move. Slowly. Steadily. The woman would be first. He had to break down her defenses, and he had no doubt that she had many. He'd already felt her reticence, and she had no idea what he was up to. He couldn't tip his hand. He had too much riding on the outcome.

The woman was a beauty, though. Standing with her in the quiet room, staring at the big bed, he'd felt a surprising surge of desire. With her hair mussed and her face high with color, she'd been damned tempting. Like she'd just had a satisfying tumble between the sheets.

He swore and shook himself, continuing to study his daughter through the open window. With Mumser snuggled in her arms, she was curled up under a weeping willow, the branches drooping around her as if already protecting her from outside forces. Perhaps from him. He sighed.

"Dawn?" Liberty O'Malley's voice called from the porch below.

His daughter's gaze went toward the house. "Yes, Mama?"

"It's time to get at your sums, dear."

Dawn's distress was visible, even from the third-floor window. "But, Mama—"

"No buts. You've wasted enough time. And Miss Parker is willing to help you if—"

"I can't let the *teacher* help me, Mama!"

There was a moment of silence. "Dawn, I don't want to argue with you anymore. The sooner you learn to do sums, the better life will be for both of us. Schoolwork is more than writing stories and poems, and it's time you realized that."

"But what about the berries? I promised Mahalia—"

"Bert and Burl have gone into the woods to pick the berries, dear, now take that . . . that *dog* up to Mr. Wolfe. He's in the room on the third floor."

A smile tugged at Jackson's mouth as he stepped away from the window. He went to the desk and rolled up the top. He was sitting there, pretending to struggle with something when Dawn Twilight knocked on the door.

Libby stepped into the kitchen and poured herself a cup of coffee. Mahalia stirred what smelled like pudding on the stove, the wooden spoon making smooth figure eights over the bottom of the cooking pot to prevent burning.

Libby peered into the vessel. "Tapioca? Isn't that a bit bland for your taste, Mahalia?"

Mahalia snorted. "You'll never catch me eatin' the likes of this." She grimaced. "How you white folk can swallow such tasteless bird shit is beyond me."

Libby gave her a sweet smile. "But it's nice of you to think of the boarders once in a while. Since," she added, arching an eyebrow, "that's who you're supposed to be cooking for in the first place."

Mahalia lifted her chin, appearing offended. "I just try to expand their culinary experience." Suddenly her face changed, and she gave Libby a wicked grin.

"What's that look for?" Libby slumped into a chair by the table and watched the steam rise from her coffee.

Mahalia shrugged expansively. "It's nothin'. We just ain't rented that room out in months, is all."

"We need the money, Mahalia, and the weather is cooling off. Also, the back stoop slopes so far down on one side, I'm afraid someone will take a tumble. The extra four dollars a week will help toward fixing it."

"Yes, ma'am," she said in her most subservient voice. "If you say so."

Libby threw her a jaundiced look. "Say what's on your mind, Mahalia. You will sooner or later, anyway."

Her assistant gave her a wide-eyed look of innocence. "What could be on my mind, Miss Liberty?"

Libby squirmed. Mahalia used formality only when she was making fun of her.

"Why, it don't matter a whit that he's the nicest piece of male flesh that's passed through Thief River in months, now, does it?"

Feigning indifference, Libby took a sip of her coffee. "I really hadn't noticed."

Mahalia's snort was anything but delicate. "Shore, and you didn't notice them clear blue eyes, either, or them wide, hard shoulders. Did you notice his thumbs?"

Libby gave her a puzzled glance. "His thumbs?"

The schoolmistress entered the kitchen and fixed herself a cup of tea. Cyclops was pressed close to her ankles, purring loudly.

She took a chair across from Libby, making room for the cat on her lap. Since her arrival in July, she'd bonded both with the battered one-eyed cat Libby had rescued from the dump, and with Dawn. Libby attempted to squelch the nip of jealousy she experienced each time Dawn and Chloe Ann went off together, searching the woods for injured birds or unusual berries. When she wasn't in the schoolroom, Chloe Ann Parker was merely a young, curious, energetic girl. She and Dawn had much in common, despite the difference in their ages.

"Did you notice the new boarder, Miz Chloe Ann?"

Chloe Ann poured a dollop of cream into her cup and stirred with dainty strokes; then she dropped some cream onto her spoon and watched Cyclops lick it off.

"I've just come from school, Mahalia." She stroked Cyclops, who showed her gratitude by nuzzling Chloe Ann's hand.

Libby had always been intrigued by Chloe Ann. Although she appeared both prissy and vulnerable, she had a strength beneath the surface that Libby felt was waiting to erupt. She was an eighteen-year-old girl, teetering on the brink of full-fledged womanhood. She enjoyed doing girlish things with Dawn, yet when she taught school, she commanded each child's attention.

Libby envied her ability to change roles. Libby never had such a chance. Ever since her childhood, she'd worked to put food on the table. She'd never learned to play. That was why she didn't begrudge Dawn her wistfulness. Perhaps she should have expected her own daughter to be more helpful around the rooming house, but Libby didn't want Dawn to miss out on her childhood, as she had.

Chloe Ann's youthful vigor included a romantic heart. She and Libby had shared a secret or two, and although Chloe Ann had suitors galore, Libby knew she was waiting for the man of her dreams. Libby had had to bite her tongue to keep from telling her that dream men simply didn't exist, and the sooner poets stopped filling women's heads with such nonsense, the better off everyone would be.

Chloe Ann turned to Libby. "We have a new boarder?"

Libby opened her mouth to speak, but Mahalia rushed right in.

"Yes, ma'am. A big, tall, handsome son of a—"

"Mahalia," Libby warned, giving her a hard glare.

Mahalia chuckled, her large frame jiggling beneath her loose dress. "I was just askin' Libby if she'd noticed the man's thumbs."

Libby and Chloe Ann exchanged looks.

"His thumbs?"

"Exactly my response, Chloe Ann." Eyeing Mahalia, Libby asked, "What in the world can you tell about a man by studying his thumbs?"

Mahalia continued to chuckle. "Same thing you can learn by studyin' his ears or his nose, or maybe even his big toes or the size of his feet."

Libby hadn't seen a man's bare feet since before Sean died. An automatic memory triggered in, and she remembered that all of his toes had been rather small. "And that is . . . ?"

"Their size, of course."

Although Chloe Ann's face was pinched into a look of puzzlement, Libby had an idea where Mahalia's discourse was leading.

"Mahalia—"

"The size of what?" Chloe Ann interrupted.

Mahalia clucked and dropped the spoon onto a plate, then moved the pot off the heat, covering the hot handles with the sides of her apron. "Oh, come now, gal. You're dense as a tree trunk. Ain't you ever wondered how big a man is 'tween his legs?"

Chloe Ann gasped, her fair skin turning a bright shade of pink while Libby nearly choked on her coffee.

Mahalia turned as her smile lingered, showing her large white teeth. "My, my. You gals ain't as coy as all that, are you?"

Libby's eyes watered, and she continued to swallow and cough. "Mahalia Jones, you are a wicked, wicked woman. Look what you've done to poor Chloe Ann. You've embarrassed her to tears, and you almost caused me to choke to death."

Mahalia harrumphed and tossed Chloe Ann a jaded glance. "Don't tell me a woman grown don't wonder about them things."

Chloe Ann's face continued to color.

"Whether women do or don't isn't the issue, Mahalia," Libby scolded. "We don't go around talking about it, that's all."

Mahalia poured the tapioca into a bowl, covered it, and set it near the window to cool. "Don't know why we can't talk about it. Them is facts of life." She turned on them, her fists on her ample hips. "Men talk about us, you know."

Libby gave her a look of warning, but Mahalia ignored it.

"Ain't you ever noticed the blacksmith's hands?" She rolled her eyes. "Big. And that hawklike nose of his is another dead giveaway. Why," she added, a sly smile sliding across her lips, "don't tell me you ain't ever noticed the peddler man. He might be scrawny, but his hands and his feet is *big,* and I can't help wonderin' what it'd be like to—"

"Enough, Mahalia." Libby felt heat rise to her cheeks.

Feigning offense, Mahalia lifted her nose in the air. "All's I'm sayin' is that the new boarder, he got nice big thumbs."

One side of her mouth lifted in a sassy grin. "The rest of him ain't bad, neither."

Dawn rushed into the room, her eyes glittering with excitement. "Mama, Chloe Ann, guess what?"

Libby sensed something had sidetracked Dawn from her homework again. "Have you finished your sums, dear?"

"Well, no, but—"

"I don't want to hear any more excuses. I'm tired of them, Dawn. Sick and tired of your excuses." Libby was close to losing her temper and had to force herself to hold back.

"But I'm trying to tell you, Mama. Mr. Wolfe showed me a way to do them that I understand. You know how I always have trouble carrying a number?" She plopped her arithmetic paper on the table and swiftly worked one of the problems. "See?" She held the paper toward her teacher.

Chloe Ann squinted a little as she studied the work, then smiled at Libby. "She's done it right."

Frowning, Libby looked at the paper. "Mr. Wolfe showed you how to do this?" It rankled that a stranger could wheedle his way into their lives with such ease.

Dawn gave her an eager nod. "And it didn't take any time at all, Mama. He told me to break down the numbers into pennies. Not only that," she continued, "he was writing a letter, and I helped him with some of the words."

Libby raised her eyebrows. "You helped him compose a letter?" She was tempted to ask who it was to, but knew it was none of her business.

Dawn's smile was blinding. "See? He helped me, and I helped him. He said it was recip—" She pinched her dark brows together. "Reciprocal."

"My, my," Mahalia crooned. "Ain't he just the finest man to help a young girl like that?"

Libby could feel Mahalia's wicked gaze on her and forced herself not to look her way. Naturally she was grateful he'd helped Dawn get a grip on her sums, but she was also very, very leery. Maybe she was being overly protective and acting foolish, but few people did something for nothing.

She studied her daughter, who had flung herself into a chair and was concentrating on finishing her sums. Perhaps Mr. Wolfe saw that Dawn was a special child. Perhaps that was all it was . . . but it sure didn't feel like that. Libby felt a knot of apprehension in her stomach, and no matter how hard she tried, she couldn't get rid of it.

3

THE FOLLOWING MORNING AS SHE PREPARED BREAKFAST, LIBBY heard a commotion outside. She took the skillet off the heat and hurried to the front door. Her breath caught in her throat when she stepped onto the porch.

Squatting beside her mums, Jackson Wolfe pounded a picket-shaped stake into the ground, one of many that made up a tiny fence that surrounded her precious flowers.

There was a fluttering in her chest, and she pressed her hand over her heart. No man had ever done anything for her without being asked. And this man was so beautiful to watch. Dragging in a quiet breath, she gazed at his wide shoulders. She could detect the muscles beneath his shirt as he moved. His shirtsleeves were rolled up, and his sinewy forearms bunched and relaxed as he worked.

The dog wiggled and leaped at him, barking and nipping at his elbow. He ignored it, continuing to work. Seeming to sense he was no longer alone, he glanced up, giving her a blinding smile. Libby swallowed the lump in her throat and returned one, surely not as beautiful as his.

"I hope you don't mind. It's the least I can do."

"I don't mind," she answered. "It's very thoughtful."

He finished and stood, checking his work. "I'll fence the other flower beds later. If I take the dog with me to the jail, the flowers should be safe."

She flushed, knowing he'd sensed her overprotectiveness toward something as inanimate as her mums. "That . . . that's fine. Thank you." She turned to the door, then said, "Breakfast is ready, Mr. Wolfe."

"I'll be there as soon as I clean up."

She returned to the kitchen, feeling off-balance and giddy. Dawn sat at the table, flanked by Bert and Burl, who shoveled in mounds of hot cereal, smacking their lips approvingly. Dawn's glance kept going to the door as she toyed with her food.

"Eat your breakfast, Dawn, or you'll be late for school."

Libby stood at the counter, her back to the door, when Jackson entered the kitchen.

Dawn fairly gushed. "Good morning, Mr. Wolfe. How's Mumser today? Did he sleep all right in a strange place? Are you taking him to the jail with you?"

"Dawn, really," Libby scolded. "Give the man a chance to take a breath." She motioned to an empty chair, which he slid into, unfolding the napkin onto his lap.

"The dog's just fine this morning, young lady. And, yes, I'll be taking him to the jail with me." He studied her. "Are your sums done?"

Dawn graced him with a wide smile. "I finished them last night. That trick you showed me made them easy to do."

Libby placed a plate of eggs and ham in front of him, along with a bowl of hot cereal. He glanced up, his eyes so blue and twinkly that Libby thought she might faint. He certainly did something to her insides she'd never experienced before.

"So," Burl began, gumming a piece of bread and jam, "yer gonna be the sheriff, huh?"

Jackson nodded, finished chewing what was in his mouth, then answered, "Until Vern gets back on his feet, anyway."

Burl continued to chew and talk. "Got experience?"

Jackson appeared to bite back a grin. "Some."

"Whatcha been doing afore this?" Bert wiped his cereal bowl with a piece of bread, then stuffed the bread into his mouth.

"Gentlemen," Libby began, using the word lightly, "let the man eat in peace. You can interrogate him later." She glanced at Dawn, who was resting her chin on her palm, staring at the man.

"Dawn? It's time to get ready for school."

With a weary sigh, Dawn wiped her mouth and rose from the table. "I'd like to play with Mumser later today, Mr. Wolfe. May I come by the jail and get him?"

"Dawn, I don't think—"

"That's a fine idea. He'll be bored, having to stay with me all day." A sudden, concerned expression etched his features and he turned to Libby. "That is, if it's all right with you, ma'am."

Libby suppressed a sigh. "As long as you get your schoolwork done, Dawn. But remember, that comes first."

Dawn gave her mother a quick hug, then raced from the kitchen.

Bert and Burl dawdled with their coffee, quiet as church mice. But Libby knew that in no way meant their wrinkled old brains weren't working. After over a dozen years under the same roof, they knew her about as well as anyone. If she showed the slightest bit of interest in Jackson Wolfe, they would somehow know it. Their rheumy old eyes never missed a thing.

Jackson wiped his mouth with his napkin, then stood. "I'll start on the rest of those fences later today, ma'am." He crossed to the door, then turned. "Thank you for the breakfast. It was delicious."

She gave him a wavery smile, then followed him with her gaze until she could no longer see him.

"Ya fancy him, don'tcha?" There was a sly note in Burl's voice.

She returned to the table and began clearing it. "Don't be ridiculous," she huffed. "He's merely a nice man who is making sure his dog doesn't ruin my flower beds."

The Bellamy brothers finally rose from the table. "Seems

a right friendly gent," Bert mused. "Why, helpin' the little gal with her sums and buildin' fences around yer posies— I'd say he was tryin' to get in good with ya. Don'tcha think so, Burl?"

Burl downed the remainder of his coffee and smacked his lips. "'Tain't normal fer a man to do somethin' fer nothin'."

Libby rolled her eyes. "Go on, get out of here. If Mahalia catches you loitering in the kitchen, she'll have you washing dishes."

The threat worked. They cackled as they left the room, leaving Libby to wonder if there was any truth to their words. She was a pragmatic woman, although she normally didn't read ulterior motives into other people's acts. But in spite of all that, their parting words niggled at her brain. Again, as the day before, she got a funny feeling in her stomach when she thought about Jackson Wolfe's good deeds.

The minute Jackson stepped into the sheriff's office, Mumser squirmed from his arms and raced around the room, sniffing the corners, as he'd done every morning for the past week.

With both hands, Sheriff Roberts lifted his leg onto a chair, on which sat a flat, dirty cushion. He winced, cursed, and shook his head.

"Damned game leg," he muttered as he watched Mumser scurry about. "That dog'd better not be looking for another place to take a leak."

Giving him a half smile, Jackson tossed his hat onto the desk, then crossed to the coffee pot, poured himself a cup, and took a sip. He grimaced, disappointed that it wasn't as good as the coffee he'd had at breakfast.

"If he does, it'll most likely be because the place has an encouraging smell."

Vern Roberts grunted. "No doubt his own. So some Chinese high mucky-muck gave you that piss-poor excuse for a dog, huh?"

Jackson raised an eyebrow. "Don't start with me. I've

been ridiculed from here to China about that dog not being fit lunch for coyotes."

Vern chuckled, his graying mustache twitching. "Did you find a room at the boardinghouse?"

Nodding, Jackson hid his rush of pleasure at having found Dawn Twilight. He would tell Vern about her eventually, but not yet. He savored the knowledge, holding it close to his heart. "Yes. Thanks for recommending it."

"Ah," Vern mused. "The widow O'Malley is a mighty fine-looking woman, wouldn't you agree?"

Jackson felt Vern's scrutiny but ignored it. Vividly remembering the surprising effect she had on him, he gave the older man a noncommittal shrug and studied the wanted posters on the far wall. "I suppose. Although white women never interested me much."

"With them dark eyes and hair, she's a real looker."

Jackson tossed him a sardonic look. "I'm not looking for a woman, Vern, white, green, or otherwise."

"Oh, that's right," Vern commented. "You've been courting foreign women of all different shapes and colors." He chuckled. "Just as well, I guess. Ethan Frost's been sniffing around her for nigh onto a year now." His laughter deepened. "Don't seem to get too far with her, though."

"Ethan Frost? Any relation to John?"

"His son, of course. Ethan took over the bank when old John died."

Jackson felt his stomach clench with an unrecognizable dread. His next stop was to have been the bank to discover why he hadn't heard from John for so many years. "When did John die?"

Vern brushed at his mustache with his index finger. "Let me see. Has to be nearly four or five years now."

Jackson turned away so Vern wouldn't see his concern. Perhaps he was worrying for nothing. Maybe, in the confusion following John's death, the records had simply been misplaced. Or maybe his mail just hadn't caught up with him before he left China. Surely there was a reasonable explanation.

He felt Vern's curious gaze.

"You've been gone a mighty long time, Jackson. How did it feel to live among them foreigners?"

Jackson got weary simply thinking about it. He was home; he wanted to put his travels behind him. "They're people, just like the rest of us, Vern."

Vern chuckled. "You've always been that way, you know it?"

"What way is that?"

"Never seeing the differences in people, like you never even noticed they was a different color. I guess it probably all started when you first lived with them Injuns. What tribe was that, again?"

Memories, swift and strong, nudged him. "The Yuroks."

"Yeah, I remember now. You'd been living with that tribe of Indians for, what, five years? Lord, you was only eight or nine when you was rescued." His voice became introspective. "First time I ever saw a grown man cry was the day your pa told me the news. He was so damned relieved . . . like the Almighty had given him a brand-new chance. You know, he came back from that war a hard, angry man, considering as how he thought he'd lost the both of you. You and your real ma, I mean."

Jackson knew what he meant. He barely remembered his own mother, who had been killed by a mine explosion. They had been picking wildflowers in a field nearby. She was struck by flying debris. His father had been away, fighting for the Union. Jackson didn't have much memory of his first year with the Yurok tribe that had saved him, but four years was an eternity to be away. When it was time to go home to a father he didn't remember, he hadn't wanted to leave the tribe. But a few weeks with the woman who would become his stepmother had changed all that. She'd loved him as she loved Corey, her own child. And the boys had become close. Five years his junior, Corey had adored him.

A smile threatened. It wasn't hard to like someone who considered you his hero.

His father and his stepmother had always had an intense relationship, although Jackson had never felt that they had ever excluded their children. When he met Flicker Feather, he'd known in his heart that theirs would be that sort of love, too. Unfortunately, they hadn't had a chance to find out.

"The tribe treated me like one of their own. It took me a while to adjust to Pa again. And the ranch."

"You and your pa became closer than ticks on a hound." Vern continued to study Jackson. "How long has it been since you've seen the family?"

Beneath his dark stubble, Jackson felt the hot rush of old hurts and anger flood his face. "A long time."

"What'd you and your pa fight about, anyway? Christ. It's been over twelve years. Don't you think it's time to mend that fence? Your pa might be strong as an ox and stubborn as a mule, but despite it all, he ain't gonna live forever, you know."

A painful band twisted around Jackson's heart. The very idea that his father might die before he had a chance to see him again made him anxious for a reunion. He wanted to apologize for his youthful pride and self-centered behavior. And for running away like a coward.

"Do your folks even know you're home?"

"No. And I know you're itching to tell them, but let me do it, Vern. I'll get around to it as soon as I'm settled." As soon as he had his daughter and they were a family again.

The sheriff offered a heavy sigh, rummaged through a desk drawer, and lifted out a bottle of whiskey.

Jackson raised an eyebrow. "A little early in the day, don't you think?"

Vern shook his head and took a swig, baring his teeth and clenching his jaw as he swallowed. He found Jackson studying him. "It's medicinal. Goddamn knee never stops throbbing."

Jackson hid a smile. He rather envied a man who could take a drink any time of the day and not come off acting like an ass. Lord knows he himself had tried it often enough, without success. Every so often he attempted to drink again, hoping that maybe his body had changed with age, and he could handle the stuff. It hadn't happened. Yet. He hadn't given up on the possibility, although he thought he probably should.

He took his coffee cup to the window and studied the street. Two scrawny mutts fought over garbage tossed from the hotel. A gust of wind flapped the sign over the mercantile against the eaves, the sound clattering through the street. Two women, busy in conversation, entered the store, disappearing inside. A wagon stopped out front, ready to be filled with supplies. Horses clip-clopped through the street, their hooves sending spirals of dust into the air.

Home. So different from everything he'd discovered elsewhere in the world. He'd missed the little nuances that made up the West.

Admittedly, Jackson missed his family. He'd been tempted to wire them when he landed in San Francisco, but he wanted to wait, hoping he'd find Dawn Twilight. He remembered the last time he'd seen any of them, remembered it well. . . .

With a heart broken and shattered, Jackson had left his mount in the yard and trudged toward the barn. Pa was there; he could hear him. It wasn't easy to swallow his pride and ask for help, but he had nowhere else to turn. He knew he had a lot of gall coming to his family now, after he'd left and hadn't even told them of his marriage or his daughter. But Flicker Feather's death had been so sudden. So brutal. So final. And the baby . . .

His throat was thick, and he swallowed, unable to dislodge the lump of grief that had settled there. He longed to burrow into the warmth and safety of his family, but he needed to know that his father understood his reasons for having left home in the first place: his aversion to working the land. Corey was there; he'd be all the help Pa needed. There had been no choice for Jackson. His desire to return to the tribe that had rescued him after his mother was killed all those years before had been stronger than his need to follow in his father's footsteps and till his land, raise his stock.

He also had a wanderlust that wouldn't be quenched. Flicker Feather had understood his hunger for travel and his desire to fight for the underdog. He'd been doing the latter ever since he was old enough to understand what the white man was doing to the Indian.

And most of all, no one would understand the peace he'd found living with the tribe. And the love.

Jackson could still hear his father's voice, raised in anger, when he'd told him he had no intention of spending the rest of his life on the ranch. But now, under these circumstances, he was certain that his father would take pity on him and forgive him for not wanting to be a rancher. After all, now he was a widower with a baby to care for. Surely his father could identify with that.

Nathan Wolfe emerged from the barn and strode toward the shed, the front of his shirt and his jeans smeared with muck. His acknowledgment was less than Jackson had hoped for.

"Unless you've come to help, stand clear, son. I'm up to my elbows in cow innards. Damned calf is breech."

Jackson's stomach dipped. "Can I talk to you?"

His father marched toward the shed. "Sure, if you're willing to lend a hand."

Jackson shot a glance toward the barn, knowing his father hadn't been in there alone. "Can't you spare me even a minute?"

Nathan rummaged around in the shed, picked up the supplies he needed, then returned to the barn, stopping briefly at the door. Jackson trailed after him like a child.

"Jackson, I'm sure what you have to say is important, but right now nothing is more important than getting that calf out alive. If I lose it, the mother could die, too. And we can't afford to lose another one." He glanced away, unwilling, to Jackson's mind, to look him in the eye. "You'd understand if you gave a damn about the ranch."

His father's remark stung, and Jackson's stomach pitched

downward. Obviously, to his father, a damned calf was more important than his son's pain. Clenching his jaw in hurt and anger, Jackson turned and marched toward his mount just as his mother stepped onto the porch.

She looked surprised, hurt. "You're leaving already? You just got here."

The lump in Jackson's throat expanded. "He's too busy to talk to me."

She hurried down the steps and touched his arm. "You know how he feels about foals and calves, Jackson."

Yeah, Jackson thought, self-pity burning in his gut, he values them above human life.

"Come for supper tonight," she pleaded. "You can talk to him then. We've all missed you, dear. Corey's been dying to show you his bug-and-butterfly collection, and Mandy asks about you every day. Katie, too. She wanders from room to room, calling your name."

There was a hopeful note in her voice, but he ignored it as he swung into the saddle. "Ma, I'm leaving."

She gave him an indulgent smile. "I can see that, dear. But come for supper tonight, all right?"

She didn't understand, and Jackson was too cowardly to explain. He wasn't simply leaving the ranch, he was leaving the country. If he'd had the guts, he'd have left the world. He was grieving over Flicker Feather's death, and nothing would appease him. His mother would only be hurt by his decision. . . .

Twelve years. Almost thirteen. After so much time, Jackson knew that although his youthful dignity had been injured by a father who had merely been trying to keep his ranch together, his main reason for leaving was his need to escape his pain and guilt over Flicker Feather's death. Now Jackson firmly believed that if he'd returned that night and explained what had happened, things would have been different. His mother would have taken Dawn Twilight in a heartbeat and raised her. His father would have loved her as he loved Corey, who was not of his blood. But so much time had passed. And they had both been so damned prideful. Jackson couldn't change things. Now he simply wanted to pick up where he'd left off, before he and his father were estranged.

Jackson examined the ache in his chest. It was homesickness. He hadn't seen any of his family for years, but that hadn't meant he didn't know how they were. Physically, at least. He knew he'd hurt his stepmother. That still bothered him. She was the only mother he remembered, and she'd been a good one. Hell, she'd been great.

Every year he was gone, he'd dropped his family a note at Christmas. His stepmother had answered him, but it was often six months to a year before he'd get to an American embassy to retrieve his mail. The letters he did receive were filled with news of his brother and sisters, their friends and neighbors. News that contained a forced cheerfulness and careful editing, always skimming over any news about his father, probably because she was afraid that once she started, she wouldn't know when or how to stop.

"Thinking about the old man, are you?"

He jerked his head toward Vern's voice. "How is he, anyway?"

"Fine, last I heard. I haven't seen him since that pretty ma of yours invited me out for his fiftieth birthday bash." He paused. "Them sisters of yours are real beauties, Jackson."

Jackson felt the twist of pain again. He wouldn't know his brother or his sisters if they came up and bit him on the ass. He swore under his breath. He must be getting old, for the urge to reacquaint himself with his siblings was so strong he could almost taste it. Over the last few years he'd begun to miss everything about his family. He would have it all again, once he had reclaimed his daughter. Together they would be welcomed into the fold.

"What happened between you two, anyway?"

Jackson took a chair next to the desk, and Mumser jumped into his lap, circled three times, then settled down for a nap.

"It's been so long, I hardly remember," he lied.

"Then it should be a pleasure to let them know you're back," Vern countered.

Before Jackson could respond, the door swung open, and a gangly young man with a red face and unruly hair rushed in.

Vern nodded a greeting. "Morning, Axel. Meet the new sheriff."

The red-faced young man stepped forward and extended his hand. "Axel Worth, your deputy."

Jackson shook the bony fingers and answered, "Glad to know I've got some able help around here."

The door flew open again, this time slamming against the wall, and two men entered. The older man was short and thickly muscled with a drooping black mustache. His eyes were wild with fury. The younger man was taller, as thickly muscled as the other, and sported thick black hair that hung down almost to his shoulders.

The older man strode to the desk, spread his bulky arms, and planted his hands on the desk. "That son of a bitch burned down my camp last night, killing half my sheep."

Vern winced as he repositioned his knee. "Jackson, this is Danel Mateo and his son, Dominic. Tell him your troubles from now on," he ordered, turning toward the men. "My damned knee aches so bad, it fuzzes up my head."

Cursing, the younger man stepped forward. "This has gone on long enough, Sheriff. If we don't get some satisfaction, we're going to take matters into our own hands."

Vern sighed and settled deeper into his chair. "Well, Jackson, you might as well get your feet wet. Someone's been forcing the sheepmen off their land, burning buildings and barbecuing their woolly-backs alive." He heaved a sigh and took another gulp from his bottle. "Damn. I'm getting too old for this. Sure glad you're on board, son."

Jackson grabbed his hat and dumped a snoozing Mumser into Vern's lap. "Let's have a look at your problem, gentlemen."

Jackson dismounted, requesting the other men to stay back. "How many horses have trampled this site, Danel?"

"None. I was so angry when I saw what they'd done, I didn't get this far."

Jackson squatted and studied the ground; the deputy hunkered down beside him.

"What do you make of it, Sheriff?"

Jackson studied the prints. "Looks like three separate mounts, Axel."

Axel Worth gawked at the ground. "How can you tell?"

For some strange reason, Jackson was reluctant to share everything he knew. "I see three separate sets of shoes. And at least one of the mounts was a mare."

Axel continued to study the ground, his blotchy forehead creased with intensity. "How can you tell that?"

Jackson picked up a dry stick and pointed it at a damp circle in the dirt. "This is urine. See how—"

"Horse piss? How in hell do you know it's horse piss?"

Jackson gave the deputy a weary glance. "Do you want to get down there and smell it?" When Axel sullenly shook his head, Jackson continued. "The stream is away from the back shoe marks. If it were a gelding or a stallion, the urine would be between the front and back prints. Does that answer your question?"

Axel shrugged. "I guess."

What Jackson didn't offer was that while two sets appeared to have been made by cow ponies, the third set was distinctively that of a high-stepper—an unusual mount for a cowboy.

He rose and returned to Danel Mateo and his son. "How many sheep do you think were slaughtered, Danel?"

"I'm guessing about one hundred and twenty-five. Can't say for sure." Danel shook his head. "Christ, I hope you can do something. If this happens again, I'll be wiped out."

Promising to speed up the process, Jackson returned to town, telling Axel to keep Vern informed. Before returning to the jail, he stopped at the bank. The room seemed smaller, somehow, yet nothing appeared to have changed. It even smelled the same: old dust and stale air.

A thin, bespectacled man with long wisps of hair that were swept across a balding pate in a futile attempt at camouflage glanced up from a stack of papers. "May I help you?"

Briefly touching his inside jacket pocket, Jackson said, "I'd like to check on an account, please."

"The name on the account?"

"Wolfe, Jackson and/or Dawn Twilight."

Nodding, the man rose and disappeared behind a partition. He reappeared shortly, his expression bemused. "I'm afraid I don't find such an account, sir."

A spasm rolled through Jackson's gut. He retrieved the leather pouch from his jacket pocket, opened it, and took out the papers. "These are receipts. They prove that I've been sending money to this bank for the past twelve years." Actually, they proved that the bank had received the money up until five years before.

The balding man took the receipts and studied them carefully. "Yes. Art McCann. I recognize his signature. He was John Frost's bookkeeper."

"And where is Mr. McCann now?"

The colorless man stroked his smooth chin. "Hmm. I think he retired shortly after the elder Mr. Frost died."

Jackson picked up his papers and stuffed them into the pouch. "I hear John's son is running the bank now. Is he around?"

"No, sir. He won't be back until next week."

Stifling a sigh, Jackson asked, "Do you know how I can get in touch with Mr. McCann?"

"I believe he went to live with his son. He has a ranch about four miles south of here, along the river. You can't miss it; there's a row of eucalyptus trees lined up all the way from the road to the house."

Jackson brought his mount to a halt at the beginning of the long, winding driveway. The eucalyptus trees gave off a pungent medicinal odor, not entirely unpleasant. He took the road to the house, where he found an elderly man on the porch, sitting at a table, carving something out of a hunk of wood.

"Afternoon," Jackson called.

The old gent stopped working. "Afternoon, yourself. Can I help you?"

"If you're Art McCann, you can."

"That's me." The old man rose. He was lean and wiry, his eyes were sharp. "What can I do for you?"

Jackson dismounted and joined the man on the porch. He drew out the pouch. "I believe you signed some receipts for me. From the bank." He handed them to McCann, who pulled out a pair of spectacles and perused the papers.

"Yes, sir, I remember these." His gaze returned to Jackson. "You Wolfe?"

"I am. I've just been to the bank. Ethan Frost is out of town, but the current bookkeeper couldn't find a record of our transactions."

Art McCann snuffled a laugh. "I'm not surprised."

The familiar spasm returned to Jackson's gut. "Meaning?"

"Mr. Wolfe," McCann began, motioning Jackson to a seat, "I retired shortly after John died. He was a good man. I tried to stay on and make for an easier transition when Ethan took over, but . . ."

He sighed and hiked up the jeans that hung low on his bony hips before resuming his seat. "Well, Ethan wasn't exactly my idea of a good replacement. I'm not telling you anything most people don't already know, but when Ethan was growing up, poor John was getting him out of one scrape after another, paying his debts, smoothing things over with the law. He had a terrible problem with money and women, that boy did. Let's just say that when poor John died, I took it as my way out. I didn't want to work for the kid."

"So, as far as you know, the account was active and accurate until you left."

"Sure was," McCann answered. "If I were you, I'd go straight to young Frost."

Jackson thanked him and stood up. As he took the road to town, he had an uncomfortable feeling that his first meeting with the new banker was not going to go very well.

4

LIBBY HEARD DAWN'S LAUGHTER AS SHE APPROACHED THE parlor. Peeking inside, she found her daughter sitting cross-legged on the floor in front of their new boarder, whose long legs were stretched out on the ottoman.

Libby briefly closed her eyes and sighed. Jackson Wolfe had been her boarder for only a week, yet he'd completely mesmerized her daughter. As usual, Dawn's expression was rapt as she gazed up at him. His dog was asleep in her lap.

"And they really keep their babies in a pouch on their stomachs, just like the pictures show?"

He nodded. "They most certainly do." He glanced up, catching Libby's perusal. His expression was guarded, as she knew her own would be.

Dawn turned. "Oh, Mama! Mr. Wolfe's been all over the world. He's even been to Australia and has seen a kangaroo up close, and they really do keep their babies in a pouch, just like Chloe Ann said they did." Her eyes were bright with excitement.

Libby didn't know how to feel. On one hand, she was grateful the man had taken a liking to her daughter, because the good Lord knew she needed the presence of a normal male in her life. Bert and Burl weren't any kind of role models. She supposed she should consider Ethan Frost, since he'd been calling on her for nearly a year, but for some reason, Dawn and Ethan had never gotten on well together. Probably because his sons had been among those who constantly chased Dawn home. It angered her that Ethan didn't have better control over his boys, but he seemed to think it was merely what boys did to girls. For as charming as Ethan could be, he could also be a prize boob. Oddly enough, this was the first time she'd given Ethan a thought since Jackson Wolfe rode onto her property.

On the other hand, she was leery about Jackson Wolfe's motives, if, indeed, he had any. She had no basis for her reluctance and sensed it was a problem within her, and it would be unfair to take it out on him or Dawn.

Libby stepped into the room. "I'm sure he has many stories you'd love to hear, dear, but it's time for bed."

"All right, Mama, but did you know he can ride a horse so good that he can jump over a river? And his horse is so smart, it can swim."

"Very impressive, Dawn, but—"

"Mama is afraid of horses, Mr. Wolfe."

Libby flushed. "I'm not afraid of them, dear. I just refuse to ride them." Which was a lie, considering that every time she thought of Sean, all she saw was his horse lying on top of him, crushing the life out of him.

Her boarder's gaze appeared interested. "Afraid to ride them?"

Before Libby could explain, Dawn did. "When she was a little girl, she saw a horse trample one of her friends. Then, when she moved here, she saw it happen again to another man. She's afraid of horses. She won't ride them."

Of course, the other man had been Sean, but Libby hadn't felt it was necessary to burden Dawn with her past.

"I guess we all have our fears," Jackson offered.

Somehow it didn't make Libby feel better to know that he was aware of her weaknesses. "It's bedtime, Dawn."

Dawn screwed up her face but didn't argue further. "All right," she said on a sigh as she rose, lifting the dog into her arms. She skipped toward the door, then stopped. "Will you tell me more stories, Mr. Wolfe?"

He smiled, and Libby noted that it reached his eyes. That was something no one could fake.

"It would be my pleasure."

Dawn started out the door.

"Dawn?"

She stopped but didn't turn. "Yes, Mama?"

Libby bit the insides of her cheeks to keep from smiling. "Where do you think you're going?"

"Why, to bed, like you told me to." She kept her back to her mother.

"With Mr. Wolfe's dog?"

Dawn turned, emitting an enormous sigh. "But, Mama, I—"

"The dog doesn't sleep with you, dear."

Air sputtered out through Dawn's lips. "Oh, all right." She lifted the dog close to her face and kissed his nose. Libby shuddered and grimaced, unable to understand why anyone would want to kiss a dog.

"Sorry, Mumser." Dawn returned the dog to its master and left the room, tossing her mother a crushed look as she passed her.

Libby stood in the doorway, her arms crossed over her chest, suddenly feeling awkward. "It's kind of you to entertain Dawn. I'm afraid she can be a nuisance at times. She's at that age, you know."

He said nothing for a moment, merely returning her gaze with a pensive one of his own. "She's not a nuisance. I enjoy her; she's a good audience."

Libby's resolve was melting fast. How could she possibly resist a man who spoke with such warmth about her daughter?

"I want to thank you for helping her with her sums." She smiled. "They've been her nemesis. She's wonderful with words. I mean, she's quite a poet and she loves to draw and sing. She dances rather than walks most of the time, and I constantly find her doodling when she's supposed to be

48

studying. I've often been tempted to purchase a piano, because I know she'd love to take lessons, but—" She gave him a self-conscious smile. "I'm sorry. I'm blathering, aren't I?"

He said nothing, just continued to stare at her with those bright blue eyes. He probably thought she was a bore.

"Well," she finally said. "I'll, ah . . . if you want, there's an old bottle of brandy in the sideboard." She pointed toward the cupboard in the corner. "Help yourself."

She scurried to her room but discovered she was too itchy to sleep. She undressed and slipped into her dressing gown, then removed the pins from her hair. With methodical strokes she brushed it, letting her mind wander, for although Sean had been gone for six years, it had been something he'd done for her, and she still didn't like to do it herself. Though they hadn't had the perfect marriage by any stretch of the imagination, they'd had their moments.

And those moments had ended the day Sean's mount stepped into a gopher hole, crushing his ribs as it fell on top of him.

A wistfulness spread through her, and she tossed the brush on the vanity and simply sat there, staring into the mirror. *Sean.* He'd been a good man. Kind. Generous. In more ways than one, he'd given her a freedom she would never have otherwise known. He'd given her far more than she'd ever given him.

A sadness at her inability to make him happy settled around her heart. It wasn't that she hadn't tried; she'd simply been too young to know how. How could a fourteen-year-old girl who had been taught nothing possibly know how to please a man? And, she thought, anger surfacing, why should a fourteen-year-old girl have to? It wasn't until she was older that she realized Sean had a problem with intimacy. Grown men often laughed about it, but to Sean it was no joke. Try as he might, he could never become aroused enough to make love to her.

In two very short years, Dawn would be the same age Libby was when she'd married. Emotions tumbled through

Libby like acorns on the grass, snagging at pieces of her heart. No one knew the fear that Libby had experienced when she'd been shoved at Sean, as if she were no more important than the piece of paper the deal had been written on. No one ever would. She'd learned to keep her shameful secrets to herself.

With a shaky sigh, she rose from the vanity table and swung away from the bed, knowing she wasn't ready to sleep. She stepped into her slippers and left her room, noting the night sounds in her house. Deep, heavy snoring erupted from the Bellamy brothers' room, and she wondered with a bemused smile how either could sleep through such a racket.

She tiptoed to Dawn's room, opened the door a crack, and looked inside. Her daughter was curled into a ball, one arm under her pillow and the other around the cat's neck. Cyclops looked at Libby, the light from the hallway glinting off her yellow eye.

Although no one realized it, Libby did not care if the cat slept on the bed, nor would she care if Mr. Wolfe's dog slept with him, which she assumed it did. She was not the ogre she appeared to be, but someone had to make grown-up rules and try to enforce them, even if, in the dark of night, the pets found their way to the beds and the rules were ignored.

A brisk breeze billowed out the curtains, and Libby entered the room to make sure Dawn had enough blankets. Cyclops watched her, then extricated herself from Dawn's clutches and disappeared under the covers. She was merely a lump at the bottom of the bed near Dawn's feet when Libby left the room.

She managed the stairs in the dark, knowing them by heart, sidestepping the squeaky spot on the fourth step from the top. A light flickered in the parlor. The fireplace, no doubt. She stepped inside, gasping in surprise when she discovered Jackson Wolfe in the easy chair holding a glass of brandy. The firelight drenched half his face; the other half was darkly shadowed. It was so odd to see a man sitting there as Sean had. But the resemblance stopped there. Sean had been spare, almost gaunt. Jackson Wolfe was muscular and vital. He certainly wasn't the first man to sit in that chair since Sean had died, but he was by far the most compelling.

"I'm sorry. I thought everyone was in bed." She clutched at the front of her dressing gown, keenly aware of how little she wore under it.

His gaze raked her; she should have been insulted, yet she wasn't. She found the look deliciously flattering. She wasn't unattractive, she knew that, but Jackson Wolfe was the first man whose interest she appreciated.

Lifting his glass toward her, he said, "I applaud a woman who doesn't truss herself up like a turkey at bedtime."

Heat flared in her face and she felt her nipples tighten. "Just how many glasses of brandy have you consumed, Mr. Wolfe?"

One side of his sensual mouth lifted. "What makes you think this isn't my first?"

She shivered beneath her lightweight dressing gown and eyed the fire, aching to be closer to the warmth. But that meant being closer to him, and she sensed that wasn't a good idea. "Because your demeanor is totally out of character with the gentleman you appeared to be earlier this evening."

He took another swig, his gaze never leaving her. "Yeah, you're right. I have one hell of a rotten demeanor when I drink." He smirked, his eyes glittering as he studied her. "I'm likely to say a bushel of things I'll regret, but you're a damned fine looking woman, and I don't usually find white women attractive."

With hesitant steps, she moved closer. "Is that supposed to be a gentlemanly compliment?"

"Didn't it sound like one?"

His gaze moved over her so slowly she almost felt it. "A sober man is a gentleman. A man who imbibes seldom is."

He winced. "'Imbibes.' Damned fancy five-dollar word for something as simple as taking a drink, don't you think?"

She stepped closer still, beginning to feel the warmth of the fire. This arousal, this . . . excitement was new to her. It was so seldom that she allowed herself to let go, to explore dangerous sensations. "What word would you use, Mr. Wolfe?"

He expelled a healthy sigh and pulled a thoughful expression. "Let me see. How about 'bibulate'?"

She repressed a smile. " 'Bibulate'? That's good, but 'guzzle' and 'swill' seem more appropriate."

Frowning, he shook his head. "Too crass. How about . . ." His gaze found her mouth, and Libby held her breath. Her tongue came out to wet her lips.

"Oh, you shouldn't have done that." His voice was husky and deep. Like warm whiskey. She shivered, repeating the gesture, nervous to the bone.

One side of his mouth lifted into a half smile. "You did it again."

She shook her head. "No. I . . . I was taking it back." Lord, what kind of foolishness was this?

A warm, raucous chuckle escaped. "You know what that means, don't you?"

Her face was on fire. "It means I was taking it back."

"Oh, no," he argued. "It's an invitation to a kiss. It's part of an obscure Australian ritual."

If nothing else, he was an intriguing drunk. In spite of her discomfort, she had to smile. "Since I'm ignorant of Australian rituals, obscure or otherwise, rest assured that what I did was *not* an invitation." Her body hummed beneath her gown, and the pulse at her throat hammered against her skin. His gaze continued to tease. Taunt.

"How 'bout 'suck'?"

She shook herself. "What?"

"Suck." His gaze moved from her mouth to her chest.

She swallowed, feeling an odd pulling sensation on her nipples. "Suck?"

He lifted his glass. "You know, 'bibulating'?"

An exquisite yet foreign feeling scudded through her stomach. She folded her arms across her chest and pressed them against her waist. "I don't believe that word makes any sense in this context, Mr. Wolfe." Why was she bothering with him at all? Sober, he was gentle and solemn. Drunk, he was disgusting, just like every other liquored-up boob she'd ever known. Yet she was fascinated.

He waved the glass in her direction. Some of the liquor sloshed over the brim, spilling onto the floor. "I disagree. So does Mr. Webster. Wanna look it up?"

She watched the liquid seep toward the rug, then lunged, using the hem of her dressing gown to stop the stream. Finding herself on her hands and knees in front of him, she slowly lifted her head. He was staring at her chest. She glanced down to find her gown gaping open. He had an unrestricted view of her bosom.

Their eyes met. Libby's heart continued to pound, and her body thrummed as she folded the neck of her robe in her fist.

He touched her arm, his grip a light pressure. "I've been all over the world, Mrs. O'Malley, and you are as intoxicating as any woman I've seen."

With a twinge of reluctance, she drew her arm away. "Intoxi*cated* is the word, Mr. Wolfe, although it describes you, not me."

His hand drifted onto her thigh, and Libby stood up so quickly she saw spots before her eyes.

He sighed and took another swig of his brandy. "I shouldn't drink."

Why she didn't turn and run, she didn't know. "Nothing is good unless it's done in moderation," she answered.

"Except sex."

His lack of inhibition shocked her. No man had *ever* spoken so boldly to her before. He probably deserved a sharp smack across the face, but oddly, she'd been lured into the conversation like a trout to a fisherman's fly.

"Sex in moderation is truly a bore," he announced, his words beginning to slur. He raised his finger at her and shook it. "I oughta know. I've been searching for the cure to boring sex all over the world."

Libby's gaze roamed to his thumb, and she swallowed hard, remembering Mahalia's comparison. It wasn't just his thumb that was big; his entire hand was huge.

She shook her head, trying to empty it of foolish musings. "It's just like a man to think his problems lie elsewhere, when they usually begin within the man himself."

He frowned, tossing off the remainder of his brandy. "Are you insulting me?"

She pushed her hair away from her face. "I'm surprised you're sober enough to realize it."

He sat before her, grinning like a wicked cat, his arms resting on the chair and his legs spread wide. "Your hair shimmers in the firelight like rich red wine. I'd love to bury my face in it."

She turned abruptly toward the fire, allowing the image to form in her mind. Her insides were a-tumble, her blood ran hot. Despite his drunken state, he was beside her in an instant, his huge hand enveloping hers.

Tingles sped up her arm, yet she continued to study the fire, her heart racing. "What are you doing?"

"I'm collecting my kiss."

"Don't—" She gasped, attempting to wrench free, but he tugged her close. His body was hard against hers, and she was forced to tilt her head back to look into his face. Desire should have softened his features, yet they were tight and as hot as iron freshly pulled from a furnace. The intensity in his eyes both excited and frightened her.

"Let me go."

"I should." His fingers raked her hair, and his palm cupped the back of her head. "I would, if I were sober. Hell, if I were sober, I'd be in bed, thinking about kissing you instead of doing it."

She was just getting used to the smell of brandy on his breath when his mouth came down on hers. He blatantly parted her lips with his tongue. She pressed her fists against his shoulders, yet she had no strength to ward him off or push him away.

The kiss deepened. The stubble around his mouth chafed her skin, and she liked it. Oh, God, she liked it. . . . He tasted of brandy, and as if that small tidbit had power of its own, it gave her a feeling of intoxication, as if she'd had a drink herself.

His mouth was harsh one moment, then soft, pliant . . . pleading. His tongue played with hers, and something inside Libby burst, sending hot seeds of pleasure tumbling through her blood. His knee parted her thighs, a movement that brought her closer to him, and she captured his leg between hers, as if by doing so she might satisfy the ache in her belly.

He finally lifted his head, but Libby was swimming with desire and didn't have the strength to open her eyes.

"I gotta tell you something, Libby."

The sound of her name on his tongue was almost as arousing as the kiss. Almost. Libby took a deep breath and forced herself to move away. She touched her face, aware of the tingling left not only from his kiss but from his beard. In an instant she felt ashamed, the sensation a strong antidote to her desire.

"I don't think we have anything more to talk about." She moved awkwardly toward the door. Her legs felt like useless water-soaked pegs.

"Oh, I think you're gonna wanna hear what I have to say. Hell, Libby, I gotta say it or I'll bust wide open."

She waited near the door, eyeing him warily. "So say it."

Several emotions flickered across his face, and his gaze never left hers. "You're not gonna like it."

His slur was becoming worse. His plastered state began to disgust her. "Just say it, you drunken lout, and let me go to bed."

He rested his hand on the fireplace mantel. "Do you sleep alone?"

Her insides jumped; her nerves were as taut as piano wire. "That's none of your business. Tell me what you want to say, so I can go."

There was a mysterious shimmering in his eyes, and his smile disappeared. It appeared again, although it was a smile of an entirely different sort. "You've got a damned fine ass, Mrs. O'Malley."

She gasped. *"That's* what you had to tell me?"

"No," he answered, his eyes bleary, "but it'll do for now."

"Well, I hope that in the morning you'll have a damned fine hangover, Mr. Wolfe."

She marched to her room, wondering at her tottering feelings. She hated herself now; she would despise her weakness in the morning. But she was also disappointed. She'd thought he was different. She'd hoped he was. Even so, she'd thrown herself at him with no more reticence than a hungry whore. Perhaps she was no better than he.

5

MOUNTAIN GOATS CLAMBERED UP THE SIDES OF JACKSON'S head, their spiky antlers jabbing at his skull. He ran his tongue over his teeth and shuddered at the taste left there, which was comparable to that of Himalayan goat shit. Not only did he wish it were tomorrow, he deplored the thought of having to face today.

Throwing a protective arm over his eyes to ward off the morning sun, he groaned and cursed, hating himself for drinking again. When would he learn? Had he really thought this time would be any different than the others?

He knew why he'd done it: it had been damned near impossible to sit and talk with his own daughter and pretend to be a stranger, even though, in essence, he was. That was what had driven him to the brandy. He'd wanted to announce to the world that he was the father of this beautiful, bright child. He'd wanted to scream, "She's mine, you miserable peasants. Show me something you've created that's anywhere near as perfect as this! I dare you!" Of course he couldn't do a damned foolish thing like that, but it was getting harder and harder to keep his mouth shut.

When Liberty O'Malley offered him brandy, he'd

thought, Why the hell not? Then one glass had become two, and after that, he couldn't remember most of the conversation he'd had with her.

He winced. No doubt it was awful. Drinking made him stupid. Insensitive. Crude. If he'd stayed true to form, he would have a lot of making up to do just to get back into her good graces. How in the hell could he purport to be a good father if he came off as a sloppy drunk? Most women found drinking itself offensive, and he had no doubt Liberty O'Malley was like most women in that respect.

He didn't recall much about their conversation, but he recollected how she looked in that dressing gown. One of the last things he remembered was gazing at her ample bosom while she was on her hands and knees, attempting to clean up the booze he'd spilled.

Now, in spite of his pain, his body responded. There was nothing wrong with him below the neck, he thought with a wry grimace, and mornings usually rendered him horny, anyway. Reliving the moment when he'd gazed at her dusky breasts made him harder, causing the quilt to tent over his groin.

Like most men he knew, he was a breast man. He admitted it. He never quite believed men who professed to prefer legs or asses. Everyone had those. But breasts . . . ahhh, breasts. So many different shapes and sizes. And colors.

To him, a handful was never quite enough. He was ready for a woman with a full, lush figure, ample thighs and breasts with nice perky nipples. He loved it when a woman teased him with just enough clothing to accentuate her curves.

Not that his landlady had consciously sought him out wearing that flimsy thing she had on last night. But the moment she'd walked in, he was lost. The fabric had clung to her breasts, and he could almost tell exactly what shape they were. And though ample, they didn't sag. They were taut and opulent, and had sent carnal sensations racing through him. And the nipples. Ah, yes, the nipples.

He let out a whoosh of air. Even though in his experience

dark-haired women often had dark brown nipples, he would bet hers were pale, nearly the color of her skin.

Abruptly, he swore and groaned. That wasn't all he remembered, dammit. He'd kissed her. Even now he recalled how her lips had glistened with the moistness of that kiss. And she'd responded.

He swore again. Everything was coming back to him, every detail of his vile behavior. He'd almost told her who he was. Surprisingly, a tiny shred of sense had kept him from blurting out the truth.

He swallowed, ignoring the putrid taste in his mouth as he returned his thoughts to the kiss. His erection grew, heightening the hungry itch of lust at his groin.

Suddenly the door opened, slamming against the wall.

"Laundry day, Mistah Wolfe. We gotta have that quilt."

Jackson attempted to grab his bedding, but it was whisked off the bed, leaving him bare and cold.

"What in hell!" Dumbfounded, he discovered the big black cook standing over him, her eyes dancing with amusement. Before his brandy-soaked brain could react, Liberty O'Malley raced into the room.

"Mahalia, don't wake—"

Both women stood there, gaping at him. Too late, he snatched the extra pillow off the bed and covered himself.

Mahalia chuckled all the way down the stairs and outside, while Libby brought up the rear, holding the other end of the quilt. Neither spoke as they dunked the quilt into the tub of hot, soapy water, and Libby refused to look at her assistant, for Mahalia continued to laugh the sort of laugh she used when she was highly amused.

"Stop that," Libby ordered, attempting to sound firm.

Mahalia stopped poking at the wet quilt with the paddle and wiped her eyes with the back of her hand. "Can't help it. Did you ever see such an expression on a man's face? Did you?"

Libby hadn't been looking at his face. What she *had* looked at had shocked her. She wasn't entirely innocent, but never had she imagined one that size. It was reprehensible to allow the thought to materialize at all, but she couldn't ignore it. She gave herself a good strong scolding, then smirked. A lot of good a reprimand would do. There were some things she simply couldn't banish from her thoughts, and she was afraid this was one of them.

Earlier, she'd awakened, feeling that odd sense of dread that people have when they've said or done something they can't take back and can't quite recall. Then she remembered the kiss, and her feelings of shame returned. She'd kissed him with the fervor of a seasoned trollop.

She gripped her paddle tightly so Mahalia wouldn't notice that her fingers shook. Truth to tell, she was shaking all over, inside and out. Her heart fluttered against her ribs, and her stomach quivered.

The kiss had been one thing, but seeing him lying in his bed, naked as a jay, with his . . . She expelled a whoosh of air. It had been like . . . like a pole, thick and long, slanting toward his flat, hair-covered belly, the base nestled in a profusion of dark hair. And hair grew over his chest, too, dense and dark. Her first thought had been a shameful one: Could she have touched her thumb to her index finger if she'd tried to span the pole?

Her cheeks flamed. How had such a brazen thought found its way into her head? She could never look him in the eye again. And heaven help her if she inadvertently glanced lower.

In spite of everything, the sight of him was emblazoned in her brain. There were scars aplenty, she remembered that. Now, as she thought about it, she wondered just what kind of work Mr. Wolfe had done to incur such a physical battering.

"If it had been stickin' straight up, it would've been tall and upright as a lamppost."

Libby's face continued to burn. "Mahalia," she warned.

"Didn't I tell you?" Mahalia ignored the warning. "His thumbs said it all, yes, they certainly did."

Libby had gone to bed the night before, disappointed to learn that he drank so much. She should have known that no man was as perfect as Wolfe had appeared to be. Any decent man would be embarrassed by what had happened this morning, and she had no doubt he would be. She prayed he had a roaring hangover as well.

"I asked you to see if he was up. Otherwise, I told you not to bother him."

Mahalia snorted. "I ain't runnin' this place like a grand hotel. I got my schedule to keep. Besides," she added with a sly grin, "he's usually up and gone by this time."

Libby raised her eyebrows. "You can tell his daily routine after only a week?"

"He didn't seem like a slugabed to me." Mahalia continued to pound the quilt with her paddle. "I think we're gonna have to take these feathers out or they won't dry till spring." She stopped working and adjusted her bosom beneath her loose-fitting frock, the motion causing her breasts to look like puppies squirming in a sack.

"We'll put another quilt on his bed. I have an extra one in my room," Libby answered. "Meanwhile, you go in there and see that he gets breakfast, and I'll—"

"Oh, no, you don't. I've taken care of the beddin' since the day I arrived, and we ain't changin' the rules now. *You* get in there and see that he's fed."

Libby gave her a jaded look. "I guess it's too late to remind you who's the boss here."

"I only do what's best for you, Libby honey."

"And in this case that would be . . ." Libby stopped, waiting for her to explain.

Mahalia laughed again, her shoulders shaking. "I think it's best that you face that man. How long do you think you can avoid him after what you seen this mornin'?"

"Maybe I didn't see anything."

Mahalia's eyes were filled with amusement. "If that's true, why is that hollow in your throat jumpin' like there's a frog trapped behind it?"

Libby didn't have to feel her neck to know that was true. "I don't know what you're talking about. I discovered Mr. Wolfe in the parlor last night, drunk on brandy. If I'm having any reaction at all, it's that I hope his embarrassment is overshadowed only by his hangover."

Mahalia continued to enjoy herself. "Yes, indeed. I don't doubt that there's wild horses gallopin' through his head about now, droppin' their turds on his tongue."

Libby shook her head. "Very crudely put, Mahalia."

"Hangovers ain't a pretty sight, Libby, especially to those havin' them. I had a few of my own in my time."

Libby hadn't had much experience with drunks. Her father, as thoughtless and insensitive as he'd been, had many failings, but drinking wasn't one of them. Sean had taken one drink a week. Jackson Wolfe could have learned something from him, she thought, with a shake of her head.

She turned and marched to the kitchen, only to discover there was no hotcake batter left over from breakfast. Evidently Bert and Burl had packed away more than the usual number. She was trying to decide what to fix when Jackson stepped into the room.

Their gazes met.

The pulse at her throat continued its attempt to escape.

She forced herself not to react to the sheer size of him, concentrating instead on his squinty bloodshot eyes and the thick stubble of beard that covered his face and neck. Libby swore she could see a pulse throbbing at his temple, and she could only hope his head felt close to exploding.

She slammed a frying pan onto the stove and heard his groan. It gave her a satisfying sense of power.

"What are you hungry for this morning, Mr. Wolfe?"

"Coffee will do." His voice was like gravel tumbling into a well, all cavernous and harsh.

She affected her most sympathetic look. "Oh, but I think you should eat breakfast, don't you? Liquor is likely to eat a hole in your stomach. If you don't coat it with something good, you'll probably belch up that awful bitter green stuff."

At her words, he turned a bright shade of green himself. She hid a smile.

"Coffee." He slumped into a chair, propped his elbows on the table, and put his face in his hands.

Libby's lips curled into an evil smile. "I know just the thing." She removed two eggs from the basket on the counter, cracked them into a dish, and brought it to the table.

The yolks, yellow and round as twin harvest moons, floated atop the clear, thick whites. "How about eggs?"

Without looking up, he shook his head. "No eggs."

"Oh, I think eggs would be good for you, Mr. Wolfe. And these are so fresh, too. Why, look."

When he didn't, she prodded, "Please, it's the least you can do. Dawn gathered these herself."

He opened one bleary eye, then quickly closed it again, but not before she wiggled the dish under his nose. His cheeks briefly bulged with air before he swallowed.

"See? The yolks are so yellow and perky, and the whites are thick and nice. They haven't gotten to that runny, slimy stage."

He raised his head, and the look he gave her would have curdled milk. "I said no eggs."

She waved them under his nose again. "You're sure? They're so good when they're fresh. Not like after they've gone bad." She made a disgusting sound in her throat. "You know, when the smell is putrid enough to make a man retch. Nothing as bad-smelling as rotten eggs, I don't believe."

She saw him gag, so she put the eggs aside, intending to use them in her baking. Feeling only a slight twinge of pity, she poured him a cup of coffee and put it on the table in front of him.

He grabbed the mug between his hands and raised it to his mouth, slurping the hot brew slowly.

"I do have baking-powder biscuits, Mr. Wolfe. Perhaps they would go down easily." Oh, how quickly she took pity on him! Her bark was always worse than her bite.

He nodded, but didn't open his eyes. "I have to apologize."

She knew what was coming. "Apologize?" *She* should apologize. After all, she'd been the sober one, and she'd acted like a hussy just the same.

"I don't usually drink. I mean, I *can't* drink. I've never been able to in my entire life."

Curious, Libby poured herself a cup of coffee and sat down across from him. In spite of his disheveled appearance, he commanded her attention. He hadn't dressed with as much care as she'd noticed before. The three top buttons on his shirt were unbuttoned, and the dark hair that covered his chest now shoved its way through the buttonholes.

She swallowed hard, forcing her gaze elsewhere.

His shirtsleeves were rolled up, exposing thick forearms with an abundance of dark hair, and wrists she knew she couldn't span with her fingers. She attempted to ignore the fluttery feeling in her stomach and concentrated on his failings.

"Are you telling me you can't hold your liquor?"

"That's exactly what I'm telling you."

Surprised, she asked, "Then . . . why do you continue to try?"

He sighed and rubbed his face again, as if doing so would banish the pain she knew was throbbing inside his head. "Every now and again I think maybe my body's changed and I can handle it. And every time I try, I suffer for it." He gave her a bloodshot look. "The eggs were a dirty trick."

Libby suppressed a smile. "I'd apologize, but I enjoyed your reaction too much."

His look said everything. "Somehow I knew you would."

"Why do you drink?"

He cleared his throat. "Something usually triggers it." He took a bite of biscuit and seemed to have trouble getting it down, but finally succeeded.

She rose, lifted a jar of honey off the shelf, placed it in front of him, and resumed her seat. "And what triggered it last night?"

His smile was mysterious as he slathered the biscuit with honey. He didn't answer for a long, quiet moment, then finally said, "Probably the job. I thought it was going to be a piece of cake."

"And it's not?"

"Seems I've stepped smack dab into a bit of a range war."

"Oh, yes. Those poor sheepmen." Ethan had talked of little else for months.

"What do you know about it?" He suddenly seemed quite alert.

"Oh, not much. Ethan—that is, Mr. Frost, the banker—

is a friend of mine, and he holds the loans against much of the property around here. He hears things."

Jackson Wolfe gave her a noncommittal nod. "I see."

They sat together in silence for another long moment. Finally he said, "Again I apologize for last night."

Libby ran her finger over the rim of her cup and waited.

"I must have said or done something stupid. I usually do when I'm in that state."

She recalled every second of their little tryst. It was just as well that he didn't. "You don't . . . remember anything?"

His gaze flickered to her chest, then to her mouth. "Not much."

Heat crept into her neck. So. He did recall ogling her bosom.

The silence was thick again, and just when Libby decided she couldn't bear it, Mahalia glided into the room.

"Well, Mistah Wolfe. You feelin' better now with somethin' in your stomach?"

He gave her a weak smile and took another swig of his coffee.

"Tell you what," she began. "I'm gonna start on dinner. It's gotta cook a long, long time, and this house'll be filled with smells that'll make your mouth water. I'm cookin' New Orleans vittles tonight, complete with Cajun spices and sausage drippin' in grease." She winked at him. "Bet you can hardly wait."

With a shuddering swallow, he pushed himself away from the table, rose, and rushed from the room.

Libby's lips twitched. "You did that on purpose."

Mahalia chuckled. "Every man what imbibes oughta pay the price, is my feelin'."

"I gave him a little of my own," Libby admitted. "I described eggs gone bad, then stuck a couple of fresh raw ones under his nose."

Mahalia threw her head back and laughed. "You're learnin', gal. You're learnin'."

Later in the morning, after Mahalia had opened the quilt and spread the feathers on the attic floor to dry, Libby continued to think about Jackson Wolfe's body. It upset her that thoughts of him took control of her mind. He was, after all, just a man. It had been hard enough to remember that when he was clothed. But at least she could have told herself that, like Sean, he probably looked terrible without attire.

However, the sight of him with nothing on at all was completely and utterly impossible to forget. That was one body against which she could easily consider curling up. And if nothing else, that admission shocked her into doing something that totally occupied her mind. She sat at the desk in the parlor and went over her accounts. It was the only thing that could take her mind off everything else. Even at that, it was a struggle, for every other word she read reminded her of him. Sheets—that he slept on and that molded his manly form. Quilts—that were whipped off, revealing his glorious nudity. Pillows—which he belatedly used to cover himself.

It was a wonder she got any work done at all.

Dawn poked her head around the kitchen door. "I'm looking for Mumser, Mama, have you seen him?"

Libby thumped her knuckle on a loaf of bread, testing the firmness of the crust, then slathered the top with butter. "I imagine he's at the jail with Mr. Wolfe." She placed a cloth over the bread.

Dawn danced into the room. "Burl said Mr. Wolfe didn't take the dog with him this morning."

Libby frowned. Obviously the man couldn't handle a hangover and a dog all in one day. "I wish he'd tell me when he's not taking the dog with him. I wouldn't appreciate having to look after it, but at least I could keep it out of trouble. Hopefully, the dog is shut in his room."

"He's not."

Libby pulled the apple crisp from the oven and slid it onto a table. "How do you know?"

Dawn glanced at the floor. "I checked."

Libby gave her a soft, scolding look. "You know we don't go into our boarders' rooms without good reason."

"I know, but I wanted to play with Mumser. He's probably lonesome and bored, having been alone all day."

Libby ground coffee beans, then poured them into the coffeepot strainer, placing a coarser strainer over the top. "Have you finished your sums?"

Dawn flittered about the room. "Everything is done. That trick Mr. Wolfe taught me is great, Mama." She stopped in front of Libby, her gaze a bit dreamy.

"He's been so many places. All over the world. Can you imagine? He's been to Africa, India, and even China, Mama. *China.* That's where he got Mumser." She hugged herself and twirled. "I've never known anyone who's been to so many exciting places."

She danced to the stove and sniffed, wrinkling her nose. "Mahalia's cooking that smelly stuff for supper?"

Libby winked at her daughter. "Better see that the horse trough is full."

Putting her hand over her mouth, Dawn tiptoed closer to Libby and giggled. "Remember the first time Bert tasted Mahalia's Cajun cooking? He nearly drowned in the trough trying to put out the fire in his mouth."

Libby remembered, too, and joined her daughter with soft laughter of her own. "He was facedown in the water with his arms and legs hanging over the sides."

Dawn's giggles grew. "He looked like a drowning scarecrow."

Laughing harder, Libby drew her handkerchief from her apron pocket and wiped her eyes. She pressed her forehead against Dawn's. "We shouldn't laugh at him, dear."

"Oh, pooh, Mama. He laughs at everyone else, all the time."

Libby gave Dawn's braid a loving yank, then stepped away. "It's time to set the table." She lifted the plates from the cupboard and put them on the counter.

Dawn grabbed handfuls of silverware and started making place settings while Libby gave Mahalia's stew a stir.

"Evening, ladies."

Libby's pulse jumped at the sound of Jackson Wolfe's voice, and both she and Dawn turned toward the door. Libby had to admit his appearance was much better than it had been at breakfast.

"I . . . er . . . thought I should tell you that I've finished putting fencing around your flowers."

Libby felt warm, almost content. "Why . . . how thoughtful of you. Thank you."

He appeared contrite. "It was the least I could do. After . . . ah . . . ." He glanced at Dawn, then at Libby, and smiled sheepishly.

In spite of Libby's warm, cozy feeling, the cynical side of her wanted to inquire if he was merely trying to make up for what he'd done the night before, but she was wise enough not to put the thought into words.

"Oh, Mr. Wolfe," Dawn gushed. "Where's Mumser? I wanted to play with him, but I couldn't—"

A shrill, eardrum-piercing shriek interrupted Dawn's sentence, and all three of them glanced toward the stairs.

Libby was the first one out of the kitchen. "Mahalia?" Hiking her skirt up to her knees, she ran up the stairs, the clatter of Dawn's and Mr. Wolfe's footsteps not far behind her.

Libby reached the attic, her heart pounding from fear and exertion. "Mahalia? What's wrong? What is it?"

Mahalia threw open the door and stood over her, her fists slammed against her hips and smoke nearly coming out of her ears.

She flung a fleshy arm toward the attic floor. *"This.* This is what's wrong!"

There, amid a flurry of feathers that appeared to be falling from the ceiling, scampered Jackson Wolfe's damned dog. He was chasing after the tiny plumes, leaping and snatching at them, catching them in his mouth, then flicking them out with his tongue. The hair on his chin was thick with feathers and wet from his slobber. The room looked as though a storm had dumped several inches of snow on the floor, then sent in a whirlwind to bring every flake to life.

6

JACKSON TOOK THE BROOM LIBBY OFFERED AND BEGAN sweeping the floor. He'd insisted on cleaning up the mess his dog had made, and he was apologetic as he swept up feathers.

"I hope some of these can be salvaged." He uttered a mild curse. "I'm sure sorry this riled your cook the way it did. I should have taken the dog with me today, but"—he stopped sweeping and ran one hand through his hair—"I guess I thought I had enough to worry about without wondering what he'd get into at the jail."

Libby allowed a small smile. "He's a nuisance at the jail?"

"According to Vern, he is."

"I wouldn't imagine there's much to get into there," Libby reflected.

He gave her a boyish smile, one that tugged at her. "You'd be surprised."

They worked quietly. "I know Mumser's a poor excuse for a dog," he said, "but you have to understand. He was a gift from the emperor of China, and I wouldn't feel right palming him off on someone else. I guess, according to

69

Chinese customs, I should feel honored. Mumser's a breed of dog that's highly valued there."

Intrigued, Libby asked, "You've recently been to China? What on earth did you do there, Mr. Wolfe?"

"Jackson. Please. You know what they say—Mr. Wolfe is my father." His eyes closed briefly, but not before Libby saw a twinge of pain.

"What kind of work are you in that takes you clear to China?"

"I'm a soldier-for-hire. At least I was."

Libby crossed her arms and leaned against the wall. This man became more and more interesting as time went by. "You mean a country planning a revolution would send you an invitation?"

He caught her cynical tone and smiled. Again it transformed him. "Something like that."

"You said you *were* a soldier for hire. You've retired?"

He turned, sweeping with his back to her. "I've done enough fighting to last me a lifetime. War changes people, ma'am." He stopped working and stared out the window.

Libby's gaze followed. On the bare branch of a dying cedar, blackbirds loitered like hooded highwaymen. From the tone of his conversation, she imagined they bespoke his mood.

"Before we go into war, we're chaste. Naively innocent. After a few battles, we change color, like cities that become blanketed in soot."

My, she thought, lifting an eyebrow. For a large, battered man, he was quite poetic. "Do you think that standing in for Sheriff Roberts will fulfill your lust for adventure?"

He turned, his china-blue eyes cautious. "Wanderlust is a hard impulse to resist, but I'm going to try." After a moment he added, "I have some other plans."

The way he looked at her almost made Libby believe she would be a part of those plans. Which was ludicrous, of course. She mentally shook herself. Too much time spent listening to her daughter and Chloe Ann blather on about fantasies and dreams.

The door creaked open, breaking the silence between

them, and Cyclops sashayed in, her scarred and scabby nose in the air as she perused the room. In spite of her appearance, she no doubt considered herself quite a feline. Rather like Lila Sanders, the aging prostitute who had rented a room from Libby a few years ago, unaware that her looks had gone bad and her figure had gone south. The cat sniffed at the floor, smelling the area where the dog had been. Growling, she arched her back, then sashayed out again.

"We've . . . never had a dog around here. Only cats," Libby explained.

Jackson continued to sweep. "I was raised on a ranch. Cats were left outside to control the rat and mouse population."

Another boyish smile, another tug at Libby's heart.

"I had a dog, though. Well," he amended, "he ended up being mine. Max was a big black bruiser. He fell down an empty well shaft and was as close to death as a creature could be."

Interested, Libby asked, "What happened?"

Jackson scooped up another handful of feathers and dropped them carefully into the wicker basket. "My pa thought we should put him out of his misery."

Libby gasped, pressing one hand to her chest.

"Don't worry." Another heart-stopping smile. "My stepmother convinced him that the dog deserved a chance. It was her dog, actually, but I'd recently been . . . Well, let's say that she knew how much Max meant to me. They put the dog in a room at the back of the barn, and I slept there and took care of him. My stepmother brought me meals. Didn't even demand that I sleep in a proper bed until Max was out of the woods."

He stopped working, his eyes filling with warmth, his harsh features softening. "It was almost as if she and I understood each other from the beginning. Hell, I was only eight at the time, but . . ." He sighed, then smiled again, and Libby thought she'd never seen anything quite so beautiful.

She said nothing, but immediately envied that kind of relationship with a parent. And that kind of childhood.

She glanced at the room. "Well, it looks like things are in order again. Thank you for cleaning up."

"It was the least I could do."

The grandfather clock that stood in the downstairs foyer tolled eight. "Oh, dear. I'm afraid you've missed dinner."

"As have you," he reminded her.

The thought of dining alone with him appealed to her. "I can prepare something for both of us, if you don't mind potluck."

His mouth twitched, almost creating a smile. "Cajun sausage, swimming in grease?"

Libby laughed, then bit her bottom lip. "Not unless that's what you want. Undoubtedly there will be enough left for another meal, considering that the last time Mahalia cooked this dish, we had leftovers for nearly a week. She tried to disguise it by hiding it in tortillas and in hash, but the boarders complained so much that I'm surprised she dared concoct that meal again."

His gaze was warm, sending Libby's heart palpitating. "Anything will be fine." He gripped the basket by the handles and lifted it into his arms. "Just let me know what to do with these."

"Leave them here for the time being. If you'll come to the kitchen in a half hour, I . . . we . . . I can have something for you . . . us . . . you to eat." Lord, he had her tongue-tied.

"I'd appreciate it." He returned the basket to the floor and left the room. His door opened, then closed. She heard him scolding the dog—not in cruel tones, but she knew it was a reprimand.

She took the stairs, stopping by Dawn's room. Her daughter was reading, the light from a kerosene lamp fanning across the pages. She glanced at her mother and gave her a mischievous smile. "With all those feathers around his mouth, Mumser looked like he'd swallowed a chicken."

Libby tried not to return her smile, but failed. "It's not amusing, dear."

72

Dawn continued to grin. "Then why are you smiling?"

She crossed to where her daughter sat and began unbraiding her hair. "What are you reading?"

Dawn showed her the cover.

"Ah, yes. *Little Women.* One of my favorites." For a girl of twelve, Dawn was exceptionally bright. Although when Libby first took Dawn into her home, she hadn't known how to read at all. Now she read everything she could get her hands on.

Dawn sighed. "Mine too. The only thing is . . ."

Libby threaded her fingers through Dawn's luxuriant hair. "Yes?"

Her daughter sighed again. "I love you, Mama, please don't feel bad, but I wish I had sisters. Lots of family, like those girls. Aunts, uncles, you know." She giggled, a soft, wistful sound. "Even a bratty brother might be fun."

Feeling the melancholy in her own stomach, Libby picked up Dawn's brush and began brushing her daughter's thick, shiny hair. "I understand, dear. When I was a girl, I wished for the very same thing."

"But you had brothers and a mama and . . . and a papa."

"Indeed I did." She'd never gone into any detail about her unhappy childhood. It wasn't important.

"Mama?"

"Hmm?"

"I don't want to upset you, but I've been thinking about, you know, my real mother again."

Libby stopped a sigh. What was a *real* mother, anyway? "Your curiosity is natural, dear." Even though she believed her own words, Dawn's curiosity about her natural mother was a hard pill to swallow. But she knew better than to upset Dawn with her own petty feelings.

"I wonder if she was White or Indian."

"It's hard to say." Libby couldn't imagine a mother of any color willingly abandoning a beautiful child like Dawn. In quiet moments she often thought perhaps both parents were dead. It was the only sensible conclusion she could come to.

Many things between her and Dawn had continually gone unsaid. Every so often, as now, Dawn admitted to being curious about her own family. The first six years of her life had been miserable: the first three she couldn't remember, and the next three she'd been a virtual servant on a ranch to the north of Thief River.

"Tell me again how you found me, Mama." Dawn's voice had a dreamy quality.

They'd done this a dozen times before, but Libby continued to gratify her child. "I was on my way home from Eureka when I saw this pitiful little girl lugging water from the pump to the house."

"Yes, and I tripped and fell and the water spilled onto the ground."

"Then that woman"—

"Mrs. Fitzsimmons," Dawn offered.

—"came out and scolded you, ordering you to bring in another full pail of water."

"And you didn't like to see a little girl working so hard."

Libby gave her a sad smile. "It broke my heart."

"Then you stopped and pretended to ask for directions so the woman would quit being so mean to me."

Libby nodded. "I was surprised to find her so talkative." And Libby had had to mask her anger at the way the woman treated Dawn.

"And she said my name was Dawn. That's what I remember being called. And they'd found me on their doorstep one cold winter morning. I was maybe three, but no one really knows for sure."

"That's right."

Dawn twisted in her chair and looked at her mother, suddenly understanding. "Does that mean that I really don't have a birthday on August tenth?"

"That's the day I found you. As far as I'm concerned, it's the day you were born."

"I guess that's not such a bad thing." Yet there was a wistful tone to her words.

Libby recalled that the woman—a pinched, work-worn

rancher's wife who had long since stopped feeling sorry for anyone but herself—had told her that Dawn should be grateful they'd taken her in at all and not left her to die. She'd been useless to them for the first few years, too young to work and too stupid to learn anything. Breeds were like that, she'd said, her whiny voice a grating annoyance. Libby remembered how her jaw had ached that night from keeping a close rein on her fury.

The woman had been anxious to get rid of Dawn, despite the fact that she'd been a useful servant. Libby had whisked the girl away before the woman could change her mind. Even at six, Dawn had been a beautiful child. To this day, Libby remembered the depth of emotion she'd seen in the girl's eyes.

"And all the way home," Dawn repeated, knowing the story by heart, "I sat next to you, and you put your arm around me. I remember that, Mama. I felt so safe with you."

Libby swallowed the lump in her throat. It was a poignant memory. One she would never forget.

The only memory Dawn had of the time before that was of a frail elderly woman who had loved her and kept her safe. There was a gap in her memory that she couldn't account for. And Libby had not pressed.

Dawn turned and gave Libby a hug around the waist. "Don't look sad, Mama. I love you so much."

Libby bit into her lower lip, pressed her daughter's head against her, and kissed the top of her head. "I love you too, dear. Very, very much, but you know," she added, "we don't always get what we want."

"I know that," Dawn whispered. "I'm happy you're my mama. The day you took me away from that place was the happiest day of my life."

"Mine too." Libby's words caught in her throat, and she felt the sting of tears. She sniffed, a sound that brought Dawn's head up. Her eyes were shining too.

They giggled together like best friends, boldly wiping away their happy tears.

Libby stepped away and dug out her handkerchief. "Well," she said, wiping her eyes and blowing her nose, "aren't we just pitiful?"

Dawn's grin was wide. "I like it when you cry, Mama. Then I know you're happy."

Libby laughed. "That's kind of contrary, don't you think? Most people cry when they're sad and laugh when they're happy."

"But when you're happy, you laugh and cry at the same time. And . . . and I've never seen you really sad. Or mad, even."

Libby drew Dawn's hair into a loose braid, drawing through it a ribbon, which she fastened at the end. "I've had no reason to be sad since you came into my life, dear. And angry? Oh, that takes far too much energy, and it's all wasted."

Libby pressed a kiss on Dawn's cheek. "I have to get to the kitchen and fix Mr. Wolfe something to eat." She started toward the door.

"I hope you make him something nice, Mama, and not that awful stuff we had for dinner."

Libby stopped and turned. "You're fond of him, aren't you? And it isn't just because he has a cute little dog."

"Mumser's darling. I know he's a bit too playful, but he's still a puppy. One day he'll mind, I just know he will." She searched Libby's face. "Mr. Wolfe is a real nice man, Mama. I kind of wish—"

"Don't say any more, dear. You know what Mahalia says—"

"I know, I know," Dawn interrupted. "Fill one bucket with cow turds and the other with wishes and see which one fills up first."

Libby raised her eyebrows, but said nothing. "I think you should get ready for bed."

Dawn rolled her eyes. "Whenever you can't think of anything else to say, you tell me to get ready for bed."

Libby gave her daughter a warm smile. "It's late, dear. I'll come up after I've fed Mr. Wolfe."

"Don't close the door, Mama. Leave it open a crack so Cyclops can come in."

Libby blew her daughter a kiss, then briefly checked herself in the mirror before she left the room. She was jittery with excitement and anticipation as she made her way to the kitchen.

Jackson took a moment to watch Libby from the darkened hallway. She reached for something high on a shelf, a movement that accentuated her full bosom beneath the bodice of her gown. She couldn't reach the object, so she dragged a chair from the table and unceremoniously lifted her skirt to her knees before stepping onto the chair. The brief glimpse of her stocking-clad calves warmed him.

So far, he thought he'd repaired any damage he might have done the night before. Amazing what little favors would do. He'd planned to put fencing around all the flowers anyway, but after last night, he made sure it was done quickly. He also wanted to repair the back porch, which slanted dangerously. He'd hoped to have that done before he told her he was Dawn Twilight's father, but he was getting anxious to visit his family, and he wanted his daughter at his side when he did.

A niggling voice persisted in his head, attempting to remind him that he couldn't simply whisk Dawn Twilight away now that he'd found her. That thought had been solidified when he'd watched her and Libby together earlier, before Mumser had gotten into the feathers. Jackson got a strange feeling in his stomach whenever he thought about their relationship.

Whatever else it was, they laughed and giggled together like sisters, yet Libby O'Malley was definitely a mother to his child.

But dammit, anyway! He couldn't let that influence him, because one way or another, he would reclaim his daughter. And, he reminded himself, the sooner the better.

"Oh, there you are."

The sound of his landlady's voice cautioned him to say

nothing, although he knew he couldn't wait too much longer. It was time to learn more about Dawn's arrival on Libby O'Malley's doorstep. Chances were that once Libby found out who he was, she wouldn't offer any information. He'd be lucky if she didn't kill him and serve him up in stew.

He stepped into the kitchen and took a seat at the table.

Libby placed a plate of scrambled eggs, ham, and bread in front of him.

"I hope this is all right."

His mouth watered, but he gave her a wary glance. "Eggs, huh?"

"They're cooked this time," she answered with a smile.

"It's fine. Looks real good. Thanks."

She worked at the counter, cleaning up pots and pans while he ate.

He swallowed a mouthful of buttery eggs. "Aren't you eating?"

"I had a bite while I was making yours." She tossed the words over her shoulder.

"Mind if I ask you a question?" At her nod, he asked, picking his words carefully, "Dawn's a half-blood, right?"

Libby stopped working and rested her hands on the counter. She didn't turn. "Yes, she is. I thought we established that the day you moved in."

He cleared his throat. "Oh. Of course. I, ah, guess I'd forgotten."

He waited for her to offer more information. When she didn't, he asked, "How did she come to be here, with you?"

Libby turned, her expression guarded. "What an odd question. What makes you think she isn't mine?"

Take a step back, he cautioned himself. "I rather doubt Sean O'Malley was an Indian."

She smiled, her guarded expression gone. "You're right, of course. After Sean died, I was very lonely. The house was his, so after his death it became mine. We'd lived here, of course, from the time we were . . . were married. Although the house was always full of boarders, something was missing from my life, and when I found Dawn, I knew what it was."

She offered an apologetic smile, as if he might find her words foolish. Instead, he was enthralled. "How did you find her?"

"I found her living with a family between here and Eureka six years ago. She's been with me ever since." Libby wiped the stove, then moved on to the other tables and countertops in the room. "They were using her as household help, even though she wasn't more than five or six years old." She stopped and smiled wistfully. "Poor darling, she doesn't even know when her real birthday is."

Christmas Day, he thought, pain slicing through him, enhancing his guilt. "She had no family?"

"No. Well, not unless she was abandoned, which is the case with so many of the half-bloods around here."

Abandoned. He mouthed a curse. He had abandoned her. Neglected her. How many years would he pay for his sins?

Libby sighed. "I'll never understand what sort of person could reject a child."

His mood threatened to sink lower, but he caught himself. He was here now, and that was what mattered.

She kept busy at the counter. "To me, the only excuse for abandoning a child is death."

In spite of his resolve, his mood worsened. "There could be other reasons."

"None that would make any sense to me," she answered. "A woman simply wouldn't leave a child." She paused, then shook her head. "A man might, but I know a few fine men who have lost their wives, like Ethan Frost, and just because they're hurting and child care is a lot of work, they don't abandon their children."

Her words were hard and pragmatic. It was as if she knew everything about him. But up through his guilt swam his rationalization: "There are always extenuating circumstances, you know."

"When it comes to children? I don't think so."

He realized that if he told her his reasons for leaving

Dawn, she would call him the worst kind of man. Hell, he'd called himself every name in the book, but he was here to change all that.

Sufficiently battered, Jackson merely grunted a response. His appetite gone, he shoved his plate to the center of the table. She would undoubtedly find him a poor excuse for a parent, but if he lived to be a hundred, he'd make it up to his child.

Again he chose his words carefully, although his heart pounded with anticipation. "Dawn was lucky you took her in." He was angry with Libby for her firm stand, and he knew it was because she made him feel like the slacker he was. Or had been.

Libby snorted a laugh. *"She* was lucky? Oh, Mr. Wolfe, I'm the lucky one. Not a day goes by that I don't thank God for bringing Dawn into my life."

His guilt continued to eat away at his insides. Cursing quietly, he knew he couldn't stand it another minute.

"I'm her father." He held his breath, his heart drumming in his ears.

Libby gave him an absentminded look. "What?" The word was barely audible.

"I'm Dawn Twilight's father," he repeated, surprised and relieved at her mild reaction.

It didn't appear that Libby understood him, although her face slowly changed expression. "Dawn . . . Twilight?"

"That's her name," he answered, rather abruptly. "I'm her father, and I've come to take her home."

Comprehension was swift and violent. Fury turned Libby's eyes to flame. With the swiftness of a cat, she lifted a skillet off the counter and hurled it at him, shrieking like a banshee. He deflected it with his forearm. It clattered to the floor.

"Out!" The word was a mere whisper, yet her message was clear.

"Now just a damned minute—"

"Get out," she hissed, her hands pressed over her ears. "Getoutgetout*getout!"*

"I had a damned good reason for doing what I did, no matter what you might think."

She took his dish from the table and threw it at him. He cringed as it flew past him and shattered against the wall behind him.

"Get out!" She grabbed the handle of another skillet. "You . . . you miserable, miserable excuse for a man. How dare you come here and . . . How *dare* you!"

Not wanting another skillet flung in his direction, Jackson made tracks for the door. "We'll talk about this tomorrow, dammit, and you'll hear me out."

"Get out of here you . . . you loutish, putrid *drunk.* And don't you *dare* say anything to my daughter. *Don't you dare."*

"I had no way of knowing I'd find my daughter here, with you." His excuses sounded whiny and pathetic, but he couldn't seem to stop himself.

Libby's chest heaved, and her face was an angry red. "If you utter one more peep, I'll cut out your tongue while you sleep, damn you."

Sensing he had no options, Jackson left, uncomfortable with his own anger yet not at all surprised by hers.

7

LIBBY STOOD IN THE CENTER OF THE ROOM, HER FINGERS pressed against her mouth and her chest still heaving. Blood rushed into her ears, thrumming like a waterfall. She continued to stare out into the darkened hallway long after Jackson had gone. The only sound she heard was the drumming of the grandfather clock as it stroked nine, mimicking the pounding of her heart.

The door to Mahalia's quarters opened, then squeaked closed. Turning slowly, Libby found the housekeeper looking at her, her expression almost contrite.

Shuddering with anger and fear, Libby swallowed. "You heard?"

"I heard." Mahalia surveyed the damage, then, with broom and dustpan, swept up the mess.

"How . . . how can this be? How can it possibly be true?" Libby crumpled into a chair and rested her forehead on her arm. Her head was crowded with noises: Jackson Wolfe's paralyzing words, her own dread and skittering heartbeat.

Usually quick with her answers, Mahalia had only questions. "Why'd he come back now? What'll happen to that poor little gal when she hears this? What are you gonna do?"

Gathering strength, Libby sat up, but felt the need to press her shaky fingers over her lips. "What am I *going* to do, or what do I *want* to do?"

Mahalia chuckled, her good humor returning. "Well, I know what you'd *like* to do, so tell me what you're *gonna* do."

Libby narrowed her lids. "I'm not sure yet, but believe me, I'll think of something."

"I have no doubt you will," Mahalia answered, a smile in her voice.

Libby continued to fume. She stood and paced. "If that man thinks he can sashay in here after all these years and simply pick up where he left off, he has another think coming. I mean, he left her, Mahalia. He *left* her! I can't imagine any reason to do such a thing that wouldn't sound like a feeble excuse."

Mahalia made a consenting noise in her throat. "Little Dawn's gonna have quite a shock."

"Oh, not just Dawn, but Dawn *Twilight.*" In spite of her rage, Libby had to admit it was a beautiful name. "He might assume my anger was for myself, but it wasn't. My first thought was how Dawn would react to this . . . this monstrous news."

"Well," Mahalia interjected, dumping the broken glass into the wastebasket, "by the looks of this kitchen, *your* reaction was pretty danged violent."

Libby was remorseful. "I'm sorry about the mess, Mahalia, I didn't even think. I threw the first thing I could lay my hands on." She tried to push stray strands of hair into the braid at the back of her neck, but her fingers shook so badly she couldn't.

"Hmm. Good thing you didn't grab the meat cleaver."

"Men," Libby muttered with a huff. "They have no instincts at all. Did he expect us to fall into his arms, grateful he'd finally decided to return? Kiss his feet as if he were some conquering hero?"

Mahalia tsked. "You need a cup of tea with a splash of whiskey in it." She crossed to the cupboard to prepare the concoction.

Libby expelled a harsh sigh and rubbed her temples. "I need something, all right." She needed her head examined, that was what she needed. How cleverly he'd played her, doing just enough little chores around the place to endear him to her. The kiss loomed in her mind, and despite her fury, her lips tingled at the memory. She mouthed a mild curse. He'd probably calculated that as well. And fool that she was, she'd actually begun to fall for him.

Mahalia set a cup of steaming tea on the table and motioned Libby to drink. She took a sip, grimacing at the taste of the whiskey, then took another. After the fourth swallow, she finally felt the knots in her stomach loosen.

"He doesn't have a prayer of reclaiming her, you know." She ran her index finger around the rim of the cup, suddenly feeling very clever and quite confident.

"That a fact?" Mahalia poured more tea into Libby's cup, then added another dash of whiskey.

"I hold the winning card." Oddly, the tea tasted far better now.

"Yes, honey, but if he really is Dawn's daddy, that's a powerful thing. Why do you s'pose he's waited all this time to come forward and claim the little gal?"

Libby took a slurp of the tea. "He'd better have proof, that's all I can say."

Mahalia agreed. "He shore do need proof, but even without it, why would he claim to be her daddy if he ain't? It ain't like she's an heiress or somethin'."

"I don't know," Libby whispered, her confidence flagging once again. "Still, unless he has proof, he has no real claim." She tossed Mahalia a cunning smile, knowing that in this game for Dawn's custody, she held the ace.

"You'd best get to bed, Libby," Mahalia suggested, eyeing her carefully.

Perhaps, she thought, but what she really wanted to do was give that man a piece of her mind—while her brain was numb. She stood, the whiskey-laced tea making her bold.

Without thinking twice, she marched up the stairs, intent on confronting the man again. Out of the corner of her eye, she saw a dark shape lurking at Dawn's bedroom door. Her heart took a leap.

She rushed across the carpeted floor and grabbed his arm. He turned, surprised.

She refused to relinquish her hold. "Get away from her door." Her voice was a cross between a whisper and a hiss.

With a swiftness that belied his size, Jackson lifted Libby off the floor and carried her down the hall, away from Dawn's room.

She pummeled his chest. "Put me down, you ape!"

"Keep screaming, and you'll have everyone out here gaping at us."

Dawn poked her head out and squinted into the hallway, her glossy hair in tangles around her face. "Mama?"

Jackson released her, and Libby ran a fluttery hand over her own hair. "I'm sorry, dear. Did we wake you?"

Dawn's expression was puzzled as she looked from Libby to Jackson. "What's wrong? Is something wrong?"

Libby hurried to the door. "Nothing's wrong, dear. I . . . I thought I saw a mouse, that's all. Go back to bed."

"Cyclops is in my room. Should I put her out in the hallway so she can catch it?"

Libby hustled Dawn to her bed. "Yes. Of course. We'll let Cyclops take care of it."

Once Dawn was snug under her covers, Libby tiptoed out and shut the door. Jackson hadn't moved.

She marched toward him, fists on hips. "Now see what you have me doing?" she scolded. "I've never lied to her before. *Never.*"

His eyes were dark and his expression explosive. "If you have anything else to say to me, let's get out of the line of fire. All I need is for those nosy old coots to come out, sniffing around for scandal."

He took Libby's arm, but she pulled it away. "I don't need any help from you," she snapped, then tramped to the third floor.

Once in his room, she rubbed her arm where his fingers had been and glared at him. She hoped she had bruises in

85

the morning, but unfortunately all she felt was tingles racing up and down her flesh. "What were you doing at Dawn's bedroom door?"

He loomed over her, his wide shoulders and thick arms menacing. "I was watching my daughter sleep. I have that right, you know."

Libby swallowed a jagged lump of fear. "How many times have you done that?"

He turned away from her. "A few."

True fear seeped into her chest and the buzz from her tea dwindled fast. "What if she'd seen you?"

"She didn't."

Libby surveyed the room, noting the masculine touches he'd inadvertently added to his surroundings, like his saddlebags, his battered leather travel bag, and a pair of boots that looked big enough to plant trees in.

"So." His features were cautious when he faced her. "Where does this leave us?"

Libby would save her trump card for morning. "I want to see some proof."

He jabbed his index finger at his chest. *"I'm* the proof."

She inched toward the door, suddenly feeling uncomfortable being in the same room with him, behind closed doors. "That's not good enough."

"It'll have to be," he snarled.

The fury she'd felt earlier returned, burning in her stomach and radiating everywhere. "You're insane if you think I'll let you take Dawn away from me."

He gave her a mocking smile. "I don't think you'll have much choice."

She gripped the doorknob and twisted, wishing it were his throat or, heaven help her and God forgive her, his all-fired precious manhood. "We'll see about that."

The following morning Libby awoke with demons thrashing around in her head. Besides the effects of the whiskey in her tea, she suffered from sleeplessness, because all night long, thoughts of her conversation with Jackson had kept her awake.

She also had to deal with the fact that never before in her entire life had she unleashed her temper. Never. And even though she'd been out of control, throwing things like a raving lunatic, she'd held back. Lord help the world if she ever truly let go.

After Dawn had left for school, Libby retrieved the precious papers from her safe and marched to the third floor, knowing that his room was the only place in town where they might have privacy. She knew he was there, because he hadn't come down for breakfast.

With her papers in one hand, she pounded on the door with the other. Before he answered, she took a deep breath, expelling it slowly.

From the other side of the door, he told her to come in.

Libby stepped inside, her gaze moving swiftly away from his wide, hard chest as he slipped into his shirt. The hair that covered him looked soft and lush, and how she could think about running her fingers through it not only surprised her but made her angrier than she already was.

Her eyes drifted to him again, and they studied one another, neither speaking. Battle lines were drawn.

The damned dog leaped off the bed and greeted her, yapping, growling, and wiggling at the hem of her skirt.

"Mumser." He snapped his fingers and pointed to the bed. The dog took a running leap, landing on a pillow.

"Stay," Jackson ordered. To Libby he offered a chair.

"I'll stand, thank you." She sounded perfectly prudish, relieved that her feelings didn't show, for in spite of everything, he was still a physically compelling man. She couldn't turn off her feelings, although she wished she could.

He continued dressing, an act that should not have been sensual but was. Even though he was fully clothed, Libby continued to imagine the naked chest beneath the shirt. Oh, she *hated* this feeling!

She clenched her papers in her fist and jumped right in. "As I said last night, I won't let you say a word to Dawn unless you have some proof that you're really her father. You can't imagine what a shock this will be."

Muscles clamped in his jaw. "Why would I claim her if she weren't mine?"

Mine. The word shivered through Libby, rekindling her anger. "Do you know what kind of father you are?"

He swung away and crossed to the dry sink. "I imagine you're going to tell me."

"As far as I'm concerned, if you truly are Dawn's father, you've lost all the privileges that go along with it. What makes you think you can come here and step right into her life? Did you imagine she'd have no feelings about being orphaned? Actually, 'abandoned' is a better word. 'Orphaned' would mean she no longer has parents, which obviously, if I'm to believe your claim, isn't the case."

"You don't know anything about my reasons, you sanctimonious harpy."

She ignored the insult. She simply didn't care what he thought of her. "And unless you've been in a coma for the past twelve years, which I doubt, I don't have to know your reasons. Did you think Dawn was some . . . some empty vessel that only *you* could fill?"

He retrieved a brush from the marble top of the dry sink and drew it through his thick hair, seemingly unperturbed by her ranting. "I'm her father, and there's not a damned thing you can do about it."

She took a deep breath and slowly counted to five, her anger simmering at his blasé attitude. "Oh, but I think there is."

He arched an eyebrow in her direction, but continued grooming his hair. "Now *this* I've got to hear."

She stepped forward and shoved the papers under his nose, holding them there until he took them.

"What the hell—"

"Read them." She folded her arms across her chest and waited.

He tossed the brush onto the dry sink, his expression changing as he thumbed through the papers. When he finally raised his head, his eyes were so hard and cold they appeared chiseled from marble.

"You adopted her?"

Libby almost sagged with relief. "All nice and legal. She's been my daughter in every respect for almost six years."

Jackson strode to the window, presenting her his back. "All nice and legal," he repeated. "I see."

"No, I don't think you fully understand the consequences of adoption, or you wouldn't be so calm about it."

"She's still my daughter. My blood." He didn't sound threatened at all.

"And she's my daughter, too." Keep your head, she thought, pulling in a long, deep breath.

"So we're at an impasse?"

"Not as far as I'm concerned. I'm right, and you're wrong," she informed him.

He snorted a sardonic laugh. "Too bad you lack confidence."

"The law is on my side, Mr. Wolfe." She wasn't nearly as confident as all that, but she'd be damned if she would let him know it.

"How much does she know about her heritage?"

Libby frowned. "She knows she's a half-blood, if that's what you mean."

"That's not what I mean." He faced her again, his eyes still cold. "Does she know anything about the religion of her people? Their customs?"

Libby retreated a step. "Why . . . why no. I know nothing about those things."

"So basically," he began, slowly approaching her as if he were a prosecutor and she were on trial, "she's simply a nice little Christian girl with unusually brown skin who goes to a school for Whites and learns their fabled history."

Libby's anger stirred, but she didn't step away. "Fabled? What do you mean?"

His smirk was almost hungry. "The history of conflict always has two sides to it, although we read about only one."

"And you're saying that our white history is a lie?"

"Graphically colored in favor of the Whites. No mention is made of the horrors the Indians suffered when our ancestors trampled them and wrested away their land."

At the harshness of his statement, Libby flinched. "And you know the whole truth, is that it? You and no one else?" She forced a cynical laugh. "You'll do anything to shift the guilt, won't you?"

"I have no guilt."

The haunted look in his eyes told Libby otherwise. "I'd like to believe that, for it would make you even less worthy than you already are, but I don't."

He yanked his jacket off the chair and shrugged into it. "I don't give a damn what you believe. She's my daughter, and I'm going to claim her."

Reflexively, Libby grabbed his arm again.

His eyes revealed a dispirited look that took the simmering edge off Libby's anger.

This constant battling would get them nowhere. She was becoming as callous about Dawn's future as he, and it had to stop. As much as she hated to, she had to use another tactic. "Please," she pleaded softly. "If I need time to adjust to this, think about Dawn. And," she added, feeling the hardness of his muscled arm beneath his sleeve, "let me be there when you tell her."

"I'll consider it." He whistled for the dog, who jumped into his arms, then both were gone.

Libby stood in his room, feeling an ache so deep that it went into her bones. As far as she could determine, the conflict over custody could have no favorable ending.

Ethan fumbled for a cigarette as he approached the abandoned shed. His palms were sweaty and he felt like shit. If he kept losing thousands at his monthly poker games in Eureka, as he had been doing over the past six months, he would run out of funds. Hell, he'd gone through his own money a long time ago. What he was doing now, and had been for years, was clear-cut embezzlement.

So far, he'd gotten away with it. So far. Ethan winced and pressed his fist against his stomach. Christ, it burned like the devil. The cramping had become worse lately, and none of his old remedies worked anymore. He'd had enough plain milk to choke a calf, and if he ever saw another cup of wintergreen tea, he was afraid he'd vomit.

He pulled the flask from his inside coat pocket, removed the cap, and took a long pull on the contents. Milk and whiskey. A decent compromise. It had become the only thing he could tolerate when his stomach began to rebel.

Tossing a quick glance over his shoulder to make sure he hadn't been followed, he stepped to the door of the shed, opened it, and hurried inside. Cleb Hartman, one of his poker partners, sat at the battered table, smoking a cigar. Axel Worth, Vern's deputy, stood beside the cold, dead fireplace.

"'Bout time you got here." Axel fidgeted with his gun belt.

"I had some business to take care of." Ethan took a seat across from Hartman. "So what have you found out?"

Cleb clamped the cigar between his teeth, preparing to talk around it. "It's pretty damned certain they're going to put in a railroad line between Thief River and Fort Redding."

For the first time in a week, Ethan felt the knots in his stomach relax. "And the ranchland between here and there is truly paved with gold."

Cleb huffed a laugh. "In a manner of speaking."

"We got a new sheriff, Ethan." Axel strolled to the table and took a seat.

Ethan felt a frisson of fear, but dismissed it. "So what's that got to do with me, kid?"

"He ain't old and he ain't laid up. He's already been out to Mateo's sniffing around." Axel swore. "He could even tell that one of our mounts was a mare by the way she took a piss."

Ethan tapped his index finger against the scarred table-top. His plan had begun, and he didn't want anything to stand in the way, especially not a new lawman.

Danel Mateo was close to caving in, and he was one of the two sheep ranchers whose land Ethan coveted. Whose land lay between Thief River and Fort Redding. Whose land would be available for a song after Mateo fled, in fear of his life, soon followed by Ander Bilboa and his tow-headed brood. Since Ethan held the mortgages, both ranches would be his. Then he could sell the land to the railroad for a sweet, sweet price.

Jackson refused to let Dawn Twilight's adoption ruin his plans. Hell, he wasn't even sure it was legal, especially if a blood parent showed up. He had no doubt that being her natural father superseded an adoption by a stranger. And a widow woman at that.

Who was he kidding? Sure, he was still confident he could get Dawn Twilight back, but Libby O'Malley was no ordinary woman. She was far more complex than he'd imagined, and he appreciated that. *That* was what rankled. She wasn't some narrow-minded, dried-up, Bible-thumping prune. She was warm and loving, generous and wise. She was a damned good mother, he'd seen that from the very first day.

It changed nothing. He was sorry she'd be hurt in all this, but that couldn't be helped. His daughter needed him. Or maybe, he thought, his heart racing, he needed his daughter.

He planned to teach Dawn Twilight about her tribe. Tell her about her sweet, lovely mother. About the beautiful and peaceful ways of the Indian, not to mention their customs and religion. Then she could choose. At least, armed with information about her heritage, she'd have that choice and wouldn't have to live a white life if she didn't want to.

But he knew she probably would. And that was all right too. At least she'd know the other part of her. If he didn't teach her, no one would. They sure as hell didn't teach that kind of thing at a white school.

He was itching to tell her. And although he hadn't come out and told Libby he'd wait, he would. If he was nothing else, he was a man who kept his word.

As he rode toward the jail, his thoughts shifted to Libby O'Malley once again. A jumble of emotions stampeded through him, for until now he hadn't given much thought to the concept of mother love, that fierce, protective love of a woman for a child, the kind of love that eclipsed everything else, even a mother's own needs.

Did Libby have it? Did she understand that by telling Dawn Twilight the truth, she would lose her?

Jackson would not have placed a sure bet on anything, but if he'd had to take a wild guess, he'd have bet Libby O'Malley's mother love was as strong as any woman's. She considered Dawn Twilight hers in every way.

He also sloughed off the idea of the adoption, certain that as Dawn Twilight's natural father, he could get her back without a fight—or with one, if it came to that.

Libby felt like a criminal hiding in the alley across from the jail, but she wanted to talk to Sheriff Roberts and hoped Jackson would leave so she could. She was relieved when he finally went on an errand, accompanied by Deputy Worth. She slipped inside; Vern Roberts was there, nursing his bad knee with a bottle of whiskey.

He gave her a sheepish grin. "It's medicinal."

She raised her eyebrows. "Then shouldn't it go on your knee, and not in your stomach?"

"Don't start with me, Libby. I never much pictured you as the nagging wife type."

Libby allowed a smile. "That's a compliment, I guess, and I wasn't going to say anything until you thought you had to justify your actions."

"No, but you'd have thought it, anyway."

Her smile widened. "So how *is* the knee coming along?" She studied it through his pant leg, noting it was still swollen.

"Ah, hell. I don't think it'll ever be good as new again. The doc tells me I'm too old to even think that it will be. I'll prob'ly have to rely on a cane for the rest of my life." He scrutinized her. "What's on your mind, Libby?"

She perched on the chair beside him. "What do you know about the law?"

He snorted a laugh. "I'm a lawman, ain't I?"

"But do you know anything about adoptions?"

"Ah," he said with a nod of understanding. "Little Dawn.

93

It ain't no secret you adopted her, Libby. What's the problem?"

She studied him for a long, quiet moment. "Did Jackson Wolfe tell you he's Dawn's natural father?"

Vern's expression was incredulous. "Naw. He ain't."

"He is. At least he claims to be."

"Well, I'll be a dad-burned monkey's uncle . . ."

"What I want to know is this: could he have the adoption overturned?" She didn't want to weigh her words with her emotions, so she swallowed a comment about Jackson being an unfit, undeserving parent.

Vern scraped his fingers across his jaw. "Guess you'd have to get legal advice, Libby. And since the closest law firm is in Sacramento, that's where you'd have to find help."

She let out a whoosh of air and sagged into the chair. "That's what I was afraid of. The attorney who drew up the adoption papers moved east, and I have no idea how to reach him."

"Well, I guess you could wire just about any lawyer and get the information you want. By the way, did you know Jackson's got family hereabouts?"

Libby's stomach dropped. "Family? Where?"

"Up near the state line. His pa owns a big spread near Broken Jaw. Raises cattle, sheep, and horses."

So, she thought, her stomach continuing to pitch and toss, he probably has money and can afford to fight for custody. It was also a man's world. She swallowed the sour taste of impending defeat in her mouth. "Do you know them?"

A smile spread across Vern's craggy features. "Sure do. His pa is an old friend of mine. Nice fellow. And his stepma is a real wonderful lady. Them kids grew up with everything a kid could ask for. Love, a good home, and plenty of teaching. If I was asked, I'd say Jackson don't have a selfish bone in his body."

This bit of information depressed her further. She would never intentionally wish a hard life on anyone, considering that she knew firsthand how miserable it could be, but to learn that Jackson Wolfe appeared to have everything a man could want made her furious. He'd probably *always* gotten what he wanted, and now he wanted *her* daughter and assumed it was only a matter of time before he'd get her. *Over my dead body.*

"'Course," Vern went on, unaware of the turmoil in Libby's head, "Jackson's been gone a long time. Ain't had contact with the family for twelve years or so. Why, he ain't even told them he's home."

A thread of hope. "Then . . . then they don't know about Dawn?"

"Can't say as they do. Hell, I didn't know about it, and I think his pa would've brought up the fact that he has a grandchild if he knew about it. He'd have scoured the countryside for her. Alerted every lawman from here to the Mexican border. Believe me, if the Wolfe family gets wind of this—and they will, sooner or later—they'll dote on Dawn like she was a princess. Yep, damned fine people."

Libby continued to feel sick. "And . . . they're a large family?"

"Oh, yeah. Well, a clan, of sorts. There's Corey, Jackson's brother, and Mandy and Kate, his sisters. Then there's a Negro family what's lived near them for as long as I can remember. Damned fine blacksmith, the fellow is. Their kids grew up with Jackson. Well, he was the oldest, so all of them, black and white, followed him around like he was the Pied Piper or something."

He stroked his chin again. "Don't know what them kids is up to these days. Haven't seen Nate Wolfe for nearly a year."

Libby swallowed a dejected sigh and smiled. "Thank you, Vern, you've been very helpful. I'll send a wire to the lawyer in Sacramento and see what he says."

"It'd be a damned shame for you to lose the girl."

Libby bristled. "I have no intention of losing her, Vern."

"Jackson's a fighting man, you know. Stubborn, too, just like his pa. He don't give up on something he wants."

From the door, Libby threw the sheriff a forced smile. "Neither do I, Vern, neither do I."

She stepped outside, nearly colliding with Chloe Ann. "Is school out already?"

Chloe Ann fell into step beside her. "It's past three." She raised a package toward Libby. "I had to stop and pick up some supplies at the mercantile." She put her hand on Libby's arm. "What's wrong?"

Giving her a bright smile, Libby answered, "What makes you think something is wrong?"

Chloe Ann chuckled. "I may be as blind as a bat, but I'm close enough to see those frown lines gathering between your eyes."

With a sigh, Libby fell into step beside Chloe Ann. "Jackson Wolfe is Dawn's natural father." At Chloe's gasp, Libby nodded. "My reaction was a little more expressive, I'm afraid."

"Hmm. Broken dishes?"

"How did you know?" Libby felt the return of remorse at having destroyed the crockery and put a hole in the kitchen wall with the skillet.

"I saw the shards in the wastebasket on the back porch this morning before I left for school."

Libby's sigh was filled with disgust. "That . . . that wretched man. He comes here, slowly and carefully spins a web around all of us, then slithers in for the kill."

"Imagine how *he* might feel, Libby."

"Him? He's feeling pretty smug, if you ask me. But I shoved the adoption papers under his nose this morning, and although he didn't show it, he has to be worried." She could hope.

"I don't know . . ." Chloe Ann's voice trailed off.

"Oh, don't tell me you think he has a chance at regaining custody," Libby accused, suddenly feeling betrayed.

"I hope for your sake you win, Libby. You know I do. It would be so cruel for him to take Dawn away from you, but . . . the law is a funny thing. Not only is he her legal parent but he's also a man. Men seem to have the upper hand in almost anything. They make the rules, you know."

As they turned the corner, a rider galloped past, coming dangerously close to the wood-plank sidewalk.

Libby gasped and clutched her chest, her heart pounding, her ears ringing. Every time she heard the thundering of horses' hooves, all her good sense fled. She staggered into Chloe Ann.

Chloe Ann gripped her arm. "Are you all right?"

Libby expelled a shaky breath, her knees weak. "I'm sorry. It's foolish to be afraid of horses, but . . ."

"Don't worry about it, Libby. Why, that one got my heart pounding too." She made a disgusted sound in her throat. "You'd think it would be against the law for anyone to ride that fast in town. See? That's what I mean. Men make the laws to suit themselves."

As her equilibrium returned, Libby felt her confidence flag. She knew men made the rules. She knew Jackson had a good case against her, on paper at least. She knew he loved his daughter and wanted her to be with him. She *knew* all of those things. But she hoped that just this once they wouldn't matter and the law would be on her side.

8

JACKSON MADE SURE HE WAS AVAILABLE FOR HIS DAUGHTER AS often as possible, if only to say hello. When he could spend enough time, he regaled her with stories, amused her, entertained her, and virtually gave her his dog. Which, if he truly examined the gesture, was inevitable, because the Shih Tzu adored Dawn Twilight, and Jackson knew the feeling was mutual.

As anxious as he was to start a new life with her, he dragged his feet about telling her who he was. It had finally hit him, like a rock to the head, that Dawn Twilight really considered Libby her mother and he was half afraid that she'd consider him an outsider, unworthy of her affection. Hell, for him to tell her he was her father would be harder than fighting a legion of armed Chinese thugs.

But each evening he looked forward to any time they might have together. It had been two weeks since he'd admitted to Libby who he was, and they still treated each other like enemies teetering on a fragile truce. He had to hand it to her though, for she didn't do or say anything to lessen him in Dawn Twilight's eyes. That was not to say she wasn't probably thinking the worst about him. The old saying, "if looks could kill . . ." seemed to flow from her eyes like poison from a rattler's fang.

On his return from the jail, he stopped in the kitchen and found it empty. Bread cooled on racks, and the aroma from the oven made his mouth water. It reminded him of home, and the nostalgia was so strong it twisted like a knife inside him.

Glancing outside, he saw the top of his daughter's head. He pushed the door open and found her bent over something, concentrating hard. When he stepped onto the porch, she glanced up, then quickly returned to her task. But not before he saw the tears in her eyes. Something queer happened to his heart.

"Now, now. I don't like to see a pretty little girl cry. What's wrong?" He rarely called her Dawn, for he was afraid he'd slip and call her by her full name. He wasn't yet prepared to answer her questions.

She sniffed. "Oh, it's just this dumb mark on my knee." She hiccuped, then sniffed again. "I scrub it and scrub it, but it just won't go away."

A shaft of memory slashed through him, weakening him. "A mark on your knee? Do you . . . Would you mind if I took a look?"

With a shrug, she extended her bare leg in his direction. "I've had it as long as I can remember. It's ugly," she added, on the verge of fresh tears.

The tattoo. God, why hadn't he remembered? Forcing himself to stay calm, he studied the raindrop-shaped mark. Memories of the day the tribal holy man had put it there gusted through him like sleet on a winter wind.

This would have been the perfect opportunity to tell her who he was. Yet he couldn't. And it wasn't just because Libby wasn't around. It was because he was still a coward about Dawn Twilight's reaction, even though he knew she'd eventually thank him for coming back. He hoped.

"Do you know the story of the raindrop clan?"

Dawn Twilight sniffled and wiped her nose with the back of her hand. "N-no," she stammered.

"It's a very fine story. Want to hear it?"

She gave him a halfhearted shrug. "I guess so."

He settled down next to her. "The people of the raindrop clan lived near the great ocean," he began, his voice taking on the cadence of the tribal storytellers.

"Their days were always filled with good things. Fog shrouded their mornings, sunshine warmed their afternoons, and rain fell every night while they slept. They had the perfect world. Then, for no reason they could understand, everything changed."

Interested, Dawn Twilight asked, "What happened?"

"One season passed, and they had no rain. The people of the clan didn't panic, for they had experienced the passing of a dry season once before, but always before, the fog had continued to kiss their mornings."

"But this time was different?" She drew her legs up and rested her chin on her knees.

Jackson nodded. "This time the fog didn't greet them each morning, only the sun. And as the days grew long, and the shadows bent across the dry, parched earth, the sun continued to beat down upon them and their crops. The crops shriveled up and died. The fish, always so abundant, disliked the warmth of the water, so swam north, where the water was cooler. The animals, too, left for wetter, cooler places, many going into the mountains where rain came more often."

"So . . . so the people didn't have any food?"

"The people were starving."

She chewed on her lower lip, her expression pensive. The mannerism was like Flicker Feather's, and he waited for the pain, but there was only a distant memory.

"And what did they do, Mr. Wolfe?"

He ached for her to call him Papa. "An ancient holy man, so old no one remembered him ever being young, recalled the story of a beautiful maiden who lived on top of the mountain. A maiden who had special powers to speak with the spirits of the heavens."

"Did they go to her?"

"Oh, they wanted to, but it wasn't as simple as that. The

100

mountain on which she lived was often an angry one, spewing dust and fire into the air. They feared its temper. They assumed the maiden was responsible for the anger. Only a special person could be sent up there safely. Unfortunately, they had no guess as to who that special person might be."

"So who did they send?"

Jackson crossed one booted ankle over the other and leaned into the chair. "As luck would have it, the holy man sent the most handsome, most courageous brave to plead with her to intercede on the tribe's behalf. His only flaw was his eyes. One of them was blue, like the fresh mountain springs. The other was a deep, rich brown. If the maiden didn't approve of their choice, not only would their request for rain be refused, but they would see drought for ten more seasons."

"And did she accept him?" Dawn Twilight's eyes were wide, pulling Jackson in.

"Not at first," he explained, "for it was dark when he arrived. Her first command was that he prove he was willing to sacrifice himself to save the tribe."

Her dark brows pinched together. "He had to die?"

"He had to prove to her that he was willing," he amended, smiling into her upturned face.

"What did he do?"

"He vowed that he would throw himself into the mountain's burning, flaming mouth if that would save his people."

Dawn Twilight gasped, placing her sweet, delicate hands over her mouth. "Did he die?" Her question was a shaky whisper.

Jackson graced his daughter with a warm smile. "No. When the maiden was confident the brave would give his life for the others, she called him away from the rim of the crater. As they stood together, they discovered they shared a unique feature, for the maiden also had one blue eye and one brown."

"So what does that mean?"

"It means that for every lovely young creature on God's earth there is a mate. Have patience, little one. Consider your mark a kiss from the gods."

Glancing at her tattoo, Dawn sighed. "I suppose it isn't such a bad mark after all."

Jackson couldn't conceal his smile. "I think it's beautiful. It makes you special, Dawn Tw—" He cleared his throat. "It makes you very special indeed."

She continued to gaze at the tattoo, her expression so wistful it twisted at Jackson's heart. "The mark would be more special if a handsome prince had one just like it, like in the story."

He choked back a surge of emotion, wondering how long he could keep up the charade.

Carefully hidden beside the window, Libby had listened to the story. She pressed her fingers against her eyes to stop the sting of tears. Since his shocking admission, he'd risen a bit in her estimation, for he'd kept his promise not to tell Dawn who he was until she could be there. It had to be killing him. Still, she wondered why he hadn't told her it was time.

Not that she wanted him to. Lord, no. If he never told Dawn who he was, it would be soon enough for her. But, she realized with some disappointment, that was her opinion. As nice as he was to his daughter, he didn't know anything about raising a child, especially a girl-child. That, unfortunately, was the only thread she had to hang on to. And as she listened to him now, that thread had begun to grow thin.

Suddenly Dawn came through the door, barely stopping as she spoke. "Gotta get my sums done, Mama. I'll be in my room." She sounded, well, positively . . . positive.

Jackson followed her inside, his gaze on Libby. "You've been listening."

"That's what you were talking about before, the legends of her ancestors."

"Yes," he answered, his gaze not leaving her.

She should have been apologetic, but she wasn't. There were scores of reasons why she didn't believe he was best for

Dawn. "This still doesn't prove to me that you're her father."

"I've got proof now," he answered cryptically.

Libby got a funny feeling in the pit of her stomach. "What proof?"

"The tattoo."

"That . . . that mark on her knee? How is that proof of anything?"

"I've got one just like it."

Libby felt as though she were drowning. "You . . . you've got one?"

One corner of his mouth lifted into a sexy smile, causing her heart to flip-flop. "You don't remember seeing it the other day?"

The fateful morning when Mahalia had stripped him of his bedding sprang to her mind. But she hadn't been looking at his knees. . . . Warmth crept over her skin at the memory, making her cheeks hot.

"But you weren't looking at my legs, were you?"

Her flush deepened, for he'd obviously read her mind. Sometimes she didn't understand him at all. One minute he was cold and aloof, the next he teased her. He'd knocked her off-balance from the very first day.

She didn't know how to respond to such banter. She'd never learned. It was best simply to ignore the innuendo. "So you have proof. That's all fine and good, but how do I know you won't get itchy feet and leave again?" At this point, his wanderlust was her best defense. Maybe her only defense.

His eyes hardened. "What makes you think that's what happened the first time?"

"Do you want to argue the point?"

His gaze shifted to one side. "I'm here to stay."

"So you say. Seems to me, though, that once a man has tasted that kind of freedom, he can't quite kick the habit. What happens to your daughter if the lure of adventure becomes too strong to resist, and you go gallivanting off to fight another revolution?"

"That won't happen."

The fact that he couldn't meet her gaze gave her the real answer. So this was the way it would be. She couldn't refuse his request to be with Dawn, but she would fight with everything she had to keep him from taking Dawn away from her.

"You can continue to see Dawn, under my supervision. I will also determine some of the activities you must attend with her."

"Activities?"

She hid a triumphant smile. It was a good idea for him to see the pain Dawn went through on a daily basis. Pain because of her mixed blood. Perhaps the hardships of her life would drive him off once and for all. Libby had no doubt that he'd dreamed up some sort of fantasy life with his child. He had no idea how hard the reality was. Perhaps the reality would change his mind. She could only hope.

"Before you tell her who you are, you must observe her life, Jackson. Not just what you see here but what she goes through at school, on the street, everywhere."

He shrugged. "That'll be a pleasure."

Her smile was melancholy. "We'll see. There's a box social at the school tomorrow at noon. I want you to come with me."

Stroking his chin, Jackson watched the progress from the back of the schoolroom. Libby sat next to him. Besides Chloe Ann Parker, the teacher, they were the only adults in the room. She'd agreed to let them observe the box social. In fact, she'd been quite enthusiastic.

Beside him, Jackson felt Libby's tension. She was taut as a wire, her gaze never leaving Dawn Twilight. And even though his daughter sat among the other children, Jackson felt she was alone. She was the only breed in the class. A ton of emotions thrashed around in his gut, and he was unable to sort them out.

The bidding for the baskets began. Jackson knew that Dawn Twilight's, tied with a bright green bow, was filled with Mahalia's delicious fried chicken, buttermilk biscuits, and apple pie. His mouth watered just thinking about it. Unfortunately, only the boys in the class were able to bid.

The first basket to go belonged to a pretty blond girl with long pigtails. A tall, gangly boy offered for it and was not challenged. Jackson sat forward, his hands clenched into fists on his knees as he waited.

"I want the one with the green bow." A tough-looking boy barely into his teens stood up and pointed at Dawn Twilight's basket. Jackson grabbed Libby's hand and squeezed it while he held his breath.

Libby leaned close. "That's Willie Frost, one of the banker's sons."

Jackson noted that Libby's eyes were hard. Dawn Twilight turned her face to the side, affording Jackson a view of her profile, and her expression of dread. He waited, his jaw set. The boy, Willie, leaned across to a friend and whispered something, which caused the other lad to emit a wild snicker.

Jackson nearly came out of his chair; Libby dragged him back.

"You can't interfere," she ordered, her voice soft yet stern.

Jackson sat down but didn't relax. Couldn't. "If he does anything to hurt my daughter—"

Libby pinched his arm. "Just wait a while. See what happens."

It appeared no one else would bid on Dawn's basket, and Jackson knew a pain he'd never experienced before, not even in all the years he'd been fighting.

"I'd like that basket." The voice was husky, on the verge of manhood. Dawn swung around, facing the back of the classroom. Jackson's gaze followed.

Libby leaned into him. "He must be new. I've never seen him before."

Jackson studied the lad, looking for the same snide attitude he'd seen in the Frost boy, but found none.

"Hey," Willie Frost sputtered. "The breed's basket is mine. I asked for it first."

"Willie," Chloe Ann warned. "You will not use that word in this room. Have I made myself clear?"

"Well, that's what she is," he answered with a sneer. "She's a digger's brat, and she's—"

"Willie Frost, close your mouth."

"But—"

Chloe Ann's ruler came down hard on Willie's knuckles. The boy yelped. "Go to the corner and stay there," she ordered.

He glared at her but rose from his desk. "I'll tell my pa, and he'll have you fired."

Chloe Ann prodded him with the ruler. "By all means," she answered, "tell your father. I'd be delighted to talk to him once and for all. Your disrespect for others is appalling, and you've disrupted this classroom often enough."

Willie tossed her a glower as he slunk toward the corner. "I don't care what you say. She's a breed."

Ignoring him, Chloe Ann turned to the other boy. "It's your basket, Danforth. You'll be sharing the lunch with Dawn O'Malley."

Jackson caught his daughter's shy smile as she looked at the boy. Again, something akin to pain twisted inside him. He'd missed so much. All the years between birth and adolescence. All those years when a child learned about living, he'd missed. He hadn't been there when she took her first step or when she spoke her first words. There were times when he didn't think he could bear the loss of those years.

He quietly wondered if he truly deserved her, and he knew he didn't. But he sure wasn't going to give her up. He couldn't, not when he'd just found her. Libby O'Malley would have to accept that.

A twinge of conscience sounded silently in his head, but he ignored it.

Libby rose to leave, Jackson followed. Once outside, he turned on her, his face etched with fury.

"What was that all about?"

"It's what Dawn must go through every day of her life, Jackson."

"Then why subject her to it?"

Libby crossed her arms over her chest and met his glare. "I suppose, after witnessing this one incident, you have an alternative?"

Jackson huffed. "She could be taught at home."

"Oh, that's a sensible solution," Libby answered, her voice laced with sarcasm. "She must learn to cope with reality, Jackson. After all, one day she'll be all grown up and will go out into this cruel world. She must be armed, and her armor must be strong enough to withstand the cruelties of the Willie Frosts everywhere."

Jackson said nothing for a long, quiet moment, then murmured, "I thought Ethan Frost was a friend of yours."

She gave him a sidelong glance. "That doesn't mean I condone the way he's raising his boys." She stepped away and plucked dried leaves off a sad-looking rosebush. Ethan was coming by after dinner tonight. She needed to talk with him. She couldn't go on watching her child endure such bullying. Of course, she thought with a weary sigh, Ethan would probably propose again, and she would refuse. Again. No way would she tie herself to a man whose children were hooligans.

Besides, she didn't love him. She would never marry again without love.

"I got the impression he was more than a friend," Jackson said.

She crushed the dying rose petals in her fist. "Well, he's not. He's a widower with four ruffians, and I'm not the least bit interested in taking on a responsibility like that. In fact, I think what he really wants is a housekeeper. I already have a house to keep. I surely don't want to keep his."

"Does the boy pick on Dawn Twilight often?"

She ignored the pain in his voice. He needed to know the truth. "He and a few of his little bully friends have chased her after school. She comes home with rips in her stockings and bloody knees, and I know she's fallen or been pushed. She won't tell me what's happened, but I know. I know."

"Believe me, I'd—"

"You'd what?" She stopped and turned on him. "She refuses to make an issue out of it, Jackson. She's learning to deal with these incidents herself, and although it breaks my heart, I have to let her."

"Well, I don't."

"Yes, you do. And at this moment you have no rights whatsoever."

"I can't go on like this," he mumbled. "I can't stand to watch her in so much pain."

"And you think I can?"

He was tense beside her. "I don't know how you do it."

Sometimes she didn't know how she did it, either. "Dawn is often far more mature about it than I am. My instincts are the same as yours, Jackson. I die a little inside every time she comes home hurting."

"I've got to tell her who I am. I can't stand this silence any longer. I want to become part of her life. I want to protect her from snotty little bastards like Willie Frost."

Libby had been expecting this, but the words were like rocks weighing on her heart. She wanted to warn him, to tell him not to expect too much from Dawn's initial reaction to the news that her father had been living with them for weeks. But Libby wasn't sure how her daughter would react. Though she was eager for news of her "real" family, Dawn was basically a dreamer. And dreamers created fantasies, not realities.

"You don't agree."

Libby rubbed her neck. "I don't honestly know what to tell you. No matter how you tell her, the truth is going to be a shock."

After clearing the dead grass and leaves off the back porch, Jackson stepped into the kitchen. Bert Bellamy nodded at him from the table. Or maybe it was Burl. Hell, he couldn't tell the two old coots apart.

"Evenin', Sheriff." The wizened man stuffed a plug of tobacco against the inside of his cheek and gave him a sly smile. "Seems someone's tryin' to weasel in on yer territory."

"My territory?"

"Yep. That slick feller Ethan Frost is courtin' Miz Liberty on the front porch. I was sittin' there, comfy as ya please, and she shooed me out like I was a fly on butter."

Jackson frowned. "And how do you figure that's my territory?"

Bellamy cackled. "Ya think yer yellin' back and forth ain't been heard by anyone but yerselves?" At Jackson's look of surprise, the old man continued. "So ya got yerself a daughter, have ya? Danged fine gal, that Dawn. I don't suppose me an' Bert is much of a threat to ya, but if ya harm one hair on that little gal's head, actin' sheriff or not, you'll have to answer to us, mister."

With a shake of his head, Jackson left the old coot alone and walked toward the front door. He heard voices on the porch.

"It's my final offer, Libby."

"And 'no' is my final answer. Oh, Ethan, why can't we just be friends?"

Jackson noted a hint of annoyance in her voice, and for some perverse reason, he was glad.

Frost sputtered a mild curse. "Because I don't want to be your friend, Libby. I want to be your husband."

"And I've told you I will not step in and try to tame those boys of yours. They have absolutely no respect for people, and I especially resent the way they treat Dawn."

"Oh, Libby, they're just being boys."

"Not that it will ever happen, let me assure you, Ethan, but suppose I accepted your proposal. I would be subjecting my daughter to harassment day and night instead of a few hours every afternoon."

Frost made a growling sound in his throat. "Is that what this is all about? Your daughter? Hell, Libby, she isn't even your blood."

Jackson felt a surge of anger. He hated the bastard already, and they hadn't even met.

The porch swing squeaked.

"Ah, come on, Libby. Don't leave. You know what I mean."

"Yes. Yes, I do, Ethan Frost, and if you think—"

"I'm sorry. I know I can be callous at times. Please sit down. I'm sorry I ruined the mood. I wouldn't hurt you for the world, Libby. I care too much for you."

Jackson stood in the shadows and shook his head. Yeah, he thought, but he didn't give a shit about her half-breed daughter. Anger continued to boil in his stomach, and it took all his strength to keep from storming onto the porch and tossing the man off onto the grass.

Still, he felt like a voyeur, especially when he was drawn to the window. Libby and the banker were seated on the porch swing, the banker's arms closing around Libby's shoulders. Libby squirmed away. Ethan Frost followed. Their faces came dangerously close together.

Jackson froze and swallowed the knot in his throat. If he hadn't known himself better, he'd have sworn he was jealous.

Suddenly a horrendous sneeze exploded from Libby's mouth.

Frost swore and pulled away. He moved toward her again, and once again Libby sneezed loud enough to shake the windows.

When he lunged for her a third time, Jackson could hold back no longer. Springing onto the porch, he charged at Frost, grabbed the collar of his jacket, and dragged him off the swing.

Frost's strangled gasp of surprise was offset by Libby's cry of alarm.

"Jackson! What are you doing?"

Jackson roughly hauled Frost down the steps. "Get on your mount and get the hell out of here."

Frost struggled under Jackson's grip. "Get your hands off me. I'll leave when I'm good and ready."

In spite of his words, Frost made a quick getaway, leaving Jackson seething as he watched his retreat.

"Just what was that all about?"

Libby was at his side, the moonlight glancing off her eyes. He was surprised by the anger he saw there.

"He wouldn't leave you alone," Jackson murmured.

She made a sound of disbelief. "And you thought it was your duty to leap out onto the porch and save me, like the hero of a bad farce?"

He suddenly realized how foolish he must have looked. "Well, you were sneezing. I thought you needed help." He paused a moment, then added, "Maybe you should see the doctor."

"Nonsense," she said with a snort. "That's my standard defense against his ardent pursuit."

"You mean you did it on purpose?"

"Of course." There was a smile in her voice. "I'm just surprised he hasn't caught on by now. I thought he was smarter than that."

As Jackson watched her escape into the house, he had the oddest sensation in his chest. He couldn't decide if it was pleasure or relief. Maybe it was a little bit of both.

9

JACKSON DREADED FACING ETHAN FROST AFTER HAVING tossed him off Libby's porch the night before.

He stepped into the bank, nodding a greeting toward the clerk he'd spoken to the previous week. "Ethan Frost in?"

The clerk rose, crossed to a door, and knocked, then disappeared inside. He reappeared shortly, followed by Frost, who was handsomely dressed and impeccably groomed. He looked as if he repelled lint and dirt. Jackson's dislike for the man was reaffirmed.

Frost gave him a cold, sly smile. "Perhaps I should throw you out of here. Then we'd be even."

Jackson didn't feel like apologizing. "I've come about my daughter's trust fund."

Frost sighed and nodded toward his office. "Let's go inside."

Jackson followed him and took a seat in front of the desk while Frost settled into his opulent leather chair.

"I was sorry to hear about your father. He was a good man."

Nodding slightly, Frost cleared his throat. "What kind of arrangement did you say you had with the bank?"

"Your father set up a trust fund for my daughter." Jackson studied the son, who was so very different from the father. John had been a rumpled, apple-cheeked, elflike man with cottony white hair, a generous smile, and twinkling blue eyes. The son bore no resemblance to him. Despite his handsome features, fit posture, and gleaming bronzed hair, his eyes were flat and hard. Cold.

Frost frowned. "Under what name would it have been?"

Jackson drew out the leather pouch and dumped the papers onto the desk. "Under mine, of course. Jackson Wolfe. My daughter's name is Dawn."

There was a brief flash of recognition in his eyes, but it was quickly masked. "Dawn O'Malley?"

Remembering Frost's callous remark regarding Dawn the night before, Jackson gave him a terse nod, then shoved the papers across the desk. "I have receipts for the gold I sent to this bank up until approximately five years ago. The receipts stopped coming at about the time your father died."

Frost studied the papers one by one, stacking them neatly on top of each other when he'd finished. "They certainly do seem to be in order."

Art McCann's analysis of Ethan Frost flashed in Jackson's mind. McCann hadn't liked him. Jackson didn't either, for a number of reasons. "Damn right they're in order." He leaned across the desk to make his point. "I was in here last week, and your clerk wasn't able to find a trace of my account. Can you?"

Another brief flash of discomfort. "Of course. I'll certainly look into it, Mr. Wolfe."

"That would be smart, Mr. Frost. Otherwise I'm afraid we'll have to get the authorities in here to find out what's going on."

Frost narrowed his gaze, his jaw clenching. "There won't be any need for that, I can assure you."

Jackson met his gaze. "Then maybe you'll check into this matter now, while I'm here."

Frost steepled his long, thin fingers and stared at Jackson

over the tops. "If you wish, although that could take some time. It would be better if—"

"I've got the time."

Frost stood. "Yes. Well. I'll see what I can find, but—"

"I'll wait right here."

Frost hesitated a moment before leaving Jackson alone in his office. Jackson studied the window, absently watching a pine tree flicker in the wind outside. An odd feeling in his gut told him Dawn Twilight wouldn't see a penny of the thousands he'd set aside for her.

Ethan mopped his face with his handkerchief, then ran a finger between his collar and his neck. He suddenly had a choking sensation, as if his collar were too tight. And his armpits prickled. Damn, but he hated to sweat. He sucked in a breath, attempting to regain control.

So. Libby's little half-breed was Jackson Wolfe's daughter. Ethan felt certain he wouldn't have touched that fund if he'd known it would get him into trouble. Hell, who was he kidding? All that money made his mouth water. He'd have wrestled the devil for it.

After taking over the bank upon the death of his father, he'd discovered Wolfe's trust fund simply sitting there, collecting dust. And interest, of course. Ethan hadn't thought ahead to this moment. True, there was always the fear that someone might return and claim it, but so many years passed, and no one came. He'd felt safe; he began using the fund as his own private reserve. And he'd gambled it all away. So many times he'd been close to making a killing, to wiping out everyone else at the poker table. So many times. Now, with the railroad deal, he was close to making a killing again, and he wasn't going to let anything or anyone stop him.

Ethan knew that Wolfe couldn't prove he'd embezzled the money. He would have to tell him the fund wasn't here, but he would also have to find a way to keep Wolfe from bringing in the authorities. Ethan's books wouldn't bear scrutiny.

His stomach burned. He dragged his flask from his inside

jacket pocket and took a long swallow. Afterward he took in greedy gulps of air to calm himself. Somehow he had to buy time regarding the trust fund. Unfortunately, with the news of the railroad about to become public knowledge, he had little time to waste.

The next afternoon Libby met Dawn on her return from school and ushered her into the parlor. Jackson sat in the chair by the fire, and Libby closed the door so the three of them could be alone.

Dawn's expression was one of puzzlement as she looked from one to the other. "What's wrong?" She gasped, pressing her hand to her mouth. "Did something happen to Mumser?"

"It's nothing like that, dear."

Dawn frowned at her mother. "Then what is it?"

Beneath his stubble, Jackson appeared pale.

"Mr. Wolfe has something to tell you," Libby began. She couldn't imagine how he was going to get through this, much less how he would start. Already he looked about to collapse under the strain, and he hadn't even begun.

"Your . . . mother tells me you often ask about your real family. Is that right?"

Dawn's eyes widened. "Do you know them? Do you know who they are?"

He flashed Libby a fearful look. "Yes. I . . . er . . . I do."

She ran to him, fell to her knees, and grabbed his arm. "Oh, please tell me something about them, please."

Another fear-filled glance. Libby could tell he was struggling. She had no sympathy.

"You . . . you have a grandma and a grandpa who live not far from here."

Dawn tossed Libby a look of shocked surprise. "Did you know that, Mama?"

Unable to speak, Libby merely shook her head.

Dawn's gaze returned to Jackson. "Didn't they want me?"

Libby's stomach hurt; it had been roiling and convulsing ever since morning when Jackson had finally told her it was time to tell Dawn the truth. She hadn't been able to eat all day, and her jaws ached from clenching them. Now Dawn's emotions were in shambles, just like her own.

"Let Mr. Wolfe finish, dear."

Jackson's color had not returned. Under different circumstances Libby might have had pity on him.

"They don't know about you. If . . . if they had, they would have wanted to get to know you. You . . . also have two aunts and an uncle," he added.

Dawn's face changed, softening some. "Oooh," she said on a sigh. "Do you know their names?"

His eyes appeared shiny. "Your uncle's name is Corey. Your aunts are Mandy and Kate."

Dawn tossed her mother a heavenly smile, one that made Libby's stomach convulse again.

"Mandy and Kate," she repeated dreamily. "And cousins? Do I have cousins, Mr. Wolfe?"

He attempted a smile, but it wavered and was gone. "I'm not sure about that, but I don't think so. One of your aunts, Kate, isn't much older than you are, though."

Dawn was edgy with a cautious happiness. It made Libby's stomach clench harder.

"Why didn't you tell me sooner?"

Jackson ran his hand through his hair, rumpling it. "Because . . . I had to be sure."

Dawn was noticeably confused. "Sure about what?"

"I . . . I had to be sure that you were my . . . my daughter." The word came out choked, and he appeared to have trouble breathing.

As if in slow motion, Dawn stood up and stepped away. "Huh?" She looked to her mother for further explanation.

Libby put her arm around Dawn's shoulders. "I think Mr. Wolfe is trying to tell you that he's your father."

Dawn swung toward him, her hands clenched into fists. "My . . . my father? My real father?"

Jackson smiled, a beatific expression on his face, his eyes glowing with an eager warmth. "You are my daughter. Dawn Twilight."

Libby could have anticipated Dawn's reaction, but it was obvious that Jackson hadn't.

Dawn flung herself from her mother's arms and edged toward the door. Her eyes were wide with fear and apprehension. "I don't believe you. I *don't.*" She nailed Libby with a glowering stare. "Why didn't someone tell me?" Her gaze swung to Jackson, and she glared, her throat working wildly. "What were you waiting for? Did you have to approve of me first? Did you have to wait and see if I was good enough for you?"

She was breathing hard, her tiny chest heaving. "Why did you leave in the first place? Why did you? And . . . and why did you have to come back now? Oh, I hate you! I hate you!" She burst into tears and ran from the room.

Libby felt sick; she could have predicted this. "Well!" she exclaimed, her voice laced with sarcasm. "That went rather well, don't you think?"

Jackson sat in the chair, stunned into silence. Finally he murmured, "I didn't think she'd be so angry. Why is she so angry?"

"Oh, I don't know," Libby began conversationally, "just a hunch, but maybe it's because you came waltzing into her life after being absent for twelve years. Not only that, but you didn't identify yourself until you'd been here a while. That might make her the teensiest bit angry and upset."

Seemingly unaware of her mockery, he continued to stare at the door; then he drove his fingers through his hair again. "I didn't know what else to do."

Had Dawn not been her daughter, she might have even felt sorry for him. He truly hadn't a clue about children and their feelings. "You've been living in a fantasy world. You might be a crack revolutionary, but you're ignorant about fatherhood." She refused to sugarcoat her words simply to make him feel better.

He didn't even argue with her. "I hadn't looked at the situation from her point of view."

Libby strode to the window, pulled back the curtain, and glanced outside. Dawn was huddled beneath the weeping willow, Mumser clutched to her chest. "Obviously."

"You tried to warn me."

"Yes, I did."

"How could I have done it differently?"

Libby sighed and turned to face him. "It wouldn't have mattered how you approached it, Jackson. As much as she's always wanted to know about her family, she's frightened by the truth. Before this, she used her imagination. She daydreamed about her family. It was her fantasy of what might have been. Try to imagine what she's going through now that she's learned she actually does have a family out there—a family that might not want her, that might not live up to the family of her dreams."

He leaned his head into the cushioned back of the chair and closed his eyes. "I had so many plans."

Libby wanted in the worst way for him to give up. Admit he couldn't simply step in and take over. "So now you're going to quit?" Her words were hopeful, although she knew he wouldn't back down.

He shook his head. "No. I can't quit. I just don't know how to proceed."

She sighed again, wishing she weren't quite so damned honorable. As much as she wanted him gone, he was, after all, Dawn's father. "I'll talk to her."

"I didn't mean to hurt her. I honestly didn't know she'd be so upset."

Libby crossed to the door. "I know you didn't, but no matter how many times I tried to warn you, you wouldn't listen." She didn't add that because of his ignorance, he wouldn't make a good parent, especially to a sensitive child like Dawn.

"I suppose you have the right to know why I left in the first place."

Libby nearly held her breath. And waited.

"Dawn Twilight's mother was gunned down by vigilantes one day while she worked in her garden."

Libby bit into her bottom lip, moved by the words.

"I was just a kid. Hell, we both were, but she was wise beyond her years. And I loved her. When she died, I didn't give a damn about anything. Not revenge against her killers, not even the daughter she bore me." He expelled a heavy sigh.

"I had the presence of mind to set up a trust fund with John Frost, leaving it up to him to make sure Dawn Twilight and my wife's grandmother were taken care of. That's the kind of coward I was, Libby. I didn't even face up to my responsibilities like a man. And the worst of it is, the trust fund seems to have disappeared. There's no proof anywhere that I was anything but a chicken-livered coward who just up and ran away."

Despite her anger, Libby felt her throat clog with unshed tears. "And you merely left the country without looking back?"

Another sigh. "I'd like to tell you differently, but that's about the size of it. But all those years I sent money to John Frost, soothing my guilt, only to discover Dawn Twilight hasn't seen a penny of it. That's why it's so important for me to become part of her life again. I've got a lot to make up for. You can understand that, can't you?"

Understand? Libby expelled a shuddery breath. Yes, she understood, but that changed nothing. She could understand his motives but she didn't have to approve of them.

A spasm clutched at her heart, for she felt her hold on Dawn slipping away like the ebbing tide. "I'll talk to her," she repeated.

Libby stepped into the circle beneath the willow branches and sat on the grass beside her daughter. "This has always been one of your favorite spots."

Dawn said nothing. Tears stained her cheeks, and she sniffled.

Libby fussed with Dawn's hair, attempting to tuck stray strands into her braid. "He had the best of intentions, you know." God, why was she defending the man?

Dawn pressed Mumser close; the dog wiggled to get comfortable, seeming to sense her anguish. "Why didn't he tell me right away, Mama?"

Her voice was filled with such pain it tore at Libby's lungs, rendering her nearly breathless. "I think he was afraid."

Dawn snorted a tear-filled laugh. "He's a big man. He's been all over the world, fighting all sorts of bad men. He's been shot and stabbed and beaten up. He's not afraid of anything."

Libby was forced to smile. "Things that frighten big men like Mr. Wolfe would surprise us. Why, I think he was afraid of you."

"Afraid of *me?*" She was incredulous. "Why would he be afraid of me? I'm just a little girl."

Libby nodded. "A little girl he left twelve years ago, and for whatever reason, he feels guilty about it." It wasn't up to her to explain; Jackson had to do that.

They sat in a silence that was punctuated only by Dawn's sniffles.

"But why didn't he tell me?" Dawn asked again.

"I think deep down he was afraid of your reaction, dear. How does a person go about explaining to his child that he wants to be part of her life again?"

Mumser squirmed from Dawn's grasp and chased a dried leaf across the grass.

"What's gonna happen now?"

The odd discomfort returned to Libby's stomach. "Nothing will change, Dawn." Beneath the folds of her gown, she crossed her fingers.

Dawn snuggled closer, and Libby put her arms around her. "It's funny, isn't it?"

"What?"

"How I've always wanted to know my family, and now that I have one, I'm afraid."

Libby studied Dawn's face. "What are you afraid of?"

Dawn shrugged. "I don't know. It's . . . it's just that my stomach hurts now whenever I think about . . . them. Those people I don't even know. What if they don't like me?"

Libby's throat tightened. "How can they not like you?"

120

"I don't know. If my own papa wasn't sure he wanted me—"

"Don't say that. Don't even think it. That's not the reason he didn't tell you who he was, Dawn."

Dawn expelled a watery sigh. "He knew my other mama, didn't he? Do you think she's alive?"

Libby stroked Dawn's hair. "Why don't you ask him, dear? In my mind, no mother would have willingly given you up. And no mother who hadn't loved her daughter very much would have given her such a beautiful name."

"Dawn Twilight," she repeated. "It *is* pretty, isn't it?"

"It's the most beautiful name I've ever heard," Libby answered, and meant it. "You know, he probably has a lot to tell you."

Dawn raised her head and gazed at the house, her anxious expression mingled with hope. "I guess so."

"Why don't you find him?"

Dawn stood. "Things won't really change now, will they?"

Libby's gaze was cautious. "Change?"

Dawn swallowed repeatedly. "I mean, you'll still be my mama, won't you?"

Libby rose and took Dawn into her arms. "You're my daughter. I adopted you. I chose you. You will always be my daughter, and I'll always be your mama."

Dawn gave her a quick hug, then sprinted toward the house.

Libby stood beneath the weeping willow a long while after Dawn had disappeared, having come to the conclusion that the tree aptly expressed her own feelings. She knew she needed to have a good cry. She just had to make certain no one was around to see it.

Jackson raised his head, sensing someone at the door. His daughter stood there, as if uncertain whether she wanted to enter. At least she'd returned. "Please, Dawn Twilight. Come in."

Dawn Twilight stepped into the room but hovered near

the door. Each time Jackson saw her he was struck by her beauty. Indeed, she looked like her mother, but in truth, she was going to be even more beautiful.

"I imagine you have many questions for me."

Dawn Twilight dug the toe of her slipper into the rug, twisting it nervously. "Did you know my other mama?"

Jackson noted that she didn't say her "real" mama. "Of course. She was my wife, and I loved her very much."

Studying him through cautious eyes, she asked, "Did she die?"

The memory, though no longer painful, was vivid even now. "Yes, she did."

Dawn Twilight moved closer. "How?"

"She . . . she was killed. Shot by . . . by some white men who called themselves vigilantes. They wanted to get rid of the Indians, but I think they were also angry that I lived among them."

"Then why didn't they kill you instead of her?"

He smiled at her candor. "The way to inflict lasting heartache is to harm someone you love. It forces you to live with your guilt and your pain."

She looked at him strangely, the words affecting her on some level. "What was her name?"

"She was called Flicker Feather."

Dawn Twilight gazed past him, toward the window. "Flicker Feather. That's a pretty name too. Was she pretty?"

"She was beautiful. You look like her."

She accepted the compliment casually. "But I don't look like you."

"We do share a similarity," he explained.

"What?" She was still cautious.

"The raindrop tattoo. I have one, too. We all did."

She sidled closer. "You have one?"

"I do indeed."

She studied him, her gaze becoming less cautious. "Why did you leave me?"

Jackson's heart felt as if it had been squeezed. "That's a story I'm not very proud of."

Dawn dug the toe of her shoe into the carpet again and stared at her hands. "Who did you leave me with?"

"Grandmother," he answered softly, remembering the strength of the old woman.

"She was an Indian, wasn't she?"

"Flicker Feather's grandmother. She was a wise, wonderful woman, Dawn Twilight. I admit that I ran away like a coward, but there was no one better to leave you with than her."

Dawn Twilight toyed with her sash. "I sort of remember her. Not very much, but I remember an old woman. Why didn't you leave me with my other grandmother?"

Jackson rubbed his hands over his face, pressing them against his eyes. "At the time I thought I was doing the right thing. You can't know how sorry I am. You can't know," he murmured, unable to meet her gaze.

"What about my grandpa and grandma? What are their names?"

Her resilience amazed him. "Your grandfather's name is Nathan. Your grandmother is Susannah."

Dawn Twilight cocked her head to one side. "Is she pretty?"

Jackson gave her a warm smile. "I've always thought so."

She sat on the arm of his chair. "Do you think they'll like me?"

"I think," Jackson began, taking his daughter's hands and squeezing them between his, "they will absolutely adore you."

All of her reticence fell away, exposing the vibrant child beneath. "I hope so."

"I know so. We'll go there one day soon, if you like."

Uncertainty flickered across her face. "They don't know about me?"

"No. But that's a long story, Dawn Twilight, and I want you to know that it has nothing to do with you and everything to do with me and my stubborn pride."

She appeared to digest this, then said, "And . . . and you're sure they'll like me?"

He longed to take her into his arms, but he knew he didn't yet have the right. "They will love you."

Expelling a great sigh of relief, she asked, "When is my real birthday?"

"When do you celebrate it now?"

"August tenth. That's the day Mama found me."

"You were born on December twenty-fifth," he answered.

Her eyes widened and she grinned. "Christmas?"

With a nod, he repeated, "Christmas."

Another sigh. "Now I've got two birthdays."

"And we'll celebrate them both, I promise you."

Giving him a quick grin, she leaped off the chair and darted to the window. "Oh, no! Mumser has chased Cyclops onto the roof, again." She whirled away and skipped to the door. "I'll see you later, Mr. Wolfe."

Jackson sat and studied the door. Again her resilience surprised him. But she'd called him Mr. Wolfe. Hell, what had he expected, that she'd call him Papa?

Libby stepped inside, her expression cautious.

Jackson gave her a grateful nod. "Thank you for not nailing me to the wall."

A cool smile spread across her lips. "I wasn't doing you any favors, Jackson. She has a right to know who you are, that's all."

He was beginning to get his strength back. "Yes, I suppose we should talk about rights, shouldn't we?"

Her gaze narrowed and she faced him, fists on hips. "Dawn is my daughter. I don't believe there's a law in the land that would overturn the adoption and return a child to an itinerant father."

A swell of anger washed over him. "I've told you my footloose days are over. And, I might add, my family is virtually riddled with good women who will accept Dawn Twilight with open arms."

The threat reached its mark. Libby paled and leaned against the wall, as if to keep herself from falling. "If you try to take Dawn away from me, Jackson Wolfe, you'll lose her forever. Not only that, but I will personally drive a stake through your heart while you sleep."

Her black eyes smoldered. In spite of everything, he liked her fire. He wished the circumstances were different, for she was a woman worthy of knowing. Worthy of his respect. Yet he was unable to keep from baiting her, for she was the enemy.

"The fact that you think about me in bed, Libby O'Malley, gives me hope that we can reach a satisfactory conclusion."

Her face flushed. "The only satisfactory conclusion I can imagine is you riding off into the sunset . . . alone, never to return. Maybe being swallowed up by an earthquake."

"Then we've reached an impasse, haven't we?"

Her gaze was hard, her mouth set. Even so, she was appealing in her anger.

"An impasse is a stalemate, a tie, a standoff," she said. "As far as I can see, I still have the upper hand. I am the person she calls Mother. I am the person she turns to when she's unhappy. When she's had a bad dream. When she's had a bad day. I'm the one with whom she shares her secrets. Somehow I can't picture you taking my place."

He couldn't stop his cocky smirk. "Don't be so sure. Remember, blood is thicker than water."

She huffed, an angry, impatient sound. "And *nothing* is thicker than a man's head." With that, she spun away and sailed out the door.

10

LIBBY STORMED FROM THE ROOM, HER FACE HOT AND HER temper flaring. The man wasn't fit to care for a pig, much less a child. Lord, just about the time she thought he wasn't a bad sort, he revealed his true colors. There was no way in hell he would take Dawn away from her. She'd fight him to the death—his, preferably. *Damn* him, anyway!

But she knew that fighting over Dawn would be detrimental to the child. A court battle would upset everyone, especially Dawn. And Libby refused to even consider allowing Dawn to choose which one of them she wanted to live with. That would tear the child apart.

Libby saw no happy endings, either. Even though she had legal custody, this was a man's world. Men made the rules to suit themselves. She feared that Jackson *could* take Dawn away from her. Somehow. Some way. At the very least he could bring her to his family, which he admitted was "riddled" with good women who could care for her.

Libby went to her room and threw herself onto her bed. At times like this she wanted to curl up into a ball and escape from the world. She'd never allowed herself that privilege, however, and now wasn't the time. But she was tired of being strong. Unfortunately, now she needed her strength more than she ever had before.

And if all of this wasn't bad enough, she was still attracted to him. Oh, why wasn't he homely? Chinless? Spineless, for that matter? Why in the devil did he have to be big and strong and ruggedly handsome? Why did he have to be clever, and smart and . . . and poetic?

She rolled over and stared at the ceiling. Wouldn't you just know it? The man of her dreams—if she'd ever allowed herself to have one—was her sworn enemy.

Dawn Twilight skipped along beside Jackson, holding his hand. The dog raced ahead of them, stopping often to root in the dead leaves that covered the ground.

"And that story you told me about the maiden on the mountaintop was true?"

"As true as any legend." Jackson hadn't felt so light-hearted in years.

"Do you suppose she was related to me?"

"Oh, I think she was. Definitely." He couldn't believe how terrific he felt, now that Dawn Twilight knew the truth. And now that she'd accepted it.

"There are other half-bloods in Thief River," she announced.

"I'm aware of that."

"They aren't very happy. Some of them are drunk all the time. Others, the girls, are prostitutes. Some of them, anyway."

Jackson clutched Dawn Twilight's hand tightly in his. God Almighty, what would he have done if Libby O'Malley hadn't taken his child in? "How do you know such things?"

His daughter shrugged. "Everyone knows. A prostitute sells her body for money. Some even get pretty trinkets."

He was uncomfortable with the conversation. "Who told you this?"

"Why, Mama, of course. She answers all of my questions."

Jackson swallowed a groan. Didn't the woman understand the meaning of discretion?

"I wish she could have come with us," Dawn Twilight mused.

Jackson cleared his throat. "I'm sure she has too much to do to go cavorting in the woods for berries."

"Yeah, but sometimes I think she needs to. She never has any fun." Dawn Twilight danced away, basket in hand, and plucked some dark blue berries off a bush, dropping them into the container.

Jackson studied his child. That was a very mature concept for someone so young. "I thought she was seeing someone."

Dawn Twilight continued her task. "Seeing someone?"

He was uncomfortable with this, too, because it wasn't any of his business. Although anyone who had seen him toss Frost off the porch the other night would have thought otherwise. "You know. A gentleman caller."

His daughter snorted a laugh. "Oh, you mean Mr. Frost. I don't like him."

It suddenly occurred to Jackson that Libby would have a better chance of keeping Dawn if she had a husband. That thought rankled like the very devil. It would absolutely kill him if Ethan Frost, a man he didn't trust, somehow wound up raising his daughter. And even though Libby had as much as said she'd never marry the man, women up and did strange things.

"Does your mama like him?"

Dawn Twilight wrinkled her nose. "I don't know. She likes him as a friend, I think."

"Yeah, that's what she said." Pulling out his timepiece, he checked the hour. "I have an errand to run before I return to the jail. Do we have enough berries for a pie?"

"Maybe for one, but we need enough for three. I'll stay here and pick more."

A surge of protectiveness overpowered him. "No. I don't want you out here by yourself."

"But I come here alone all the time."

He shook his head, resolute. "Not if I have anything to say about it."

Her mood suddenly turned pensive. "What am I supposed to call you?"

Something in Jackson's gut fluttered. "What would you like to call me?"

Dawn Twilight traced the handle of the basket with her index finger. She wouldn't look at him. "Well, you *are* my papa."

Jackson's throat worked as he attempted to swallow. "You can call me Papa if you want to."

She slid a shy glance his way. "Do you want me to?"

He hoped he could smile without frightening her with his enthusiasm. "Yes. I want you to."

Returning a smile of her own, his daughter took his hand, and they strolled through the woods. The schoolmistress waved at them from the path.

"Oh, good!" Dawn Twilight exclaimed. "Now I don't have to go home with berries for just one pie. Miss Parker will stay with me."

Jackson watched them stroll into the trees, tempted to stay near. But he had work to do. The deputy should have returned with his report on the latest sheep incident by now.

And he had to learn not to smother his daughter, throwing the net of his newly acquired overprotectiveness over her, driving a wedge between them and weakening their fragile relationship.

Jackson retrieved his mount and rode north and east, toward the lush valley land that fed the sheep. He had ridden perhaps an hour before he saw Dominic Mateo riding toward him.

Dominic reined in his steed beside Jackson. "Something I can do for you, Sheriff?"

With a nod, Jackson answered, "How far does your land go, Dom?"

Dominic raised a thickly muscled arm. "Nearly to Fort Redding to the north and Thief River to the south."

Jackson's gaze wandered over the tide of grass. "Anyone else have as much land as you?"

"Ander Bilboa's land butts up against ours. We're almost on the line now. He and my father bought their land together. Ours spreads west, his spreads east."

"Any other sheep ranchers with land close by?"

Dominic shook his head. "We have most of the land. There are a few farther east, into the foothills, but their land isn't as extensive."

"What are your thoughts on the trouble, Dom?"

Dominic's dark eyes hardened. "I wish I could tell you. I can't think of a reason for this. The cattlemen don't seem hostile."

"I agree. They all profess their innocence, and although there could be some lingering animosity, I'm not at all sure they're to blame for your troubles." Something gnawed at Jackson. Something he couldn't put his finger on, but something he couldn't dismiss.

"Where does a man go if he wants to, you know, let off some steam? Spend a little money on a good game of poker or a woman?"

Dom smirked. "You don't look like the sort of man who'd spend his money that way, Sheriff. Or even have to, for that matter."

Jackson shifted in his saddle, trying to piece together the puzzle that involved Ethan Frost, McCann's comments about the banker's wild younger days, and Dawn Twilight's misplaced trust fund. "Say I was that sort of man. But say I didn't want anyone to know about it. Where would I go?"

"Eureka would be the closest place. Or Sacramento."

Jackson felt Dom's earnest perusal, but wasn't ready to explain himself. Not even about the shoe prints he'd discovered earlier. "Has anyone ever approached you about buying up your land?"

"No one. What have you heard?"

Jackson shook his head. "Not a thing. I'm just thinking out loud, that's all."

Dominic hesitated a moment before nodding and riding off toward the ranch. Kicking his own mount into a gallop,

Jackson rode toward town. It was time to probe into Ethan Frost's private life.

Corey Wolfe urged his mount through the trees, avoiding the roads whenever possible. Nothing happened on the road. At least nothing that interested him. But in the woods, the trees and underbrush teemed with life.

Something rustled in the bushes ahead of him. He brought his mare to a halt and pulled the notepad from his breast pocket, along with the stub of a pencil.

From behind the brush sauntered a wolverine. He wrote quickly: *"Gulo gulo*—the wolverine, or skunk bear—this far south is unusual."* A hare emerged from a hole in the ground, sniffed the air, and disappeared as the young man slipped the notebook into his pocket. The wolverine pounced on the hole, digging desperately to gain entry.

Man and mount picked their way through the trees, bypassing the animal, anxious to avoid its notice. Through the leaves, a brilliant autumn sun spattered a patchwork of light onto the ground. The sky held a mixture of unthreatening altocumulus and cirrus clouds, which occasionally glided across the sun.

Thrasher song floated toward him from the trees, a pleasant, variable warbling. With ease he mimicked the sound.

The young man sucked in a noisy breath of air. "Ah, it's a perfect day, Maris." His mare whickered and, in response, tossed her head coquettishly. He ran a hand down his palomino's shiny mane. "You're a beauty, my girl."

In the distance he heard voices. Young voices. He smiled. Female voices. Maris moved toward the sounds, stopping behind a fireberry shrub at her master's gentle command.

There were two of them. One quite young—a breed, he suspected—and a promising beauty. He'd never had many prejudices. One of his oldest friends was a descendant of slaves.

The other one took his breath away. Hair the color of spun gold and a laugh that tinkled like fine crystal in the wind. They sat resting against the trunk of an oak, eating berries and sharing secrets. That's what he imagined, anyway, for he had sisters, and they were always escaping into the woods to laugh and whisper.

He whistled a melodic robin's song, and the younger one stopped giggling and looked straight at him. "Mumser," she called.

A dog—at least that was what it appeared to be—burrowed through the dead leaves at the base of the tree, then lunged at the horse, yipping frantically.

Maris whinnied and sidestepped the nuisance.

"Mumser, heel!"

The moppish mutt obeyed, but continued to growl.

Both girls stood up, wary.

He nudged Maris forward. "Good afternoon, ladies."

The golden one squinted at him, not as one would squint into the sunlight, but like someone who could not see into the distance. Her nearsightedness disarmed him, for it made her vulnerable and, to his mind, in need of protection.

The young one stepped forward, thrusting a pugnacious chin his way. "Was that you whistling?"

"Indeed it was." Even as a boy, he'd had the gift of mimicry.

"What do you want here?"

Ah, an alert protector, not amused by his talents. She'd been taught well. The mutt continued to growl. The golden one continued to squint. "I'm looking for the sheriff."

"Well, you won't find him here," the young one announced, a hard edge to her voice.

He chuckled. "Of course not. I'm on my way to Thief River. I'm going in the right direction, aren't I?"

The golden one gently tugged the young one toward her, trying to put the girl safely behind her. "Why don't you use the road? Most people do." There was a hint of sarcasm in her tone. She had fire. He liked that.

"Ah, the road. Roads are so boring, don't you think? I, like you, much prefer the woods."

Both women appeared startled, and he hastened to reassure them. "I don't mean to frighten you, ladies. Actually,

I'm looking for a man who is *acting* sheriff. Perhaps you can tell me how I can find him. His name is Jackson Wolfe."

Recognition flared in the young one's dark eyes. "Who are you, and why are you looking for him?"

Spunky little thing, he decided. "How ungentlemanly of me." He tipped his hat. "My name is Corey Wolfe. I'm looking for my long-lost brother."

The young one's eyes widened as she continued to stare. "You're Mr. Wolfe's brother?"

He gave her a dazzling smile. "You've heard of him, then?"

She appeared to have trouble swallowing. "He . . . he's staying at my mama's rooming house. But . . . but he's at the jail now. Or he should be soon."

His gaze settled on the golden one, who watched him like a vigilant feline. A *myopic* vigilant feline. She was delicate and sweet. And he'd been lamenting his inability to find the perfect woman all of his young life.

"Try the jail." The young one pointed toward the road. "That way."

He tipped his hat again. "Good afternoon, ladies. I hope we'll meet again," he added as he rode away, mimicking the bubbling sounds of the meadowlark.

Jackson returned to the jail. The deputy hadn't made an appearance in days. Jackson was beginning to wonder just how much help the young fellow would be. Engrossed in paperwork when the jail door opened, he didn't look up. "About time you showed up. Where in the hell have you been?" He turned to file a stack of papers in the drawer, barely glancing at the door.

"I don't believe it. I heard it with my own ears, but I didn't believe it. Jackson Wolfe a lawman?"

It wasn't the deputy. The voice was filled with good humor and a certain familiarity. Jackson glanced up. Standing before him was a tall, tightly muscled young man whose tawny hair fell in unruly waves around his ears. His heart thumped hard. "Corey?"

With a nod of his head, his brother grinned at him, his eyes brimming. "God dang it, I still don't believe it's you."

Jackson came around his desk and pulled his brother into a bear hug. Though Corey was leaner, they were the same height. "Christ," Jackson murmured, his voice thick with emotion, "you're all grown up."

Corey pounded him on the back. "Mother'll think she's died and gone to heaven when she learns you're home."

They pulled apart and studied each other, eyes shining, grinning like fools.

"How did you know I was here?"

Corey refused to release him. "Vern sent Pa a wire. I intercepted it. Thought it best to find out for myself before throwing both him and Ma into a tizzy."

"That's Vern for you. Sticking his nose into business that doesn't concern him." Strangely, Jackson wasn't angry. He'd put off wiring them himself only because he didn't know how to begin to repair all the damage he'd done. "So they don't know I'm back?"

Corey studied him, continuing to shake his head in disbelief. "Why didn't you let us know you were home?"

Jackson let out a whoosh of air and ran his fingers through his hair. "I had something to settle before I did."

"And is it settled?"

Jackson turned away, remembering Libby's claim on his daughter. "Not completely."

"Jackson, if they find out you're home from someone other than you, they'll be devastated."

A wealth of emotions clamored through him. "How are they?"

"They're fine. They grieved for you, you know."

Jackson muttered a curse. "I don't have to hear that."

"I think you do. It's like you died, and they never got the chance to bury the body. Why in the hell did you leave the way you did?"

He cursed again. "At the time I thought I was doing the right thing. I didn't want to run the ranch, Corey. That was all. Can you believe it? It was all because I didn't want to run the damned ranch."

Corey continued to study him. "There was more to it than that, wasn't there?"

Jackson's pulse leaped. "What makes you think that?"

Corey settled comfortably into a chair and scratched his smoothly shaven chin. "I've been gnawing on that for a long time, brother." He shook his head. "You weren't that shallow. You wouldn't have fled the country in search of something elusive if you'd just hated ranching. No, I figure there was something more to it." He slanted his brother a glance. "Tell me I'm wrong."

"I can't."

"Didn't think so. What was it? A woman? You went back to the Indian village, didn't you?"

Jackson drew a hefty breath, then expelled it noisily. "She was killed by marauding Whites. Vigilantes. I . . . I couldn't bear it when she died. We had a daughter. I left the baby with my wife's grandmother."

Corey whistled softly through his teeth. "Why didn't you tell the folks? They'd have helped, you know that."

"Pride, I guess. I stopped by to do just that, but to my mind, Pa looked too busy to care about what happened to me. He had a breech calf that day, and he was so damned concerned about that animal . . ." His voice trailed off at the memory.

"Did you come back for the child?" At Jackson's nod, Corey expelled a sigh of his own. "Find her?"

Another nod. "I told her who I was a few days ago."

"What is she, about twelve?"

Jackson nodded, his expression grim. "Yeah. About twelve."

"So what's the problem?" Corey poured himself coffee and brought the cup to his mouth.

Jackson swung toward the window and studied the street a moment, allowing his gaze to follow a stray dog as it nosed through the dirt. Then he turned back to his brother. "She's been adopted."

Luckily Corey hadn't taken a drink of his coffee. "What?"

"By the woman who runs the rooming house."

A slow smile spread across Corey's face. "Well, I'll be

damned. I think your daughter and I have already met." He explained what had transpired in the woods.

"Who is the golden one?"

Jackson smirked. "Always the poet, Corey. The 'golden one' is the schoolmistress, Chloe Ann Parker."

"Chloe Ann Parker." The name came out of Corey's mouth sounding like a chant.

Now it was Jackson's turn to study his little brother. He was a handsome devil, his golden curls mere shades darker than he remembered. He was lean and tightly muscled, like a circus acrobat. When Jackson had left, Corey was a gangly boy of twelve, with knobby knees and a squeaky voice. Now he had to be almost twenty-five. Thickness gathered in Jackson's throat, and he cursed himself for missing out on so much of his brother's life and everyone else's.

"No woman in your life, little brother?"

"I've been too busy." He winked. "Until now."

"Doing what, may I ask?"

"I'm compiling a book on California flora and fauna."

Jackson arched an eyebrow. "A writer in the family. Mother must be very proud." He waited a beat. "And Father?"

Corey's smile was grim. "I help him when I can. Actually, Kito's boys, Abe and Ash, have been working for him for a few years. Abe is as tall as his pa and almost as strong."

"And . . . and Mandy? Kate?"

Corey's smile turned warm. "You wouldn't recognize them. Mandy's been away at school. She's home now, for a short time, anyway. Ah, Jackson," he said, his voice luxurious with awe, "she's a beauty."

"She's almost twenty," Jackson mused.

"And beating young suitors off with a stick."

They looked at each other and grinned.

"Pa's worried sick she'll take up with someone he doesn't approve of." Corey's grin widened.

"I'm surprised she hasn't already. And Katie?"

"She'll be fourteen next week, remember?"

He hadn't. "God," he muttered, stretching his back, "with my sisters and brother all grown up, I feel ancient."

Corey gulped his coffee, then put the cup on the desk. "So when do I get to formally meet your daughter?"

Jackson clamped a hand on his brother's sinewy shoulder. "You'll come home with me. As long as Dawn Twilight knows who you are, you can bet she's told her mother."

Corey gave him a quizzical look. "What about this woman who adopted your daughter? Can we expect anything to happen there, or is she a toothless crone with a wart on her nose?"

Jackson gave him a mysterious smile, remembering Libby's lush curves and sensuous mouth, her cautious pride and the fire in her dark eyes. Warm wine and sultry Spanish nights.

He steered his brother toward the door. "She's no crone, and there's no wart on her nose, but the most we can expect to happen is that she's undoubtedly working on a menu plan to serve my head on a plate."

Corey appeared fascinated. "Sounds interesting."

In spite of himself, Jackson chuckled. "'Interesting' doesn't begin to describe it."

11

LIBBY HAD WATCHED DAWN'S TRANSFORMATION. SHE'D COME flying into the kitchen from the woods, nearly skidding to a stop, to announce that she'd seen Jackson's brother and that he could whistle like a bird and had yellow hair and a beautiful horse. Now, with everyone seated around the dinner table, Dawn had become a mute. Her eyes darted toward her father, then across the table to her uncle, and Libby noticed that not only had she not spoken a word, she hadn't touched her food.

It was a tense meal to look forward to for Libby as well. For some inane reason she wanted to make a good impression on Jackson's brother, so had taken pains to choose the right dress for dinner and had even put the Spanish combs in her hair that Sean had bought her after their wedding.

If Corey Wolfe's look was one of interest, Jackson's was one of fire. Lord, she hadn't meant to dress for *him*. Her intention hadn't been to seduce, for pity's sake. She merely wanted Corey Wolfe to know that she was someone to be reckoned with in this battle for Dawn's affections.

Bert and Burl ate nonstop and spoke little, which wasn't that unusual, for they never liked to mix food and conversation. However, Libby noted with a sinking feeling, they took everything in just the same. No doubt tomorrow they would sit on the porch and discuss every detail of this meal in their own inimitable way.

Chloe Ann appeared to be the focus of Corey's attention, although Libby noticed he never ignored Dawn in favor of the schoolmistress. Chloe Ann blushed throughout the entire dinner.

Mahalia served them, making noises in her throat which, fortunately, only Libby understood. They translated to "This is an interestin' situation we've got here, Libby. How're we gonna handle it?"

Later that evening, Libby found Dawn in the parlor with Jackson and Corey. They had her full attention, regaling her with stories of their boyhood. Stories of their sisters, their friends, their parents. The get-togethers they had enjoyed, the parties they'd attended, the traditions they had delighted in as children.

An emotion Libby was reluctant to name climbed up her throat, leaving a bad taste in her mouth. Plainly, she knew it was jealousy. And fear. A whole lot of fear.

She stepped into the room. "Dawn, it's time for bed." Whatever she did, she couldn't let her daughter see what she was feeling.

Dawn bade the men good night and was quiet as she and Libby climbed the stairs to her room. Yet Libby noticed that she nearly vibrated with unleashed energy.

"I wonder if you'll be able to sleep," Libby pondered.

Dawn turned her shiny dark eyes on her mother. "I don't think I can, Mama. It's all so exciting." She giggled, then pressed a hand to her mouth.

Libby touched her stomach, in which her supper churned. "Do you want to talk about it?" The last thing Libby wanted to hear about was Jackson's wonderful family, but she hid her somber mood.

"Oh, Mama, they're gonna have a big party for me! Uncle Corey said so, even though no one knows about me but him. He said everyone would love me. *He* already loves me, and he only just met me! Isn't it exciting, Mama? Isn't it?"

She had never seen Dawn this euphoric, this filled with joy and happiness. It depressed Libby further. "Very exciting, dear. But you have to get up early in the morning. You'd better think quiet thoughts."

"I'm gonna write a story about my life," Dawn announced.

Libby hid a smile. "It should make for exciting reading."

With a dreamy yawn, Dawn pulled her nightgown on over her head. "It'll start when I was a baby. About being alone, near death's door," she said dramatically. "Uncle Corey told me he'd help me."

Cyclops was already under Dawn's covers when she slid into bed, and Mumser hopped up beside her, growling at both Libby and the lump the cat made at the foot of the bed.

Libby shook her head. "Does that dog do nothing but growl?"

Dawn bent and kissed him. "He doesn't mean anything by it, Mama." She pulled the covers up to her chin, her gaze on Libby. "What's wrong?"

Libby's smile was as warm as she could muster. "Hmm?"

"You're smiling, but your eyes are sad. What's wrong?"

Libby sat on the bed, ignored the dog's menacing growl, and smoothed Dawn's hair away from her forehead. "Nothing's wrong."

Dawn's eyebrows were pinched together. "Something looks wrong, Mama."

Libby squeezed her daughter's arm, then tickled her, making Dawn laugh. "Oh, I'm just envious of all the attention you're getting from the two most handsome men in the house, that's all."

Dawn relaxed. "Papa is handsome, isn't he?"

Libby's stomach pitched to her knees. "Papa?"

Nodding, Dawn answered, "He said he wanted me to call him Papa, and I want to. It's all right, isn't it?"

Libby was dying inside. "Yes. Of course. After all, he has the right to that much, I guess."

"What do you mean, Mama?"

Libby straightened the bedding and rose. "Nothing, dear. Now try to sleep. It's late." She crossed to the door.

"Mama?"

"Yes, sweetheart?"

"I love you."

Libby couldn't turn, for her eyes stung with tears. She wasn't even sure she could speak. "I love you too, Dawn."

Meeting Jackson in the hallway, she quickly swiped at her moist eyes with her fingers. She wanted to fly at him, pummel him with her fists, knee him in places no lady would, but her frustration had no outlet. She'd already lost her temper with him once, and she refused to let him believe she had no control. One day her inability to express her emotions would be the death of her, because her head would probably explode.

Jackson loomed over her. His nearness sent her pulse pounding, making her angrier still.

"I wanted to say good night."

In spite of everything, the sound of his deep baritone made her quiver. "She's already in bed." Her arms crossed over her chest, Libby stood in front of Dawn's door like a jailer.

Jackson's eyes glittered in the dim hall light. "You can't stop the inevitable."

"I can try," she answered, grasping at straws.

"Don't—"

His words were cut off by screeching and growling from Dawn's bedroom.

Libby flung open the door. "Dawn? What's happening?"

"It's Mumser and Cyclops," she wailed. "They're fighting, Mama. Get them off my bed!"

A light came on behind her, and Libby realized that Jackson had lit the lamp. Cyclops stood on one side of Dawn, her back arched and every hair standing straight up. She was alternately screeching and growling at the dog, who barked and yipped and growled on the other side of Dawn's quaking supine body.

"Mumser!" Jackson's terse command made the dog quiet, but he continued to growl deep in his throat. Jackson picked him up off the bed, drawing him away from the fight.

Libby dived for Cyclops, who shimmied away and slunk out of the room, into the darkness.

Dawn's eyes were wide and filled with tears. "They were gonna fight, Mama. How can they fight when I love them both?"

Libby rubbed her face and pressed her fingers against her eyes. "You can't have it both ways, dear. Obviously they can't sleep in the same bed. You'll have to choose."

Mumser wiggled from Jackson's grip and leaped onto the bed, licking Dawn's tears as they dripped down her cheeks. She gave them a watery smile and hugged the dog. "Oh, I do love Cyclops, Mama, really I do, but . . . but Mumser is more cuddly."

A queasy feeling stirred inside Libby. "Is that your choice?"

Mumser snuggled beside Dawn, preparing to stay. "Can Cyclops sleep with you?"

How can they fight when I love them both? Libby's head told her the choice had nothing to do with her, but her heart told her differently. She and Jackson were no better than the animals, fighting for Dawn's affections. However, the dog was Jackson's, the cat hers. Emotionally, Libby felt her daughter was rejecting that which she'd known longest for something new, something more exciting and more promising. With all that had happened, and what would happen once Dawn was introduced to Jackson's family, Libby feared her daughter's choice of a parent had been made as well.

She prayed she would hear from the attorney soon. She'd wired him shortly after Jackson told her who he was, and now the lawyer appeared to be her only hope. But even if the adoption held up in a court of law, she knew she would never get Jackson out of her life.

Corey bent over his notebook, leaning toward the light. Leaves and berries, each in a small pile, were heaped up on one side of the kitchen table. A shadow fell across his book, and he glanced up.

A timid Chloe Ann Parker stood nearby. "Hello." Her voice was sweet. Soft. Melodic.

He slowly shoved his notebook to one side, afraid that any swift movement would drive her off. "Hello." He couldn't stop the sound of pleasure he knew was in his voice.

She moved to the table. "What are you doing?"

"Oh," he answered with a shrug, certain she was merely being polite, "nothing, really. I'm just cataloging some samples."

She reached across him, her lilac scent hovering between them, and plucked up a leaf. With dainty fingers, she touched the thick, shiny surface, then turned it over, exposing the dull, flat underside. "California laurel."

Pleased and surprised, he answered, "Not a very exciting specimen, I'll grant you."

"Oh, but you're wrong. When it flowers, it's lovely." She continued to handle the leaf, then snapped it into two pieces. A pungent aroma wafted toward him, obliterating the lilac-scented air.

"I love this smell," she murmured, drawing in a long breath. "It's so . . . so earthy."

Well, well, well, he thought, his interest mounting. "How do you know so much about trees, Miss Parker?"

"They're a hobby of mine." She leaned close to the notebook. "How do you?"

"I'm compiling a book on the subject." His smile was quick. "Are you impressed?"

She rocked onto her heels, her hands clasped behind her, her head cocked to one side. In the light of the lamp, her golden hair shimmered with fire. "Should I be?"

"By all means," he answered with mock seriousness. "I would be disappointed if you weren't."

Examining him carefully, she asked, "You're truly Mr. Wolfe's brother? You look nothing alike."

"We're not related by blood. My mother married his father."

"And little Dawn is his daughter." She pondered the

statement, then added, "From his first day here, he seemed to be interested in her."

Noting the dry tone, he asked, "You don't approve?"

She raised a tawny brow. "Approve? I don't think it's my place to make a judgment. However, Libby is a dear friend of mine, and anything that hurts her, hurts me."

Corey shrugged. "Why should she be hurt?"

Chloe Ann graced him with a sly smile. "You aren't that naive, are you?" She gave him no chance to answer. "Your brother hopes to take Dawn with him, doesn't he?"

"He *is* her father."

"And Libby is her legal mother. Tell me, Corey Wolfe, how such a dilemma can have a happy ending for all?"

This side of her showed a wisdom he hadn't imagined. His interest in her grew. "Life doesn't always have a happy ending, Chloe Ann Parker."

There was a sadness in her eyes as she turned to leave. "That's true, I guess, but who do you figure will be the most unhappy if he takes Dawn away from her mother? How would you have felt if you'd been ripped from your mother's arms?"

A dusty corner of Corey's memory was jarred, and he suddenly remembered that that very thing had nearly happened to him.

Jackson glanced at Miss Parker's retreating form as he stepped into the kitchen. His brother's gaze was still on the door.

"You don't waste any time, do you?"

Corey gave him a lopsided grin. "When I see what I like, I go after it." His grin turned wry. "I'd think you'd do the same."

"What in the hell does that mean?"

Corey laughed softly. "You're not that dense, are you?"

"I must be, because I don't have the faintest idea what you're talking about." At least he didn't want to think he was that obvious.

Jackson went to the stove, checked the pot, and poured

himself a cup of coffee, then sat across from his brother. He felt Corey's probing appraisal.

"Seems to me the solution to your dilemma is right under your nose."

"I don't have a dilemma," Jackson grumbled, knowing full well that he did.

"Whatever you say, big brother," Corey answered under his breath.

"I'll . . . er . . . wire the folks in the morning. As soon as I can get away, we'll take a trip north to the ranch."

"Dawn, too?"

"Of course, Dawn, too. That's the purpose of the trip, isn't it?"

Corey folded his arms over his chest and studied him. "You have no qualms about taking Dawn away from here?"

Jackson glowered into his coffee, attempting to ignore his conscience. "She's my daughter."

"What about her mother? Haven't you given any thought to how she'll feel? Or, for that matter, if she'll even let you take her?"

"I've contacted an attorney. We'll see who has legal custody," he growled. "I have no doubt she's sent word to one, too."

"Ah, a standoff."

"I'll win," Jackson answered, and meant it.

"Possibly, but what will you win, big brother?"

"My daughter, of course. What else is there?"

"If you do win, don't you think Dawn would be more willing if you considered a union with the mother, too?"

"So that's what you were getting at."

Corey chuckled. "Either your head's made of wood or you're a little light in the heels. Somehow I don't think you're either."

In the quiet recesses of his mind, maybe the thought of a union of some sort with Libby O'Malley had occurred to him. Other than Dawn Twilight, however, he had little to offer a woman. He wasn't interested in remarrying. He didn't feel it was fair to give a woman false hope.

"A long-drawn-out court battle would be detrimental to everyone involved, don't you think?"

Jackson muttered a curse, knowing Corey was right. "When did you become so almighty brilliant?"

"A natural gift, I guess." Corey's smile was charming.

Jackson had no doubt that his brother had won many arguments with his smile alone. "I know the separation would be bad, especially for Dawn Twilight. I've thought of that. But we can't make her choose between us. That wouldn't be fair, either."

Corey's examination of him made him uncomfortable. "Well, say something, will you?"

Corey heaved an exaggerated sigh. "Mrs. Libby O'Malley is a handsome woman."

Jackson snorted. "What's that got to do with the price of tea in China?"

"Don't tell me you hadn't noticed."

Oh, he had, all right. At dinner he could hardly take his eyes off her. Sultry Spanish nights. Warm wine . . . He shook himself. "Of course I've noticed. I'm not blind."

"And you don't see any possibilities there?"

"Possibilities for what?"

Corey threw his head back and laughed. "Are you purposely dense, or is that *your* gift?"

"Ah, Corey, get serious. She'd sooner carve me up and use me as mulch in her garden."

"A little honey goes a long way toward sweetening the tea, brother."

Hearing the idea spoken aloud made Jackson uncomfortable. "I'm not like you. I'm a plain, straightforward kind of man."

"You're as poetic as the next guy, Jackson. You could try courting her."

Court Libby? He swore again. She'd laugh in his face, then carve out his heart.

A door squeaked open, and the housekeeper stepped into the room. She wore a voluminous multicolored tentlike garment that could have kept the sun or the rain off a small army.

"What you two doin' in here? Lord, I'm tryin' to sleep, and all's I hear is chatterin' and clatterin'."

Instantly contrite, Jackson murmured an apology.

She made a tsking sound in her throat. "Can't you take your business into the parlor an' leave me in peace?"

"Immediately, Mahalia." Jackson caught Corey's gaze and nodded toward the door. Corey gathered his samples and rose.

In the parlor they settled into the chairs that flanked the fireplace. Corey grinned at him.

"Intimidating sort, isn't she?"

"Hell. Mahalia doesn't like me."

"Can you blame her? After all, whether you planned it or not, you're here to make her boss's life miserable."

Jackson glowered into the dwindling fire. "What a helluva mess."

"I still say there's a way to save it."

Jackson dug the heels of his palms into his eyes, pressing hard. "You're crazier than a bedbug." Still, the idea had been planted, and try as he might, Jackson couldn't shake it off.

12

*E*THAN WAS PLAYING BALL WITH HIS TWO YOUNGEST BOYS when Cleb Hartman rode up. He tossed the ball to the younger of the two, Eddy, who caught it, raised his arm, and grinned at his father.

"Good catch!" Ethan said.

The boy tossed the ball to his brother, who returned it.

Ethan watched as Hartman dismounted. "News?"

Hartman nodded. "Except for contacting the ranchers whose land is involved, it appears to be a done deal."

Ethan's stomach convulsed, but he caught his son's throw and returned it. "When will that be?"

"As soon as all the paperwork's done, I suppose. You know the government doesn't move very fast. I'm surprised no one's contacted the landowners yet." Hartman gave a casual glance toward Ethan's boys.

"Then there's no time to waste. We've got to give them at least one more good scare. Do it tonight."

Hartman mounted his horse. "Tonight it is."

Ethan didn't watch him ride away. His thoughts were already elsewhere. After his run-in with Jackson Wolfe at the bank, he kept expecting the man to hound him about the "lost" money.

The sheep ranchers were keeping him busy, fortunately for Ethan. Of course, that was another problem. How long would it be before Wolfe put it all together? He was a worthy adversary, the first Ethan had met, and it wouldn't take too much for a reasonably intelligent person to figure out what was happening with the sheep ranchers. If that person had any contacts at all, he was probably close to knowing the truth right now.

"Eddy? Would you get your papa's flask out of his saddlebag?"

Little Eddy hurried to do his father's wishes. He retrieved the flask and returned to Ethan, who took it and swallowed the milk and whiskey, hoping to settle his stomach.

"You got another bellyache, Pa?"

Ethan ruffled his son's golden curls. "It's nothing for you to worry about, boy." Before long he might not need another swig of the concoction for his stomach. Mateo's and Bilboa's land would soon be his to purchase for a song. Then he could sell it to the railroad for a hefty price and get himself out of a passel of money troubles.

His gut rebelled again. If only Jackson Wolfe didn't get in his way.

Dawn had insisted that Jackson and Libby accompany her to the general store to see a particular bolt of fabric she'd been admiring. Libby knew she wanted a new dress to wear to the party Jackson and Corey had promised her. And Libby knew, too, that she wanted her daughter to look her absolute best. She would work harder on this frock than she'd ever worked in her life. No one was going to suggest that Dawn wasn't well provided for.

They strolled home with the fabric, a bright yellow calico with sprigs of green ivy, wrapped in a package under Jackson's arm. They each held one of Dawn's hands.

Stalemate.

Standoff.

Dawn gazed up at her mother, then looked at her father. "Are you two going to get married?"

Surprised and embarrassed, Libby felt her insides flutter and her face flush. "Certainly not. What made you even think such a thing?" She avoided looking at Jackson, but noted out of the corner of her eye that he appeared to concentrate on something far in the distance.

"Well," Dawn drawled, "you're my mother and he's my father."

Libby tossed Jackson a pleading glance, but he refused to make eye contact. Typical, she thought. She couldn't even count on his help with the simple things. How could he possibly handle something serious?

"I can be your mother and not be married to your father, dear. It's as simple as that."

Dawn grew quiet. They strolled along in silence, Libby's brain buzzing. Married to Jackson Wolfe? Hardly something she would have given a thought to. Certainly she was attracted to him, but . . . marriage? *I think not!*

Finally, Dawn said, "But if you two don't get married, Papa could leave me again."

Libby raised her eyebrows. Her fear exactly. Even with Jackson's emotional promises to stay and his obvious love for his daughter, he could go meandering again. She doubted that even Dawn's pull was strong enough to stop him. And there was no way that she herself would marry a war-loving wanderer—if the chance ever presented itself. However, she kept quiet.

Jackson stopped, turned Dawn toward him and bent to meet her questioning gaze. "Dawn Twilight, I'm not going anywhere that I can't take you with me."

Dawn tossed her mother a quick glance. "But . . . what about Mama? Can she come, too?"

Libby glanced to one side, attempting to focus on the awning that flapped over the millinery shop. Dawn's innocent questions were exactly what Libby had feared from the moment she learned who Jackson was. Dawn did not understand the situation, and there was no way to explain it to her. Libby curiously awaited Jackson's answer.

"It's not as simple as that, Dawn Twilight."

Quiet again, Dawn suddenly brightened. "It would solve everything if you two would get married."

A warning of sorts went off inside Libby's brain, traveling the length of her body, creating uncomfortable yet provocative sensations everywhere. She knew it was up to her to field the question. "People don't get married for any old reason, dear."

"Why not? When Janelle Anderson's mama married Mr. Wilson, Janelle said it was because her mama couldn't run the ranch by herself. And besides," she added, "it wouldn't be for any old reason. It would be for me."

Libby tried not to squirm with discomfort. "There are those . . . situations, I guess, when such unions are profitable for both people, but . . . but our case is different."

"Different, how?" Dawn probed.

"Well," Libby answered, trying not to stammer, "you see, I have a business to run. I don't need to marry someone to help me with it. And . . . and Mr. Wolfe is . . . well, he's . . ." She threw him a frantic, troubled look, hoping for help.

"Remember, Dawn Twilight," he said patiently, "I have a family, and they're waiting for me. Waiting to meet you. Waiting to welcome you as one of their own."

Libby felt nauseated.

Dawn squeezed her hand. "But . . . I can't leave Mama. I . . . I want to meet my new family, Papa, but . . . but I want to stay with Mama."

The relief Libby felt was nearly overshadowed by Jackson's long, deep sigh.

"Dawn Twilight, we can't—"

"I won't leave Mama. I won't!" She wrenched herself free from both of them and ran on ahead. Libby knew without a doubt that her daughter was in tears.

Libby and Jackson continued on in silence.

"Should one of us go after her?"

Libby glared at him. "And tell her what?"

"I'm, er, meeting a lawyer this afternoon. He . . . he

151

suggested that you come, too and . . ." He cleared his throat. "And bring the adoption papers."

Libby nearly sagged to the ground. "I haven't heard from the lawyer I've contacted yet."

"Well, at least we can meet, can't we?"

Bolstering herself, she replied, "I suppose. But just because your lawyer is there and mine isn't, don't think that this thing is anywhere near settled." She wanted to believe the adoption would hold up in any court in the land. She had to believe it, or her world would come to naught.

Like the adversaries they were, they sat across from each other. Beneath the table, Libby gave her handkerchief several anxious twists. Otherwise she tried to show no emotion. She was desperate, she knew that. She even allowed herself to wonder what she would do if she lost this battle for Dawn. The sinking in the pit of her stomach told her it was possible.

She'd checked with the telegraph office on her way over, but there was still no word from the lawyer. Even though Dawn had told them both she wanted to stay with her mother, Libby knew that Jackson was adamant about gaining custody.

As desperate as she was, marriage to a man like Jackson Wolfe wasn't a consideration. Never mind that he hadn't asked her. He had a few good qualities—she'd decided that long ago—and granted, she was attracted to him on a baser level, but she couldn't imagine marrying him.

After all, what was to prevent him from growing bored with the bucolic life and taking off again? In spite of his avowal not to, she didn't trust the words, because the possibility hadn't yet arisen.

Oh, why didn't anyone understand that a man was not a natural parent? A father was not a mother and, in Libby's mind, could never replace one. They were entirely different entities. She recalled the time, years before, when two young parents were watching their small children splash in the river. The current was strong, and one of the children ventured out too far and was caught up in it. The young mother screamed for the father to fetch the child, but he had told her the child would be all right. The mother, dressed in frock and petticoats, threw herself into the river to save her child. Before the father could reach them, both had drowned.

Oh, Libby thought, remembering the father's anguish, no one had better tell her that a father could easily replace a mother, especially one who had done nothing with his life but kill people for money. That was not the sort of experience a father should have for raising a gentle daughter.

The door opened and Jackson's lawyer entered, causing Libby's head to spin and her stomach to churn. He sat at the end of the table between them.

"Mrs. O'Malley? I'm Daniel Green."

Libby lifted her gaze, finding an earnest appearing man of middle age. She shoved the adoption papers toward him. "Mr. Green," she acknowledged with a nod. "These are the papers you asked for. I have contacted an attorney of my own, but unfortunately I haven't yet heard from him."

He studied the documents briefly, then looked at her over the rims of his glasses. "As you know," he began, "Mr. Wolfe has asked me to discover if he could regain custody of his daughter."

Libby swallowed, hoping none of her turmoil showed. "I'm aware of that, Mr. Green."

He folded the papers and placed them on the table. "These appear to be in perfect order," he announced.

Libby felt a wave of relief. "I knew they would be."

Jackson's face was unreadable.

"However . . ."

Bad news was always prefaced with "however." Libby had a sinking feeling and was comforted in the knowledge that she was seated. She couldn't fall any farther.

Daniel Green heaved a sigh. "However, in cases like this, when a natural parent shows up, the court generally finds it prudent to return the child to that natural parent."

Libby blinked, stemming her angry, anxious, fearful

tears. "Prudent? What about . . . what about feelings and . . . and love and emotions? Oh, not mine. Don't for a minute even consider how I'm feeling."

She shook with fury. "Men are always so logical about things. What place does logic have when it comes to human emotions? Think about Dawn, Mr. Green," she pleaded, her anguish exposed and as painful as raw flesh. "She's almost thirteen years old. How can you possibly find it reasonable to tear her away from everything she's known simply because it's *prudent?*"

The lawyer removed his spectacles and bit on the end of the bow. "I know it seems cruel, Mrs. O'Malley, but whatever you might think about it, it is the law."

Libby pressed her hands over her mouth, her heart pounding, her stomach threatening to toss up her lunch. "You mean, no matter what I do or how hard I fight, the adoption can be overturned?"

Daniel Green studied her, his gaze sympathetic. "We can always go to court and have a judge decide. Perhaps that would be the best solution."

Her panic was raw. "But . . . but Mr. Wolfe is an itinerant and thoughtless parent," she said accusingly, sensing defeat but unwilling to give up. "Surely you can see that. He sent no word for the past twelve years. What kind of concern is that? Oh, Mr. Green, if you only knew under what circumstances I found her—"

"I've been informed, Mrs. O'Malley."

Her mouth worked frantically. "You . . . you have?"

With a nod, he stood up and gathered his papers, leaving Libby's adoption papers on the table. "You've done an exemplary job of raising the child, Mrs. O'Malley. Mr. Wolfe admits to that and more. However, you should know that he didn't reject his daughter. He set out with good intentions, placing her in the care of someone he firmly believed in. He sent money regularly for her care, unaware that the money wasn't going where it was supposed to."

Libby had heard all of this before. To her, it didn't matter. All of Jackson's good intentions did nothing to dissolve the ferocious knot in her stomach. "Then, you're saying that the only way to resolve this is to go to court?"

"I'm afraid so. Please let me know your decision." He bade them a good day, and left them alone.

Libby's gaze swung to Jackson. "A court battle. Exactly the sort of thing I'd hoped we could avoid."

"It's for you, Libby, not me. I don't have to establish proof, but I can," he murmured from across the table. "What's more important is that I have proof that she's my daughter. That's all I need."

There was pity in his eyes. God, how she hated that look from anyone! "You heard Dawn this morning. She . . . she said she wouldn't leave me."

"I know," he answered. "And I've thought a lot about that." He drove his fingers through his hair, then muttered something under his breath.

"Well? I hope you've decided she'd be better off with me," Libby continued. "Naturally I would allow you to visit often, and I'm sure she would want to know your family. I have no problem with letting her visit them as well. But above all, I don't want her to be put into the position of having to choose between us." She was babbling, she knew. It kept her from taking a swing at him.

There was just one more thing she had to ask. "If you do decide to fight me and she refuses to go with you, will you force her?"

"How can you even ask such a question?" His voice was soft with disbelieving anger.

"That question keeps swimming through my head, Jackson. You might think I'm selfish, but truly, I'm concerned for Dawn, and how she will react to all of this." Libby took a deep breath, hoping to slow the pounding of her pulse.

Fearful of his silence, she finally said, "Surely in all of your brilliance, you have a solution."

"Yes, I have a solution."

Interested, she studied him. His expression was guarded. Unreadable. "Well? Don't keep me in the dark."

"We could get married."

Her jaw dropped and she was out of her chair, leaning on the table for support. *"What?"*

"It would solve everything, Libby."

"It would solve *nothing.*"

His grin was sly. "Don't tell me that, since Dawn suggested it this morning, you haven't considered it, even for a second."

She expelled a sharp burst of laughter. "A second is about as long as the idea deserves to be considered."

"Well, don't think for a minute that you can get her away from me by marrying someone else and providing a home with a mother and a father. Like that . . . that *thief,* Ethan Frost. It wouldn't work, anyway. I'm still her legal father."

"I have no intention of marrying Ethan or anyone else," she shot back. "And you have no proof that Ethan took your money." Why she was defending the man, she couldn't say.

"So we continue to butt heads?"

It was the plot of a melodrama. If it hadn't been so serious, she might have laughed. Two people marrying merely to hang on to a child's love. "I need time to think about it."

He rose. "If it helps make your decision, I can promise you that I won't bed you . . . until or unless you want me to."

Libby's flagging spirits sagged further. Oh, great, she thought morosely, another unconsummated marriage. "That's very . . . gentlemanly of you."

"It isn't that I wouldn't want to—"

"Stop." She held up her hand. "Don't say anything you might regret, Jackson."

An odd emotion flashed in his eyes. "Well, don't take too long to make up your mind. I'm not a patient man."

She glared at his retreating form, wishing he were unattractive. But his wide, hard shoulders tapered to a narrow waist and long, strong legs. The muscles of his thighs were outlined beneath his snug jeans.

Turning at the door, he sent her a questioning look. "Are you coming?"

She gathered her papers, anxious to be alone. "I'll be along."

When he'd gone, she went to the window and watched him stride down the street to the jail. She could do worse. But again, the question rose in her mind: what was to prevent him from growing weary of family life and taking off again?

On one hand, if he did leave, at least by marrying him she'd be there to pick up the pieces when Dawn began to fall apart after being abandoned by him yet one more time.

On the other hand, she'd been quite happy with her life since Sean's death. Her emotions had been carefully filed away, and until Jackson Wolfe rode into her yard, she hadn't expected to have feelings for a man again, nor had she wanted to.

But for Libby, it all came back to Dawn, and what she would do to keep her daughter. Yes, she could do worse than marry Jackson Wolfe. He was basically good and kind. He loved their daughter passionately.

Ah, those words, "love" and "passion." She meandered to the table and picked up her papers, shoving them into the pocket of her cape. It was silly, she knew, for even though she'd loudly professed to both Dawn and Chloe Ann that dreaming was a waste of time, Libby yearned for both love and passion in her life.

She had no doubt that if she allowed herself to, she could love a man like Jackson Wolfe. And her passions ran deep, although they were dormant, and had been forever, until he came along. She longed to unleash them, discover an excitement she'd read about but hadn't expected to experience. But one couldn't find passion in a one-sided relationship.

Jackson had offered marriage as a way to keep Dawn happy, Libby was aware of that. Being the sort of man he was, he couldn't merely spirit his daughter away, knowing her feelings. And Libby was grateful for that sensitivity. What were his choices? She groaned. What were hers?

She would seriously consider his offer. Dawn was worth

any price she had to pay, even if it meant tossing away her dignity. Even if it meant selling the rooming house. She'd poured her heart and soul into her business, yet it was, after all, just a business. Dawn and Dawn's happiness were Libby's life. Without Dawn, the business meant nothing.

Still, it wasn't a decision she would come to quickly. Or lightly. Or without personal pain.

13

JACKSON STEWED, PACING THE JAILHOUSE FLOOR. WHAT DID the woman have to think about? As Dawn Twilight's natural father, his custody was assured. He was offering to share his daughter with Libby, and it wouldn't be a bad life. He was eager to settle down. He knew she suspected he'd leave again, but if she dragged her feet because she didn't want to live with him, then she ought to be grateful if he *did* leave, for she'd still have his daughter.

But he wasn't leaving, and it rankled that she wasn't more amenable to his offer. Never again would he abandon Dawn Twilight. He'd lost too much precious time as it was. And as his thirty years pressed in around him, he longed for a peaceful life, one filled with many children and a warm, willing woman.

He'd been attracted to Libby O'Malley that very first day. Who wouldn't have been? Not only was she capable, sensible, and strong, but there was a lushness about her that she couldn't hide, no matter how tart her tongue. Her fury at discovering who he was had only added to her passion. Pasty, passionless people neither loved nor hated. Libby O'Malley did both with a vengeance.

Jackson cursed. Ever since Corey had suggested the possibility of a union with Libby, it had been on his mind. But he'd seen the fear in her eyes. Fear of what? She wasn't a naive little virgin, afraid of intimacy; she'd been married before. Even so, fool that he was, he'd assured her he wouldn't touch her until she was ready—if ever.

Other than that, what more could he promise? He'd do anything to keep Dawn Twilight's love. Why wouldn't she?

There had been a time when he would not have given a damn about any person who stood between him and his daughter. Even though it wasn't intentional on her part, Libby had made him see that for Dawn Twilight to be happy, she must have both of them. Now he had to convince her that getting married was the right thing to do. But that had to be done properly. He'd have to court her, and courting wasn't an easy concept for him. Women were usually more interested in him than he was in them. It had been a long, long time since he'd had to work at it.

His thoughts continued to grind away in his mind until the door opened behind him. It hit the wall with such force that the windows rattled.

Jackson turned, finding an impatient Danel Mateo filling the doorway. "Danel, what can I do for you?"

"They done it again, Sheriff. They done it again. They poisoned another herd of my sheep."

Grabbing his hat, Jackson ordered, "Take me there, Danel. I want to see for myself."

They rode east, into the low hills that rolled at the foot of the mountains, into the land of lush grasses and tree-lined rivers.

"Damned s.o.b. gunnysackers," Danel growled, his drooping black mustache twitching with anger.

Gunnysackers, as Jackson had come to learn, was the term for the marauders who, wearing old cloth sacks over their faces with holes cut out for their eyes, continued their reign of terror against the sheepmen.

As they rode onto Danel's land, Jackson detected the faint scent of saltpeter, which he'd discovered was poisonous to sheep but not to cattle.

Danel's wail of despair alerted Jackson to the carnage. Sheep carcasses lay everywhere. Dominic was dragging them into a pile.

Jackson dismounted and picked his way through the battlefield. Saltpeter had been spread in the path of the flock during the night, so the hungry sheep would eat it, along with the grass, in the morning.

The sheep that had been killed the day after he'd arrived in Thief River had been burned alive. Others, he learned, had eaten grain laced with strychnine. Two nights after that, a herd of sheep had been rimrocked, stampeded, and driven over a cliff.

"You gotta do something! If you don't, I will." The pain in Danel's voice was shattering.

"Don't do anything foolish, Danel."

Dominic, nearly as tall and as thickly muscled, stepped up to Jackson. His black eyes held sparks. His jaw was clenched. "Then *you* do something, Sheriff. Look at this slaughter. How much more are we expected to take?"

"I'm working on it, Dom. I just don't want either of you getting hurt or doing something you'll regret. We'll catch him. This has been going on a long time. As much as you want it to, it can't be settled and put to right overnight."

"We're not giving you much more time, Sheriff. We're law-abiding men, but this," Danel said, swinging his arm wide, "is more than a man should have to take."

Jackson would make a trip to Eureka in the next day or two to check out his idea. If that didn't pan out, he'd ride to Sacramento and do the same. Meanwhile, he'd continue to look for someone riding a high-stepper.

As he returned to town, he tried to recall the kind of horse Ethan Frost had ridden the night he'd tossed the banker off the porch. He swore at his lapse. He'd been so intent on getting Frost out of there, he hadn't paid any attention to his mount. But in Jackson's mind, all threads appeared to lead to the banker. Danel Mateo and Ander Bilboa, like most of the other sheep ranchers, were strapped to the gills with mortgages and loans, and Ethan Frost held the deeds to all their land.

After finishing the evening dishes, Libby grabbed her shawl and stepped onto the porch. She loved this time of day, when her work was done and the house was quiet.

A glittering field of stars caught her eye as she glanced upward, and for a brief, foolish moment, she made a silent wish.

I wish I were adored and cherished as someone's beloved.

A wry smile touched her lips at her fanciful thinking. Wishes and daydreams belonged to the likes of Chloe Ann and her daughter, both of whom had yet to face the hardships of life, not to pragmatic women like herself. Not to someone who had been married off to a man twice her age when she was barely into her teens. Nevertheless . . .

Wrapping her shawl tightly around her, she leaned against a porch pillar and gazed skyward again. She hadn't come to a decision about Jackson's less than enthusiastic proposal. A part of her knew it was the sensible thing to do, because it would allow her to keep Dawn, but emotionally, Libby had a difficult time with it. Yes, if Jackson got itchy feet and went away, she would be left alone with the daughter she loved. But she couldn't abide another man leaving her, whether it was voluntary or not.

For so many years in her life she'd felt unnecessary, extraneous. Her father had openly admitted he'd wished for another son. Her mother had been a useless ally, for as far as Libby could tell, she'd merely been a receptacle for her father's lust, never once telling Libby she was loved or wanted.

She might appear strong on the outside, but Libby had discovered, with the appearance of Jackson Wolfe in her life, that there was a soft inner core that was vulnerable and passionately impoverished. For some reason, he'd touched that core, and Libby couldn't bear the thought of him marrying her out of pity.

The door opened behind her, and she knew immediately

who had opened it. His presence affected her physically, making her want something from him that he undoubtedly wasn't willing to give.

He stood beside her and followed her gaze into the sky.

"'She walks in beauty, like the night of cloudless climes and starry skies.'"

Libby's smile was brief. "So you quote Byron. Is there any end to your list of accomplishments?"

"Hmm. Sarcasm. Here I thought I'd impress you with my poetic soul."

He smelled good. An undefinable scent that she'd come to expect only from him. It wasn't cologne; it wasn't sweat. It was simply . . . him.

"Nice night for a stroll."

She pulled in a breath of crisp autumn air. "Yes."

"Care to join me?"

She slanted him a wary glance, quietly questioning his objectives.

"You're wondering about my motives."

The smile she heard in his voice softened her. "So you're a poet and a mind reader, among your other talents."

He touched her elbow, sending tingles over her flesh as he guided her down the steps. "My other talents? Ah, yes. I know you've seen them; it's nice that you noticed . . . and remembered."

She flushed, grateful it was dark. Oh, she'd noticed, all right. Rarely a day went by that she didn't remember how she and Mahalia had caught him wearing only his birthday suit.

Ignoring the remark, she fell into step beside him. "You can read minds. I thought perhaps you were a magician as well."

He took her arm and drew it through his, a common enough gesture. Although Libby had the urge to lean into him, she stifled it.

"A magician?"

She nodded. "How else do you account for the fact that you've mesmerized Dawn?"

They strolled down the incline to the river. It rushed over the rocks. If she listened hard, she could hear the burbling echo of the water as it raced through the caverns that dotted the landscape along the riverbank.

Frogs croaked lazily. Crickets chirruped. The hoot of a gray owl sounded from somewhere in the trees.

"Not entirely. She won't be happy with me unless you're there, too."

"I know that," Libby admitted.

"Then why are you unwilling to marry me?"

She smiled sadly to herself. "I've been married once. And although it was a cruel thing to do to a fourteen-year-old girl, it turned out not to be so bad. If Sean taught me nothing else, he taught me survival and independence."

Jackson muttered a mild curse. "Then what are you afraid of?"

Dared she tell him? Dared she bare her soul and tell him she wanted passion? Love? Commitment? "I don't need your pity, Jackson."

"Pity?" The word rumbled up from deep within his chest. "What makes you think I pity you?"

"I saw it in your eyes when we were with the lawyer."

He snorted a harsh laugh. "You're about the least likely candidate for pity I've ever met. Dammit, woman, you're creating obstacles where none exist."

She stopped walking and turned to face him. "I am not. I merely want—"

"What? What do you want? Love?" The word came out like a curse. "I can't promise such a thing, Libby. Look what happened to me when I lost one woman I loved. I abandoned my daughter, fled to foreign lands, and made my living killing people."

Of course. She hadn't expected him to promise his undying love. What was wrong with her, anyway? A marriage between them was foolish. She was very possibly half in love with him already, but what did her love matter if it wasn't returned?

"I can promise you a lot of things, Libby. Whether you want to believe me or not, I can promise you that I won't abandon Dawn Twilight again. I can promise you that I'll stay on here as sheriff, the town willing, so you won't have to give up your business. I'll be as considerate as I'm capable of being, whether we . . . er . . . you know . . ."

He cleared his throat, clearly uncomfortable. "But I'll warn you right now," he went on, "that if you agree to marry me, I intend to coax you into my bed by one means or another."

Oh, my. There was that feeling again, that lush heaviness low in her belly. Hunger for him rose up to meet it. She didn't know what to say, so she said nothing.

"There's something between us, Libby. You can't deny that."

She took some solace in the knowledge that he felt it, too. Heavens, she continued to feel—that . . . that overwhelming urge to be with him, to touch him, have him touch her. It had been that way since he'd kissed her. But were those feelings enough? Surely they wouldn't be, at least not for her, if it weren't for Dawn. Even so, it was hard to commit herself. For once she said yes, there would be no turning back.

The fervent daydreaming side of her that she'd vowed didn't exist came roaring to the forefront, and her emotions were a-tumble. She knew without a doubt that if she married him and fell completely and totally in love with him—and she very well could—she'd be devastated if he found love elsewhere. But she'd still have Dawn. If he broke his promise and set out again for the far corners of the world, she would feel as though she'd failed as a wife, but she would still have Dawn.

He drew her close. "Look at me, Libby."

She lifted her gaze, slowly meeting his. He was a dark silhouette against the moonlight.

"You have some feelings for me," he announced, his beautiful baritone rumbling through her. "I can see it in your eyes."

She immediately lowered her gaze, but he tipped her chin up with his forefinger.

"As I said, Jackson," she repeated, her own voice holding a slight quaver, "I don't want your pity."

His lips came down on hers, insistent, probing. She tried to remain passive, but that wasn't possible. The force of his mouth opened hers. She slid her hands up his chest, grasping at the fabric of his shirt while he laved her with his tongue. A thrill raced through her, causing her to gasp.

At the sound, he groaned into her mouth and his hands moved to her waist and down over her bottom. He pressed her to him, allowing her to feel the hardness behind his fly. Keeping one hand on her rump, he moved the other up her side, to her breast. Even through her clothing her breasts swelled and tingled.

"A kiss is not enough," he growled against her mouth. His fingers moved to her bodice, fumbling with the buttons. Libby knew she should stop him, but she couldn't. She didn't want to.

He cursed at his awkwardness, and she helped him, sliding the buttons quickly from their holes. He tugged her dress down over her shoulders, camisole straps and all, leaving her bare to the waist. Vaguely she felt cold air on her skin.

She pressed him close when he bent and pressed his mouth over the pulse that throbbed at her neck, then down over her freed breasts. He laved her nipples with his tongue, sending quivering spasms throughout her body until she was afraid her legs wouldn't support her.

Raising his head, he kissed her again and took one of her hands, drawing it between them. He cupped her palm around him; he was long and hard the full length of his fly. She bit back a groan of pleasure.

"Is this pity, Libby? I dare you to tell me that what I'm feeling right now is pity."

She was swimming with desire, allowing her fingers to touch him, stroke him. The memory of his nudity those weeks before spun inside her again, and she felt a yearning new and insistent, a yawning chasm of hunger.

Grabbing her arms, he wrapped them around his neck

and crushed her to him, raising her, supporting her so that her pelvis met his.

"There's heat between us, Libby," he whispered against her mouth. "You feel it too." He hiked up her skirt, his palm grazing the back of her thigh.

For the first time in her life, she thought she might swoon. "I . . . I . . . can't stand up, Jackson."

He sank to the ground with her in his arms and pulled her, facing him, onto his lap, drawing her legs to either side of his hips. His hand returned under her skirt. She unbuttoned his shirt and ran her fingers over his chest, loving the feel of the hair as it teased her palm.

The ache between her legs was impossibly strong. Her blood felt thick as warm honey as it pulsed through her veins. She pushed herself closer to him, pressing against the hard bulge, moving her burning flesh over it.

Beneath her, he fumbled with his fly, and in her eagerness, she assisted him, gasping in surprise when he sprang free. Unwilling to think further, she drew him into her through the slit in her drawers, sinking onto him, feeling an urgency well up inside her even through the pain of his entrance.

He stopped briefly.

"No, no," she murmured, her hunger causing a madness she yearned for.

She sank deep, gasping as she felt him inside her. His hands were on her hips, helping her move, teaching her to please him as his thumb nudged the hot, wet flesh at the apex of her thighs.

He lowered himself onto his back, so that he was lying on the ground. His hands still guided her hips, his own jutting upward with each thrust.

Something was building, boiling inside her, a pressing urgency that had nothing to do with logic and everything to do with passion. She loved it. She wanted it. She let herself go, reaching and grasping for that which she'd never known before.

When it came, rolling over her in swelling, spasmodic

waves, she bit her lip to keep from crying out. The sensation was too strong, but before her keening moans of satisfaction echoed through the night, he pulled her to him and kissed her, swallowing her sounds of pleasure.

A brief moment later he stiffened beneath her, gripping her hips hard. He came inside her, groaning into her mouth once again.

She lay on his chest, the drumming of his heartbeat against her ear. She should get up. Really, she should. But having him fill her was glorious. Blocking out conscious thought, she gave herself up to her feelings and nuzzled his neck with her nose.

"Ah, Libby, Libby . . ." He stroked her rump through her underwear, dipping inside to run his fingers over her flesh. When he couldn't seem to touch enough, he tugged at her cotton drawers, loosening the string that was tied at her waist. Both of his hands went beneath her dress, and she dragged herself to a sitting position, allowing him to touch her.

His thumbs nudged her where they joined. She felt the urgency build, causing her to move again, slowly, seductively, on his shaft. Her breathing became erratic, and she knew nothing but the eagerness of impending fulfillment.

Suddenly he rolled her beneath him, moving inside her once again. She drew her legs up, pressing her heels into his back, rising to meet his thrusts.

The explosion was no less exquisite than the first time, and Libby wept as the wild pleasure of climax rocked them both. They stayed joined, Jackson resting on his elbows over her.

He bent to kiss her. "God, Libby, you were a virgin?"

"No! N-no, of c-course not," she stuttered. "Don't be a fool. It's just been a while, that's all," she lied.

All at once, regret reached like clammy fingers into the farthest recesses of her soul. She pushed him off her, sat up quickly, then rose, fastening her drawers.

He gazed up at her from the ground. "That wasn't pity, Liberty O'Malley."

As usual, his baritone touched a chord inside her, but her shame went deeper.

"I'm sorry," she murmured. "I shouldn't have . . . I mean, I've never . . ." Shaking her head, she picked up her skirts and raced toward the house, trying to ignore the stinging pain between her legs.

14

Libby TOOK THE STEPS TWO AT A TIME AND TORE INTO HER bedroom, stopping short of slamming the door behind her. She sagged against it, pressing her palms into the wood. Good Lord, what had come over her?

Still awash with shame, she stumbled across the room and threw herself onto the bed, covering her face with her hands. They shook. And why wouldn't they? In one reckless moment she'd not only lost her virginity, which, in her mind wasn't that big a thing at her age, but had experienced something she'd heard about but hadn't believed existed: ecstasy. It was almost absurd. Lord, they'd rolled around on the grass like a couple of dogs in heat.

Her misery deepened. She had to be some sort of freak. How could the feelings she'd experienced be right, or even normal, for that matter? And why, God help her, hadn't she had any inkling of this feeling before now? It wasn't as if she hadn't been kissed and groped before.

She crossed to the dry sink, poured water into the bowl, and wet a cloth. As she dabbed at the soreness between her legs, she scolded herself again for submitting to Jackson.

There was a quiet rapping at the door.

She threw the cloth into the porcelain bowl and slipped quickly into her nightgown. "Who is it?"

"Jackson."

She gasped. "Go away."

"Libby, if you don't open the door, I'll make a scene and wake up the Bellamy brothers."

Leaning her forehead against the door, she ordered, "Go away and leave me alone."

"I mean it, Libby."

When he started to sing "Nobody Knows the Trouble I've Seen," she flung open the door.

"You are such an ass," she said accusingly.

He stepped inside, his size dwarfing her. "I wanted to make sure you were all right, that's all."

She swung away. "I'm fine. Now will you leave me alone?"

Out of the corner of her eye, she saw him step to the dry sink. And at that very moment, she realized what she'd left there. She sprinted to beat him, but was too late. She felt such a richness of embarrassment that her skin prickled with sweat.

In the porcelain dish, immersed in water tinged pink with her blood, was the soiled cloth she'd used to cleanse away the remnants of her maidenhead.

With a soft curse he took her hands, and although she tried to pull away, he held her firm. "I don't know what to say, Libby."

Through her misery, she heard herself say, "It doesn't matter. It's nothing."

"I'm sorry. I'm so very sorry."

She couldn't look at him. "Fine. I accept your apology. Now please just leave me alone."

He left without another word, and Libby rinsed out the cloth and poured the water into the chamber pot, all the while feeling her heart pounding so hard, it gave her a headache.

How in the world was she going to face the man in the morning?

* * *

When she woke, nothing had changed. She still felt shame deep inside for allowing herself to be seduced by him. And she was sore, both in mind and in body as well as angry, with herself and with him. He wanted her—of that she was certain—but only because Dawn wouldn't go with him if she didn't marry him. At least not willingly. She rose and dressed, cringing at the soreness between her legs, then hurried downstairs.

She prepared oatmeal, viciously stirring it, the metal spoon clanking angrily against the sides of the pot. Each movement reminded her that the night before, she'd lost something on which most women placed great value. But not her. She'd decided long ago, after Sean died, that she would give away her virginity whenever she pleased. It just so happened that she hadn't found anyone she wanted to give it to.

She wrinkled her nose. Until now, it appeared.

Mahalia stomped into the kitchen wearing a frown, Libby's tan frock—the one she'd worn the day before—over her arm. "What's this on your dress?"

Libby glanced at it. "Where?"

Mahalia spread the fabric, exposing a green stain. "This."

Libby felt herself color. "My, my. What do you suppose that is?"

"Looks like grass stain to me. Now," she continued, "if this were Dawn's dress, I could understand. I'm forever scrubbin' grass stains off her clothes. But yours . . ." She clucked, her gaze probing, as if she expected an answer.

"You're waiting for an explanation? Sorry," Libby apologized, continuing to stir the cereal, "I can't imagine how that stain got there." Had Jackson not so boldly entered her room and discovered her secret, she might have felt embarrassed about a little thing like grass stains. Now she was angry, and the stain only served to remind her of her shame.

Again Mahalia made sounds in her throat that foretold her mood. "If'n I didn't know you so well, I'd be givin' you some suggestions." She cackled. "Or maybe some advice."

Libby slanted her a look. "I don't think I care to hear either."

"I didn't expect you would," Mahalia answered with a chuckle that jiggled her breasts and her belly. She turned to leave as Jackson entered the room.

"Why, good mornin', Mistah Wolfe. I was just showin' Libby, here, these funny green stains on the back of her skirt—"

"Mahalia." Libby's voice had a threatening ring to it, but Mahalia merely chuckled, then was gone.

Libby's heart was bumping her ribs, but she kept an icy facade, until Jackson stepped up behind her. Oh, heavens, he was so close she felt the heat of him the entire length of her, and her body began to betray her. Her facade nearly melted. Nearly.

His hands touched her shoulders, and she swung away, the pot of oatmeal in her grip. "Be careful," she threatened. "I wouldn't want this hot kettle to slip and accidentally land on the front of your jeans."

"Libby, I had no idea—"

"Stop right there," she interrupted. "The status of my innocence is my business."

"The hell it is."

His deep, rich baritone sent involuntary shivers over her flesh. "Well, it certainly isn't your concern."

"But you were married, dammit."

"So that makes seduction all right?"

He straddled a kitchen chair. Her gaze automatically went to his spread thighs, but she forced it away.

"I was seduced as well," he informed her.

She flushed and turned on him, the spoon gripped in her fist. "Listen. I may have been . . . celibate, so to speak, but I was in no way innocent. It was . . . it was time to get rid of the thing anyway."

"The thing?"

Ignoring the laughter in his voice, she put the cereal on the table with a thud. "You know precisely what I'm referring to."

He studied her for a long, taut moment. "Most women save themselves for the man they love."

"Well, I'm not most women. And that's hogwash, anyway.

I'd have gotten rid of it years ago if I'd had a mind to." And she would have. She was almost certain she would have.

"I'm surprised you were still virginal, considering you'd been married."

"Well, there are all sorts of marriages. All of them don't lead to the bedroom." Her anger simmered.

"Obviously yours didn't," he offered.

"Brilliant deduction," she said, her voice laced with sarcasm. "It changes nothing. Don't think I'm going to capitulate and marry you. If that was your plan, you'll be sorely disappointed." She was foolish to accuse him of such a thing, but at the moment, she wanted to blame him for everything.

"My plan?" He snorted a laugh. "We were both ready to explode, Libby. Don't deny that."

"Be that as it may," she retorted. "What we . . . what we did last night in no way expedites my decision."

"You think I purposely seduced you so that you'd feel obligated to marry me?" He sounded more amused than surprised.

She turned away, fussing with the bowl that held the bread dough. "Don't try to tell me that idea didn't occur to you."

"No. It didn't."

"I find that hard to believe." She dumped the dough onto the counter and laced it with flour.

"Why?"

"Because you know that without me, Dawn won't go with you." From behind her, she heard him chuckle. "And what's so darned funny?"

"You are."

She gave the bread dough a savage punch, picturing his arrogant face. "I'm happy you find me so amusing."

"You're itching for a fight, aren't you?"

She continued to attack the dough, kneading, pummeling, folding. "I'm simply telling you your plan didn't work."

The chair scraped, and suddenly he was behind her. "Do you want to fight, Libby?"

She didn't rise to the bait, but his breath ruffled the hair on her neck, causing a recurrence of the feelings he'd stirred within her the night before.

"Don't take your anger out on the bread dough. Look how you're punishing it." His hands caressed her shoulders and her neck, and as hard as she tried, she couldn't pretend to feel nothing.

"Wouldn't you like to do that to me? Ah, think of it, Libby. Think how much you'd like to come at me, pounding and screeching and screaming."

She clamped her jaw tightly. "It's rude to lose control," she managed.

"It's not healthy to keep your anger inside, either. Come on, Liberty O'Malley, let it go. Show me how you *really* feel."

His voice had an annoying baiting quality, a tone she abhorred because it was so often used to intimidate.

"All right, you bully." She swung around, her hands sticky, and shoved at his chest, leaving splotches of dough and flour on his shirt. He didn't budge, so she pushed him again. The twinkle in his eyes and his smug smile were enough to make her want to double up her fist and punch him.

"Come on, Libby, you can do better than that," he coaxed, egging her on. He put his fists up, fighter style, and danced the boxer's dance before her.

She bit the insides of her cheeks to keep from smiling. "You're an ass."

"Come on," he urged, punching her lightly on the shoulder.

She brushed him off and went back to her bread dough, but he continued to annoy her, tapping her shoulders, her spine, even her rump.

She swung at his arm, and missed.

"Oh, is that what it takes?" He tapped her rump repeatedly, all the while cajoling her.

"Stop that!" Turning, she swung at him, landing a punch on his arm.

"That's better, Libby girl. Much better." He continued to

spar with her, touching her nose, her chin, her arm—in essence, becoming a prize nuisance.

She waved him away with both hands, fending off light punches, and felt a wonderful freedom. They remained locked in playful battle, Libby fighting off his feathery punches and biting back the urge to scream with laughter.

One of his hands grazed her side, just above her waist, and she gasped and pushed him away.

"Aha! The maiden is ticklish." He touched her again, getting another rise out of her, and she shoved him. He was immovable and relentless.

Unable to stand his teasing and unable to keep from laughing and shrieking at his touch, she turned, grabbed a handful of flour, and tossed it at him.

He stopped, momentarily stunned, flour cascading from his long eyelashes and his nose. His expression was so comical that Libby doubled over, holding her sides as she laughed.

"Think that's funny, do you?"

In a swift movement that belied his size, he spun her around and doused her with a handful of her own ammunition, causing her to sputter and cough.

Unable to keep the laughter from her voice, she shouted, "You wretch!" She brushed at her face and hair, flour filtering through the air between them.

"What in the devil's goin' on in here?"

The merriment stopped, and Libby turned toward the door to find a curious and puzzled Mahalia staring at them.

Apologetic, Libby began to stutter. "Oh . . . oh, Mahalia, I-I'm sorry we've made such a mess."

"I don't give a damn about the mess, honey, but I sure am curious about why y'all made it."

Smoothing her hands over her dress and her hair, Libby tried to think of a logical explanation. There wasn't one.

"I'm afraid it's my fault," Jackson interceded. "I was trying to get her to let her hair down a bit, and . . . well, I guess we kind of got carried away."

Mahalia arched her brow, appearing not quite certain she believed him. "Well, that bread won't get baked that way."

"Never mind, Mahalia. I'll finish up in here," Libby promised. "After all, this mess is my fault. You shouldn't have to clean up after me."

"And I'll help her," Jackson offered.

Libby glared at him, her good humor having fled. "Don't you have to arrest someone or something?"

He studied her, his eyes continuing to glisten. "Yeah, I guess you're right. We'll continue our discussion later, though. Count on it."

Mahalia snorted. "In some other room, I'm hopin'. My kitchen ain't safe with the two of you around."

Jackson gave her a quick wink and was gone.

Libby studiously began to clean up the flour that had spilled onto the floor.

"Lan' sakes. I don't know about the two of you. One week you're tossin' plates and skillets at him, the next you're dousin' each other with flour. Am I missin' somethin'?"

"I could no more explain it than I could fly, Mahalia." Libby felt her housekeeper's gaze on her.

"Uh-huh." She clucked her tongue. "You'd best go up and change that frock, honey. I'm just gettin' clothes together to wash." When Libby continued to wipe up the floor, Mahalia added, "Scoot, now. Let me finish in here. I'll bring you fresh towels in a minute."

Too embarrassed to argue, Libby took the stairs to her room and stepped out of her flour-spattered gown. Standing in her camisole and drawers, she finished rinsing the flour from her face, then took down her hair and was brushing it free of debris when there was a soft knock on the door.

"Come in, Mahalia," she called out. "I'm as decent as I'll ever be." When she didn't enter, Libby crossed to the door, realizing she probably had her hands full.

She flung it open and stood, rooted to the spot, as her gaze traveled up the tall, perfectly honed body of Jackson Wolfe.

"Oh, Lord," she muttered, attempting to close the door.

His foot became a doorstop, and he eased his way inside, closing the door behind him.

She swallowed, her heart in her throat and her pulse hovering somewhere between her navel and her knees.

"This isn't one bit proper." She tried to sound indignant. She failed.

"God." His voice was a husky rumble, and his gaze moved over her slowly and thoroughly. "Look at you." He picked up one of her long, loopy curls and raised it to his face, his eyes never leaving hers.

"Jackson, please. You're embarrassing me. I'm . . ." Belatedly she crossed her arms over her breasts. "This isn't proper, and I'm not decent."

"Propriety and decency belong in stuffy drawing rooms, Libby. What we have between us is hot and intense, and I'm not going to let you forget it." All the while he spoke, his hands traveled up and down her arms, making her quiver.

He placed her hands on his shoulders, then turned her right arm to expose the sensitive inner surface, and ran his mouth from the elbow to beneath her shoulder.

She shuddered at the sensation, closing her eyes and forcing herself not to melt against him. "I'm still not ready to marry you, and . . . and if you think that by constantly assaulting me with your . . . your . . ."

His eyes twinkled, and he drew her close, so close she could feel him growing behind his fly. "My . . . what?"

She swallowed. "You act like a rutting ass." She tried to sound incensed, but knew she failed, for his hands were on her hips and he was slowly drawing her back and forth across the front of his jeans.

"I know, but I'm good at it, don't you agree?"

She raised her head to scold him, which she instantly realized was a mistake, for his mouth came down on hers, clamping hard. The kiss was one of possession, and Libby had no strength or desire to resist.

He broke the embrace, stepping swiftly to the door. "Sooner or later you're going to give in, Liberty O'Malley."

Feigning anger, she answered, "Not before I fight you with every breath I take."

His smile was devastating. "If the little overture in the kitchen is any indication of our future together, Libby girl, I'm going to enjoy the struggle." Returning briefly, he kissed her hard on the mouth, and before she could fight him, he was gone.

On shaky legs she crossed to the dry sink and studied her reflection in the mirror. Her lips felt swollen; there was high color in her cheeks. And that telltale pulse bounded relentlessly behind the flesh at her throat.

She knew she was a strong woman. Unfortunately, she sensed that the one thing that could break down her defenses was her own reaction to this incredibly handsome, virile, powerful . . . annoying man.

Burl Bellamy spat a stream of tobacco into the spittoon, briefly taking his eyes off Corey's work while his brother snoozed in his chair. "So," he said, shoving the plug against his cheek with his tongue, "someone pays ya to draw fancy pictures, huh?"

Corey carefully sketched the lobes of the big-leaf maple. "They sure do," he answered. He was eager for his niece to get home from school. He had a surprise for her; that was why he was working outside, on the porch.

Burl cackled. "Dang, now I've heard it all. Can't 'magine why anyone would pay a body fer such work."

Corey smiled. "No, I don't imagine you could."

Bert snorted and awakened. He sat up straight, blinking his rheumy eyes at the other two. "Cain't you two talk a bit quieter? How's a body to get a nap with such racket?"

Burl chortled. "By dang, Bert, ya woke yerself up."

Bert scowled, his mouth working and his flabby jowl wagging like a cock's wattle.

The Bellamy boys were amusing, Corey would give them that. And it didn't matter how many times they found him drawing and writing, they repeated their expressions of disbelief that anyone would pay him for it.

Lifting his head, he saw Dawn Twilight approaching, her schoolbooks under her arm. "Have a good day?"

She gave him a brilliant smile. "For a change. It's the first time in days that bully Willie Frost hasn't chased me."

Corey jumped to her defense. "Do you want me to take care of that hooligan?" At her giggle, Corey added, amazed at her good humor, "I mean it, Dawn. I'll thrash the rascal with a hickory whip."

"You don't have to. Chloe Ann has already taken care of that part."

Corey raised his eyebrows. "She takes a stick to him?"

"Well, only his knuckles. And she uses a ruler. I don't think she really likes doing even that much, but Willy is such a bully that nothing else seems to work."

He could hardly believe that shy, delicate little thing could stand up to schoolhouse bullies.

"Well, if I can't jump to your defense, at least let me give you a present." He pulled the leather-bound journal from his inside coat pocket and handed it to her.

Her eyes big, Dawn slowly took it, running her fingers over the cover. "What's this for?"

"Look inside," he instructed, anxious to see her reaction.

Dawn dropped her schoolbooks on the step and opened the journal, her expression turning puzzled. "There's nothing on the pages."

"It's a journal, or a diary. And it's only blank because you haven't written in it yet."

She smiled, biting down on her bottom lip. "Oh, Uncle Corey. A journal, for me? How did you know I liked to write?"

"Oh," he answered, leaning into his chair, "I have my spies."

"You mean Papa and Mama." She leafed through the blank pages, her expression rapt. "I must take after you. I want to be a writer someday, too, but I want to write stories about people I know."

Corey jerked his head toward the Bellamy boys, who were both snoozing and snoring. "You could start with those two characters."

She giggled again, then touched his arm. "Thank you so much, Uncle Corey. I love my present."

He glanced at her hand on his arm. "Is that all I get?"

With a happy sigh, she flung herself into his arms. "I'm so lucky," she murmured against his neck.

Corey hugged her, hoping she was right. Oh, she was a

lucky little girl, but if Libby and Jackson didn't get together, how lucky would she feel if she was taken away from her mother?

Jackson had left his mount at the livery, requesting that he be reshod. As he walked to the boardinghouse, he found his thoughts absorbed with images of Libby. God, what a life they could have together, if only she'd agree to marry him. Their union might not be based on love, but it sure as hell would be filled with passion.

But . . . a virgin? He couldn't get over his surprise. Shock, really. And her reaction . . . He'd slept with enough women to know when they were faking and when they weren't. Libby definitely hadn't been faking. Even now he felt the bite of desire at the thought of bedding her again.

He mouthed a curse. Of course, he'd promised her that if she married him, he wouldn't bed her without her consent. He wondered if what they'd done the night before would make her more amenable to the whole idea of marriage or merely strengthen her resolve against it.

She'd been wound up as tight as a pocket watch before breakfast. But once she loosened up, she was delicious. Tussling with him, laughing when she threw flour in his face, letting loose when he attempted to tickle her . . . Lord Almighty, what a woman she was. How could any man married to her not take her to his bed? Who was this Sean O'Malley, anyway, and why hadn't he touched her?

He continued to be deep in thought as he approached the porch.

"Papa!"

Smiling at his daughter, he held out his arms for her. She scrambled down the steps and went into his embrace. "Oh, Papa, look what Uncle Corey gave me." She stepped away and held out the book. "It's a journal, Papa. I can start writing all my thoughts and stories down in this book. Isn't that wonderful?"

He caught Corey's gaze, and they winked at each other. "Leave it to your uncle to think of a wise gift for such a talented girl."

She expelled a satisfied sigh. "Everything's so perfect. The only thing that would make it better would be if you and Mama got married."

Again Jackson's gaze met his brother's. Corey gave him a quirky smile and wiggled his tawny eyebrows.

Jackson smoothed his hand over his daughter's thick braid. He wanted to marry Libby, and Dawn Twilight wanted it, too. What would it take to convince the woman that it was the only thing to do?

15

THE FOLLOWING MORNING LIBBY WAS INFORMED THAT SOME-
one else from Jackson's family had arrived at the jail.
Despite her reluctance to appear to have done anything
special in order to make a good impression, she bustled
around the rooming house, dusting, straightening, and
making sure Mahalia's evening meal wasn't as hot as a
Cajun summer. She had two vacant rooms, which she
aired out and provided with fresh linens, in case whoever
had arrived hadn't made arrangements to stay anywhere
else.

And for some inane reason, as afternoon waned and the
dinner hour approached, she felt the need to primp. She
rushed to her room, took a quick bath, and changed into
one of her nicest frocks. She supervised Dawn's dressing as
well.

As they waited for Jackson's return, Dawn displayed the
nervous fidgets that Libby felt but tried to hide.

"Do I look all right, Mama?"

The new yellow frock with the ivy sprigs made Dawn's
skin look like polished sand, and her long, freshly braided
hair gleamed with health.

"You look absolutely beautiful," Libby answered, straightening the bright green ribbon at her daughter's waist.

"You look pretty too, Mama. You hardly ever wear that dress."

That was true. The dusty rose lawn was one of her best. "Well, I want to make a good impression, too."

Dawn twirled away. "Did you know that Papa has an Indian name?"

"No, I didn't." But she wasn't surprised.

"When he was little and was rescued by the Indians, Papa said that at first he was very bel . . . bel . . ."

"Belligerent?" Libby suggested.

"Yeah, belligerent. The Indians knew he was scared, but he acted tough, like a little warrior brave. So they called him Warrior Heart.

"Did you know that his real mama was killed?"

Libby digested this, seeing the similarities in Dawn's and Jackson's lives. It was no wonder he was so obsessed with regaining custody. She suddenly felt a bite of pity for a little boy who must have been so very frightened at having his world destroyed.

Dawn studied her. "Are you gonna marry Papa?"

Libby's stomach dropped. "I . . . I don't know."

"Papa says he wants you to."

Interested, Libby answered, "Oh, he does, does he?"

Nodding, Dawn announced, "Then we'll be a real family. I'm gonna write a story about it, Mama. Everything will be *perfect.*"

Libby stifled a weary, anxious sigh. Perfect, indeed. For Jackson and for her daughter, but certainly not for her. The idea had begun to grow on her, however. She knew that living with Jackson Wolfe wouldn't be dull, and she couldn't deny that she was attracted to him. On top of that, he made her laugh. Who could resist a man who could make her shake off her inhibitions and squeal with glee? And, of course, there was that bedroom incident. . . .

A commotion on the porch and the sound of Jackson's

mellow baritone caused her already nervous stomach to lurch again.

"We can't begin to thank you for putting us up on such short notice," Susannah Wolfe acknowledged.

"I'm glad I had the room," Libby answered graciously.

Mrs. Wolfe hugged Dawn and kissed her temple. "I was thrilled to discover I had a granddaughter, and such a pretty one at that."

Jackson's stepmother sat on the settee in the parlor, Dawn's hand clasped between both of hers. Dawn gazed up at her in awe. Again, as when she'd met Jackson's brother, she'd become a mute.

Libby hid her hands in the folds of her skirt and clenched them into fists. Susannah Wolfe was a beautiful woman. Her hair, a rich mahogany, was youthfully lustrous. Her skin bore a smattering of freckles, and she looked years younger than she probably was. She, like Libby, was full-bosomed, and Libby decided that if she could look that good when she got to be Susannah's age, she'd be elated. Mrs. Wolfe's brown eyes were kind, and her smile sincere.

Though Libby tried to act normal, she continued to feel ill. "Dawn has talked of nothing but Jackson's family since he told her who he was." She forced a smile at her daughter, then returned her gaze to Susannah Wolfe. "She isn't a mute, you know. Actually, this is only the second time in her life I've noticed that the cat had her tongue."

Dawn flushed beneath her dusky skin and looked at her lap. "Oh, Mama . . ."

Katie, Jackson's youngest sister, a pretty little blonde of perhaps fourteen, sat on the other side of Dawn. "Mama says I'm Dawn Twilight's auntie. It seems funny because we're almost the same age."

The girls exchanged shy grins, and Libby experienced a heaviness that weighed on her heart.

"And I'm happy to know that she's living so close to us, because my older sister, Mandy, is away at school," Katie informed Libby.

"It will be nice for Dawn, too," Libby commented. This entire situation was fine and dandy with everyone but her.

Her back was to the door, but she knew immediately the moment Jackson entered, for the faces of the other three lit up like candles on a Christmas tree.

Susannah, beaming with love and pride, lifted her hand toward her son. "I've been waiting twelve years to touch that face again."

Jackson took his stepmother's hand and kissed it, then allowed her to caress his features.

Libby continued to feel ill.

He went behind his mother, resting his hands on her shoulders. She imprisoned one between hers, occasionally touching it with her cheek.

The scene caused a hollowness in Libby's stomach.

"Dawn Twilight," Jackson murmured, "why don't you take Katie to your room? I'm sure Mumser is anxious to play."

Dawn flashed her mother a quick look, and when Libby smiled, she took Katie's hand and they left the room, Dawn chattering about the dog, the cat, and the time they started to fight on her bed.

After the girls were gone, the silence in the room was stifling. Libby had nothing to say, but her mind was rushing like a freight train barreling along a downhill track.

Susannah broke the quiet. "You've done a wonderful job with her, Mrs. O'Malley. Jackson told me where you found her, and, oh, my," she whispered, her free hand on her breast, "I don't know what would have happened had it not been for you."

To Libby's ears it sounded like "Thank you very much; we'll take over now," but she held her tongue. "Dawn's an easy child to care for, Mrs. Wolfe. She's bright and loving. I haven't done more than any mother would do." They had to know her position. She wasn't about to hand over her daughter without a fight.

"Please, I'll call you Libby if you'll call me Susannah."

Libby forced her smile not to waver. Oh, if only the woman weren't so nice! "Of course."

Jackson cleared his throat, then glanced at the chime clock on the mantel. "It's almost eight. Where are Corey and Dad?"

Susannah patted her son's hand. "They'll be along. You've become fretful, dear. Of all my children, you were always the one with the most patience." She turned and smiled up at Jackson, who winked at her and squeezed her shoulder.

"I have patience when it suits me," he answered, his knowing gaze resting on Libby.

Susannah gazed at her as well, and Libby had the uncomfortable feeling that everyone knew her dilemma. As for the impending reunion between father and son, Libby wasn't sure she could sit and watch it. The first one, between Jackson and his stepmother, had been hard enough. In fact, it had been heart-wrenching. Susannah Wolfe had clung to her son, sobbing with joy. Libby's throat had clenched up, and she'd had to rush from the room or she'd have been in tears, too.

But Libby's pain came from the knowledge that this family had so much more to offer Dawn than she had.

Hearing footsteps on the porch, Libby rose and excused herself, anxious to get away.

She met Jackson's father and brother in the entry.

"Libby! This is my father, Nathan Wolfe," Corey said. "Dad, this is Liberty O'Malley, the woman who rescued your granddaughter."

Unsure of what to expect, Libby extended her hand, only to be drawn into a gentle hug by the bear of a man.

Nathan Wolfe pulled away and looked down at her, his eyes shiny with emotion. He was an older version of his son, but Libby sensed that Jackson was a handsomer man than his father had been. Even so, it took nothing away from Nathan's magnetism.

He smiled, his eyes crinkling at the corners. "The minute I heard, I wanted to take my son out behind the barn and tan his hide, but from what I'm told, he's now bigger than I am."

Corey laughed. "Don't listen to him, Libby. We got punished, all right, but he never laid a hand on us."

How different from her own childhood, she thought, swallowing a wistful sigh. Even now she could almost feel the sting of her father's belt on her thighs.

She attempted a smile. "The . . . others are in the parlor, Corey."

He looped his arm through hers. "You're going to join us, aren't you?"

Flustered, she began to stammer. "Oh, I-I don't think so. I'll . . . bring you some pie and coffee, though."

"Point me to the parlor, son. I'm anxious to lay my eyes on your wayward older brother."

They left her in the entry. She turned down the wall lamp and was going into the kitchen to brew a fresh pot of coffee when she heard the girls' voices on the stairs. From the darkened doorway, she watched the scene.

"Papa!"

"Katie! I've missed you, girl. Come give your papa a hug."

Katie Wolfe offered a girlish giggle. "I saw you yesterday morning, Papa." She clattered down the stairs.

"That's too long, my girl, too long." He swung his daughter into his arms and gave her a noisy kiss.

Katie squealed. "Your beard, Papa! You're giving me whisker burn!"

Dawn stood at the top of the stairs, her eyes as big and round as black buttons. Libby bit her lower lip, then pressed her fingers to her mouth. Dawn wore her emotions on her sleeve, and Libby knew that if Nathan Wolfe was reticent in any way, it would break her daughter's heart.

The bear of a man put his daughter on the floor and gazed at the landing. "And who is this beautiful creature?"

"It's Dawn Twilight, Papa."

Libby couldn't see his face, but she could imagine his expression. Dawn stood, stiff with anxiety, and graced him with a wavering smile.

"Come down here, granddaughter, and give your grandpapa a hug," Nathan ordered, his voice gentle and his arms outstretched.

After a brief moment of hesitation, Dawn raced down the steps and flew into the man's arms, pressing her face against his neck.

Her fists against her mouth, Libby turned and made her way into the dark kitchen. She stumbled to a chair and slumped into it. Her stomach churned. She hadn't felt so ill since she'd had the grippe.

She forced herself to stay calm, knowing it would be one of the most difficult things she'd ever have to do. A question kept running through her head: how could she possibly compete with a family like Jackson's? Over time, there would be nothing to prevent Dawn from making the choice to live with Jackson on her own. How much more exciting for her to be part of a large, noisy, happy family than to live in a rooming house with her mother, a schoolmistress, and two crazy old coots who had been around longer than dirt.

Long after the others had gone to bed, Jackson and his father sat by the fire, talking quietly. It felt good, this peace of mind. It felt right.

"So what are your plans?" Nathan asked.

Jackson poured his father another shot of brandy but took none for himself. "I'm not sure. A few things are going on around here that, as sheriff, I have to clean up. A couple of ranchers have been losing their sheep to poison and rimrocking."

"Could cattlemen be behind it?"

Jackson shook his head. "I don't think so. Even the ranchers themselves don't think so."

Nathan scratched his stubbled jaw. "Where is the sheepmen's land?"

"Both men own grazing land north of here. One spreads east to the Nevada border, the other west."

"You know," Nathan began, "I had lunch with the governor's brother a few weeks ago, and he implied that they're going to build a railroad line, starting at Fort Redding."

Interested, Jackson perked up. "From Fort Redding to where?"

"I'm not sure," his father answered. "It hasn't been announced, as far as I know."

"Isn't that interesting. What do you suppose would happen around here if that line were to come through Thief River?"

"I'd say anyone with land along the track site would become very wealthy." Nathan lifted an eyebrow at his son. "Would those sheep ranchers' land happen to be in the way?"

Jackson smirked. "Right smack dab."

Nathan settled deeper into the overstuffed chair. "So now you have a motive. Any suspects?"

"I'm not sure." He studied his father. "Do you want to take a trip to the bank with me in the morning?"

Nathan shrugged. "Sure. Why?"

Not ready to voice his jumbled thoughts about the sheepmen, Jackson instead told his father about the disappearance of Dawn Twilight's trust fund, and his suspicions about who was responsible.

"Flicker Feather was killed by vigilantes. In order to put that whole part of my life to rest, I have to find out who they were. But that'll have to come after I've cleared up the problem with the sheepmen. I can't let it rest, though, Dad. For years I felt responsible for her death."

Nathan heaved a dark sigh and rubbed his face with his hands. "God, but I wish we'd settled things all those years ago. If we both hadn't been so stubborn, you and Flicker Feather would have been safe with us. And we would have had the joy of watching your daughter grow up."

Jackson nodded. "I was stubborn and muleheaded. I also felt extremely sorry for myself." He gave his father a small grin. "Maybe I just wanted to drown myself in pity. Hell, telling you about Flicker Feather and Dawn Twilight would have solved my problems. I honestly think I wanted my grief hanging around my neck like a damned albatross."

His father studied him, a tenderness in his eyes. "We missed so much time together."

Jackson grinned confidently. "I'm glad we get a chance to make up for it."

"I am too," Nathan growled through his smile. "And what will you do when everything is cleared up?"

Jackson studied a scuff on the heel of his boot. "It all depends."

"On the lovely woman I met earlier?"

A note of caution crept into Jackson's voice. "What makes you say that?"

His father smiled. "Corey mentioned that you'd suggested she marry you."

Jackson muttered a curse under his breath. "She hasn't accepted."

"Son, I've been around women a long, long time, and I can tell you right now that very few, except the desperate, will jump into marriage, no matter what the circumstances."

"What am I going to do, then? She's more of a mother to my daughter than I am a father to her," he grumbled. "And Dawn Twilight won't come with me willingly if her mother doesn't come too."

"It's no longer up to you to decide," his father said quietly. "But I have a feeling your Liberty O'Malley will come around."

A sprout of hope. "Whatever gives you that idea?"

"Women like her are selfless, Jackson. She'll do what's best for the daughter you share, even if it's not in her own best interest."

"But I don't want her to be reluctant. I want her to come willingly."

"Don't expect too much right away, son. You know, I may be an old fool, but I detected something between the two of you. I think your mother did, too."

Jackson felt it, too, but he wasn't ready to announce it to the world. During their flour fight in the kitchen, he'd sensed her coming out of that taut shell she'd protected herself with. His attraction to her grew, but he could still never promise to love her.

"Did you fall in love with Mother the first time you saw her?"

His father's smile was warm. "No. I'd been sent to bring her back in for supposedly murdering her husband, remember?"

"Oh, right. And she didn't fit the profile of a cold, calculated murderess." Jackson laughed quietly. "I can't imagine anyone thinking she could do such a thing."

"It was easy to believe until I met her," his father replied. "Susannah had been beaten, son. Even when I began to fall in love with her, I saw such a haunted look in her eyes every time I got too close that I had to back away. And Corey, poor tike, was only three years old, yet I saw evidence of the abuse he'd received as well."

"I don't think Libby's marriage was abusive, but it sure as hell wasn't happy. Or normal." She still hadn't confided any of the details about her marriage, and on some level he knew he had no right to know. But he wanted to. And he hoped that at some point she would have enough faith in him to tell him. Of course, a lot had to happen between them before that would occur. In spite of everything, he felt pleasure every time he remembered that he'd been the first. And he felt a restless need to be the only man to have her.

"Your mother would be the first one to remind you that all women don't want the same things out of life."

Jackson was resolute. "Libby wants what's best for Dawn Twilight, and since I have custody, what's best is that she take me up on my offer."

"That may be obviously what's best for you and Dawn Twilight, but is marriage to you best for her?"

Jackson stared into the waning fire. What he'd offered Libby had been generous, and he'd meant every word. And after having her, he knew he'd want her again. And again.

The following morning Jackson and his father stopped at the bank. Ethan Frost met them. Although the banker's manner was cool, Jackson sensed tension beneath the suave veneer. His eyes, as usual, were expressionless.

He offered both men chairs in his office.

Without preamble, Jackson asked, "Have you found my money?"

Frost's gaze went from one to the other, and Jackson detected a brief flash of fear in his flat eyes.

"I've had my people searching the records, but we haven't come up with anything, yet." Frost's gaze was focused somewhere between the two men. He didn't look Jackson in the eye.

He's lying, Jackson thought.

"It's amazing to me that there's no record anywhere of my daughter's trust fund," Jackson mused.

Frost fidgeted slightly behind his desk. "My father wasn't quite right toward the end. The whole transaction could have been misplaced."

Jackson bit back an angry retort. "He seemed fine to me when I left."

Frost gave him a cool smile. "You didn't know him like I did."

"Maybe not. So let's say you're right. Let's say your father completely mishandled the trust fund. So be it. No matter what happened on this end, I sent money to this bank for nearly twelve years." He paused, pinning Frost with an icy stare of his own. "Where in the hell is it?"

"I told you. We have no record of having received any money from you. I saw your receipts and I believe you. I just can't help you."

Jackson fumed, but held his temper. The bad feeling he'd gotten from Frost at their first meeting intensified. Though tempted to threaten him again with the bank examiner, Jackson decided to try another tactic. "Well, I'd appreciate it if you'd continue to look into the problem."

A flash of surprise. "Certainly, Mr. Wolfe. I'll keep looking."

"By the way," Jackson began in an offhand manner, "do you hold the mortgages on most of the ranchland around here?"

There was another brief flash of fear in the banker's eyes. "Certainly. I'm the only banker."

Jackson gave him a wide, hungry smile. "Of course you are."

Frost stood up and leaned across his desk. "Listen. If you're trying to implicate me in the troubles the sheepmen are having . . ."

Jackson held up his hand. "I didn't mean to imply anything, sir. I'm just curious, that's all."

A wariness spread over Frost's features. "I've been perfectly willing to help those sheepmen out, Mr. Wolfe. I've extended them credit. What more can I do?"

"Yes," Jackson answered as he moved toward the door. "What more can you do?"

As Jackson and his father reached the door, Frost said, "I'll keep looking for your money, Mr. Wolfe, but I wouldn't count on us finding it."

The two men were silent until they exited the bank.

"The bastard is lying."

Nathan nodded. "I've never met the man before, but I know his type."

"I've got to make a trip to Eureka. Want to come with me?"

"Eureka? What for?"

Jackson muttered a curse. "It's just a hunch, but I need some answers, and I need them now. I have a tense feeling in my gut that Frost is somehow involved in all the sheep slaughter, and I want to know why. I've had a bad feeling about him from the day we met."

"What'll you find in Eureka?"

"An ongoing poker game, I hope," Jackson answered, crossing his fingers behind him. "Frost is lying about the trust fund, I'm sure of it." He briefly told his father of his visit with McCann, the retired bookkeeper. "Frost is hiding something else, too. I can feel it. Hell, he's so full of shit his eyes have turned brown."

Nathan chuckled, slapped his son on the shoulder, and turned toward the street. "We'll have to return to the ranch in a couple of days. Why don't you ride with us as far as Eureka? After I've checked things at home, I'll rejoin you."

Jackson watched his father stride toward the rooming

house, tall, handsome, and self-assured. God, but it was good to be with him again. He loved the man.

The hunch in Jackson's gut about Frost wouldn't let up. The only thing he feared was that the situation with the sheep ranchers would escalate before he discovered for certain who was behind it. He wanted to have the job done before someone got killed.

16

MAHALIA REMOVED THE BREAD FROM THE OVEN, THUMPING the crust with her knuckles.

Chloe Ann sat at the table, paring apples for a pie.

Libby knew something was on her mind; Chloe Ann rarely had time to visit until after her lessons were done. Yet today she'd stopped in the kitchen immediately upon returning from the schoolhouse. They were alone, Jackson's parents having gone to visit Vern Roberts and his wife. The girls were in Dawn's room, sharing secrets. She hadn't seen Corey all day.

"What do you think of Jackson's brother, Libby?"

Libby cut the lard into the flour for her piecrust and hid a smile. So that was it. "He's quite a catch, isn't he?"

"Oh, y-yes," she stammered. "He's handsome and all, but he's also brilliant, don't you agree?"

"I'm afraid we haven't discussed matters of much brilliance, Chloe Ann."

Undaunted, Chloe Ann announced, "He's writing a book on the flora and fauna of California. Did you know that? He has a publisher in San Francisco."

Impressed, Libby nodded. "No, I didn't know, but I guess I'm not surprised."

"So you admire his mind," Mahalia interjected with a snort. "Is that it?"

Chloe Ann leaned across the table, her expression rapt. "Oh, yes. I've never met anyone like him before. He's . . . he's so different. So interesting. So intelligent."

Mahalia made the telltale sounds in her throat, and Libby cringed, sensing what was coming.

"An' the fact that he's got a nice tight little butt don't have nothin' to do with it?"

"Mahalia," Libby scolded, noting Chloe Ann's blush.

Mahalia swung around, an empty bread pan in her fist. "Don't 'Mahalia' me, Liberty O'Malley. I don't know why you white folks don't say it like it is. Hell, it's just us women here. Can't we at least be honest among ourselves?"

"But, Mahalia," Chloe Ann argued, "I *do* admire his mind."

"That might be true, girl, but don't you be tellin' me you'd be as enthused if he was bald and fat and broke wind at the dinner table."

Libby threw up her hands. "Oh, Lord, Mahalia, must you?"

"I just don't believe she ain't noticed how nice he'd look wearin' nothin' but a smile."

Chloe Ann's blush deepened, but she allowed a shy smile of her own. "He is rather nice to look at, isn't he?"

"Now, was that so danged hard to admit?"

Chloe Ann busied herself with the apples and continued to blush. "He's asked me to go birding with him on Saturday morning."

"Now, that sounds like a heap of fun," Mahalia said with a smirk.

"Don't be sarcastic, Mahalia," Libby warned.

"I ain't. I mean, think about it. Out in the woods, just the two of 'em. Why, there's nothin' more excitin' than bein' alone in the woods with a handsome man." She made a whistling sound and fanned herself. "It gets my blood up, it does."

The apple parer clattered to the table, and Chloe Ann gasped, covering her cheeks with her hands. "Oh, I hadn't meant that—I mean, we don't—we won't—"

Mahalia's full-bellied laughter interrupted her. "But you will now, I'll bet."

Libby shook her head and sighed. "Did it ever occur to you, Mahalia, that they might actually be going out bird-watching? Not everyone is interested in, well, what you are."

Mahalia continued to laugh. "Maybe not. But she's sure gonna think about it now, ain't she?"

"You are incorrigible," Libby scolded.

"No, I ain't. An' when are you gonna admit you've done a little walkin' in the woods yourself, Liberty?"

Now it was Libby's turn to blush. "We don't have to get into that."

"Oh, I think we do. Grass stains on the back of a grown woman's gown ain't somethin' I'm likely to forget."

"Maybe I was merely sitting on the grass."

Mahalia slanted her a wry look. "They weren't just on the skirt, Liberty, they was *all over* the back of that dress."

From beneath her flush, Libby shot her a stern look. "Isn't it time to get the clothes in from the line?"

Mahalia left the room, still chuckling.

Chloe Ann continued to prepare the apples, but her gaze kept moving to Libby. "Are you going to marry him?"

Libby sighed again. "What are my choices?"

Chloe Ann stood and brought the bowl of apple slices to the counter. "Would marriage to him be so bad?"

Smiling sadly, Libby dusted sugar and cinnamon over the apples before placing them in the prepared pie tins. "Those usually aren't the words that should accompany a question like that."

Chloe Ann fixed herself a cup of tea, then returned to the table. "I know you haven't asked for my advice, but . . . aren't you being a bit stubborn?"

Libby should have been at least a little offended, but she wasn't. "Yes," she admitted. "Maybe I am. I don't see any solution other than to marry him. It's just that . . . well, I'm not all that eager for marriage, and I don't want him to think I am."

Still, the thought of marriage to Jackson filled her with an abundance of emotions, and now, after much thought, not one of those emotions was accompanied by reluctance. She did know, however, that she would not admit this to him, nor would she encourage him to share her bed. It wasn't a matter of wanting to or not, it was the fear that accompanied her growing attraction to him.

Though she'd experienced a few heartaches in her life, she knew without a doubt that if she let Jackson Wolfe into her bed, she would fall totally and utterly in love with him. That would never do, for although he had promised to give her many things, love had not been one of them.

After a lively dinner, made so by Jackson's exuberant family, Libby waited for everyone else to retire before informing Jackson of her decision. His family had announced that they would return to their ranch in the morning. Libby would miss them. In spite of her continued trepidation about Dawn's growing closeness with them, she thought they were wonderful people.

Once the house was dark and quiet, Libby crept to Dawn's room and peeked inside. The girls were asleep, one dark head facing the window and one blond head facing the door. The dog was curled up between them, and when Libby took a step into the room, he growled at her.

"Blasted mutt," she murmured. She'd tried feeding the monster, and he took her treats, all right, but continued to growl while he gobbled them up.

She quietly closed the door and tiptoed past the Bellamy brothers' room, relieved to hear them snoring soundly. Pulling in a breath, she took the stairs to the third floor and rapped gently on Jackson's door.

He opened it and stood silhouetted in the lamplight. "Why, Mrs. O'Malley," he taunted, feigning surprise, "I'm delighted that you'd seek me out in my bedroom."

"Don't be foolish." She pushed at his chest to gain entrance, startled when she discovered he wore no shirt.

She tried to pull her hand away, but he trapped it against his warm flesh. The hair tickled her palm, sending goose bumps over her skin.

"You've wanted to catch me naked again for weeks, haven't you?"

He refused to release her hand, and the teasing laughter she heard in his voice annoyed her because she liked it. "You are nothing but an arrogant ass."

"Come on," he teased, taking both of her hands and rubbing them over his chest. "Wanna see my tattoo?"

She forcibly freed herself, stepping away to put much needed space between them. "Not if it means removing your pants." As nervous as she was, she couldn't resist a smile.

He returned a grin. "It's inevitable, Libby. You'll see it sooner or later."

And wouldn't that be a sight, she thought, continuing to gaze at his chest but envisioning his long, muscular legs.

Her smile slid away. "I've . . . um . . . come to a decision."

His entire demeanor changed and he appeared to grow tense. "I see." To her disappointment, he shrugged into his shirt, his gaze probing. Intense. "I'm not sure I like the way this sounds."

She swallowed hard, and clasped her hands in front of her, wondering if she'd made the right decision, despite the fact that there ultimately was no other choice. "I will marry you, but . . ."

"But?"

She feigned an aloofness she would never feel when around him. "But you will not share my bed."

He expelled a long sigh and slowly paced in front of the bed. "I see."

Oh, he did *not* see! But she couldn't very well tell him that if she slept with him again, she would surely fall in love.

"So this is to be another platonic marriage for you. Is that really the way you want it, Libby?"

She wanted to shout that it wasn't what she wanted at all,

but what she wanted he wasn't able to give her. She lifted her chin. "Yes."

He stepped close. Her body reacted to the intensity of their attraction, but she kept herself indifferent. At least on the outside.

"What if you're already pregnant?"

Her head shot up, but she quickly glanced away, because she saw danger in his expression. Her pulse galloped; her blood raced. "I . . . I couldn't be. It's too soon."

"You could be. Would that change your feelings for me?"

She opened her mouth, then closed it. How could she respond to such a question? The thought of having his child caused an unbearable ache in her heart, for what woman wouldn't want a child by a man like him?

"Your past history with babies doesn't give me a lot of confidence," she was able to say.

"Ah, dammit, I've promised you that won't happen again. Why can't you believe me?"

She forced herself to study the shadows that the lamp made against the wall. "I don't know you well enough to believe you."

He dragged his fingers through his hair and spat a mild curse. "You can't deny the attraction between us."

Rubbing her arms with her hands, she paced to the dry sink and straightened his towels. "I won't acknowledge it."

"The hell you won't. Your response on the grass, when we were locked in each other's arms and having wild, erotic sex tells me different. It tells me you want me as badly as I want you."

Although she remembered it vividly, she pretended disdain. "Don't be crude."

He cursed again. "Crude? You think that's crude? No, Libby O'Malley, crude would be to tell you that right now I could touch that place between your warm, soft thighs, that place that I know is covered with cottony brown curls, and find it wet, swollen, and hungry."

"Stop it, Jackson." Crude though his words were, they elicited a feeling of excitement within her.

"Crude would be to whisper in your ear that I could flip your dress over your head and bury my face against that place and make love to you with my tongue."

The idea aroused her, which angered her. "Stop it!"

"I could even use a vulgarism for that soft, warm part of you, to prove what crudeness truly is, but I have more respect for you than to say the word even in jest."

Heat raced to her scalp, sinking into the roots of her hair. "Be that as it may," she answered, attempting to keep her facade intact, "we will not share a bed. If I am pregnant, which I sincerely doubt, we will deal with it when and if it becomes necessary."

He studied her for a long, quiet moment, then went to the door and jerked it open. "If that's what you want, then fine. I won't try to bed you. Just remember," he warned, "if you ever change your mind, you'll have to tell me, because I damned well won't force myself on you."

Before she stepped into the hallway, she asked, "When do you want to do this?"

He shrugged, appearing to have lost interest. "It's up to you. Isn't the bride supposed to make the arrangements?"

"Fine," she answered, moving into the hallway. "I'll see what I can do."

He closed the door, and Libby felt a heavy sense of sadness and regret. This wasn't what she wanted. But she could live with it. It would be hard enough to keep from falling in love with him without letting him know how much control he had over her body. Once he had power over her mind as well, she would be lost.

Jackson stepped to the window and stared out into the moonlit night. He didn't understand her. There was fire between them; she couldn't very well deny that, when the flames had nearly consumed them both.

It would be different if she were a frigid, cold woman, but one look at her and he'd known she wasn't. And one touch had confirmed it.

All right, so he couldn't promise to love her. He wished he could. She'd already had one less than satisfying marriage;

he understood her reluctance to have another. He had . . . very strong feelings for her. And they were compatible. They had chemistry. He could make her laugh, and when her defenses were down, she was damned desirable.

He wondered if she was punishing him for disrupting her life. For having the law on his side and taking Dawn Twilight away from her. For having a family with so much love to share that they'd taken his daughter in and made her feel that love immediately.

With a curse, he turned away from the window, picked up his boots, and pulled them on. There was no way he could sleep. Not tonight. Not after this.

He left his room, quietly feeling his way down the stairs in the darkness. As he reached the first-floor landing, he noticed a low light moving toward him, Libby carrying it.

She wore a shiny robe that cinched in her waist and accentuated her round hips. The moment their gazes met, his dropped to her breasts, which were pressed against the lapels that folded over them. The shadowy lamplight played upon her bosom, and her succulent nipples hardened before his eyes. He knew that her refusal to be intimate had nothing to do with her reaction to him.

He touched her breast, eliciting a gasp from her, but she didn't move away. His thumb moved over her turgid nipple, and he felt her quiver beneath his touch.

"Whatever has provoked you to insist on a chaste marriage is going to be the death of you, Liberty O'Malley."

Fear and distrust swam behind the desire in her eyes. "Oh, don't worry," he promised. "I'll honor your request, but you didn't ask that I not touch you."

"Don't . . . don't touch me." Her voice was a shaky whisper.

His hands roamed her hips, then her sweet, savory fanny. With one hand he stroked her low on her belly, feeling the curls beneath the fabric of her robe.

She shuddered beneath his touch.

He bent and kissed her, using his tongue to gain entrance into her mouth. When she began to weaken and answer his kiss, he lifted his head and smiled down at her.

"Too late."

Anger and embarrassment glinted in her eyes, but she said nothing.

"By the way," he began, almost hating to change the subject. "I'm leaving in the morning. I'll ride as far as Eureka with my parents."

She swiftly met his gaze. "You're leaving?"

He gave her a half smile. "Will you miss me?"

The hollow at her throat pulsed visibly. "Of course not. I simply wasn't aware that you were going with them."

If her body hadn't visibly responded to him, he might have believed her. "I have some business to attend to." He hoped to discover that Ethan Frost continuously dropped money at a monthly poker game. It was a long shot, but he had nothing to lose. And with his father's connections in state government, he might also learn the route of the railroad. If he was lucky, he'd learn that it was coming straight through to Thief River.

17

WITH HIS BINOCULARS SLUNG OVER HIS SHOULDER, COREY guided Chloe Ann through the woods to his favorite spot, a fallen log behind a common manzanita. The shrub was green, for it was too early in the autumn for the teardrop flower buds to form.

Chloe Ann smelled like lilacs again. What need did he have for flowering shrubs when she was near? He forced himself to concentrate on his task, although he wanted to kiss her.

"What are we looking for?"

Her whisper was so sweet, it almost brought him to his knees. He stood behind her, his gaze finding the soft swell of her bosom beneath the neckline of her gown.

Bending to her ear, he answered, *"Passerina ciris."* If he didn't drag his eyes from her, he'd miss the purpose of the trip, although getting Chloe Ann off by herself was also part of his plan.

He noted that the pulse at her neck throbbed.

"That's the . . . the Latin name for the painted bunting, isn't it?" She turned and gazed up at him, a nervous excitement emanating from her.

He swallowed hard. She was such perfection. "You're familiar with it?"

Her eyelashes fluttered prettily. "I've never seen one up close. Only in books."

He almost smiled. He'd been studying her since the day he first saw her, and knew that her nearsightedness prevented her from seeing much of anything unless it was near her dainty nose.

He'd stood in the back of the schoolroom and watched her squint at the students, observed how she got right up to the blackboard and wrote, so close he was surprised her nose didn't get in the way. He doubted that she'd ever seen the beauty of the distant mountains or of an eagle in flight.

Saying a quick prayer, he reached into his pocket and drew out the slender box.

"Here, these are for you."

She gasped. "Oh, you shouldn't have—"

"Please," he interrupted. "I want you to have them. I only hope you won't be offended."

Aware of her puzzled expression, he sat on the log beside her and watched her open the box. A flush stained her cheeks when she saw the eyeglasses inside.

"Oh. Oh, dear!" she wailed softly.

Corey grasped her hands. "Come, now, I didn't mean to distress or embarrass you."

She drew a deep breath. "I hadn't known I was so transparent."

"Maybe only to me," he answered.

Another sigh. "I've been meaning to get a pair, really I have, but—"

"Now you have them." He took them from the case and put them on her, wrapping the curled ends of the stems behind her ears. She looked delectable. The eyeglasses didn't detract from her beautiful eyes.

"I must look atrocious!" she wailed again, trying to pull away.

Corey merely smiled. "Now you finally look old enough to teach that bunch of rascals. I swear there were times when I glanced into the schoolroom and wondered if you weren't one of the students."

She bit her lower lip and gave him a shy smile. "You're just trying to make me feel better."

"No, I'm trying to help you see better." Their gazes remained locked. At last he took her face in his hands and brought his mouth close to hers.

"This," he suggested, "will make you feel better." With that, he kissed her, drawing her sweet nectar into his mouth, feeling exhilarated when she rested her arms on his shoulders. He deepened the kiss, but held back for fear his desire might frighten her.

Drawing away, she gave him a languid smile. "Oh, my." She gazed into the trees, her expression changing to one of surprise. "Oh, my! Look at that!"

Corey followed her gaze. He saw nothing but the toothed leaves of the white alder.

"Why, I had no idea a person could see the leaves that far away." She rose quickly and spun in a circle, clasping her hands to her mouth. "Look!" She pointed to the distance. "I can see the mountains. Oh, Corey, I can see the mountains!"

Her joy was intoxicating. Heady. "Then you're not angry with me?"

She turned to him, the round wire frames perched on her nose. "I guess my vanity got in the way of my good sense." She touched the spectacles gently with her fingers. "You're sure I don't look . . . odd? Like . . . like a spinsterish schoolmarm?"

He kissed her again, letting the kiss display his feelings. When he finally lifted his head, he asked, "Does that answer your question?"

She drew in a sharp sigh. "Corey, behind you," she whispered.

He turned and found a painted bunting perched on one of the alder branches.

"It's so beautiful." Her voice was hushed, partly because she didn't want to frighten the bird away and, Corey guessed, partly from wonder.

He had to agree. The male painted bunting truly appeared to have been painted, with its purple head, yellow and green back, and red rump and underparts. With its silver beak, and the red that rimmed its eyes, it was like something created from a painter's palette.

He whistled, mimicking the clear warbling notes for which the bird was noted. It cocked its pretty head, then answered the sound.

Corey lifted his binoculars from around his neck. "Here," he said, handing them to her.

She raised them to her eyes, peering through the magnifying lenses at the bird, and expelled a rapturous sigh. "Why, it's as if it were right here, perched on the end of my nose."

She flung her arms around Corey's neck and kissed him. "Oh, thank you. Thank you for the eyeglasses."

They stared into each other's eyes. Suddenly Chloe Ann blushed and laughed.

"Tell me," he ordered, his voice gentle.

Her blush deepened. "I just remembered something Mahalia said to me the other day when I told her you'd asked me to go birding."

"Mahalia, huh? I can just about imagine." Her smile was so damned exquisite. "Did she warn you not to be alone in the woods with me?"

Her shy smile spread. "Not quite so eloquently, but she said something like that."

"And you came anyway?"

She met his gaze squarely. "Yes."

His heart soared. "Miss Parker, would you do me the honor of accompanying me to my brother's wedding?"

Her smile turned sad. "I'm afraid I can't."

"Why not?" Disappointment washed through him in waves.

"I'm to play the organ at the ceremony." She tucked her arm through his. "But I'll be happy to be at your side afterward."

He tugged her closer, feeling light, buoyant, free. He was falling in love, and he didn't care who knew it.

* * *

Libby hauled the box out of the attic and carried it to her room. She cringed as she lifted out the gown, which had been buried among countless other treasures since before Sean's fatal accident with his mount.

He'd bought it for her, and it had been a thoughtful gesture. Also incredibly expensive, if she were to judge by the fabric and the workmanship. The trouble was—

"Gawd Almighty!" Mahalia exclaimed from the doorway. "That's the ugliest gown I've seen in a powerful long time. Looks like it belonged to a whore."

"I know," Libby said on a sigh. "It *is* ugly, but surely we can do something with it." She held it up, fingering the magnolia satin with the rosy tints. "The fabric is priceless." She flicked at the frippery that had been stitched onto the gown. "The problem is the geegaws."

Mahalia clucked her tongue. "How old is this, anyway? It has a bustle."

"Sean bought it for me after we were married. I never wore it. It just didn't seem like me." She uttered a mirthless laugh. "It still doesn't."

Grabbing the gown, Mahalia examined it. "You're right. The fabric is mighty expensive."

"Can we do something with it?"

"When's the weddin', again?"

Libby swallowed her apprehension. "In two weeks."

Mahalia tossed the gown onto the bed, then bent over it. "Well, I'd best get started. Now, these have to go," she announced, tugging at the clusters of various colored roses that were sewn on the bodice, at the waist, and around the hem. "They look like they've been killed by a good frost.

"And this shouldn't be here," she said, ripping out the stitching around the lace panel at the bottom.

Libby bit back a cry when the lace was torn from the hem. "Mahalia, I can make the dress over. You have enough to do."

"Like hell," the housekeeper mumbled. "You'll prob'ly end up lookin' like you're goin' to a funeral rather than your own weddin'."

"Well," Libby answered hesitantly, "don't get carried away."

Mahalia snuffled. "Somebody ought to. I don't know what happened between the two of you, but suddenly you look like you're gonna be hanged by a rope and left to twist in the wind. And he's no better, grouchin' and growlin' around like a bear with a thorn up his butt."

She grabbed the gown and marched to the door, her weight causing the bottles on Libby's dressing table to shake and tinkle. "You might pretend to be happy, even if it's an act. Dawn ain't no dummy, you know. She can sense when things ain't right, and believe me, honey, things ain't right."

Libby sank to the bed and stared at the door long after Mahalia had gone. No, things weren't right, and to Jackson's mind, it was her fault. It was her stubborn pride, she knew that. She would be more than willing to share his bed if she knew for certain that he would never leave them, and that he might come to care for her.

Vern Roberts's wife, Jennie, led Jackson into the parlor where Vern sat, his bad leg once again resting on a pillow.

Jackson shook his head and smiled. "You keep sitting around, and you'll get fat and lazy."

Vern spat a curse. "If I don't get some relief pretty soon, I'm gonna tell the doc to cut the damned thing off." He peered around Jackson toward the door.

"Do you see the wife?"

Jackson glanced into the hallway, noting that Jennie Roberts was in the kitchen. "She's busy."

Expelling a noisy sigh, Vern reached behind a pillow and pulled out his flask. "Gotta have a drink now and then when she ain't around." He took a swig, then wiped his mouth with his sleeve. "If she finds this, she'll pour it out.

"Have a seat," he offered, swinging his arm toward the chair opposite him before hiding the flask again. "What's on your mind?"

Jackson settled into the chair. "I'm taking a trip to Eureka. Can you cover for a few days?"

"Eureka, huh? What do you expect to find way up there?"

Jackson tried for a casual grin. "I'll let you know when I find it. Meanwhile, what do you remember about the vigilantes?"

"Hmm." Vern scratched his stubble. "There ain't been any activity for years."

"Did you ever discover who any of them were?"

"Yeah, one. But he died, oh, 'bout six years back. Name was Clyde Worth."

Jackson cocked his head. "Any relation to Axel?"

Vern nodded. "Axel's pa."

Interesting. "And you weren't able to find out who worked with him?"

Vern toyed with the end of his mustache. "Well, I knew who he run with, if that's what you mean, but I couldn't prove any of 'em were involved in the troubles."

"Who were some of his pals?"

Vern appeared to study the question. "Ethan Frost, for one. I always thought that a little strange, 'cause Ethan's a good bit younger than Clyde was. It was even suggested that Ethan was the ringleader of the trio, but I never found any proof, and the burnings and killings stopped after they destroyed that village where your squaw's family lived."

Jackson bristled. "She was my wife, Vern."

"Sorry, meant no disrespect, son."

Mollified, Jackson asked, "Why do you suppose they stopped?"

"Aw, the times were changing. Oh, there was killing here and there, but you know as well as I that most of the vigilante groups were formed years back, when California was first being settled. I think they was afraid of getting caught, is all."

Jackson rubbed his hands over his face. Could Ethan Frost have been a vigilante? He didn't know why not. Of course, uncovering that bit of information had to be secondary to stopping the slaughter of the sheep. Once that was done, he would concentrate on Frost's possible involvement in the destruction of Flicker Feather's village . . . and her death.

"I think Ethan Frost embezzled Dawn's trust fund."

Vern scratched his chin. "You don't say."

"I don't have proof yet, but as soon as I do . . ." He shook his head and sighed. "Things are coming to a head, Vern. It won't be long before all hell breaks loose."

Vern slapped his good knee. "I have a feeling you'll do fine, Jackson. I have faith in you."

Jackson wished he had as much faith as Vern. "Frost holds all the loans and mortgages on the ranches around here."

"Nothing unusual about that. He's the only banker for miles."

"Have you never given a thought to his possible implication in the sheep killings?"

Vern heaved a sigh. "It's been on my mind. I just ain't had the energy to do anything about it."

"Then you won't be offended if I do?"

"Hell, no. Be my guest. By the way," he added, his mood lifting, "congratulations on your upcoming marriage."

Jackson's gut twisted. "Thanks."

Vern gave him a quizzical look. "You don't sound too enthusiastic. I hear it was your idea in the first place."

"Of course it was my idea. How else would my daughter come with me willingly?"

"Aw, treat Libby right and she'll come around. You know, your folks are mighty happy about all this."

Jackson knew it. This entire arrangement was perfect for everyone involved—except the bride and groom. And he'd done everything possible to assure Libby that her fears were unfounded. He would never leave again. But once she understood that, would it be enough for her?

Jackson bade Vern good-bye and stepped outside. The deputy stood on the stoop, appearing a little embarrassed.

"Axel," Jackson said with a nod. "You looking for me?"

Axel Worth stepped nervously from one foot to the other. "Um . . . yeah. You weren't at the jail, so I thought you might be here."

Jackson stepped off the porch and unhitched his mount. "Is something wrong?"

"Well, um . . . we just got a load of mail. Thought you should know."

Jackson frowned as he swung himself into the saddle. Why would his deputy seek him out just to tell him about the mail? He glanced around, looking for Axel's horse. "Did you walk over?"

Axel reddened. "My . . . um . . . horse is around back."

"I see." He really didn't. His deputy had always been a nervous kid, but today he was more skittish than usual.

Perhaps he should have told Vern about the possibility of Thief River getting a railroad. Unfortunately, he'd learned that Vern was as gossipy as an old woman. It wasn't wise to tell him something that might have no truth to it at all.

18

Sitting at a back table in a Eureka bar, Jackson sipped gut-ripping black coffee while his father nursed a beer. Their trip had been enlightening.

"So," Nathan began, "right here in this very bar, your banker, Mr. Frost, has lost nearly a quarter of a million dollars."

And Jackson had learned the names of the other regulars in the game. He'd memorized them: Barny Wilson, a local merchant; Howard Spellman, a rancher; Cleb Hartman, a farmer down near Thief River; and Joseph Kincaid, the local newspaperman.

Nathan swore and shook his head. "I can't imagine anyone dropping that kind of money. Hell, might just as well toss it down a shithouse hole."

Jackson's smile was dry. He'd known a couple of mercenaries over the years who'd had a similar problem. Unable to get their gambling hunger under control, they had found themselves constantly broke, always sniffing around for another way to make money, merely to lose it again. One of them had told him it was the possibility of winning big that egged him on. There was always that chance, he'd said. Jackson never understood the lure.

"Well, even though I still don't have proof, I can guess that's where all my money went," Jackson answered, resigned. "It isn't hard to figure that if Frost somehow discovered there was to be a railroad built through some pastureland, it would give him the opportunity to cash in."

"Yeah," Nathan answered with a harsh laugh. "And turn around, only to lose it all again."

Jackson feared that he would never see his daughter's money again. "I've somehow got to prove that Frost took it. That won't be easy."

"You can do it," his father said. "Now, however, I think you'd better hightail it home. In a few days you'll be a married man."

Nervousness ate at Jackson's insides. "You sure you can leave the ranch again so soon? You know I want you there, but—"

"We wouldn't miss your wedding for the world. Anyway," his father added, a sly smile spreading across his face, "your mother would never forgive me if she couldn't be there."

Jackson wished he felt the same enthusiasm. He knew Libby didn't. Maybe things would change once they were married. He could only hope.

The first rain of the season spattered the windows as Libby studied her reflection in the mirror. How fitting that it should rain on her wedding day. She lifted an eyebrow, seeing the irony in it. Catching Mahalia's gaze of approval as it wandered over her gown, she said, "You did a wonderful job on my dress, Mahalia."

Mahalia stood behind her, her arms crossed over her ample chest. "I did, didn't I? It just needs a few more little tucks, and it'll be done."

Libby smoothed her palms over the magnolia silk. Gone were the geegaws, the roses, the frippery, and the bustle. The gown fit with sheathlike closeness. The lace Mahalia had so callously ripped from the hem was now stitched to the puffed sleeves, creating snug bands that came to a V just below her wrists. Another piece made a high collar. The bustle had been transformed into a graceful train.

Though modest with its high neckline and long sleeves, the gown was provocative and breathtaking.

"It's lovely, Mahalia. Thank you." Too lovely to waste on a day she'd come to dread, she decided.

But it was too late for regrets. Jackson's family had returned the night before. Libby's dress was done, the flowers were arranged, the guests had begun to arrive, and there was enough food for an army.

On a wistful sigh, Libby carefully removed the gown and threw on a wrapper, then sat at the dressing table to fix her hair.

"I'm gonna take the dress downstairs and finish it up. I also gotta see to it that the eats is ready for the reception. Chloe Ann and Corey's mama are helpin' me with that." Mahalia chuckled. "Them two is gettin' along real good."

On a smile, Libby responded, "Chloe Ann and Corey have become quite a couple, haven't they?"

Mahalia made a sound in her throat. "Yes, indeed. And unlike you and Mistah Wolfe, them two is like lovebirds. A body would think it was them that was gettin' married instead of you two."

Their affection for each other was evident to everyone. In some ways, Libby envied them. To fall in love without the anguish she was going through would certainly make life a lot simpler.

"They have no obstacles between them, Mahalia, and they're very much in love."

"I think Mistah Wolfe's feelin's for you go deeper than you think, honey."

Oh, that it were true, Libby thought, swallowing a sigh. "What makes you say that?"

"I see him watchin' you. When you come into a room, his eyes follow you like they was magnetized."

A flutter of hope. "Really? I hadn't noticed." Which was a lie, if she thought about it. Each time they saw each other, she felt something and sensed he felt it, too. Hah! It was probably their mutual animosity. After she'd informed him they wouldn't share a bed, he'd made it quite clear that he wouldn't try to change her mind.

"I can't believe you ain't noticed, honey."

"Mahalia, you don't know the half of it. Just . . . leave it alone."

Mahalia expelled a long, noisy sigh on her way to the door. "If you say so. I just don't understand you white folk. Always mincin' around, never sayin' what you mean, expectin' everyone to read your minds. Lordy, I don't know how y'all get anythin' done, much less get together long enough to have yourselves babies."

Libby's stomach fluttered at the mention of babies. She'd often thought about his comment regarding the possibility of her being pregnant, but she hadn't allowed herself to dwell on it. She was too uncertain of her feelings.

"If you see Dawn, send her in, will you?"

"I guess I can do that," Mahalia answered as she disappeared into the hallway.

Libby was brushing her hair when her daughter sprinted into the room, already dressed for the ceremony. She stopped at the dressing table, her expression rapt.

"Oh, Mama, I saw the dress, and you're going to be so beautiful."

"Thank you, dear." Beautiful was not how she felt, however. "As soon as I fix my hair, you can have a seat and I'll fix yours." She glanced at Dawn's thick braids. "We should do something special with it today."

Dawn began unbraiding her hair. "With combs, maybe?"

"I should think so. And I'll make a special coronet out of my miniature chrysanthemums."

Libby studied her daughter in the mirror. She'd made her frock from delicate pink dotted swiss. The dress was the first grown-up gown Dawn had ever owned, although the puffy sleeves and ruffles added a youthful touch.

Libby swallowed a wistful sigh. Her little girl was growing up. Her hips had begun to fill out and her waist was tiny. When had this happened?

Dawn watched as Libby brushed her hair.

"Mama?"

Libby met her daughter's gaze. "Yes?"

"When will I get to go visit Grandmama and Grandpapa?"

The invasion had begun, Libby realized, tugging wisps of hair from Dawn's temples, letting them flutter about her face. From the beginning she'd felt coerced, and this was why. It wasn't reasonable to feel so jealous. It would be different if the Wolfes were selfish and uncaring people.

"I thought your father would have that all arranged." The words came out sounding petty, though she hadn't meant them to. Had she?

"He said I had to ask you."

That was some consolation. "Well, maybe Chloe Ann can help you get ahead in your schoolwork."

"That's what I thought," Dawn agreed. "Miss Chloe Ann said it would be all right, as long as I was caught up before I left."

Libby stopped a smile. "It seems you have it all figured out."

"Papa said the two of you could take me up there, next week, maybe."

Libby experienced an odd sensation in her stomach. "Oh, I don't think I could leave the rooming house unattended, dear."

"But Mahalia will be here, and Uncle Corey has offered to stay and help."

Feeling cornered and frantic, Libby said, "How can your father leave the jail?"

"Mr. Roberts said he could come in and give the deputy a hand for a few days. Oh, Mama, please say yes!"

So Jackson had made certain there were no loopholes for her to wiggle through. "Why can't your father take you there?"

"Because I want it to be the first thing we do as a family."

Libby wound Dawn's hair into a chignon, fastened it, then added a circle of pink mums. She tried to quell her panic. As reluctant as she'd been to marry the man, she hadn't foreseen any of the stumbling blocks outside of Jackson himself. But as Dawn prattled on, she realized that her daughter expected far more of this union than she had even been willing to think about.

Her gaze went to the window; the storm hadn't let up. Of all days for it to rain. She hated to think it was an omen, but the thought occurred to her anyway. Fortunately, she'd decided to have the ceremony in the large downstairs parlor. There would be no trudging through the mud to the church.

She finished Dawn's hair. "There. You look absolutely gorgeous."

Dawn stood and preened at her reflection. "Do you want me to get your dress?"

Libby's stomach clenched. This was it. No reprieves. Unless Jackson decided to fly the coop, he would become her husband. "That would be lovely, dear."

Dawn gave her a hug. "Oh, I'm so happy, Mama, this is the happiest day of my life. I'm going to write a story about it. But first I'm going to write in my journal."

"That was a thoughtful gift from your uncle, wasn't it?"

"I don't know how I got along without one." Dawn walked from the room, leaving Libby to question her sanity in going through with the charade.

She went to the window and watched the lacy filaments of the weeping willow tree sway in the wind. She and Jackson hadn't talked about what would happen after this day. In fact, in the two weeks since she'd told him of her decision, they'd hardly spoken at all. It had been easier to avoid him than to be around him. Avoidance wasn't entirely possible, of course, since he still took his meals at her table and slept under her roof.

More than once she'd found herself staring at the ceiling at midnight, wondering if he was asleep. Of course, even though they would be married, that part of their relationship wouldn't change. No doubt she would still stare at the ceiling at midnight, wondering if he was sleeping.

Hearing a commotion downstairs, she left the window, tying her wrapper snugly around her. She hurried from her bedroom and raced down the stairs. Mahalia didn't need any extra stress today.

She cringed. Bert and Burl stood at the kitchen door, guffawing so hard Libby feared one of them would choke.

"You worthless old fools," Mahalia shrieked. "Help the girl catch them damned animals!"

Libby elbowed her way past the brothers just as Cyclops tore by, skidding on the polished floor.

"Lookit her skid!" Bert roared, slapping his knee.

Close in pursuit was a wet, dirty, muddy, stringy-looking Mumser.

Dawn squeezed past the men and raced from the room, her face pinched with panic. "Oh, Mama, I'm so sorry." She ran after the animals, calling and scolding, in a frantic attempt to catch them.

Libby stared at Bert and Burl. "Don't you have something better to do?"

The old coots wiped their eyes, attempting to muffle their laughter. "Sorry, Miz Liberty, but them animals is the best entertainment we've ever had 'round here."

Libby gave them a scathing look, then stepped cautiously into the kitchen. Mahalia hadn't stopped wailing. With a sinking feeling in her chest, Libby finally understood why.

Mahalia was on her hands and knees, bent over Libby's wedding gown. She looked up, her face filled with anguished fury. "It's them damned animals," she wailed. "Look what they done to your dress! Just look!" On the perfect train that Mahalia had attached to the gown were smudged, muddy paw prints.

For some reason, seeing Mahalia in such distress made Libby calm. "Don't worry," she said, trying to pull Mahalia to her feet.

"Don't worry? How can I not worry? Them damned animals has ruined everythin'!"

Libby lifted the dress onto the table and studied the muddy stains. "Did you throw away the roses?"

Mahalia huffed a weary sigh. "I shoulda. They was miserable lookin'. But they're in my room, in a box on the sewin' table."

Libby retrieved them, fluffed them up to revive them, then returned with needle and thread. "We'll simply hide the stains." She wiped off the paw prints as best she could, then arranged the roses to cover them. "Actually, the extra weight will make the train flow better, don't you think?" She glanced at Mahalia's harried appearance. "You'd better get dressed. I'll finish this."

Mahalia clucked as she waddled to her room. "How you can be so calm is beyond me, honey."

Libby drew in a shaky sigh. "It's beyond me, too," she whispered to herself.

"What's going on in here?"

His rumbling baritone startled her. "Oh, it's . . . it's nothing. The animals tracked over my gown, that's all."

Jackson stood at her shoulder, his nearness causing a quickening in her stomach.

"Looks like quite a mess."

Taking a deep breath, she briefly closed her eyes and pulled in his scent. As always, it made her heady, like a glass of wine. "It will be all right."

"You!"

Mahalia stood in the doorway, fists on ample hips. "You," she ordered, pointing a thick finger at Jackson, "get out of here. Go on, now. You ain't supposed to see the bride before the ceremony."

"Yes, ma'am."

He sounded contrite, but Libby knew that if she looked at him, she would see a twinkle in his eye. He squeezed her shoulder, then left the room.

Mahalia clucked. "Don't you two know nothin'? It's bad luck for the groom to see the bride on her weddin' day."

"Oh, fine," Libby murmured, as Mahalia marched back into her room. "That's all I needed to hear."

As Libby watched from the doorway, Dawn walked the short distance to the fireplace, where pots of mums graced the floor. Her gaze moved to Jackson, who beamed at his daughter. He winked, and Libby could imagine Dawn's expression, for the look on his face caused her own heart to flutter.

His earthy maleness left her weak. Suddenly, with painful

clarity, she realized that she wanted to see that face every day, into eternity. And if she wasn't given that glorious privilege, she would live the rest of her life as only half the person she could be. The realization was so shocking to her, and so painful, she feared she might stumble.

As Libby started toward him, she felt his gaze. Her heartbeat accelerated. She could hear the vows in her head. "For richer, for poorer, in sickness and in health"—those words were fine. It was "for better, for worse" that stuck in her mind, for her feelings were at war within her. He might stay and never love her. He might leave. Which was better, and which was worse?

Jackson took her arm and led her to the preacher, his touch almost possessive. She slanted him a glance, wondering if he thought she might bolt.

He gave her a lazy smile, as if reading her mind. A quickening in her stomach told her that quite possibly, if she was lucky and he learned to love her, that smile would thrill her for the rest of her life.

He glanced at her train, resplendent with fake roses. Leaning close to her ear, he whispered, "Nice save."

Libby couldn't help but smile. Perhaps things wouldn't be as bad as she'd thought.

But after exchanging the vows that Libby had dreaded, Jackson bent to kiss her. If she'd been the dreamer she sometimes wanted to be, the touch of his mouth against hers would have given her hope. A promise of more to come. But she'd already told him there would be nothing between them. Somewhere inside, a little voice told her she'd be sorry, but practical woman that she was, she quite successfully suppressed it. At least she hoped she had. For now, anyway.

Dawn stood between them, her arms looped through theirs as they turned toward the small group of wedding guests.

"Ladies and gentlemen," the preacher announced, smiling broadly, "I present Mr. and Mrs. Jackson Wolfe and their daughter, Dawn Twilight."

The knot of dread in Libby's stomach refused to loosen,

and as the reception got under way, regret surfaced anew. Jackson's family, the bane of her new existence, pressed in around her, hugging her, kissing her, and making her foolishly want what she feared she'd never have.

Ethan Frost stepped into the jail. Axel Worth was in the chair, leaning against the wall, his feet on the desk.

Funny, Ethan thought, the kid was nothing like the father. Clyde Worth had been a trusted, albeit sometimes reluctant accomplice in the days of Ethan's vigilante raids. Although far older than Ethan, he'd taken orders without question. He'd been calm and efficient, unlike the kid, who was nervous as a squirrel and not particularly dependable. Ethan would never have taken him into his confidence if Axel hadn't discovered what his father and Ethan had been up to all those years ago.

He strolled to the desk and took a seat across from the kid.

"Been to the wedding?" There was sarcasm in Axel's voice. "Bet you never thought she'd be marrying anyone but you."

Ignoring the jab, Ethan poured himself a drink. "Is Mateo ready to buckle, or do we have another go at him?"

"Most of his sheep are gone, destroyed before shearing, which means he has nothing left but a few stragglers that got away from us. He basically ain't got the money to pay his overdue feed bills, much less his mortgage."

"What about Bilboa?"

"Cleb's setting another raid on him, but it might take a few days. Bilboa has over a hundred sheep hidden away in a lonely corner near the Nevada state line. He thinks we don't know about them."

Ethan digested this, then asked, "What's Wolfe up to?"

Axel displayed an evil grin. "You mean your lady friend's new husband?"

Ethan held his temper. The wedding had come as a surprise, that was for damned sure. True, he hadn't seen much of Libby lately, but he sure as hell hadn't expected her to get married. Oddly, she hadn't been as receptive to him as he'd have liked. When he heard she was marrying Wolfe, he assumed it was because of the breed. Women were like that sometimes, marrying for the damnedest reasons. Why she should care so much for the girl was beyond him. After all, she wasn't even of Libby's own blood.

He was a little discontented having sensed a few months before that she'd begun to see through his reasons for wanting to remarry. His boys were running wild, and he had no idea how to rein them in. He loved them, but he didn't know how to discipline them. And truth to tell, he wasn't disappointed in Libby's marriage to someone else, because he didn't want that breed in the package anyway.

Still, he'd hoped to get under Libby's skirts. More than once he'd awakened from sleep hard as a bull after dreaming of being between her thighs. Now he'd have to set his sights elsewhere. Maybe someone who wasn't quite as quick as Libby O'Malley. Someone a little less likely to question his motives. God, but he hated living alone. And he'd invested too much time in Libby, ignoring other possibilities. He wasn't a monster. He admired most women and loved most children. He was handsome, he knew that. Women usually gazed at him with admiration. Surely he could find a suitable one.

Then again, maybe Libby would tire of Wolfe's brutish ways and come to regret not having taken Ethan up on his numerous offers of marriage. He frowned. He'd still have to deal with the breed, though. As often as he'd tried to be pleasant to her, she'd never smiled at him. Never had bought into his facade. Too damned clever, for a breed.

"Surely Wolfe has learned something, with all his snooping around," Ethan said in reply to Axel's question. His latest meeting with the man had been disconcerting at best. Wolfe didn't believe his claim of innocence regarding the trust fund. But the man couldn't prove a thing. Fortunately, Ethan had destroyed all of the records. He was concerned about Wolfe, though. He knew Ethan held the paper on the ranches. Maybe he and his accomplices should lie low for a while. . . .

"Yeah. Vern Roberts's jaw flaps like an old woman's. He's

got too much time on his hands." Axel polished his gun with the tail of his shirt.

Ethan downed the liquor in his glass and poured himself another. "About what?"

Axel lifted his feet off the desk and settled into the chair. "Oh, something about the vigilantes who burned down the Indian villages some years back."

Ethan went cold. He'd be forever sorry young Worth had learned about his alliance with his father. "What about them?"

"Seems the sheriff told Wolfe about your friendship with my pa." He gave Ethan a sly look. "He also told him my pa was the only vigilante they'd ever been able to identify, but he suspected you."

Maintaining control, Ethan asked, "How do know this?"

Worth shrugged. "I was waiting outside at Vern's house to give the sheriff a message. Just happened to overhear is all."

Angry and frustrated, Ethan clenched his jaw. Old Vern Roberts had been an easy lawman to evade—too old to give chase and too weary to care—but Wolfe was another story. If he decided to stay on, Ethan would have to play a different game. A very different game, indeed.

Ethan downed another shot of whiskey, wishing he could enjoy the bite, but his stomach clenched and began to burn. He should have known better. Straight whiskey would kill him.

He was so close to his goal. It was only a matter of time before both Bilboa and Mateo capitulated. Jackson Wolfe put a giant crimp in his plans. Something would have to be done about the newcomer.

19

Dawn trudged up the stairs. "It's going to be hard to sleep without Katie in my bed. Why couldn't they have stayed until morning?"

Libby heard the stifled yawn and smiled. "Your grandparents have animals that need tending, dear. You'll see them soon enough." Libby dreaded the trip.

"I thought someone was looking after their ranch."

"Yes, but it must be very hard to look after two places at once. No doubt their neighbors are eager for them to return. Your grandparents spent a lot of time here before, you know."

"Katie said the neighbors are descendants of African slaves, like Mahalia."

They arrived at Dawn's room, and Libby lit the lamp. "That's what I understand."

Dawn attempted to stifle another yawn. "Is Papa coming to say good night, too?"

Libby raised an eyebrow. "I don't imagine he'd miss it, especially now."

After Dawn had prepared for bed and slid between the

covers, she asked, "When will you and Papa have a honeymoon?"

Honeymoon. Libby hid her distress by fussing with Dawn's bedding. "We're both too busy to take one, dear."

Dawn frowned. "Oh, Mama, I think you should. I really do."

"And why is that?"

"Because—"

Mumser pattered into the room and jumped onto the bed, growling at Libby as he settled into the curve of Dawn's stomach.

Libby had the urge to return the sound. "Ungrateful mutt," she muttered. "Doesn't he know that after that stunt with my wedding dress, I could have his floppy, moppy head on a plate?"

Dawn kissed the dog's topknot, which was tied with a pink ribbon. "He's sorry." She took the pup's face between her hands and touched her nose to his. "Aren't you, Mumser?" The dog licked her face.

Libby wrinkled her nose, unable to understand how anyone could get so close to a dog's mouth. "Not as sorry as he'll be if he doesn't learn some discipline," she warned.

Dawn wrinkled her nose. "I know, I know, but you changed the subject. I really want you and Papa to go on a honeymoon."

"Why?"

Dawn pretended interest in Mumser's fur. "Because I know why you and Papa really got married."

"You do, do you?"

"Sure. It was because of me. Because . . . because I wouldn't be happy living with just one of you. You did it for me."

Libby sat on the bed, ignoring Mumser's growl. "Does that bother you?"

Dawn's smile was blinding. "Not at all. You and Papa aren't getting on very well now, but . . . but I just know that one day you will, and then it will all have been worth it." She reached out and grasped her mother's hand. "Trust me. Everything will turn out fine, Mama. Just fine."

Libby couldn't help but smile. Giving Dawn's fingers a loving squeeze, she answered, "You're the eternal optimist, aren't you?"

"Of course, I—" Her sunny grin returned. "Oh, hello, Papa."

Libby jumped when Jackson's hand touched her shoulder.

"I came in to say good night to my beautiful daughter." He sat on the other side of Dawn.

Libby wryly noted that the dog didn't growl at him.

"We're a real family now, aren't we, Papa?"

He tweaked her nose. "As real as anything."

She snuggled under the covers. "I was asking Mama when you two were going to have a honeymoon."

Heat crept up Libby's neck.

"And what did your mother say?"

Libby didn't like the sly sound in his voice.

Dawn sighed against the pillows. "She said you were both too busy, but I told her I knew the real reason."

"Which is?" There was caution in his tone.

"That you two got married only because of me."

His fingers swept the hair away from her forehead with a tenderness that wasn't lost on Libby.

"That's not such a bad reason," he said. "In fact, it's an excellent one."

Dawn heaved another sigh. "I suppose, but I was kinda hoping . . ." Her glance moved from one to the other. "Well, you know."

Despite Libby's discomfort at the implication, she smiled. Her daughter was such a romantic.

Clearing his throat, Jackson got to his feet. "I think it's time for you to get some sleep, Dawn Twilight."

Good-natured girl that she was, she nodded and curled herself around the dog. "I can't wait until we visit Grandmama and Grandpapa."

"Neither can I," her father answered.

I can, Libby thought as she stood up. "Sleep tight, dear."

"And don't let the bedbugs bite," Jackson added.

Dawn rolled her eyes. "That's what you say to little children, Papa. I'm almost thirteen, remember?"

Jackson turned out the lamp, and Libby followed him into the hallway. She had the urge to sprint away, until she looked at his worried face. "What's wrong?"

He expelled a long, miserable-sounding sigh. "I've missed out on so much of her life."

Feeling benevolent, Libby responded, "That's in the past, Jackson."

"I guess it's a waste of energy to think about it," he agreed. "I can't help but regret all the time I squandered. If I hadn't been such a coward after Flicker Feather's death, if I'd listened to Grandmother, who tried to shame me into staying to care for Dawn Twilight. If I'd at least had the sense to tell my folks about her. But all the ifs in the world won't change things, will they?"

Libby tried to smile, but her expression wavered. "If you'd told your folks about her, we wouldn't be going through this. But worst of all, I would never have been her mother. I can't imagine my life without her, Jackson."

He studied her, his expression softened by the dim hall light. "When *are* we going to take that honeymoon?"

She glanced away from his penetrating gaze. "You know very well there won't be a honeymoon."

"You'd purposely disappoint our daughter?"

She rounded on him. "Unlike my dreamy, romantic daughter, I'm a practical woman. A realist."

"There's another word for what you are," he countered.

She gave him a wry smirk before she walked away. "No doubt you have many words for what you think I am."

"You're hot Spanish nights."

A dangerous jolt raced through her, but she ignored it and started down the stairs.

"You're mulled wine, rich in spices."

She attempted to ignore him, but her body continued to respond.

"You're soft curves and hidden passions."

"And you're crazy," she managed, trying to ignore the

leaping of her pulse. "Why don't you go to bed and leave me alone?"

He followed her into the kitchen. "Is that what you really want?"

She tried to light the lamp, but her hands shook. "It's what I told you before, and it's what I just said, isn't it?"

He placed one of his big, warm hands over hers to steady it. She closed her eyes against the whirling sensation of his callused palm on her skin.

"I just wanted to be sure," he answered, helping her light the lamp.

"You can be very sure I meant what I said." Grateful to have something to do, she placed the leftover pie and bread in the pie safe, then tidied up the counter.

"Fine. I needed to be convinced that you won't get your nose out of joint if I take my pleasure elsewhere."

Her pulse raced, and a sheen of cold perspiration coated her skin. Nausea welled up into her throat. She swung around to face him, needing to know if he was serious. He appeared very serious indeed. Her nausea worsened.

She gripped the countertop so hard that her knuckles were white, but somehow she was able to look at him. "I can't tell you what you can or can't do. I suppose living the kind of life you have, unfaithfulness is natural to you."

His gaze was unreadable, although his eyes were hard. "There wouldn't be any need for it if you hadn't suddenly become so damned stubborn."

She turned away to avoid his gaze and to hide her own feelings, which she knew were mirrored in her eyes. "You could have simply done what you're planning to do instead of stopping to tell me about it."

"Ah, but I don't want there to be any secrets between us, Libby."

Knowing she could do without his blasted honesty, she continued to feel sick, hating the smug tone of his voice. "Fine. You've told me your intentions. Now get out of here and leave me alone." She tried to swallow the lump in her throat, but it threatened to bring tears.

From behind her, he mused, "I can't believe you really don't care."

With all her strength, she reined in her emotions, grateful she'd had so much practice. "The least you can do is be discreet. I don't want Dawn to hear that her father, that paragon of parenthood, is out whoring around."

Muttering a curse, he stormed from the room, leaving Libby so weak in the knees she was forced to sit down. The pressure of tears stung her eyes, and she folded her hands, pressing them against her mouth.

This was her fault, she knew that. But what choice did she have? To sleep with him would be to give herself over to him body and soul, heart and mind. She'd finally admitted to herself that for once in her life she wanted a relationship where she could give a man everything. If she couldn't trust him and give him her all, she would give him nothing.

She drew in a shaky breath, expelling it noiselessly against her hands. But it hurt to admit this to herself. With this man, it hurt, because as much as she cared for him now, she knew she would grow to love him passionately if they fully shared a life together. And what would that get her if he could never love her?

Jackson left the house, slamming the door behind him. He didn't know where he was going, but he sure as hell wanted her to think he did.

What was wrong with her, anyway? She'd enjoyed their night together as much as he had. And that was before they were married. He'd promised her more than he'd ever promised another woman. He had nothing more to give.

He stepped off the porch, the rain wetting his face, his shirt, his jeans. He didn't care. He trudged through the muddy street to the jail where he was surprised to see a light and equally surprised to see two mounts hitched at the post. His heart rate accelerated when he discovered that one of them was a Tennessee high-stepper.

Throwing open the door, he stepped inside. Deputy Worth was playing checkers with Ethan Frost. Interesting . . .

Axel Worth got to his feet so quickly that his chair scuttered along the floor. "Sheriff! Didn't expect to find you out on your . . . er . . . ." He colored.

"There were some things I wanted to pick up," he lied, going to the cabinet and rifling through some papers.

The deputy shifted his weight from one foot to the other, obviously uncomfortable. "Well, I gotta get going. 'Night." Axel grabbed his hat and was gone.

The jail was filled with a stifling silence. With a folder in his hand, Jackson casually stepped to the window and glanced outside. One mount remained: the high-stepper. He concealed his excitement.

"I've heard rumors that you're planning to stay on as sheriff," Frost said.

Jackson meandered toward the desk. "Seems likely."

"Yes, well I'll admit that since Vern has been laid up, a lot has gotten past him."

"That's true." Jackson feigned only mild interest.

"I'll have you know I've extended some of the ranchers further credit, if they want it."

Still carefully masking his newfound knowledge, Jackson asked, "And how many want it?"

Frost's expression became concerned. "Not many, I'm afraid. You know, most of them just want to move on. Try their luck elsewhere. A pity, really." He gave Jackson a falsely sympathetic smile.

"Oh, by the way," Frost added. "Congratulations on your marriage."

Cautious now, Jackson studied him again, looking for . . . what? "Thank you."

"I suppose the best man won out," Frost continued with a sly smirk as he rose and crossed to the door. "But then, I didn't have a little half-blood in my corner."

Jackson clenched his fists, itching to rearrange that perfect face. He knew he couldn't. For years he'd settled things with his fists. This adversary was different. He was a bigot, a braggart, a thief, an embezzler, a bully, and probably a murderer. And Jackson had to break him, discover his dirty secrets.

"Well, I'll be getting on home," Frost announced. "My boys are probably waiting for me to tuck them into bed."

Jackson wanted to warn him to keep his bullying son away from his daughter. He itched to tell him to watch his step, that he was right on his tail, and one false move would give him away. Instead, he murmured, "G'night," pretending to be concentrating on something else.

Jackson returned to the window and watched Frost leave on the high-stepper. It wasn't a common horse around these parts. Most men rode cow ponies. His discovery that Frost went to Eureka every month to play poker had been the beginning. "This is another nail in your coffin, you bastard," he murmured to Frost's retreating form.

Jackson raised his arms up and framed the window with his hands. His thoughts automatically turned to his dear wife. Fool that he was, he still wanted her in his bed, but he could be as stubborn as she.

Although she'd made it clear that she wasn't interested in Ethan Frost, Jackson could see why a woman might be attracted to such a man. He was smooth, suave, and pretty-boy handsome. It rankled that the pile of shit had even kissed her. Groped her. And he was certain the bastard had, because who could resist her?

He made a fist and pounded the window frame. At least Frost hadn't made love to her. Why did the very thought of it bother him? He hadn't known she was a virgin when he'd taken her, and he'd wanted her just the same. Now, however, knowing that no one else had ever touched her made him jealous of anyone who might even have dreamed of it. Or tried.

Exhaling, he returned to the desk, doused the light, and left the jail. He trudged home slowly, not at all anxious to crawl into an empty bed.

As he opened the door, the motley cat shot between his legs, into the house. In the dimly lit entry, there were tiny wet cat paw prints on the floor, disappearing where they met the carpet.

He climbed the stairs, stopping briefly to look in on his

daughter. She was still curled around the dog, one arm resting possessively on his back. Mumser wagged his tail; otherwise he didn't move.

That was some kind of devotion, he thought as he walked softly down the hall toward the stairs. He slowed his steps at Libby's room, trying not to imagine her preparing for bed. It didn't work. He remembered the soft duskiness of her skin, the lustrous richness of her hair as it tumbled around her shoulders. How ready she'd been when he'd touched her. . . .

With a dark curse, he bolted up the stairs and closed himself in his room, cursing the itch she'd caused in him that he couldn't scratch.

20

A WEEK OF MARRIAGE HAD PASSED. JACKSON'S ROUTINE hadn't changed, much to his disappointment. Daily he wanted Libby. Each time he saw her, he got a funny feeling in his stomach and his heart drummed in his ears. His gaze automatically went to her curves, to the generous swell of her breasts, the roundness of her hips, the long, smooth, graceful line of her neck. He wanted to undress her, kiss her everywhere, spread her legs wide, and make love to her with his tongue. Listen to her sweet moans and thrilling cries of ecstasy. Most days he walked around as randy as a goat.

He'd barely gotten to the jail when Dominic Mateo rushed in, his black eyes wild with excitement.

"You'd better come quickly, Sheriff. Ander Bilboa shot a man on his property last night."

Jackson grabbed his hat, hurried to his mount, and followed Dominic due east. They rode quickly, their mounts covering the ground so fast that the scenery raced by in a blur. At a line shack on the far edge of Bilboa's land, Jackson slid from his mount as it came to a stop.

Inside, Jackson found the other rancher bending over the

injured man, mopping at some blood at his temple with a wet cloth.

Bilboa gave Jackson a cursory glance. "I should have let him die, the son of a bitch, but killing just isn't in me."

Jackson looked down at the man. He didn't recognize him. "Who is he?"

"Don't know," Bilboa answered.

"What happened, Ander?" Jackson continued to study the man, noting that he hadn't stirred.

"I have this flock of sheep I've been hiding. Lately I've been spending the night here, just to keep an eye on them. Last night I heard a rider, and when I looked outside, I saw him spreading something on the grass. Sheriff," he explained, his eyes blazing, "I was so damned mad, I could have killed him. Instead, I fired a warning shot. Unfortunately, it was dark and he must have moved, because I didn't miss." He motioned to the prone man's head. "I grazed him, but the wound is pretty deep."

Jackson continued to study the stranger. "If you've got a wagon, we should take him to town. Bring him to the jail; the doc can look at him there."

"I'll give him a hand," Dominic offered.

With an answering nod, Jackson went outside and studied the strychnine-laced ground. Dissatisfied with the number of tracks that had trampled the site, he started for town.

He was supposed to leave for his parents' ranch with Libby and Dawn Twilight today. How could he go now, with this new development?

As he rode up to the jail, Vern limped out to meet him.

"Just heard about the shooting. Who was it?"

Jackson shook his head. "I didn't know him, and neither did Bilboa or Dom Mateo. They're bringing him here, though, so the doc can check him."

"Thought that's what you might do. The doc is on his way over."

"I'm dropping my horse off at the livery. He needs a good rubdown after the ride we've just taken."

Minutes later Jackson stepped into the jail. Vern was sitting behind the desk. "So we'll have a prisoner, huh?"

"An unconscious one, but a prisoner just the same. This is the first break in the case."

Vern studied him. "Aren't you supposed to leave for your folks' today with Libby and Dawn?"

"I can't leave now."

"'Course you can," Vern argued. "Hell, Jackson, I'm feeling better. I can at least get around, and there's nothing wrong with my head. Just my leg. The deputy and I can handle an unconscious prisoner, for God's sake."

Jackson was uncertain. What if the prisoner regained consciousness? Would Vern know what to do? He should, Jackson reasoned. After all, he'd been the law here for twenty years. Still . . .

"Let's see what the doc says. Then I'll decide."

Vern shrugged. "Have it your way, boy, but I'd sure hate to see you disappoint that daughter of yours."

Jackson smiled. "Are you telling me not to take my job too seriously?"

"Naw, I didn't mean that. I just think I can handle this. If you hadn't been here, I'd have handled it just the same. The man'll be a prisoner, Jackson. I've had a good many of them over the years. Conscious or not, he won't cause us any problems."

Jackson didn't want Vern to think he didn't trust his judgment. Overall, Vern was still a good lawman. Still, he'd wait for the doctor's prognosis.

"Hurry, Mama! We're waiting for you."

It was barely dawn. Because of the shooting, they had postponed their trip a day. Jackson had announced at dinner the night before that the prisoner had a concussion and wasn't expected to regain consciousness for a few days. She knew her husband was reluctant to leave, but she also knew he wasn't the kind of man who felt he couldn't be replaced.

The lamplight cast eerie flickering shadows into the kitchen corners. Even in the wavering light, Libby's worried look was not lost on Chloe Ann.

"Come, now, Libby. You've taken care of everything

possible. There isn't that much left to do. We'll be just fine. Mahalia is wonderful at giving orders, and Corey and I will follow them to the letter."

Libby dragged her feet. "Oh, but I just—"

"Mama! Let's go." From the foyer, Dawn's voice was impatient.

Chloe Ann gave her a knowing smile. "It won't be such a bad trip, Libby. Let yourself relax. Have a good time. It might be a while before you get away again."

Libby drew her cape around her, dreading the ride and the destination. "It would have been better if the two of them had gone on without me."

That would have been easier to bear, for she knew the trip would suck all of the energy out of her, merely because she'd try so hard to pretend she was having a good time. But she knew that she would die a little every time one of Jackson's relatives won over another portion of her daughter's heart.

"Go," Chloe Ann urged, drawing her away from the kitchen. "They're waiting for you."

Reluctantly Libby picked up her valise and went to join Dawn and Jackson in the rig.

A rush of unwanted pleasure flowered in her chest when she saw Jackson, his big tanned hands gripping the reins of the team he'd rented for the trip. Automatic reflex, she thought. No matter how angry or hurt she was, her emotions were the same.

She took the stairs and was startled when Jackson left the rig and helped her in.

"That's right," Dawn acknowledged. "You get in the front, Mama. I'll sit in the back so I can sleep."

Libby raised an eyebrow. Her daughter the matchmaker. She lifted her eyes, meeting Jackson's penetrating gaze. "You would have had a better time without me."

He snapped the reins, and the team lurched forward. "Now, how would that look? Why, people would say we're only a week into our marriage and there's already trouble."

She cast him a glance, noting his sarcasm. "Well, there is, isn't there?"

He concentrated on the road. "Only because you've

238

created it. And since you created it, you're the only one who can change it."

Knowing he was right, she didn't answer. Instead, she concentrated on their destination. She would have to act normal, pretending everything was fine between her and Jackson when it was anything but. In the week since their wedding, they had spoken little.

The night he had informed her he would find his satisfaction elsewhere, she'd found herself listening for his footsteps, waiting for him to return. She'd been angry with herself and with him. When she finally heard him, she knew that no matter what he'd been doing, she'd driven him to it. That knowledge made her ill.

He'd stopped at her door that night, and she'd held her breath, half in fear and half in hope . . . but of course he wouldn't have asked to enter. He had his pride, and she had let him know in very strong terms that she didn't give a damn what he did. She pressed one hand to her temple, hoping to ward off a headache. What a superb liar she'd become.

Jackson's gaze was on her, as palpable as a touch. "With Dawn Twilight asleep, and you lost in your own little world, this is going to be a mighty long ride."

She nearly groaned. He had no idea. As far as she was concerned, the ride would be the short part. The stay itself would be as long and agonizing as waiting for laundry to dry in the rain.

"I want to make a toast." Standing at the head of the table, Nathan Wolfe looked at his older son, then across at his granddaughter, and raised his wineglass. "To families lost and families found. May we all be one from this moment on."

"Amen to that," Susannah concurred, raising her own glass.

Jackson stood. "Now it's my turn."

Libby did note that he'd had a bit of wine with his dinner and seemed to be in a garrulous mood.

He raised his glass. "To . . . honesty, truth, and trust. May there be no more secrets."

After making eye contact with his father, he allowed his gaze to settle on Libby, who flushed hot. When they arrived, Susannah had shown them to the room they would share. When she left, they had stared at the bed, discomfort so thick between them that they could have sliced it with a knife.

Although it had been Jackson and Corey's room, the bed wasn't even as big as her own, and certainly nowhere near as large as the one Jackson slept in on the third floor of the rooming house.

Now he was spewing words about honesty, truth, and trust. What did he want her to do? She'd been as honest as she dared. She supposed she could inform his family that they didn't share a bed and that she'd all but encouraged him to take his pleasure elsewhere. Would that be honest enough for him?

She suffered through the remainder of the meal, knowing it was probably delicious but having no appetite at all.

Later, when Jackson was in the den with his father, and Dawn had retired to Katie's room, Libby excused herself and went to their bedroom. She didn't care where he slept, but she was taking the bed. And she was *so* tired. She'd fought to keep from yawning all evening. She'd had little sleep the night before because of her worry about the trip, and she had refused to doze off while Jackson drove the team.

After brushing her hair, she slipped into the new cotton lawn nightgown with the leg-of-mutton sleeves and the lace-trimmed collar that Chloe Ann had given her the day she learned Libby was to be married. Libby frowned at her reflection. As if a new nightgown was going to change anything.

She turned and studied the bed, then grabbed one of the pillows and the quilt that was folded at the foot, and put them on the chair. Surely he would get the message.

Leaving the lamp lit, she yawned and crawled into bed, snuggling deep into the warm bedding, but she was too tense to sleep. She knew she wouldn't be able to close her eyes all night.

Jackson cringed when the bedroom door squeaked open. He poked his head inside and saw Libby in bed. She appeared to be asleep. As quietly as he was able, he closed the door and stepped to the bedside.

His mouth lifted into a wry grin. How could such a passionate, contrary, stubborn woman appear so damned innocent and passive in her sleep? She lay on her side, her lustrous hair fanned out over her shoulder, hiding her arm. Her fist peeped out from among the shiny strands. It was clenched. So, he thought, she couldn't relax even in her sleep.

Her eyelids had a slightly violet hue, and her long, dark lashes brushed her cheeks. Her mouth, that succulent wine-rich berry, was open slightly.

He'd stripped to his underwear before he noticed the pillow and quilt on the chair. He muttered an oath. Did she expect him to wrap himself up and lie on the floor? He grabbed the pillow, turned out the lamp, and carefully climbed in beside her. Fortunately, even though the bed was narrow, she was one of those people who didn't sprawl.

Once he was curled up behind her and she didn't wake, he expelled a long, tired sigh. Hell, he was too tired to seduce her anyway. But she smelled damned good. What was it about women? They wove some sort of spell over him simply by being alive, breathing, secreting some sort of magic elixir that drove him wild. Especially this woman.

Fool that he was, he thought about her dark, secret places, hidden from him during the day by her staunch reserve and her practicality.

His nose nuzzled her hair. For at least the hundredth time since their wedding, he envisioned her naked. It hadn't been enough to make love to her, for they'd been fully clothed. He wanted to be there when she undressed, when she stood before the washstand and bathed herself. When she bent to wash her legs, exposing her breasts and her bottom.

He wanted to make love to her from behind, thrusting

deep while he fondled her nipples. He wanted to hear her cries of pleasure again. And again. And again.

Muttering a quiet curse, he rubbed his hand over his face to dispel his dangerous thoughts. He could do it. He'd learned to sleep standing up, for God's sake. He'd learned to sleep waist deep in mud. He'd become adept at catching quick naps in some of the most squalid situations. Surely he could sleep here now. He was in a bed. A warm, clean bed. The problem, of course, was that he was lying with the first woman who had made him itch in a very long time.

And as he lay there, his arm around her and his fingers grazing her stomach, an old instinct surfaced, one that he hadn't felt since his marriage to Flicker Feather. He cursed again, wondering if he should tell Libby what he knew. He was pleased, but he was certain she wouldn't be.

Libby came awake slowly, feeling as though she were in a cocoon. The weight of the blankets was heavy, but somehow it felt cozy. She knew that if she stretched, her feet would touch the cold bedding at the bottom of the bed, so she bent her knees, stretching her toes backward.

They collided with a firm, warm, hairy calf. Startled, she tried to sit up, but the weight that she'd thought was the bedding turned out to be a thickly muscled arm. Her attempts to remove it were futile, for he appeared to be deep in sleep, and truly the last thing she wanted to do was wake him.

She stayed as still as possible, barely breathing, while she pondered her situation, unaware that her fingers had touched him until she encountered the hard muscle in his upper arm.

Cursing mildly, she quickly withdrew her hand, but remembered how often she'd gazed at his strong forearms and wondered if the hair was stiff and prickly or soft. Curious, she ran her palm over it, surprised at the texture. It was neither soft nor stiff, but somewhere in between. And, oh, my, his flesh was so firm. She recalled how some of his veins had bulged as he worked, looking like rivers of granite.

Suddenly her hand flew to her mouth. Good heavens, her

feet had touched his bare legs! Did that mean he wore nothing to bed? She swallowed hard. Lord, he wouldn't be that brazen, would he?

No, he wouldn't.

Yes, he would.

As slowly as she could, she reached behind her, investigating carefully, encountering . . . She released a sigh. He wore something, at least.

"What are you looking for?"

His voice startled her so that she gasped and would have leaped from the bed had he not held her there.

"You're not supposed to be in this bed," she accused, flustered at her foolish groping.

"You didn't expect me to sleep on the floor, did you?"

Why did his voice make every part of her body quicken? "You could sleep in the barn for all I care. This bed is barely big enough for one, let alone two. Get out."

"Now, how would that look? We're supposed to be happily married. You wouldn't want to disappoint my parents, would you?"

Another sigh, although shakier. "This is insane." If only he weren't so close . . .

"You're pregnant."

"What?"

"You heard me," he whispered.

She turned and, with all of her strength, shoved him until he left the bed and hit the floor with a resounding thud.

"Dammit," he cursed. "I hit my head on the edge of the table."

"I hope you bleed to death, you . . . you pervert." How dare he say such a thing? It was ludicrous. It had barely been a month since they'd . . . Lord, she couldn't even think the words, much less say them.

There was a sharp knock on the door. "Are you all right in there?"

Libby pressed her fingers over her mouth and stared at the door.

"We're fine, Mother."

Libby heard Jackson scramble to his feet.

"The bed's a little small. I fell out, that's all."

"All right, then," Susannah answered, her voice slightly muffled from the other side of the door. "It's almost time for your father to check the stock. Do you want to join him?"

"I'll be right there."

He lit the lamp, and Libby looked up at him. "Oh," she said with a gasp. "You *are* bleeding."

He dabbed at his forehead. "It'll be all right."

Concerned, she slid from the bed, crossed to the dry sink, and poured water into the porcelain bowl. She wet a cloth. "Come here," she ordered.

"I said it would be fine."

"Come here, you fool. Let me clean you up before you go out and face your parents."

Suddenly he grinned. "Wouldn't look very good if they thought you were beating up on their little boy, would it?"

"Don't be an idiot," she huffed, trying to ignore his complacent smile.

He stood before her, bare to the waist. Trying valiantly to ignore his nudity, she dabbed at his forehead with the damp cloth.

"You call me such terrible names. I'm beginning to think you don't like me."

He continued to smile at her as she rinsed the cloth and touched it to his wound again. As hard as she tried, she couldn't keep from returning his smile. "I don't call you names you don't deserve."

"Oh? You really think I'm a fool? An idiot? A pervert?"

"Whatever makes you think you can tell if I'm . . . you know."

His hand fondled her chin, his elbows dangerously close to her breasts. "Pregnant?"

She attempted to look away. "How in the world would you know such a thing? It's my body, and *I* don't even know."

"Call it a gift, or a curse, I guess." His tone changed.

"You're serious," she said, surprised.

He continued to stand before her. "Even when I was a

boy, I could detect pregnancy in a mare before it was evident. Don't ask me how. And I was never wrong. My family came to rely on me, and soon neighbors did, too. After they'd bred their mares, they would invite me over to use my 'powers.' The last time I detected a pregnancy was when Flicker Feather was pregnant with Dawn Twilight."

Libby's hands automatically went to her abdomen. Pregnant? Joy, dread, and fear tripped over each other inside her. Still, she didn't want him to see her feelings.

Quickly rinsing out the cloth, she said, "You'd better not keep your father waiting."

He didn't move. "That's your response?"

"What did you expect? Now when you get itchy feet and go off to fight another man's war, I'll have not one but two children to care for."

He spun away, muttering a curse as he dressed. "I don't know how many times I have to tell you that I'm not going anywhere."

She held her emotions in check until he left, then sagged onto the bed and put her face in her hands. If he was right, what would she do? Even though she wanted his child with all her heart, she couldn't endure a loveless life with him. And she was beginning to think she couldn't endure a life without him, either.

21

*L*IBBY GREASED BREAD TINS AT THE COUNTER WHILE SUSANNAH
sat at the table dropping gingersnap dough onto cookie
sheets.

"I'll never forget the first time I saw Jackson," Susannah
mused, her voice filled with soft remembrance. "Corey and
I and our friends, Kito and Louisa, had ridden to this ranch
because, months before, Nathan had told me to come here if
I was ever in trouble." She uttered a soft laugh. "But that's
another story.

"Anyway, there was an old caretaker here at the time who
informed me that Nathan's son Jackson, who everyone
thought was dead, had been found living among a coastal
tribe of Indians. Nathan wasn't here and didn't yet know
the boy was alive."

Libby had heard some of this story, but was still intensely
interested. "Had he been harmed?"

"Oh, no. They had treated him as one of their own. Had
even given him an Indian name."

"Warrior Heart," Libby offered, remembering Dawn's
enthusiastic retelling of the story.

"Yes. But he was very skittish. I had a big black dog with

me at the time. Max was his name." There was a smile in her voice.

Libby remembered hearing about Max from Jackson.

"That dog seemed to sense Jackson's discomfort. Max settled down at the boy's feet and became his closest companion. Slowly Jackson came out of his shell, but it took a while. He and that dog went through a lot together."

"And . . . and as a young man? What was he like?" Libby sliced off a hunk of dough, formed it into a loaf and dropped it into a loaf pan.

Susannah rose and slid a cookie sheet into the oven. "As the oldest child, he was the most responsible. Of course, he was Corey's hero. But no matter how often Corey followed him around, Jackson never became impatient with him."

Libby hid her discomfort. He *would* have to be perfect, wouldn't he?

"But as he got older, he became distant. Nathan and I both noticed it, and we knew why. He felt the brutality done to the Indian as readily as if it were his own burden. He couldn't stand to see the underdog defenseless. He returned to the tribe often. Although he never told us this, we simply knew that's where he was. He felt they needed his protection."

Susannah released a sigh. "We had no idea he'd married a native girl and had a child, much less that his young wife had been killed by Jackson's own people. That's how far he'd drifted from us."

They worked together in silence, Libby's emotions clamoring inside her. Perhaps she'd been too hard on him. Perhaps she'd expected too much from him.

The door opened, bringing a gust of cold air.

"Ah, nothing like the smell of fresh bread and ginger cookies to make a man profess his love for a woman." Nathan Wolfe stepped to the table, bent and kissed his wife's mouth.

Libby's stomach churned, and she ached for that which she would never have. Her gaze met Jackson's as he came into the room behind his father. Her reaction to him hadn't changed; she still quivered like a schoolgirl.

Jackson poured coffee for himself and his father, then took a seat at the table, virtually ignoring Libby. She didn't miss the quick look of concern that passed between his parents. Oh, God, she shouldn't have come. She knew it!

"The place looks great." Jackson grinned at his mother. "I'd forgotten how much land we had."

Nathan took his wife's hand and caressed it in his. "We've got to get that hay up into the high country near the cabin before the first good snow."

"When do you want to do it?" Jackson asked.

Nathan uttered a sigh. "It should be done within the next day or two, but I've got a sick mare. If something should happen to her while I'm gone, I wouldn't want anyone else to feel responsible."

Jackson toyed with his cup. "I can take the hay to the high country in the morning."

Susannah brightened. "Oh, that's a wonderful idea. Libby can go with you to keep you company."

At her suggestion, Libby nearly dropped the bread on the floor. She quickly recovered, but she couldn't look at Jackson even though she knew his gaze was on her. No doubt he was as distressed as she was.

"The cabin needs to be shut up tight, made ready for winter." Susannah smiled at her husband. "Remember the year it was invaded by raccoons because Corey had taken a girl up there and hadn't secured the kitchen window?"

Nathan gave her a suggestive smile. "Remember the first time we ever used it?"

"On our honeymoon," she answered, almost shyly.

Libby tried not to stare, but Susannah's blush was exquisite. Why, they were still in love, after all these years. Imagine that. . . .

She turned to the counter and resumed her duties, but her hands shook and her knees were weak.

She wanted that. She wanted what Nathan and Susannah had. It was up to her to change things; Jackson had told her that. She swallowed hard, vowing to bring about the change.

Perhaps the trip to the cabin wouldn't be such a bad thing after all.

That night she pretended to be asleep when Jackson came to bed, for she felt a bit skittish about her plan. She was a coward, pure and simple.

"I watched you sleep last night, Libby. I know you're awake."

His hand moved over her hip, and she bit her lip to keep from crying out.

"I know how your sweet mouth relaxes in sleep, how there's tension mixed in with your peacefulness, how your face is composed, but your fists are clenched." He continued to stroke her hip.

Unable to continue to pretend she was asleep, she rolled over onto her back, a movement that brought his hand in contact with her stomach. A shock raced into her pelvis, shooting down both legs.

She swallowed hard. "I think you should remove your hand." But this was what she wanted. What was wrong with her?

"Make me," he countered, continuing his fingertip perusal.

Again he was daring her. He did it so well. Even though they were legally husband and wife, she wasn't comfortable doing anything under his parents' roof. That was foolish, but she just couldn't. Hopefully she could convince him of her feelings once they reached the cabin. Until then . . . She drew in a breath and steeled herself against his caress.

"Do what you want, Jackson. I hope you don't get bored."

His chuckle was warm and deep as his fingers traced a circular path to the top of her thighs.

She turned her head away and bit down on her lip, wondering how long she could stand such a seductive assault.

"I think your curls were soft," he whispered. "I can't remember." He continued his subtle attack. "What color are they, Libby? Almost black, like this?" His other hand threaded through the hair at her temple.

"Maybe with a hint of red, to show your fire?"

She struggled to breathe normally; it became difficult.

His hand slid down her thigh, to the hem of her gown. "Mind if I look?"

She attempted to push his hand away, knowing he wasn't serious. "You really are a pervert, aren't you?"

"There you go again, calling me names." His fingers toyed with her knees.

"All well deserved," she managed, although his touch continued to raise havoc with her senses.

His hand moved slowly up her bare thigh. "Aren't you going to fight me?"

She smiled slyly. So that was what he wanted. To tussle, as they had in the kitchen when they'd bombarded each other with flour. "No," she managed. "Do what you wish."

His eyes held a twinkle. "Really?"

She shrugged, although her body throbbed. "You want me to fight you. You're itching for it. I won't give you the satisfaction."

"You won't fight me?"

Did he sound disappointed? She thought so. "No. I won't fight you."

"Good."

He flipped the covers away so quickly that Libby gasped. "What are you doing?"

He started tugging up her nightgown. "I'm going to see what color you are down there."

She pushed at her gown, attempting to force it from his grip. "You are truly a lunatic," she muttered, fighting against the upward thrust of his hands.

"I thought you weren't going to fight me, Libby."

She lunged at him, momentarily forgetting that to do so she had to release her hold on her nightgown.

He straddled her, his hands pinning her arms to the bed.

She glared at him, shaking with desire. "You promised not to touch me."

"No," he whispered. "I promised not to make love to you. I told you it was too late to order me not to touch you."

Frustrated and weak of will, she succumbed. "Then look, damn you. It's what I'd expect from a deviate." She pinched her eyes closed, waiting for . . . she didn't know what. Another smart remark? A leer? A snicker?

Then she felt it. A whispery kiss low on her abdomen. She opened her eyes and found herself looking at the top of his head as he bent over her.

"J-Jackson?"

He planted kisses lower and lower still until she felt his lips against the sensitive folds of her flesh. Her legs shook and she rolled her head on the pillow as the pleasure built. She tugged at his hair, not certain what she wanted.

"Do you want me to stop?" The words were whispered against her, heightening her hunger.

Did she? Yes, yes, of course she did. But, oh, God . . .

"Libby?" He dipped his tongue there, where every nerve in her body appeared to be centered, and she bucked on the bed.

She forced his head away. "Y-yes, please, please . . ." She swallowed. "Stop."

He rolled off her and turned away, presenting her his back. "It's just as well," he muttered.

She was still quaking with unquenched desire, but she pressed her legs together and moved to the edge of the bed. How could she possibly sleep, with him beside her?

As if reading her mind, he remarked, "I'm not leaving this bed, Libby."

"No," she answered, her voice quavering, "I don't suppose you are."

"No matter what you think, I have some honor. I won't take advantage of you again. The scent of you drives me wild. Your skin is so soft, it makes me crazy. That fluff of hair between your legs begs to be kissed. I apologize, but I got carried away."

So did I. She curled up into a ball and clutched the bedding to her chin. She should have let him continue. Oh, God, she wanted him to. But not here, not with his parents in the next room. It was a foolish inhibition, but she experienced it all the same. Now she knew it would be twice as hard to convince him she'd changed her mind.

In the morning, she awoke, her nose pressed against his bare chest. Again, as the morning before, his arm was around her. She knew she should do something, but for a moment, she would do nothing.

So, she thought, breathing in the scent of him, this was what the rest of her life would be like—when she finally surrendered. Perhaps her stubbornness had been uncalled for. Just perhaps, she was being unfair and unrealistic.

Allowing herself to relax, she sighed and settled against him. She would tell him now. She wouldn't wait until they were at the cabin. She loved waking up like this, close to his body. She loved the hair on his chest, on his arms, on his stomach. It was masculine. Erotic. She had an overwhelming urge to absorb him into her skin.

Sensing he was awake, she spoke. "Jackson, I—"

With a growl, he removed his arm. "I know, I know. I'm getting up." He rolled to the other side and left the bed. "I'm sorry. The bed is narrow. Fortunately, we won't be here for a couple of nights, and there are two beds up at the cabin."

She heard him struggle into his clothes in the darkness. "I hope that satisfies you."

She swallowed the knot in her throat. She hoped she hadn't waited too long.

The ride to the cabin was cold, for they'd had to take the wagon, which was piled high with bales of hay.

Libby's first glimpse of the building was through a thicket of evergreens, their pine-scented needles filling the air with a spicy tang. "Cabin" was really not a proper term for the building. She'd expected a crude structure, but this was anything but crude. The exterior was made of cedar logs. A window, larger than any she'd ever seen, faced the valley, and the roof peaked high.

The interior was just as breathtaking.

Jackson put her valise in the larger of the two bedrooms. He seemed so resolute. Gone was the teasing, the gentle taunting, the seductive assault. And, as annoying as she'd thought he was, she missed his playful advances.

While he made a fire in the large stone fireplace, she strolled to the back wall, which was the kitchen. The staples were already there, and Susannah had packed enough food for a week.

As Libby began preparing a simple supper, Jackson informed her he was going out to take the hay to higher ground.

"Do you want me to go with you?"

"No. But I'd appreciate it if you'd have dinner ready when I get back. I'll be as hungry as a bear."

She went to the window and watched him leave. He turned briefly, catching sight of her through the glass. She almost waved good-bye, but the wagon had already disappeared through the trees.

Pulling in a ragged sigh, she returned to the kitchen, browned some venison and onions, and prepared a pot of stew. An hour later it was bubbling on the stove, and she had a tin of biscuits ready to slip into the oven.

She found a copy of *The Scarlet Letter* lying on a table in the great room, and curled up in a chair by the fire to read. The grandfather clock in the corner chimed, and when Libby absently counted seven bells, she put the book on the floor and rose, surprised that Jackson hadn't yet returned.

Rubbing her arms, she crossed to the window and cupped her hands around her eyes, attempting to look outside. Up through the trees, she could see no stars, and when she discovered it was snowing lightly, she felt a jolt of panic.

She threw on her shawl and stepped outside, noting the quiet, the tranquillity. The air was cold and still. Coyotes howled in the distance, sending a shiver of fear over her skin. She listened, straining to hear the wagon, but there was no noise but the drumming of her heart.

She returned to the cabin and lit the lamps that stood on the circular tables at either end of the settee, casting some light into the large room.

Expecting him any moment, she went to the kitchen and checked the stew, slid the biscuits into the oven, then squinted out into the darkness again. Nothing. She tried not to worry. After all, he was a grown man, and even though he hadn't been here for many years, he knew the country well. He'd been all over the world, for heaven's sake. He was the most capable man she'd ever known. Yet . . .

Nervous and anxious, needing to occupy herself, she pulled out ingredients for molasses cookies and stirred up a batch. When the biscuits were brown, she placed them on the back of the stove and covered them with a cloth, then began baking cookies.

The clock chimed eight, and Libby could contain her panic no longer. Fretfully wringing her hands, she paced the great room, her gaze going to the door frequently, willing Jackson to come through it.

Her imagination went wild. She pictured him lying dead somewhere, the wagon or the horses having crushed him. A brief image of Sean's broken body shot through her, and she sucked in a gulp of air. And if the horses hadn't killed her poor husband, perhaps snarling wild animals had torn at his body, dragging him through the snow into the trees.

Anxious and afraid, she was unaware that she'd been crying until she felt the tears drip from her chin. Swiping at them with her fingers, she hurried to the door and pulled on a pair of oversized boots. Someone's jacket hung on a hook, and she shrugged into it, buttoning it hastily as she left the cabin.

The snowfall was heavier now, obliterating not only the tracks they'd made earlier, but the entire road. She forced a calm through the wedge of panic that screamed through her, trying to listen for him, praying for his safe return. She wanted to search for him, but it was dark, and she was completely unfamiliar with the landscape. As anxious as she was to do something, she knew it was sensible to do nothing. Getting herself lost would do him no good at all.

She held her breath. *There.* She heard a rustling in the trees, beyond the extended porch that jutted out from the side of the cabin. But . . . She put her hand to her mouth.

The road wasn't there; it was . . . Her frantic gaze roamed the darkness. The road was there, she thought, straight out from the door.

Suddenly a series of sharp barks returned her attention to the wooden deck and she froze, unable to move. The barking and yelping seemed to close in on her, and from the trees she heard an eerie, mournful howling, the sound sending shivers of fear over her skin.

Willing herself to move, she stumbled into the cabin and sagged against the door, her heart beating a wild tattoo against her ribs.

"Oh, Jackson," she murmured, unable to quell her fears, "where are you?"

All of a sudden she heard a gunshot. Then another. Throwing open the door, she squinted out into the darkness.

"Jackson?"

"It's me, Libby," came the answer.

"Jackson!"

With tears of relief and anger tracking her cheeks, she nearly stumbled down the steps as she ran to meet him. "Where have you been? You had me worried *sick.*"

He hopped from the wagon. "I'm sorry. I guess I lost track of time—"

She took a swing at him. "How dare you scare me like this? How *dare* you!" She hit him again, her fist pummeling his chest.

He caught her to him, and she slumped in his arms, relieved that he was here and that he was all right.

"Come on," he urged, helping her to the cabin. "I'm sorry I frightened you. It was thoughtless of me to leave you here alone after dark, especially when you've never been here before."

She sniffled. "Th-there were coyotes."

"I know. I think my shots scared them off."

He removed his jacket and his boots, then helped her with the coat. He drew her to a chair, gently pushed her into it, and pulled off her boots. He rubbed her feet, then her hands.

"I thought something had happened to you." She gazed into his beautiful face and started to cry. "Oh, God, I thought something awful had happened to you!"

He pulled out his handkerchief and wiped her face. "I didn't know you cared."

She pushed his hand away. "Of course I care, you fool."

He chuckled. "Now you sound like the Libby I remember. Feeling all right now?"

She expelled a shuddery breath. "I don't think I'll ever be all right again."

He lifted his head and sniffed. "Smells good in here. Do you want me to get you some supper?"

Feeling better, she shook her head and stood up. "I'm fine. Really, I'm fine now. Go wash up."

By the time he returned, everything was ready, and she was ladling stew into bowls. He held her chair as she slid into it, then took a seat across from her. His eyes were warm and filled with regret. "I'm sorry I frightened you, Libby."

She gave him a watery smile. "I don't know why I panicked so. Probably because I expected you to return before dark."

"It gets dark early up here; the sun drops behind the mountains quickly."

As they ate their dinner in silence, Libby realized that they were in the ideal place for a honeymoon: a secluded mountain cabin. Oddly enough, it was the first time they had ever been totally and completely alone together.

22

FROM HIS BED JACKSON LISTENED TO THE SOUNDS OF THE distant coyotes and stared at the dark ceiling. What a different Libby had emerged tonight. He wouldn't have purposely frightened her for the world, but her reaction when she thought something had happened to him filled him with hope. He thought of the baby growing inside her, and he cursed himself for worrying her so. It had been thoughtless. He could never have forgiven himself if something had happened to her while he was out.

The baby. His baby. He felt a swelling happiness at the thought of having another child. And because it was growing inside his wife—his fiery, feisty Libby—he was euphoric. Did that mean he loved her? He didn't know, but the idea was no longer alien to him.

The coyotes continued to howl. They weren't far away; in fact, they sounded closer now. That wasn't unusual, but he wondered if Libby could sleep through such eerie sounds.

Feeling a chill in the air, he slid from the bed and padded to the great room to stoke up the fire.

"Jackson?"

Not entirely surprised that she was awake, he turned. She stood in the doorway, wearing the soft white nightgown with the high prudish collar. In spite of that, she didn't look prudish at all. She looked seductive, and he couldn't deny he was tempted.

"Did I wake you?"

She shook her head as she moved toward him. "No. It's the coyotes."

"I thought they might bother you." He returned to the fire.

"I couldn't sleep. I—" She gasped. "Oh, I've never noticed the scars on your back."

"Battle wounds," he murmured, suddenly remembering how he'd gotten each and every one. He hoisted a log and dropped it onto the fire.

She touched his shoulder blade. "Oh, my. This one's so deep."

"And puckered. What color is it now? I don't get much of a chance to look at it."

"It's white. White and kind of . . . kind of shiny."

Her fingers traced it, and he closed his eyes, savoring her gentle touch. "It used to be pink. Before that it was an angry red."

"How did you get it?" Her voice was tender, concerned.

"Some Aussie madman sliced me with a knife."

"In one of your wars?"

He chuckled. "I'd like you to think so, but I got that one in a bar fight."

Her fingers moved over his back in Braille-like fashion. He found it necessary to clench his jaw, for the desire to expel a sigh of pleasure was overwhelming. "And this one?" She stopped at his waist, near his spine.

"Got gouged there by a Turk."

"In another bar fight?" Her voice held a smile.

"No," he answered, pretending to be offended.

She was immediately contrite. "I'm sorry. It could have been a very serious wound. I didn't mean to make light of it. Did you get it in a battle?"

"Sort of," he hedged.

"Sort of?"

"We were fighting because he thought I was ogling his woman."

She laughed softly behind him. "And were you?"

"Damn right. It isn't often that a man sees a woman pick up coins from the top of a bar with her . . . um . . ." He felt himself color.

"Her what?"

"It isn't the thing to say in mixed company."

"But I'm your wife," she urged, her fingers lingering on his skin.

His wife. God, how those words filled him with joy. Her touch was excruciating pleasure, if there ever was such a thing. "You'd probably be offended."

"Then clean it up for me," she suggested. "Please."

He jabbed the poker into the fire, fussing with the logs. Ah, what the hell. She knew he wasn't perfect. "She could pick up coins off a bar with her—" He coughed, uncomfortable. "With her breasts by leaning over and pushing them together."

"Oh, my," Libby said with a pretty laugh. "Do people really do such things in public?"

He turned and found her eyes sparkling. "You mean you might be tempted to do it in private?"

Laughing again, she swatted him. "No. I mean I can't imagine a woman actually doing something so outrageous."

He touched her cheek. Her trembling beneath his fingers forced him to remove them. He turned back to the fire. "You'd be surprised what women in other parts of the world will do for money. Or in this part of the world, for that matter."

"I guess I'm pretty innocent," she answered.

He lowered himself to the bearskin rug in front of the fireplace, his forearms dangling over his knees.

"Are you staying up for a while?"

He nodded. "Go on to bed, Libby. If you leave the door open, it'll warm up some in there." He could warm her up, but she probably wouldn't be amenable to the suggestion.

She hovered nearby. "I could keep you company."

He uttered a harsh laugh. "You don't have to do me any favors."

Releasing a sigh, she announced, "Jackson, I have to talk to you." She took a seat beside him.

He didn't like her tone, and already knew he'd be dissatisfied with what she had to say. "So say it and get it over with."

Another sigh. She traced a pattern on the rug. "I can live with a lot of things. I can understand you not . . . not falling in love with me. I've decided I can even live with it. I was stubborn and . . . and hard-headed and filled with impossible girlish dreams."

He studied her, intensely interested, but said nothing.

"What I can't live with is you being unfaithful. And if I don't—" She coughed and cleared her throat. "I mean, if *we* don't . . . well, sleep together, I can't expect you to be a faithful husband. You promised me a lot of things and were honest with me about the things you couldn't promise me. I appreciate that, and I can live with it."

He touched her knee, eliciting a reflexive response. Sure. She could live with it, but could he? He wanted her welcome response, like the night they had first made love. "Are you saying you *want* to sleep with me or that you're simply willing to do so because you're afraid I'll be unfaithful if you don't?"

"Oh, don't be dense, Jackson Wolfe," she muttered, tossing him a frustrated look. "You know good and well I enjoyed it the first time."

Her fire had returned, and he liked it. But she'd put him through hell, and he didn't want to make this easy for her. He patted her knee affectionately. "Good. Then we'll talk about it in the morning."

"In the—" She stood up with a huff. "Fine. I'm sorry I bothered you with something so trivial as the rest of our lives together."

She started to stomp toward the bedroom, but he grabbed her ankle, tumbling her to the rug. "Come back here."

Attempting to wriggle away, she thumped his arm with the heel of her free foot. "Let go of me, you mule."

"Oh, now I'm a mule? How many other barnyard animals are you going to compare me to?"

She squirmed beneath his touch. "Just . . . just leave me alone."

"So you've changed your mind again?"

"No," she spat. "But obviously you have." She wiggled, trying to get free.

He got to his knees and dragged her toward him by both of her ankles, pulling until he could hold her legs behind him with both hands. She glared up at him, sparks of fire in her eyes.

"Now what will you do?" she demanded. "If you try to hold me with both hands, you can't use either of them."

He allowed a smirk. "Who says I have to use my hands?"

Her eyes widened, then narrowed with caution. "Now I think I've changed my mind."

He pulled her hips onto his lap, close enough so that she could feel the stiff ridge behind his underwear. Her nightgown had ridden up, and he could see her. His hunger thickened when firelight glistened off her wet curls, because he knew then that she was ready, no matter how much she fought him or what she said. Still, he wouldn't force her. He simply pressed against her softness, holding them together. Binding them.

She stared up at him from the floor. Although she feigned indifference, something else was in her eyes. He waited.

"I don't know what you're trying to prove," she murmured.

His answer was more pressure. He glanced at where they joined. Her thighs and belly were white against her luxurious dark brown curls. He remembered how she smelled, how she tasted, and his mouth watered, anticipating another taste, another time. Gritting his teeth, he forced himself not to think about being inside her.

Talk. Talking would help take his mind off his itch. "The night after the wedding, when you sent me out into the rain—"

"I didn't," she argued. "You went of your own free will."

"Aren't you even the least bit curious as to where I went?" He applied more pressure, watching her eyes.

She blinked repeatedly, appearing to concentrate. "I . . . I don't know any of the bawdy houses in Thief River, nor am I interested in learning where they are."

"I went to the one between the general store and the millinery shop." He applied more pressure, aching to rub against her, for she was so wet that the front of his underdrawers was damp.

Her eyes widened. "But . . . that's the jail."

"Exactly."

"Then . . . then you didn't—"

"I didn't, and I'm sorry I made you believe I would," he assured her, undulating slightly against her.

"And you haven't—"

"I haven't." He kept up the movement. "I will be a faithful husband, Libby, because I want to be."

He knew the moment she began to change. Her sweet mouth opened; her breathing became faster, more erratic. She made little sounds in her throat. Her eyes were dark with passion, heavy-lidded with imminent ecstasy. He almost spent just watching her.

"J-Jackson . . ." Her voice caught, and she closed her eyes, her pelvis surging toward him and her legs squeezing his waist. She reached for him but couldn't touch him.

As she stiffened and climaxed, he watched her rapture and knew a fulfillment he couldn't explain. When she went limp, he slid her to the rug, moved his hands up her hips, and gazed at the beauty of her, all damp, swollen, and satisfied.

His gaze went to her face. She stared at him through heavy lids, her cheeks flushed.

"That was a dirty trick."

Giving her a lopsided smile, he answered, "I know. I'm full of them."

Although her nightgown was pushed to her neck, she didn't attempt to cover herself. His hand wandered toward her breasts, and she held his gaze. "Thanks for the warning."

His fingertips touched a turgid nipple and he grinned again. "Shall I tell you how much I loved watching you come?"

She made a satisfied sound in her throat as he dragged his rough palm over her nipple. "Oh, Lord," she whispered, moving restlessly, "I can feel that all the way down here." She briefly touched herself.

"So can I."

She looked at the tent his underwear made over his groin, then gave him a shy glance. "May I see it?"

Pleased at her boldness, he slid his underwear down his hips and over his erection.

When she touched it, he sucked in a ragged breath.

"It's big," she whispered, examining his shaft.

The compliment wasn't lost on him. Seed leaked from the tip, wetting her fingers. He called upon all of his strength to keep it from spurting like a fountain.

"Mahalia was right."

"About what?" He gritted his teeth, attempting to hold back.

"She said any man with thumbs the size of yours has a—"

In spite of his delicious discomfort, he was amused. "A what?"

She flushed. "Has a big . . . organ."

He couldn't stop the laugh. "Mahalia is a wealth of information, isn't she?"

Libby threaded her fingers through his bush, testing his root from bottom to tip, then from tip to bottom. She put her fingers around it and gave it a gentle squeeze, eliciting from him an exquisite moan.

"I probably shouldn't do that."

"Not continuously, anyway," he answered, trying to keep his voice from wavering.

She gazed at him. "It makes me want you inside me."

He removed her hand, unbuttoned her gown, and pulled it off over her head. "In due time, dear Libby. In due time."

He studied her breasts, fighting back the red haze of his hunger. Lowering his head, he sucked one nipple into his mouth causing her to gasp and press him closer. He moved to the other, devouring it, rolling it around and around with his tongue.

Her hands roamed his chest, his back, his stomach, his groin. She rubbed her palm over him, reached under and cradled his sac in her hand.

He swiftly laid her on her back, unable to wait, and drove into her, thrusting deep into her welcoming sheath.

Her legs circled his hips and her arms drew him close. Her nails raked his back as she arched up to meet him. As they sped toward completion, his unbearable ache, the itch that she had caused, became excruciating pleasure, and he kissed her hard and deep, swallowing her cries and making them his own.

She held him tight, and he rolled to his side, bringing her with him.

Tears tracked her cheeks, but her smile was dazzling. She ran her fingers through his hair and stroked his cheek. "Sleep with me."

It was a quiet request. He would honor it. He began to realize that life with this woman would be different from his life when he wasn't yet out of his teens. He'd been so wrapped up in his pain over Flicker Feather's death that he hadn't realized what their relationship had been lacking.

She'd failed to reach many places inside him. She'd been sweet, passive, and unquestioning. That had been enough . . . when he was less than twenty.

Libby, on the other hand, had depth and texture and would never settle for less than everything he could give, because she would give back the same.

As they lay in each other's arms, his fear of the future was suddenly overshadowed by his anticipation of it.

The howling of the coyotes seemed far away, now that she was wrapped in Jackson's arms. They had made love again on the rug, then had moved to her bed.

Exhausted, they had drifted off to sleep. Now she was awake, not because she was eager to get up but because she didn't want to waste precious time sleeping when she could be savoring his nearness.

"You awake?" he asked.

She smiled. "I thought you were sleeping."

"I didn't want to waste time sleeping." He lifted aside her hair and nuzzled her neck, his fingers suddenly busy with her breasts. "Tell me about your marriage to Sean, Libby."

"What do you want to know?" she answered on a sigh.

"Why was it never consummated?"

"It's a long story." But he had a right to know. "I have to start at the beginning, I think, to help you understand.

"Sean was a distant relative of my father's. Actually they were very nearly the same age. But our age difference didn't have anything to do with . . . with him not sleeping with me. He discovered we were related while we were living and working the fields in the Central Valley. It was peach-picking time, and we always went where there was work. We were a migrant family. White trash, according to many, and they were right."

Jackson quit toying with her breasts and hugged her. "Go on."

"The day Sean showed up, I couldn't take my eyes off him. Oh, not that he was handsome, but he was refined and well dressed. And to me, he was rich, because he owned a boardinghouse. He actually owned property, something my father had never done. He had roots, something I wanted desperately. But most of all, he was kind to me, and polite. He had such understanding eyes, as if he knew exactly how miserable my life was. He almost got into a fight when my father took a belt to me because I hadn't brought in enough money that day." Libby remembered everything vividly, and it was painful.

"I was stunned when I learned that Sean wanted to take me away with him. Not that I wouldn't have gone in a minute, but I couldn't imagine that kind of good fortune ever happening to me. I wanted to leave. I prayed it would happen. When my father insisted on selling me, I didn't care. When Sean agreed to pay my father's price, I knew I would do anything for him."

Jackson was quiet, his hands moving methodically over her bare back. "Were you happy with him?"

Libby expelled a sigh. "Yes. I was happy to be away from my family. When Sean didn't insist on his rights as a husband, I didn't think too much about it. I was only fourteen, after all. But as time went by, I knew there should be something more. I even approached him, something very bold for me at the time, and asked him why he didn't share my bed."

"What did he say?"

"He didn't say anything. He actually came to my bedroom that night and tried to . . . well, you know. Poor man. He couldn't do it. Oh, God, Jackson, he wept in my bed." Libby felt tears of pity even now. "He tried a few times after that. Then he just gave up. It didn't matter to me." She rubbed her face against Jackson's furry chest. "I didn't know what I was missing. After that, we lived together more like father and daughter than husband and wife. Neither of us ever brought the subject up again."

Jackson feathered kisses over her face, her neck, her breasts. "My sweet Libby," he murmured.

Libby touched his hair, devouring his tenderness. Her belly quivered, as if reminding her that his child grew there, and she bit into her bottom lip to keep herself from weeping with joy.

23

It was light when she woke. Jackson slept soundly beside her. His beard roughened his cheeks and chin. His lashes were spiky thick and tipped with gold, and tiny wrinkles fanned the corners of his eyes. The wound on his forehead where he'd hit the table when she pushed him out of bed had begun to heal. Deep lines bracketed his mouth, which was open slightly. His lips were dry. From the cold and the wind, she thought, remembering how long he'd been out in it the day before. Her husband was no pretty boy. She grinned. She could live with that.

She snuggled against his warm body. How one man could generate so much heat, she'd never know. She had never before slept without any nightclothes. That wouldn't go over very well at the rooming house, but for here, for now, it was wonderful.

His arm came around her, and he pulled her closer. He was hard against her stomach. "Umm," he murmured into her ear. "I'm always horny in the morning."

She smiled into his chest. "I remember. Before I forget, I want to see your tattoo."

He drew his leg out from beneath the covers. Her gaze

traveled to the meeting of his thighs where his manhood stood proud and tall. She almost bent to kiss it, but caught herself. How could she even think such a thing?

"Well?"

His voice startled her. "What?"

"Are you going to stare at *that* all day, or are you going to look at the tattoo?"

She laughed, a little embarrassed. "If you only knew what I almost did . . ."

He didn't cover himself. "Tell me."

"No," she argued. "Let me see the tattoo."

He covered his leg with a pillow. "Not until you tell me what you almost did."

Her cheeks got so hot she was almost dizzy. "I couldn't tell you, Jackson. You'd think I was . . . was immoral."

He fingered her breast. "Now I *really* have to know."

She couldn't look at him. "You'd think I was terrible, really you would."

"Unless you were thinking about biting it off—"

She interrupted him with a jab to the ribs. "Of course I wasn't thinking that."

He continued to stroke her breast, arousing her. "Anything else will only make me hornier than I already am. Trust me."

Still unable to look at him, she said, "I was almost tempted to . . . to kiss it."

"I'd like that." His voice was deep and husky.

Shocked that he was so casual with the idea, she asked, "People actually do that sort of thing?"

"Whatever people want to do with each other is never off limits, Libby, as long as they both consent." He whipped off the pillow. "Now. Do you want to see my tattoo?"

Nodding, she got to her knees and bent over him. There it was. A teardrop—or raindrop, as he'd told her—exactly like Dawn's. It didn't appear to be as large as Dawn's, but then, his knee was so much bigger. "Well. I'll be," she murmured. "It's not that big. It's no wonder I didn't see it that morning."

He shook with quiet laughter. "Have you any idea what I was thinking about that morning?"

She traced the tattoo with her fingers. "I'm not sure I want to know."

"You."

She dragged her gaze from his firm, hairy thigh and looked at him. "Really?"

"Oh, yes." His answer was enthusiastic. "I was trying to imagine what your nipples looked like. I'd seen them pucker against your dressing gown the night before and couldn't get the image out of my head."

"I thought you were too drunk to remember."

"A man is never too drunk to think about nipples," he assured her with a rakish grin. "I imagined yours were nearly as pale as your skin." He cupped her breast, rolling her nipple between his thumb and forefinger. "And I was right."

The lush heaviness returned to her lower belly, and she moved to the head of the bed, flung one leg over his hip, and sighed. "How am I going to get any work done, feeling this way?"

"You don't have to work while we're here, remember? The only thing I want is for you to entertain me." His hand roamed her bottom. "And believe me, Libby girl, I'm easily entertained."

She bit back a moan of pleasure as his fingers found her. "So I've noticed."

"You're already wet." His voice was a seductive whisper against her cheek.

And she was nearly ready to shatter into pieces. "So you really think I'm going to have your baby?" She felt languid, waiting for the sensation to build.

He kissed her—a deep, wet, open-mouthed union of their tongues. "I know you are."

She wanted to believe it, too. "I don't see how you can tell—"

"Shhh," he soothed, gently rubbing her with his fingers. "Don't talk. Feel."

It did feel wonderful, but— "You shouldn't have to—"

"Shhh. I want to watch you. Don't fight it."

Fight it? She spread her legs, feeling wanton. She didn't think she could fight it if she wanted to. And she didn't.

Later they stayed under the covers and talked. Jackson told her about his suspicion of Ethan.

Libby shook her head and sighed. "It's almost hard for me to believe that Ethan had a hidden life. I knew he went to Eureka nearly every month, but I always assumed it was on business."

"Dawn's trust fund is gone," Jackson repeated. "I wonder how much more he embezzled."

Gripped by a terrible thought, Libby raised herself onto her elbow. "You didn't suspect that because Ethan and I had been seeing each other, that I knew anything about his embezzling, did you?"

He brought one of her curls to his face and inhaled. "No. I never did. I have to admit that I didn't know what I would find when I rode up to your rooming house that first day. I wondered if Dawn Twilight was your hired help, as she'd been at that other place, but the moment I saw her, I knew she was loved. I knew things were different."

"And you knew then that you were going to take her away from me."

"Yes," he admitted.

She turned toward him and smiled into his furry chest. "And look at us now." Her thoughts again turned to Ethan.

"And you think Ethan is responsible for the poisoning of all those sheep?"

"Yes, I do. The first day I was called out to Mateo's, I found three sets of horseshoe prints. One set was made by a Tennessee high-stepper. That's an unusual breed in these parts. Most ranchers and cowhands use cow ponies. The other night, the night of the wedding, Ethan Frost left the jail on a high-stepper."

Libby rubbed his chest. "All the evidence against him is circumstantial, isn't it?"

"I'm afraid so."

"So what do we do now?"

He raised her chin with his forefinger and smiled at her. "We?"

"He trusts me, Jackson. I mean, we're still . . . he still thinks we're friends. Maybe I can find out something that would help."

Jackson's mouth came down on hers, and he kissed her hard. When he broke the kiss, he looked at her, his expression stern. "You will do nothing of the sort, Mrs. Wolfe, my wife, the mother of my unborn child. Promise me you won't. Promise."

Her heart swelled with love and pride. "If you say so, my darling." She smiled to herself as she cuddled against him. *Darling.* It sounded so very natural to call him her darling. Oh, but she did love him, didn't she? The reality didn't frighten her, didn't cause her any pain at all. He might never return her love, but he was tender and concerned, and when he made love to her, she could almost believe he actually did love her.

Their time at the cabin was over too quickly. And even though it had snowed, it wasn't enough to snow them in. Libby was a bit disappointed, because she knew that once they were among Jackson's family again, their idyllic life together would never be the same. Having people around would inhibit her.

They bundled up for the ride home in the open wagon. Libby had never seen such beauty as the snow and frost-covered trees. The boughs of the pines, weighed down with snow, would move with every breeze, spraying finely sifted granules into the cold air. Sunshine glittered off the white ground, reminding Libby of millions of sparkly diamonds. Her breath clouded in the icy air, and she pulled up her scarf to cover her mouth and nose.

Jackson tugged her closer. "I don't know if I can get to the ranch without wanting you again."

She knew the feeling. The lusty sensation of his lovemaking was with her every waking minute. "It's too cold to make love, I'm afraid."

He treated her to a grin. "That's what you think."

"Jackson!" She punched him lightly.

"I mean it. Look at the blankets in the back."

She turned on the seat and saw the stack of quilts. Her body was preparing already. "Oh, we couldn't . . . not outside." She swung around to face him again. "Could we?"

His arm came around her. "Who's to stop us?"

So far they'd made love on a bear rug on the floor, in the bed, on a kitchen chair, and standing up with her legs wrapped around his waist. He was such a clever, inventive man. . . .

They rode into the yard, Libby blissfully in love and satisfied. He'd been so eager for her that he'd barely had time to unbutton his fly. She'd felt the excitement build the moment she raised her skirts. Huddled beneath the blankets on the wagon bed, they'd made breathless, exciting love.

Her gaze roamed the ranch. The snow was gone at this level, but the air continued to have a bite to it.

Her feeling of well-being dissipated the moment she saw the expression on Susannah's face as she left the house and hurried toward them.

Libby let Jackson help her from the wagon. "What is it? What's wrong? Is it Dawn?"

Susannah drew them into the house. "No. Nothing like that." She gave Jackson a telegram. "This came for you yesterday. We probably shouldn't have opened it, but your father was concerned."

Jackson read it, then met Libby's gaze.

Her heart leaped. "What's wrong?"

"It's from Vern. Danel Mateo has been killed," Jackson answered, glaring down at the wire in his hands.

Libby sank into a chair by the kitchen table. "Oh, no."

"I've got to get back," he told her.

"I'm coming with you."

With a shake of his head, he said, "You stay here with Dawn."

She stood and placed her fists on her hips. "I'm coming with you, Jackson, so don't try to talk me out of it."

He mumbled a mild curse. "Mother, can't you talk some sense into her?"

Susannah gave him a skeptical smile and merely raised her eyebrows. "I'm afraid not, dear. She's *your* wife. But I think you should let Dawn Twilight stay."

Libby's first reaction was to disagree. "But she should be home by the end of the week or she'll miss her lessons."

"Why not let her attend school with Katie for a week or so? Then, when you have this problem solved, we'll have a big party to introduce you and Dawn to the neighbors."

Libby opened her mouth to say no, then closed it. "I—I've never been away from her that long." She would miss her daughter terribly.

"Then maybe you should stay," Jackson suggested.

Libby reined in her emotions. "No. I'm coming with you."

"Mama! Papa!"

Dawn raced out from Katie's bedroom and flung herself into her mother's arms, then her father's.

"Did you have a nice honeymoon at the cabin?" She beamed up at them.

Libby felt herself color under Susannah's scrutiny. "Now, who said it was a honeymoon, dear?"

"Well, you went off by yourselves. What else would you call it?"

"Whatever you want to call it, we had a lovely time. We wish you could have come with us."

Jackson tweaked his daughter's nose. "Oh, no, we don't."

Libby's blush spread, and she caught Susannah watching her, a contented, almost joyous expression on her face. Suddenly she had the feeling that she and Jackson had been sent to the cabin on purpose. Had their problems been that transparent?

To cover her discomfort, she asked, "Would you like to stay with Katie for a while and attend school with her?"

Dawn's eyes got big. "You mean it?"

"I have to get back to Thief River," Jackson informed her, "and since your mother insists on joining me, we thought you might like to stay here for a while."

Dawn's face lit up, then darkened as she frowned. "I want to stay with Katie, but . . ." Her look was shy. "What about Mumser? Won't he miss me terribly?"

Libby smiled. "It wouldn't be the other way around, would it?"

Dawn returned a sheepish grin. "I do miss him. I hope he remembers who I am when I get home."

Jackson drew her into a fond embrace. "How could he forget you? You're the only person who sneaks him treats from the table and lets him sleep under the covers at bedtime. He won't forget you in a mere couple of weeks."

Libby glanced outside, noting that it was almost dark. "When should we leave?"

"First thing in the morning," he answered.

That night, although they were both exhausted and had decided they wouldn't make love, it was inevitable that they would. Once in bed, their bodies touching, their need grew greater than their exhaustion.

Trying to be quiet, Jackson entered her, clamped her lips to his, and rocked with her on the bed. Bliss shattered inside her, sending a quivering through her. They fell asleep, locked in each other's arms with Jackson still inside her.

Stifling a yawn, Susannah sat up and pulled on her robe, searching for her slippers with her feet.

From behind her, Nathan asked, "Is it time to get the children up?"

Susannah smiled. *Children.* No matter how old the child was, it would always be a child to a parent. "I thought I'd make sure they were awake."

Tugging at the sash on her robe, he toppled her backward. He loomed over her in the dusky light. "You can't leave this room until you kiss me."

She drew his face to hers and they kissed. Years of practice had not made their kisses stale, and even now Susannah desired the man who had rescued her from a living hell.

She raised her head and rested on an elbow. "It's been almost a week since we made love," she reminded him.

His hand roamed her hip. "I know. And watching Jackson and Libby at dinner last night made me hornier than hell."

Susannah rubbed his chest, loving the hair that grew there. "Sending them to the cabin worked, didn't it?"

"It was a stroke of genius, my love. But then," he added, his fingertips grazing her breasts, "I've always known you were smarter than I."

She kissed him quick and hard and, with a wistful sigh, slid from the bed and left the room.

At Jackson's door, she knocked quietly. When she got no response, she opened the door and peered inside. Although she felt like a voyeur, warmth stole over her as she watched them sleep.

They faced each other. Jackson had Libby cradled close to his chest, and Susannah could tell that Libby's leg was thrown over Jackson's hip.

Saying a quick prayer of thanks, she closed the door, then knocked again, this time loudly.

"Children?"

There was a rustling on the other side of the door.

"We're awake, Mother."

"Just barely," Susannah said to herself, smiling gaily as she went to the kitchen to prepare a pot of coffee.

24

AFTER LEAVING LIBBY AT THE BOARDINGHOUSE, JACKSON returned the rig, then went to the jail. When he opened the door, he noticed that Deputy Worth was there alone. Oddly, the cell door was open, and he was sitting beside the cot, talking quietly with the prisoner.

"Deputy?"

Axel Worth leaped from the chair and spun to face Jackson, his face a mottled red.

"Sheriff," he began, his Adam's apple bobbing frantically, "I didn't expect you back so soon. Have a nice trip?"

"Fine, thanks." Jackson stepped cautiously into the cell, his gaze leveled at the prisoner. "What's the cell door doing open, Axel?"

Again Axel's throat worked. "I was . . . ah . . . just giving him some water."

Glancing around the cell and finding no evidence of the water ladle, Jackson raised a skeptical eyebrow, but said nothing. He crossed to the prisoner, who eyed him warily from the cot. At least he had regained consciousness.

"Where's Vern?" Jackson continued to study the supine man, who had a large bandage on the side of his head.

"He . . . ah . . . went home for lunch," Axel answered.

The air seemed charged with energy. It got Jackson's hackles up. "Axel, why don't you take a lunch break, too?"

"Oh, but, Sheriff, I think I should stay——"

"Take a lunch break, Axel." Jackson wanted to talk with the prisoner alone. It bothered him that Axel had appeared almost chummy with the wounded man when he walked in. And that he'd obviously lied about what he was doing in the cell.

"I'd like to fill you in, Sheriff."

"Thanks, Axel. Just one thing before you leave. Has anyone else been in here to see him?"

"You mean his family or something like that?"

"Anyone at all."

Axel shook his head. "No, sir, no one at all. Just the doc."

With a nod, Jackson replied, "All right. You can fill me in after lunch."

Tossing the prisoner a furtive glance, Axel grabbed his hat and left the jail.

Jackson took the seat that Axel had vacated. The prisoner still hadn't spoken, but he hadn't taken his eyes off Jackson, either.

Jackson tried to appear comfortable, although he felt taut as a wire. He examined the bandage on the prisoner's head, noting that it covered his ear. "What's your name?"

"Maybe I forgot my name. Maybe I have amnesia."

The sarcasm in his voice told Jackson otherwise. He rose, left the cell, and locked it, then went to the desk and shuffled through the papers until he discovered what he was looking for. The prisoner's name was Clebbert Hartman. Cautious excitement flowered in Jackson's chest. Cleb Hartman was one of the monthly poker players at the Eureka saloon.

Vern's notes indicated that Hartman, who lived ten miles south of Thief River, had once been treated by the local doctor—for a gunshot wound he'd suffered while trying to rustle cattle.

Interesting. Jackson scraped his chin with the memo, then returned to the cell and resumed his seat. The man glared up at him. His eyes were wary. His nose was narrow and sharp. His face was all angles and planes. He looked like a ferret.

"So, Mr. Hartman, it appears this isn't your first brush with the law."

The prisoner said nothing.

"What were you doing on Ander Bilboa's land?"

Hartman shrugged his shoulders beneath the blanket that covered him. "Just passing through."

Jackson gave him a predatory smile. "With a sack of poison in tow?"

"Got rats on my place." The prisoner turned his face toward the wall. "The sack must have broke."

Jackson heaved a hearty sigh. "You know, Mr. Hartman, I'd like to believe you. Really I would. But you live ten miles south of here. That stretch of land you were on is out near Nevada. Got a bad sense of direction, do you?"

"It's the truth, and you can't prove otherwise," Hartman snarled.

Jackson shook his head, feigning sympathy. "It's a shame you have to take the rap for the others."

At that moment Hartman's hand moved beneath the blanket, and Jackson instinctively grabbed it. A shot rang out, whizzing close to Jackson's ear.

"Son of a bitch," he whispered, his voice thick with surprise. He pulled back the blanket and wrestled the gun from Hartman's grip.

"How in the hell did you get this?" He glared at the prisoner, who merely met his angry gaze with one of his own.

Jackson slid the pistol into his waistband, then frisked the belligerent prisoner. "Got any more surprises for me, Clebbert?"

Finding nothing, Jackson left the cell, locking it securely behind him. His heart was still drumming his rib cage, and his ears were ringing from the shot as he went to the window and stared out into the street.

Surely Vern wouldn't have let anyone smuggle a gun in. And no one had been to see him but the doc. What were the other possibilities? They came down to one: Axel Worth.

The question was . . . why? Inhaling deeply, he decided to take a wild chance.

"It's foolish to take the fall alone, Hartman. I haven't been sitting on my hands, you know. I've been a busy man. I was in Eureka and made all sorts of fascinating discoveries."

He returned to the cell, talking to Hartman through the bars. "For instance, I discovered that you're only a fair poker player."

Fear leaped into Hartman's beady eyes. "So what? I ain't the only player in that game, you know."

Another hungry smile. "I know."

Hartman clenched his jaw and looked away.

"Your good buddy Ethan Frost loses quite a bundle from time to time, doesn't he?"

Hartman's breathing accelerated, his chest rising and falling rapidly, but he didn't answer.

"Oh, by the way, are you aware that a railroad is going to be built between here and Fort Redding? Interesting, isn't it, that Mateo and Bilboa should be the only ranchers having trouble with the gunnysackers. Oh," he continued with a wave of his hand, "it's probably a coincidence that they're the only two who own land along the track site."

Hartman almost turned toward him, but caught himself. Still, he said nothing, but he appeared to struggle for breath.

Jackson merely laughed. "Such loyalty. Do you think for one minute that Frost would protect you? He's not the type, you know. If he were in your shoes right now, he'd be singing like a bird."

Hartman tossed him a frantic glance, but quickly looked away.

"That's right, Clebbert. You think about it. Think about what Ethan Frost would do in your place. Fortunately for you, we can't accuse you of murdering Danel Mateo."

This time Hartman did turn, but he merely stared at Jackson, a sly expression on his face. "No, you can't pin that one on me, can you?"

The door opened and Vern limped through. "Jackson! Good to have you back."

Jackson nodded. "I read your report on the prisoner. Anything to add?"

"Not yet," Vern answered. "The Mateo family is having a private service and burial for Danel today. Guess the rest of us can pay our respects toward the end of the week. At the graveside."

"Yes. Well, do you mind if I go home and grab a bite? I came directly here from the road. Oh, by the way, Vern," he began, knowing full well the answer to his question before he asked it, "who around here rides a Tennessee high-stepper?"

"Well, Ethan Frost does."

Jackson's gaze was on Hartman. "Anyone else?"

"Not to my knowledge. They ain't a good cattle mount for these parts. Why do you ask?"

With Hartman's beady eyes piercing him, Jackson lied, "No reason. I saw a high-stepper at the livery and wondered who it belonged to, that's all." With a smile and a wave, he left the jail and crossed to the livery to retrieve his mount.

He hadn't told Vern about his tussle with Hartman over the gun. Wrapping up this case was something he had to do himself. And though he admired Vern a great deal, he wasn't sure he could count on him to keep his mouth shut. Axel Worth was up to something, and Jackson didn't want to scare him off.

Dawn's absence had left Libby anxious for her return. Although she was expected home today, Libby tried to concentrate on the preacher at Danel Mateo's memorial service. The family had held a private burial first. Now, a week after his murder, friends and family gathered at his graveside. Danel's eldest son, Dominic, stood stalwart beside his newly widowed mother. Her younger children formed a protective arc around her.

Although they were about the same age, Libby hadn't seen Dominic Mateo in years. She'd almost forgotten what a handsome man he was, with his unfashionably long black hair and his thick, dark eyebrows and eyelashes. Of all the

Mateo children, Dom was the one Libby had felt wouldn't stay on the ranch. Yet he'd helped his father over the past years, despite having graduated from a prestigious eastern college.

Now, standing at his father's grave, Dom appeared remote and resolute.

Libby and Jackson approached him. Libby hugged him. "I'm so sorry, Dom. Your father was a good man."

He stood within her embrace, stoic as a statue.

She pulled away, noting that his gaze was on her husband.

"Have you caught the murderer?" His voice had the hard edge of one who could barely contain his anger and his grief.

"It's only a matter of time, Dom."

Dom shook with unleashed fury. "Time? Sheriff, if you don't do something damned soon, I'll do it for you."

Jackson put his arm around Dom's shoulders and drew him away from the crowd.

Libby's gaze lingered on her husband, for she knew he was trying to explain to Dom why the law appeared to work so slowly. Even now Libby found it hard to believe that Ethan was embroiled in cattle poisoning and murder. She'd had no idea he had a gambling problem. Jackson had assured her that people like Ethan would go to any lengths to cover their behinds. She knew she'd never be able to look at him the same way again.

Eager to get home before Dawn arrived from the ranch, Libby caught Jackson's eye, motioning that she was going to walk home. Jackson blew her a quick kiss, then returned his attention to calming Dominic.

She'd just left the cemetery when she met Ethan's rig on the road. Her stomach dropped, everything she'd recently learned about him making her suddenly fear him.

His smile was blinding.

She swallowed hard, hoping to show none of the emotions she was feeling. Although there was no tangible proof that Ethan had done anything wrong, Libby trusted Jackson. Even though she'd known Ethan for many, many years, she could no longer believe a word he said. That he could take money from an innocent child's trust fund made her skin crawl. That he could slaughter hundreds of sheep for no reason other than his own personal gain made her sick to her stomach, and that he could kill a wonderful man like Danel Mateo made her angry and disgusted. How could he do such a thing? How *could* he?

"Want a lift home?"

Attempting nonchalance, she answered his smile, although her heart was pounding furiously. "Oh, no. Thank you just the same." She lengthened her stride. "The walk will do me good."

He stopped the team and jumped to her side. "Libby?"

She gave him a wide, innocent look, cursing the betrayal of her rapid heartbeat. "Yes?"

He frowned. "What's wrong?"

She tried to laugh, but it sounded strained. "Why, nothing. I'd rather walk, that's all."

He didn't appear convinced. He grabbed her arm. "Something's wrong."

Wincing as his fingers pressed into her flesh, Libby tried to pull away. "Let go of my arm, Ethan."

He complied. "It's that husband of yours, isn't it? He's turned you against me."

She looked at him, her pulse jumping. Something in his eyes frightened her. Something she'd never seen before. Turning away quickly, she continued her long strides, her heart in her throat. "Dawn's returning today after a lengthy visit with her grandparents. I have to get home," she explained.

She left him staring after her as she hurried home and sprinted up the boardinghouse steps. Relieved to find Bert and Burl rocking lazily on the porch, she said, "Good afternoon, gentlemen."

Without breaking rhythm, both old men nodded.

Libby stopped to catch her breath and studied them. "Why weren't you at the funeral?"

Burl sucked air in through his toothless mouth. "Ain't a good idea fer us to set foot in a cemetery, Miz Liberty."

"That's right," Bert agreed. "The Lord might see us there and remember we're still kickin'. Don't do a lick of good to tempt him, ya know."

Rolling her eyes, she rushed inside. Corey met her in the foyer. "Where's Jackson?"

Libby allowed him to remove her cape. "He's spending some time with Dom Mateo. Oh, Corey, the man is so angry, I'm afraid he'll do something he might regret."

"He can't put his father's murder out of his mind, Libby. No doubt he feels guilty because he couldn't prevent it."

"I suppose you're right. Poor Mrs. Mateo. Now she's without a husband, most of their sheep have been killed, and they're on the brink of losing the ranch. I hope Jackson gets this case solved quickly."

Corey took her arm. "Just for a moment I want you to stop worrying about everyone else. Can you do that?"

She gave him a wry smile. "Maybe for a moment. Actually, I'm anxious to see Dawn. I've never been away from her this long."

"We've been busy preparing a surprise for her." He put his arm around her and led her into the kitchen.

Libby gasped, surprised and pleased. Mahalia stood over an elaborately decorated cake in the shape of a floppy, moppy-looking dog.

"I've been cuttin' and piecin' for near an hour now, pastin' this thing together with icin'."

"And Chloe Ann and I made this," Corey announced, holding up a string of letters that said "Welcome Home." "I thought I'd attach them to the porch so she'll see them right away. Not only that," he continued, dramatically rubbing his arm, "I've been making ice cream and my arm is sore from cranking the ice cream handle."

"Oh, she'll love a party." Libby bustled around the kitchen, getting out plates and napkins. "I only hope Jackson gets here before Dawn does."

Burl Bellamy stepped into the kitchen, his expression puzzled.

"What's wrong, Burl?"

"I just seen the little gal."

Libby's stomach fluttered with excitement. "She's coming? Oh, Corey, get those letters up. Quickly."

Burl coughed and cleared his throat. "She ain't comin' to the house, Miz Liberty."

Libby stopped. "What do you mean?"

Burl scratched his shiny bald head. "Strangest thing. I was takin' a walk to the road, and I saw her bein' helped into a buggy."

"A buggy?" Libby's insides froze with fear. Why had Dawn not been dropped off in front of the house? "Who was driving it, Burl?"

"Well, now, I cain't be certain, Miz Liberty. My eyesight ain't what it used to be." He fumbled in his pocket. "Shortly after they rode away, some kid gave me this note. Said it was fer you."

With shaky fingers, Libby took the note, but her eyes were blurred with unshed tears of fear and although she tried, she couldn't read it.

"Corey?" She handed him the piece of paper, her stomach threatening nausea. "What does it say?"

He skimmed the note and met her fearful gaze. "Ethan has taken Dawn."

Libby's hand flew to her mouth. She swallowed convulsively. "T-taken Dawn? Taken her where?"

"He doesn't say. He wants Jackson to meet him at a place called Pinkers Bluff."

Libby pressed her forearms against her unsettled stomach and glanced at Corey. The fear in his eyes was mirrored in her own. "We've got to tell Jackson."

"Where was he going after he left the cemetery?" Corey's voice was strained.

"He—he was coming home. He's as eager to see Dawn as I am."

"I'll see if I can find him." Corey ran toward the front door.

"I'm coming with you," Libby said, hurrying behind.

Corey was on the porch. "Libby, you have to stay here."

She stood in the doorway as he raced down the steps to his mount. "No! I can't. I'm coming with you—"

"Libby, please stay here. If I miss him, you'll have to tell him what's happened." He swung into the saddle and raced away, leaving Libby on the porch, staring after him. Stay here? How was she supposed to simply stay behind when Dawn had been kidnapped?

Chloe Ann stepped beside her, put her arm around Libby's waist and gave her a loving squeeze. "Let the men take care of it, Libby."

Libby turned and stared at her, her heart thudding wildly. "Let the—" She shook her head, unwilling to explain. Chloe Ann wouldn't understand. Not until she had a child of her own.

Pulling away from Chloe Ann's gentle embrace, Libby said, "I'm going upstairs to lie down."

"Yes, you do that," Chloe Ann answered. "I'll bring you a nice cup of tea."

Libby raced up the stairs to her room. A cup of tea. She almost snorted, but she knew Chloe Ann was doing what she thought was best.

Libby threw open her wardrobe and rummaged through Sean's old clothes, things she hadn't given away. Finding his leather breeches, she tossed them on her bed, then hunted for a shirt. She undressed, donned the clothes and crept downstairs, grabbing an old hat and a jacket off the coatrack on her way out.

Refusing to follow Corey's orders, she set out to find her daughter. The place to start was Pinkers Bluff, but how would she get there if she didn't ride?

For a brief, agonizing moment, she stood motionless, examining her plight. She hadn't ridden a horse in almost twenty years; she'd managed somehow always to travel by buggy or wagon. Again, the image of Sean's broken body rose before her eyes, and she clamped her lips together, trying to stay strong.

The swirling in the pit of her stomach reminded her of her fears, but she could do this. She'd always felt that she could ride a damned horse if she had to, and now *she had to*.

"I need a horse." Lord in heaven, she never thought she'd say those words out loud. With quick steps she hurried to the livery. Desperate times called for desperate measures.

Her arms and legs tied, the breed sniffled quietly beside him. "Wh-where are you taking me?" Her voice was a mere whimper.

"Someplace where your papa won't find you unless he does what I ask." It had been amazingly easy to take her. As she walked down the road toward the boardinghouse, she'd been alone. No one else had been around.

Had Ethan not been out of town, Axel would have found him sooner, and Ethan could have taken the little breed before she was nearly at her doorstep. Poor Axel, he mused. Sweating like a mule because he'd secretly slipped Hartman a gun, then had been sent from the jail like a child. The plan had been for Cleb to pretend to overpower Axel and make his escape before Sheriff Roberts returned from lunch.

It wasn't clear what exactly had happened. Wolfe apparently had said nothing to Sheriff Roberts about the gun, but Axel had been hiding out ever since he learned that Wolfe had wrestled the weapon from Cleb. Wolfe was no fool. He probably suspected Axel of giving it to the prisoner in the first place. Ethan didn't dare go to the jail to confront Hartman. They weren't even supposed to know each other. Unlike Axel, who would undoubtedly spill his guts if confronted, Cleb was a tough bastard. Maybe he wouldn't keep his mouth shut forever, but he was stubborn enough to stay quiet long enough for Ethan to get away. After that, who cared? They were on their own.

Now Ethan needed a few hours to close the biggest deal of his life, then he'd be gone. Jackson Wolfe was no fool.

Ethan would send for the boys later. Willie was fifteen, almost a man. He'd been a father to the younger ones for years. They could survive a few weeks without him.

What rankled was that Libby had been turned against him by that brute of a husband of hers. God, but he'd hated to see that look of fear in her eyes. . . .

The little breed hiccuped. "Papa will do anything you ask, Mr. Frost. I know he will."

"You just keep thinking good thoughts, little girl." She wasn't nearly so sassy now, was she?

She went quiet beside him, then murmured, "Willie's gonna be just like you when he grows up."

He laughed quietly. "Is that a threat or a promise?"

"Willie's a bully."

"You're a mouthy one, aren't you?"

She stared at her hands. "Willie's a bully, just like you."

"Watch your mouth, little breed. Willie's strong. If he comes across as a bully, it isn't his fault; it's yours for being a weakling."

"I'm not weak," she argued. "And my mama says that we're all what our parents make us."

"Wise woman, your mama. Always thought she'd make a fine mother to my sons."

The little breed slanted him a hard look. "She'd never have married you."

He reached out to touch her chin, but she yanked herself away, trembling beside him.

He pulled a quilt over her lap. "Here. I don't want you catching cold on me." He smiled to himself. Not before he got her to the cave, anyway.

Then the tide would give her a chill she'd never forget.

Seething, Jackson read the note: "Wolfe. I have your half-breed. Meet me at Pinkers Bluff and we'll talk. Frost."

Jackson crumpled the paper, his stomach churning wildly. "Corey, get back to the rooming house and make sure Libby's all right. She's liable to do something crazy."

"I thought I'd stay with you," Corey suggested.

"Go home and stay with the women, Corey. That's an order."

Corey sighed heavily, but obeyed. Before he left, he said, "Take care of yourself."

With a nod, Jackson kicked his mount into a gallop and dashed toward Pinkers Bluff, berating himself as the wind whistled around him. He'd waited too long. He should have moved on Frost immediately. This was his fault, and his fault alone. Even though he had no concrete proof, he should have done something to prevent the disastrous chain of events.

Now the bastard had his daughter. Icy fingers squeezed his heart. God, if anything happened to her . . .

He drove his mount harder, burning up the ground beneath them, unable to get to the bluff fast enough.

It loomed in the distance. The remains of Flicker Feather's village were below the bluff. To the west were numerous caverns and caves, all the way to the coast. The air was damp, and there was a hint of the ocean in it.

He saw Frost waiting for him at the top of the bluff. His gut tightened, twisting the nerves, forcing a red haze of fury before his eyes.

Calm. He had to stay calm. A foolish move could cost him his daughter's life.

25

WHERE'S MY DAUGHTER, YOU SON OF A BITCH!" JACKSON shouted the words as he closed the distance between them.

Frost was calm astride his mount. "She's safe. At least for now," he added cryptically.

"What do you want from me?" Jackson scanned the landscape in search of Dawn Twilight.

Frost laughed. "She's not here, Wolfe. I need time to get away. You're an honorable man. If you promise to let me escape, I know you won't go back on your word." He continued to snicker. "That's what makes men like you so transparent and easy to use."

Jackson wanted to rearrange his face. Focusing internally, he calmed himself. Although it grated at his sense of justice, and after all, he'd taken an oath to uphold the law, he would agree to anything to keep his daughter safe. Besides, he'd do Dawn Twilight no good if he lost his temper. "I promise. Now tell me where she is."

Frost wagged a finger at him. "Tut, tut. Not so fast. Aren't you the least bit curious to know why I asked you to meet me here?"

Flicker Feather's burned village was just over the bluff. Jackson's gaze swung to the banker. "I think I know."

Frost crossed his forearms over the pummel on his saddle, affecting a nonchalant pose. "So. You have everything figured out, have you?"

Jackson refused to let his gaze waver. "Pretty much."

"Well, as long as you promise to let me go, I guess I can tell you everything."

"Don't bother," Jackson answered. "I don't have time to listen to your rot."

A smirk. "Oh, but I insist." A malicious grin. "Don't worry. Your little breed will be fine. For a while, anyway."

Jackson had all he could do to stay on his mount and not go for Frost's throat. "Get on with it."

Ethan flicked his reins casually against the saddle. "I've been here before, as you can imagine."

Jackson waited, impatiently clenching his teeth.

"It was nothing personal, Wolfe." A chuckle. "None of the destruction was personal. I was a young man with high standards. Those damned diggers were such an eyesore," he said with feeling. He raised his index finger in Jackson's direction. "I never harmed a child. I never did. You've got to believe me."

Jackson huffed a dry laugh. "Is that supposed to make it all right?"

Ethan sighed. "I don't suppose someone like you would understand. After all, you actually slept with one of them, didn't you?"

"She was my wife." God, how he wanted to smash Frost's nose in!

Ethan made a face. "You know? I don't understand that." He shivered. "Sleeping with one of them seems so . . . dirty." He wrinkled his nose.

Jackson held his rage, sensing he was being baited. "Any other of your fine, upstanding, bigoted vigilantes alive?"

Ethan chuckled. "Nope. All dead, I'm afraid. Except me, of course."

"I don't believe you."

"Now, Sheriff. You don't expect me to rat on my friends, do you?"

"How big are your gambling debts, Frost?"

Ethan nodded expansively. "So you found out about those. Well, I'll be a rich man once I sell Mateo's and Bilboa's land to the government."

"For the railroad."

"You've done your homework, haven't you?"

Jackson suddenly laughed. "Do you expect to get away with this?"

"You've promised not to stop me, Sheriff. You have to keep your promise. You're an honorable man."

"Hell," Jackson murmured. "I'd keep my eyes open if I were you. Dominic Mateo is out for your blood."

Ethan suddenly exploded. "I didn't kill his father. I didn't! It was an accident—" He stopped, settling into his saddle, and smiling an evil smile. "Very good, Sheriff. Very good."

"You're an asshole, Frost."

"And you're a fool."

"Maybe, but in the end, I'm going to win."

"No, I don't think so. I'm smarter than anyone you've ever met, Wolfe. You know how I found your little trust fund?"

"I imagine you're going to tell me."

Ethan shook his head and laughed. "It was purely by accident, I assure you. After my father died, I found all this money simply sitting there, collecting interest and dust. I couldn't let that happen. I was already in debt; gambling has always been my downfall." He stared into the distance. "Yours wasn't the only money I embezzled."

Jackson had heard enough. "I don't need to hear any more. Where's my daughter?"

Frost raised his hand. "Not quite yet. Let me see," he mused, appearing to concentrate.

"Did you kill my wife?"

"You mean your squaw?" He grimaced. "Probably. But like I said, it was nothing personal. It was such a long time ago, and there were so many of them."

It was all in the past. Jackson didn't want to dwell on it anymore. The only thing that rankled like hell was letting Frost go. "Where's my daughter?"

"I expected to see a stronger response from you considering I've admitted killing your squaw. Knowing your kind, it's probably all bottled up inside. Well," he said, moving away, "if you'll promise not to follow me, I'll—"

"Where is she?" Having to let him go left a sour taste in his mouth, but his daughter was more important at this moment than the law. Ethan Frost would get what was due him. Eventually. That was all Jackson could hope for.

"She's in one of the caverns along here." Ethan pointed toward the west.

"Which one?"

"Oh, come now, Sheriff. That would make your task incredibly easy, wouldn't it? I'll give you a hint. She won't last long once the tide comes in, and—" He pulled out his pocket watch. "Oh, dear. It's coming in now."

Hearing the sound of approaching hoofbeats, both men looked up. The horseman was riding fast and hard, directly toward them.

With one hand clutching the reins and the other the saddle horn, Libby clung to the rented horse, her heart thudding with fear. This was insane. Insane! Her teeth jarred each time her rump hit the saddle, and she'd lost her hat before she reached the outskirts of town. Now her hair had come loose, and the wind was whipping the long, wild strands around her face. She didn't care. Her fingers were frozen; she couldn't have relaxed them if she'd wanted to.

Pinkers Bluff came into view, and she felt a combination of fear and relief. She only hoped she wasn't too late. In the distance she saw two men on horseback. Hanging on tight, she guided the horse in that direction.

Her brain told her one of the two men was Ethan; her heart and soul told her the other was her husband. She directed the mount toward Ethan, wanting to run him over. At the last minute she tugged on the reins and pulled the horse to an awkward halt.

Everything shook—her hands, her knees, her chest, even her teeth. Gasping for breath, she slid gracelessly from the mount and flew at Ethan. Catching him off guard, she grabbed him and hauled him off his mount.

"You bastard! Where's my daughter? Where is she?" She threw herself on top of him, scratching and punching, out of control. She pulled his hair, kicked him, and rammed her knee into his groin. In a remote corner of her mind, she heard him gasp for air.

"I'll kill you! I'll kill you, you slimy pile of hog slop!"

She felt herself being lifted away from him, but she continued to kick at the air.

"Bastard! Bastard! Bastard!"

"Come on, Libby. Settle down, honey."

Up through her anger, she recognized Jackson's voice. She fought him, kicked at him, screamed. "He's got her! He's got my daughter, dammit! I'll kill him, I'll kill him!"

"Libby, we have to let him go."

The words sifted through her frenzy. She swung around and stared at her husband as though he were an escaped madman. "Let him go? Jackson, we can't let him go! He's got Dawn. He's got—"

"I know where she is, honey." He attempted to soothe her, but her agitation was too strong. "We can't waste time with him. We have to get to Dawn or she'll drown."

Suddenly exhausted, she slumped against Jackson, trying to hold back her fearful sobs. "Dawn, my poor, poor baby . . ."

"We'll find her, sweetheart."

Ethan coughed, spitting out blood-tinged saliva. He swore and wiped his nose with the back of his hand. It was smeared with blood. "She's insane, Wolfe. Keep her the hell away from me."

Libby's chest heaved. "You . . . you piece of skunk vomit," she hissed, her teeth clenched in fury.

Ethan attempted to smooth his rumpled hair. "Yes, well, we all do what we have to do, Libby." He straightened his coat, mounted his horse, and rode away.

Anguish suffocated her. "We're just going to let him go? After all he's done?"

"It's the price I had to pay for Dawn's life, sweetheart." Jackson stood by his mount, his arm around Libby. "I hate like hell to let him go, honey, but I promised." He waited a beat, then said, "He's responsible for Flicker Feather's murder and the burning of their village. I suspect everyone in the village died in the fire."

Libby closed her eyes. "Then how did Dawn survive?"

"That's one thing we may never know."

She brushed tears from her cheeks. "But to let him go after all he's done . . ."

"I had no choice. I have a feeling he'll get what he deserves if Dom Mateo ever catches up with him. Now come, love, we've got a lot of ground to cover."

He helped her into his saddle, swinging up behind her. "We'll come back and pick up your mount after we've found Dawn Twilight."

They tore over the earth, slowing at the mouth of each cave where the high tidewater spilled in, calling out Dawn's name.

"Oh, God, what if we're too late?" Libby had been thinking it so hard she hadn't been able to stifle the words.

All of a sudden they heard a sound. Jackson drew his mount to a halt, and they listened.

Libby gasped, relief making her weak. "It sounds like Dawn," she whispered, straining to hear.

"It's coming from over there," Jackson stated, urging the horse toward the cave.

"Dawn? Darling?"

"In here, Mama! I'm in here!" Her voice echoed from inside.

They raced to the mouth of the cave, taking note of the swelling waters that sped through it. They waded in, squinting into the darkness.

"Dawn Twilight?"

"Papa? Oh, Papa! I'm here!"

Libby swallowed her alarm when she saw how far the tide had risen on Dawn's body.

Jackson sloshed through the waist-deep water and sliced the ropes that held his daughter. She tumbled eagerly and gratefully into his arms. He carried her outside but wouldn't put her down.

Libby hugged them both. "Oh, darling, I'm so glad you're all right." She stepped away, her heart thumping anxiously. "He didn't hurt you, did he?"

Dawn stroked her mother's hair. "I'm fine, Mama, but what happened to you?"

Jackson gave Libby a proud smile. "You'd have been proud of her, Dawn Twilight. She came to find you on horseback."

Dawn's eyes grew big. "You rode a horse, Mama?"

Libby felt the threat of tears. "I'd have ridden the devil's mount to find you, darling. Why weren't you dropped off at home?"

Dawn glanced away. "I'm sorry, Mama. That was my fault. Grandpapa's friend, Mr. Kito, wanted to drop me off at home, but I begged him to let me walk from the jail."

She looked at her mother and grinned. "Did you really ride a horse?"

Jackson's grin was broad. "She did. And she flew at Ethan Frost and yanked him off his horse, then proceeded to beat him up."

"I hope I broke his nose," Libby mumbled, bearly remembering her actions.

With Dawn on one arm, he wrapped the other around her. "I think you deserve to be called Warrior Heart, my love. I didn't like being on the receiving end of your temper, but I've never seen anything like what you did to Frost."

"He deserves to die a long, lingering death." She attempted to fix her hair, but the effort was useless. "I lost my hat."

He drew her close and looked deep into her eyes. "And I've lost my heart."

Libby blinked, surprised. "You . . . you have?"

He gave her a lopsided grin. "Have I ever. I love you, Liberty Wolfe, more than I can ever tell you."

Feeling a happiness that threatened to consume her, she breathed in the rich, salt-tinged air, careless of the tears that blurred her vision. "And I love you."

Dawn hugged them both. "And I'm going to write a story about this."

A week later Jackson brought a mysterious package home from the jail. "Come see this," he instructed Libby.

She wiped her hands on her apron and eased herself into a chair across from him, still suffering muscle aches from her fateful ride. She tried not to wince. "What is it?"

Jackson tipped the package over and out tumbled several important-looking documents.

Libby picked one up and opened it, then shot Jackson a look of surprise. "Why, it's the deed to the Bilboa place."

Jackson nodded. "Mateo's is in there, too. And there are others, of ranchers I've never heard of, who have apparently moved on. Frost was a busy crook long before the government decided to build a railroad through the sheepherders' land."

Libby looked through them, recognizing the names of many ranchers she'd thought had simply moved on of their own free will. "Where did you get them?"

Jackson shrugged. "The package was on my desk when I got to work this morning."

Libby sucked in a breath. "This is wonderful, but . . . who put them there, and what does it mean?"

"I don't know. I wish I did. I have no doubt Ethan Frost had these documents at one point. How he lost them is anybody's guess."

Libby rose, went around the table, and settled herself on her husband's lap. It certainly wasn't soft, but it felt better than the chair. "I wonder who got them away from him."

"It doesn't matter, but I could take a guess," Jackson murmured against her hair. "Axel was on the jail floor this morning, trussed up like a turkey, babbling about Dominic Mateo and promising to tell me everything if I'd protect him from the Basque. Cleb Hartman was straining at the cell bars, hollering at Axel to keep his mouth shut."

"You think they were all in this together?"

"That would be my guess."

Libby worried her bottom lip with her teeth. "So you think Dominic somehow got the deeds away from Ethan?"

"It's possible."

"Then . . . then what happened to Ethan?"

"I don't know." He caressed her shoulders, her back, her arms.

Her muscles relaxed under his ministering. "Are you going to go after Dom?"

"Would I be shirking my duty as a lawman if I didn't?"

"No," she said, smiling into his beautiful blue eyes. "There's been enough heartache. It's time to heal. What will happen to Axel and Cleb?"

"The circuit judge is on his way. They'll be dealt with properly. And I've already posted a notice that the papers have been retrieved. Anyone who wants his land back should contact me."

They nuzzled each other, kissing and nibbling.

"I do love you, my Warrior Heart. You really love me, too?"

Jackson laughed. "I've told you so every day, haven't I?"

Libby expelled a contented sigh. "And here I thought I was doomed to live with a man I loved who would never love me."

"I love you with an intensity that sometimes scares me, sweetheart. Never have I felt this way before."

Libby gazed into his rugged, wonderful face. "Never?"

"Never," he repeated. He drew back, suddenly concerned. "You didn't have any bad effects from your ride?"

She knew he meant the baby. "No. I think we're going to have another Warrior Heart to raise."

"And another one after that?"

She kissed his ear, drawing the lobe into her mouth. "Most definitely."

Growling into her neck, he stood with her in his arms. "Is there time?"

"Dawn doesn't get home for another hour. Is that long enough?"

"I guess it'll have to be," he answered. "Otherwise, she might walk in on us and decide to write a story about it."

They laughed together as they took the stairs to the third floor, to the room they now shared.

Libby's contentment went deep. Her prayers had all been answered. True to their daughter's prediction, things had worked out just fine.

Epilogue

Riverside Boardinghouse, 1895

JACKSON SPRINTED UP THE PORCH STEPS, ACKNOWLEDGING THE rocking Bellamy brothers with a nod.

"Afternoon, Sheriff." Burl spat a wad of tobacco at the spittoon, his aim slightly off as the brown sludge trickled down the side.

"So today's the day that highbrow brother of yers returns from New York City."

Jackson rested his boot on the railing and gazed out over the lawn and Libby's prize chrysanthemums. "Today's the day," he responded, feeling a rush of excitement.

"What's he done, again?" Bert questioned.

"He received an award from the publishing world for his comprehensive work on the birds of the American West."

"Studied birds, did he?" Burl spat again, his aim no better than the first time.

Jackson wondered how old the coots were. With their aversion to physical labor, they'd probably outlive everyone. He'd never seen either of them do a lick of work as long as he'd been at the boardinghouse.

"Yes, he studied birds, Burl." He entered the house, the aroma of apple pie and cinnamon buns sensually attacking his nostrils. Crossing to the kitchen, he peeked inside and was graced with the scene of his wife sitting cross-legged on the floor, entertaining their four-year-old son, Nathaniel.

He glanced up, honoring his father with a bright, toothy smile. "Papa!"

"How's my big boy?"

Jackson helped his very pregnant wife to her feet, then scooped his son up in his arms and gave him a noisy kiss. He held him high in the air, and the boy squealed with glee, settling against Jackson's shoulder when he brought him down.

Libby straightened, her hand pressing the small of her back. Jackson was immediately concerned.

"You shouldn't be working so hard, sweetheart. Where's Mahalia?"

Libby stepped closer to him and offered her mouth. There was a smudge of cinnamon and sugar at the corner, and Jackson licked it off before kissing her long and deep. He stirred, in spite of her advanced pregnancy. Or maybe because of it. Hell, he didn't know, for she was able to arouse him no matter what her condition.

"I sent her on an errand to get her out of my way. You'd think we were having royalty to dinner, the way she's acting."

Jackson smiled into her eyes, then noted the fluttering pulse at her throat. It always thrilled him to know she wanted him as badly and as often as he wanted her. "Well, it isn't every day we have a famous author to dinner."

Libby's features softened. "I can't wait to see the baby. Chloe Ann and Corey, too, of course," she amended. "It's been too long." She gave Jackson a sly look. "He writes that he has a surprise for Dawn. She's beside herself trying to guess what it is."

Libby's face was flushed, and Jackson continued to feel concern. "Are you sure you're not doing too much?" With his family coming down from the ranch, he was afraid Libby had taken on more than she could handle.

"Will you stop worrying about me? I'd go crazy if I couldn't keep busy. You know that."

He rubbed her swollen abdomen, watching her relax. "You need a break, dear wife."

As if on cue, Dawn Twilight entered the kitchen, giving her parents a crafty look. "Are you two at it again?"

Jackson's gaze lingered on his daughter. She'd been a beauty at twelve; now she was a heartbreak waiting to happen. Something clutched his heart, and he recognized it as regret. One day soon she would leave them and begin a life of her own. She was mature beyond her years, but to him, she was still his little Dawn Twilight. The daughter he would have lost had it not been for Liberty O'Malley Wolfe.

"What are you going to do about it, you gorgeous creature? Write another story?"

The crafty look became a crafty smile. "You might be surprised. But right now," she added, lifting her sleepy little brother into her arms, "Nate needs a nap before company comes."

Dawn carried her brother to the door, then turned to her parents, her blue-gray eyes warm and her smile blinding. "You two are really something."

Jackson pulled out a kitchen chair, sat down, and drew Libby onto his lap. They cuddled as he massaged her belly.

"Dom Mateo is back," he told her.

Libby sat up, surprised. "Did you see him?"

Jackson tugged her toward him. "He stopped in to say hello."

"You still think he killed Ethan?"

"It's just a hunch. Who knows, maybe Ethan's death was an accident. He was found floating facedown in the river. That could have meant he drowned."

"And the water is so swift there," Libby added, her voice cautious. "After all, that's why they call it Thief River, isn't it? Because it draws unsuspecting people into it, then snatches them into the current?"

"That's the legend." He kissed her again.

Neither mentioned the package of deeds and mortgage papers Jackson had received four years before. Now, however, every family that had been driven out had been given the opportunity to reclaim their land.

"Have you any idea what Corey's surprise is for Dawn?"

"I have a good idea," Jackson answered, trying not to act smug.

Libby pinched him, making him yelp. "You'd better tell me or I'll pinch you again."

He grinned. "If you weren't so pregnant, I'd—"

"You'd what?" Her gaze was innocently seductive. The telltale pulse at her throat continued to throb.

"God, but I love you, woman."

"And I love you."

They settled together again. "He's gotten her a scholarship, one she can use at any school she chooses."

Libby gasped, her eyes filling with tears. "Oh, Jackson, she'll be euphoric."

He hugged his wife close. "I only hope she doesn't decide she wants to go to some fancy eastern school."

"I don't think she'll want to be that far away, do you?"

"I hope not."

Mumser scurried into the kitchen, sniffed the corners, then settled near the stove on a rug Libby had put there especially for him. Not far away, Cyclops was asleep on her own cushion.

Libby shook her head. "After four years, that dog still growls at me. He has no idea that I could have his head on a plate, does he?"

"You know that old saying, 'his bark is worse than his bite'?"

She raised a skeptical brow. "Are you referring to Mumser or me?"

He chuckled. "You two have more in common than you think, you know."

"Oh, don't give me that nonsense."

"But it's true, love. Under all of your bluster and stoicism, you're a softhearted pushover. Behind Mumser's growl, he's the same. And the Shih Tzu is also known as the chrysanthemum dog because his face resembles the mum."

Libby scrutinized the animal. "He doesn't look like *my* mums."

"I'd think that after all this time the two of you would come to some sort of truce."

"Actually," she answered, "I think we've rather come to enjoy our antagonism. Why, we even look forward to it, don't we, Mumser?"

The dog perked up at the sound of his name, glanced at Libby, then growled, although his heavily plumed tail wagged.

Libby laughed. "See?"

Again, as so often happened when he thought about his life, peace stole into Jackson's heart. He couldn't imagine things turning out any other way. He was a lucky man to have found a woman like Liberty O'Malley. In his soul, he knew it was she, not he, who had the Warrior's Heart.

Dear Readers:

First of all, I must apologize to the town of my birth, Thief River Falls, Minnesota, for stealing the name and transporting it to California. I'm not even certain the legend of the river is correct, but it's the one I learned as a girl, and it was dramatic enough to stay with me and make me a cautious swimmer all those years ago.

Also, for you Shih Tzu buffs, thanks to my friend, Dorothy Lohman, I'm aware that the breed didn't come to the United States until the twentieth century, but because this is fiction, I've chosen to bring it over earlier.

Again, as always, I welcome your letters and suggestions and I thank you so much for your support. I hope *Warrior Heart* was all you expected it to be.

Best always,

Jane Bonander

Jane Bonander
Box 3134
San Ramon, CA 94583-6834

**POCKET BOOKS
PROUDLY PRESENTS**

SCENT OF LILACS

Jane Bonander

**Coming Soon
in Paperback
from Pocket Books**

**The following is a preview of
Scent of Lilacs. . . .**

Providence, Rhode Island
Late 1800s

With her medical books clutched against her stomach, Lexy stumbled up the narrow stairway to her small apartment and hurried inside. She shut the door and leaned against it, biting her lip as another cramp doubled her over. Gasping for breath, she dropped her books, letting them clatter to the floor. Black spots dotted her vision, and she felt faint, lightheaded. She couldn't make it to the bed, she couldn't. Too weak . . . too sore . . . too sick.

She slid down the wall, landing in a heap on the mat she kept just inside the door. Closing her eyes, she rested against the wall and continued to swallow, drawing air into her lungs. She put her head between her knees and steadied her breathing until her head was once again clear. Her hands shook. Her heart pounded. Sweat dampened her forehead and her neck.

She shifted on the floor, feeling the squish of blood beneath her clothing, against her flesh. It had seeped through her petticoat, and no doubt through the fabric of her gray wool skirt.

But, she thought, the state of her clothing was the least of her worries. A sick, hollow feeling burrowed into her stomach. She knew what was happening to her, yet all of her education hadn't prepared her for the reality. She was losing the life that had begun inside her. It had happened to countless women before her. Her throat closed. Her eyes began to sting, and the tears came, steady as rain.

With angry fists, she swiped at them. She never cried. She was always in control. *Always.* Until now, damnit. She sniffed. Then, like a child, she ignored the linen handkerchief in her pocket and wiped her face on her sleeve. Papa wouldn't have approved of such theatrics. Such histrionics. "Be strong, my girl," he would have said. "Let your sister be the weak one. It's better if no one knows how you feel." All of her life she'd tried to live up to those words, no matter how bad she felt. No matter how many times someone or something had made her want to cry.

He wouldn't approve of her condition either, she thought with a wry twist of her mouth.

Another cramp, sudden and violent, stole her breath, making her pant for air. She waited only briefly, wanting to get across the room before another pain struck her. Moving one hand in front of the other, she crawled to the bed, blood flowing from her like unchecked menses. She pulled herself onto the coverlet and collapsed against the pillows.

She lay there, knowing she should clean herself up and assess the damage. But all she wanted to do was escape into sleep.

Lexy stirred, wincing at the sticky sensation between her thighs. She opened her eyes and stared into a pair of vivid blue ones. "Ben?"

Muttering a vile curse, Ben Stillwater sat gingerly

on the bed and clasped one of her hands in his. With the other, he touched her forehead, then slid his strong yet gentle surgeon's fingers down her cheek.

He moved his hand away, clenching his fingers into a fist. His eyes became hard. "You could have bled to death."

She rose onto an elbow and glanced at her skirt, noting the rusty-red stain that spread through the fabric. It had begun to dry, which meant she was no longer bleeding.

"But I didn't." She saw his raw concern and patted his arm. "I came home, Ben. I knew it was happening. I'd had cramping all day." She sounded so calm. So in control. When really she was screaming inside, angry with herself for wanting a child by a man who had turned to her only because of his loss, and his grief. Then left without even saying good-bye.

Ben examined her skirt, gently pushing her to one side to study the bedding beneath her. "There's very little blood on the bedding. Your clothing absorbed much of it. Still, you should be checked. I could help you to the clinic—"

"No," she interrupted, suddenly frantic. "You do it. I don't want anyone else to know. . . ."

He smothered another curse. "Not even *him?*"

Lexy squeezed her eyes shut, attempting to block out the face of the man responsible. The man she'd loved forever—a man who had always been in love with her pretty, vivacious sister, Megan. "No. Not even him. Especially not him."

Ben pulled in an angry breath. "The son of a bitch should know what he's done. I want him to suffer, Lexy."

Her fear rising, Lexy gripped his arm. "Promise me you won't tell him. Promise."

Ben's handsome features softened, but his eyes were hard as he turned away. "Tell him? I don't even know where the bastard is. How can I tell him what he's done to you?"

She smiled, attempting to tease, trying to make light of a situation that weighed heavily on her heart. "It takes two, Ben. As a doctor, you should know that." Her gaze followed his to the window. It had begun to rain; drops spattered the pane, creating a wet, carefree pattern.

"I guess I wanted to hear that he forced you."

Lexy raised a skeptical eyebrow. "You would have preferred that he rape me?"

"Of course not." Ben drove his fingers through his thick blond hair. "God, Lexy. It isn't as if you're some innocent girl who doesn't know how babies are made. You're months away from earning your medical degree. At the very least, one of you should have used protection."

Her gaze flickered away as she recalled her attempt at the vinegar douche the morning after. "I did."

Ben swore again. "And what about him? He had more than enough medical training to know how irresponsible it was to—"

Lexy pressed her fingers over Ben's lips. "No more, Benjamin. It's over and done with. I can get on with my life. What's happened here will always be just between the two of us. Promise me."

"All right, but—"

"No buts, Ben." When she was certain of his silence, she sagged against the pillows and closed her eyes. Yes, it was over and done with. But even if she could rub it out of her mind, how would she erase it from her heart? Or him, for that matter? For a very short number of weeks, Jake Westfield had been an intimate part of her. His child—boy or girl—had been growing in her womb. She wasn't at all certain she could ever forget that.

Northern California
Two years later

"So, yer a lady sawbones, huh?"

"Yes, I am." Lexy bit the insides of her cheeks to prevent a smile. The ancient station master's lips disappeared into his toothless mouth as he gummed a wad of tobacco. His face was juiceless. Wizened. It reminded Lexy of a long-forgotten apple in the dark corner of a cellar.

"Goin' to the fort, are ya?"

This time she did smile. "Yes, I am."

He studied her, his expression serious. "They already got a doc there, ya know."

"I know that. I'm hoping he needs some help." She'd wired Dr. Monroe, explaining that she was Captain Max York's sister-in-law, and was coming to visit and willing to do anything she could to help the doctor at the fort. He hadn't responded. She wanted to believe it was because he hadn't gotten her wire. The sensitive nerve endings in her stomach told her differently. Graduating at the top of her medical class from Pembroke had yet to become an asset in her attempt to practice medicine. As far as the Providence medical community was concerned, she might as well have been a leper. Had she been one, however, she might have gotten a bit of sympathy. As a female physician, she'd gotten nothing but condescending smiles and little pats on the back. Oh, how she detested that treatment!

Anxious to be picked up, she scanned the horizon. Still nothing. Not even a distant cloud of dust to indicate someone was on the way. She strolled down the platform, grateful for the brim on her bonnet, for it shielded her eyes from the sharp sun. She'd never felt such heat. Hot and dry, like an oven. It rose in waves from the parched earth. Perspiration on her brow dried almost before it gathered.

She squinted into the distance again but saw nothing. Except for the withered station master, she was alone. Frowning, she dug in her purse, brought out her sister's letter, and read it again. As if she'd needed to, she thought with a dry smile. She had it memorized. Someone was definitely supposed to meet her. Today.

With a sigh, she returned to the shade and slumped onto a bench beneath the station's eaves, resting against the crudely built wall. Her eyes drifted closed. The heat was like a narcotic, rendering her lethargic.

She'd been examining her reasons for responding to Megan's request to visit since she boarded the train in Providence. Megan's pregnancy had been the strongest lure. Lexy noted a bit of anxiety in her sister's letter when she spoke of the fort doctor. That alone had made it easier for Lexy to make the trip. But it was Megan's announcement that Jake Westfield was scouting for the Army here, at this very fort, that had given Lexy pause. Of course, Meggie had not known Lexy and Jake's brief history. She huffed a laugh. Jake probably didn't even remember it.

Jake. She wondered if she would always have this little catch in her throat when she thought about him. This funny little ache in the vicinity of her heart. This fluttering in the pit of her stomach. A grim smile touched her lips. Even remembering that he'd called out her sister's name as he spilled his seed into her didn't rid her of her foolish feelings. Well, she thought, drawing the hot, dry air into her lungs, maybe once she saw him again she'd realize she had built him up to be something more than he actually was. Maybe.

Nothing would ever have happened between them if he hadn't lost those two patients. Ben had always called Jake a reckless man, both in his personal life and his professional one. Lexy knew it wasn't true. She knew the reason Jake laughed in the face of disaster one day, then crashed to earth, deep in despair the next. Whatever he was doing with his life now was a waste compared to what he could have done with it as a physician. But it wasn't her place to judge him. She knew the devils he wrestled with, and they were painful to her, too.

She snorted a soft laugh. As if he cared.

"Well, well. If it isn't the good little doctor."

Lexy sat forward abruptly and raised her head. Her eyes, filled with surprise, looked back at him, the gentleness he remembered from before immediately replaced by a wariness that made his throat and chest ache.

"Well, well," she mimicked, tilting her head to one side, "if it isn't the big, bad renegade."

Some of the ache left him. Only some. She still had her spunk. He hadn't taken that away from her. But oh, God, he'd taken so much. . . . "How are you, Lexy?"

She gave her shoulders an exaggerated shrug, stretched her arms out, and spread her fingers wide. "Well, let me see. I've traveled this entire country in a train that belched smoke more often than a fat man breaks wind. My constant companions included a gin-swilling banker with a wart on his chin, a boisterous rancher with *no* chin who thought that just because I was a doctor I'd enjoy the most crass of stories, and last but not least, a handsome but ignorant lumber-jack who spoke only Swedish. Does that answer your question?"

Jake chuckled, studying her. Enjoying her. "I've missed your quick wit."

She squinted up at him, her expression skeptical. "Oh, is that so?"

"That's so," he assured her, continuing to smile. "Lexy, I'm sorry—"

"Oh, pooh." She made a little sound in her throat and looked away, brushing his apology aside.

"I never meant to hurt you." He hadn't. She'd been too special. Too sweet beneath that silly pragmatic facade. He'd simply been suffering and filled with need, and she'd been there for him, taking away his pain. A selfless act, so like her.

Again, she waved the words away. "Don't worry about it. It was nothing."

Nothing? An odd feeling stirred in his gut. *Nothing?* He studied her, looking for signs of—what? How could it have been nothing to her when it had been something to him? For years he'd known how she felt about him. Funny little Lexy, so crazy about him she couldn't hide it. And now, after what they'd shared, it was nothing?

Frowning, he cleared his throat. "I was . . . I was concerned."

She toyed with the buttons on her jacket, then looked him square in the eye, her expression apologet-ic, "I'm sorry, Jake, but I got so busy with my course work after you left, I barely had time to think about what we did."

His discomfort intensified. "Well, I'm . . . I'm glad to hear it." Like hell. "You always did have a way of making the best of a situation."

Her gaze flickered away briefly. "Unlike you?"

He tried to smile. "Still trying to convince me I've make the wrong career choice?"

She grinned, that sweet, crooked way she had of twisting her full, sensuous lips to one side. "I quit trying to convince you of anything, Jake. We all have to make our own decisions."

"Thank you for that." She was one of the very few who understood him. That, too, made her special.

She stood and brushed the wrinkles from her skirt. "For what? For not telling you you've thrown away an illustrious medical career to become some silly cowboy who sniffs out helpless Indians so the Army can herd them all onto land they don't want?" She huffed. "Lord, from what I've read, those poor people are treated like cattle."

Jake couldn't stop the chuckle that escaped as they walked toward her luggage, which was stacked on the platform. "Gee, Lexy, don't hide your thoughts. Tell me how you *really* feel."

She blushed, twisting her mouth again. "Sorry. It's not easy to keep my musings to myself."

Her lips continued to fascinate him, as they always had. He had the strangest urge to run his tongue over them and prepare her for a kiss. Hard on the mouth. Tongues dueling. His groin came to life, stirring dangerously. He quietly cursed and shook off the sensation—which refused to be ignored. "I'm glad to see you haven't changed."

"In two short years? How could I possibly change?" She gave him a blinding smile, one that convinced him she was all right. It should have made him happy; it made him miserable. One night with her, and he'd wanted her again, every day since. One night with him, and she'd obviously realized she'd merely had a crush, and now it was over. Damn.

To cover his feelings, he stopped in front of her baggage, which consisted of two steamer trunks, three oversized valises, and a black medical bag. After expelling a long, disbelieving whistle, he asked, "All of this isn't yours, is it?"

She shrugged one of her dainty yet capable shoulders, another gesture he remembered well—and enjoyed. "Of course."

He bent to lift the trunk, pretending it was too heavy to budge. Groaning, he stood and stretched his back. "Christ. What have you got in here? Andirons?"

"My books, of course. And some of my favorite supplies. You didn't expect me to come all this way without them, did you?"

He shook his head, unable to hide a smile. "Every other woman on the face of the earth would have trunks full of shoes, petticoats, fancy gowns, and silly-looking hats with birds and feathers perched on top. Only you would pack them full of medical books and supplies."

She crossed her arms over her chest and glared at him. "Are you making fun of me?"

He bent again and hoisted the trunk onto his shoulder, then crossed to the waiting wagon. "I always have, haven't I? What's the matter? Can't take it anymore?" If she no longer cared, he sure as hell could convince her he didn't either. Pretend nothing happened. Pretend it didn't matter. Return to the banter they'd shared before. . . .

"Oh, I can take anything you can dish out, cowboy."

Hoisting the last of her luggage into the wagon, he

answered, "Cowboy. I like that. It fits me." He helped her in, remembering the softness of her skin, the faint scent of lilacs that always surrounded her.

"Dr. Westfield fit you, too." She settled in the seat, smoothing her skirt around her.

"Don't start, Lexy."

She gave him the one-shouldered shrug. "Can't help it. It's my nature."

He shook his head and changed the subject. "Sorry about the wagon. Your sister warned me you'd come loaded for bear." He gave her a good-natured, brotherly wink, one that wasn't easy when he wanted to press his nose against her neck and lick it. "I guess she knows you better than I do."

Lexy's expression changed; she became pensive. She wasn't pretty, not like Meggie. No, Lexy wasn't pretty, she was ravishing. But she didn't know it. At least she never acknowledged it. While her sister was slim and fair, Lexy was full-bosomed and curvaceous, and had hair the color of butterscotch candy. It wasn't fashionable to look like Lexy. But it was damned provocative. He'd watched her reluctantly grow into a woman, attempting to hide her femininity beneath a hard, pragmatic exterior, choosing a profession that few women even thought about.

He hadn't always been attracted to her. To all the men he'd known, including his best friend, Max York, and to he himself, Megan had been the logical choice. Until he began to spend time with Lexy.

He touched her chin, turning her sweet, expressive face toward him. "Hey, there. You'd better not have that long face when Meggie sees you."

Lexy gave him a small smile. "How is she? And Max? Are they . . . are they happy?"

He laughed, remembering Megan's horror at the antiquated facilities the fort afforded, even for the captain. "I think your sister would prefer to be somewhere in the civilized world, but other than that, she's fine. Max is a lucky guy."

He felt Lexy's gaze on him, but when he met it, she glanced away.

"Why did you come West, Jake?"

Jake studied the team, still feeling shame at leaving her like he had. "I had my reasons. Max is my best friend. I couldn't let him fight the Indians alone, you know," he answered with a smile.

She was quiet again, her expression thoughtful. "How far to the fort?"

"We'll be there by tomorrow afternoon."

She gasped, a tiny sound he barely heard. "Tomorrow? We're riding all night?"

"Of course not. We'll stop for a few hours tonight so the horses can rest." He'd resisted coming to meet her, but Megan had pleaded with him. Max couldn't be spared, and she trusted no one else. God, he was the last person she should trust when it came to Lexy. He'd tried not to think about being alone with her, spending another night with her in the middle of nowhere. In spite of her apparent disinterest in him, his interest hadn't changed.

He glanced at her, and their gazes met. Lexy was the first to look away. He stole a peek at her bosom, which heaved slightly, as if she'd taken a flight of stairs. He remembered the shape of her breasts, the size of her nipples, their color, their taste . . . her spontaneous orgasm, which had nearly caused an early spilling of his own seed.

He forced himself to stop his wayward thoughts. Instead, he focused on the memory of how she'd found him that fateful day. He'd been slumped on the stoop in front of her apartment building, his head in his hands, his sorrow building.

"Jake? What is it? What's wrong?" Her concern had always softened him, for she truly cared what happened to him. He'd never deserved her concern. Or her care. And certainly not her love.

He'd raised his face to hers, drowning in her beautiful eyes. "I lost them, Lexy. I lost them both."

She'd taken his hands in hers. "Who?"

"My patients, goddamn it!"

Lexy had pressed one hand to her mouth. "The mother and child?"

He'd nodded briefly before putting his face in his hands again.

Without another word she'd urged him to come into her apartment. She'd guided him to the sofa, but he'd clung to her. They had fallen to the piece of furniture together, his arms gripping her tightly. She had soothed him. Comforted him. It had started as simply as that. It wasn't long before he was caressing her breasts, tugging at her blouse. Shortly after that, she'd removed her clothing above her waist and allowed him to fondle her. Kiss her. Even now, when he thought about it, he wanted her again. He ached for her spontaneous arousal. But he'd taken that from her which women revered, and for that he couldn't forgive himself. This would be a night of hell. Pure hell.

"Jake?"

He shook himself. "Yeah?"

"Will we really be out here, all alone, tonight?"

"Yeah. Does that bother you?" If it did, there was hope.

"Why should it bother me? You'll protect me, won't you?" she asked, her tone flippant.

Disappointed in her response, he forced himself to

give her a brotherly shove, then put his arm around her shoulders. "Of course. I'll protect you from the bogeyman."

She expelled a shaky sigh. "Yes," she answered almost absently, "but who'll protect me from you?"

Look for
Scent of Lilacs
Wherever Paperback Books Are Sold
Coming Soon
From Pocket Books